W9-CZH-295

MILLIE CRISWELL
DESIRE'S ENDLESS KISS

ZEBRA BOOKS
KENSINGTON PUBLISHING CORP.

TO THE SPECIAL LADIES IN MY LIFE:

ESTHER R. PERKINS—*my agent, whose expertise and guidance has helped get my writing career off the ground, while keeping my feet firmly planted*

and

ANN LaFARGE—*my editor, whose wit and wisdom has come to my aid on more than one occasion.*

Thank you both!

ZEBRA BOOKS

are published by

Kensington Publishing Corp.
475 Park Avenue South
New York, NY 10016

Copyright © 1991 by Millie Criswell

All rights reserved. No part of this book may be reproduced in any form or by any means without the prior written consent of the Publisher, excepting brief quotes used in reviews.

If you purchased this book without a cover you should be aware that this book is stolen property. It was reported as "unsold and destroyed" to the Publisher and neither the Author nor the Publisher has received any payment for this "stripped book."

First printing: December, 1991

Printed in the United States of America

Daniel grabbed Samantha's hand and led her deep into the boxwood maze at the back of the garden. It was very dark.

"I can't see a thing," she said. "How will we find our way back?"

Daniel's teeth flashed white against the darkness. Leading her to a stone bench, he pulled her down beside him. "Are you cold?" he asked, placing his arm around her shoulders. His fingers caressed the satin of her skin, creating a warm sensation in the pit of her stomach. Her mouth was suddenly dry; she couldn't formulate the reproach she knew she should utter.

"You're beautiful, Samantha," he whispered. "You know that I'm going to kiss you, don't you?"

She nodded mutely, mesmerized by the velvet sound of his voice. His lips covered hers, branding her with fire. A rush of pleasure surged through every inch of her being. Forgetting who Daniel was, where they were, and what had brought them together, she responded with an urgency that surprised and frightened her.

Wrapping her arms about the firm muscles of his back, she leaned into him. She wanted him to kiss her again, to keep on kissing her, to kiss her always and forever.

LET ARCHER AND CLEARY
AWAKEN AND CAPTURE YOUR HEART!

CAPTIVE DESIRE (2612, $3.75)
by Jane Archer

Victoria Malone fancied herself a great adventuress and student of life, but being kidnapped by handsome Cord Cordova was too much excitement for even her! Convincing her kidnapper that she had been an innocent bystander when the stagecoach was robbed was futile when he was kissing her until she was senseless!

REBEL SEDUCTION (3249, $4.25)
by Jane Archer

"Stop that train!" came Lacey Whitmore's terrified warning as she rushed toward the locomotive that carried wounded Confederates and her own beloved father. But no one paid heed, least of all the Union spy Clint McCullough, who pinned her to the ground as the train suddenly exploded into flames.

DREAM'S DESIRE (3093, $4.50)
by Gwen Cleary

Desperate to escape an arranged marriage, Antonia Winston y Ortega fled her father's hacienda to the arms of the arrogant Captain Domino. She would spend the night with him and would be free for no gentleman wants a ruined bride. And ruined she would be, for Tonia would never forget his searing kisses!

VICTORIA'S ECSTASY (2906, $4.25)
by Gwen Cleary

Proud Victoria Torrington was short of cash to run her shipping empire, so she traveled to America to meet her partner for the first time. Expecting a withered, ancient cowhand, Victoria didn't know what to do when she met virile, muscular Judge Colston and her body budded with desire.

Available wherever paperbacks are sold, or order direct from the Publisher. Send cover price plus 50¢ per copy for mailing and handling to Zebra Books, Dept. 3608, 475 Park Avenue South, New York, N.Y. 10016. Residents of New York, New Jersey and Pennsylvania must include sales tax. DO NOT SEND CASH.

Part One

Embers of Doubt

Oh, what a tangled web we weave;
when first we practice to deceive!

Sir Walter Scott
Marmion

Chapter One

June, 1813.

Washington City. Samantha Wilder wrinkled her nose in disgust as she stared out the window of the hackney coach that would bring her to the Capitol building. The sparsely populated, indifferent city known as the nation's capital covered the banks of the Potomac like a suit of fine clothes on a ragpicker's son. Some capital! Why, her home city of Boston was far more suited to that honor than this ugly backwoods settlement, she thought uncharitably.

The city without streets. That's what Washington was called and justifiably so. Poplar-lined Pennsylvania Avenue, the road the coach presently traveled upon, was the only road in the entire town that could be remotely construed of as a street. Aside from the President's House and the Capitol building, the entire city consisted of a few boarding houses and clusters of new homes set at considerable distances from each other.

Disbelief twisted Samantha's face into a frown. This

was the seat of our nation's government? This was where great minds and political thinkers gathered to form the policies that would govern our lives forever? she asked herself, shaking her head. It was like viewing a camp of nomads.

She had been there for only a few weeks, and already she hated it. If not for the urgent nature of her visit, she would have hastened back to Boston and said good riddance to the place.

Spying the Capitol sitting atop Capitol Hill among a grove of elm trees, Samantha breathed a sigh of relief only to be overtaken with a fit of coughing when the dust from the unpaved road floated in through the open window.

"Are you all right, miss?" the portly gentleman seated next to her in the coach inquired.

Nodding, Samantha smiled weakly, pulling a white linen handkerchief out from her reticule to cover her nose. It wasn't bad enough, she thought, that the stench from Tiber Creek, which was nothing more than an open sewer, was turning her insides queasy. The situation was compounded by the malodorous smell coming from the overweight gentleman seated next to her. What had she done to deserve such punishment? she wondered.

The Capitol, whose north and south wings were connected by a crude covered bridge, stood before her, unfinished and sadly lacking the splendor that Dr. William Thornton, the architect, had envisioned. Due to the present war with Britain, funds previously appropriated for the completion of the building were now diverted to the effort of fighting the British.

Climbing the steps of the impressive sandstone structure, she couldn't stem the anger rising within her at the stupidity of such a war—a war that, in all reality, should never have begun. If not for the lack of timely communication between the United States and Great Britain, there would have been no war. Great Britain had rescinded the hated "Orders in Council" restricting American trade overseas in June of last year, their proclamation coming within weeks of President Madison's declaration of war.

If only the British Foreign Secretary Lord Castlereagh's communiqué had reached the President in time, she thought mournfully, then perhaps her older brother, Robbie, would still be with her instead of dead or a prisoner in some far-off land. First her father and now Robbie. How much grief was a person expected to bear in one lifetime? she wondered, blinking back tears.

Patrick Wilder's two-masted merchant ship, *The Fair Betsy,* named in memory of her mother who had died when Samantha was just a child, had disappeared off the coast of France in March of 1812. Enraged by what her brother had called "Britain's piracy," Robbie had signed on with the U.S.S. *Chesapeake* in retaliation. It had been three weeks since his ship had been engaged in a naval battle thirty miles off the coast of Boston Harbor. And it was his disappearance that had brought her and her grandfather to Washington and the Capitol to seek help from her friend, Adam Bainbridge, secretary to Timothy Pickering, the senator from Massachusetts.

Entering through the pair of heavy oak doors, Samantha walked down the dimly lit hallway to her right toward the wing that housed the Senate chambers. The unfinished walls and ceiling lent an air of impermanence to the nearly completed building, though she could see from the handsomely carved fluted columns of marble that the Capitol would one day be a showplace. It was no secret that former President Jefferson had decided it so, having hired Italian artisans from Carerra, Italy, to execute the intricate patterns.

Spying the door with Senator Pickering's name on it, she pushed it open, pausing at the sight of his secretary bent over a sheaf of papers.

"Hello, Adam."

Adam Bainbridge's blond head popped up; his face registered surprise and then annoyance. "Samantha, what the devil are you doing here? You know you shouldn't have come. It was most unseemly of you."

Sighing, Samantha brushed the dust from the skirts of her lemon-colored gauze gown in a gesture of impatience. "Oh, Adam, don't be such a prig. Dozens of doting mothers bring their marriageable daughters here to parade before the Senate in the hope that they'll snare a rich and powerful husband. Is it any wonder that the chamber is called the finest drawing room in Washington?"

She smiled inwardly at the look of outrage plastered on Adam's face. It was a handsome face, really too pretty to belong to a man. He had long, dark eyelashes that most women would kill for and a shock of white-blond hair that looked almost unnatural in its pearlescence.

Adam hadn't changed a whit since they'd been children growing up together in Boston. He had always been a stickler for the proprieties—always one to find the gloom in every situation. "A wet blanket," Robbie called him, though with no small lack of affection, for the Bainbridges and the Wilders were fast friends, having lived next door to one another for more than twenty years.

Rising from his chair, Adam crossed the room to take Samantha's hands in his own. Though his expression had softened, his voice remained firm. "This isn't Boston, Samantha. We are at war with England, and you are tempting fate by parading around unescorted through this uncivilized community. Have you forgotten what Admiral Cockburn's marines did to Havre de Grace? Do you wish to be accosted in a similar manner?"

Havre de Grace, situated sixty miles north of Washington, was the site of senseless cruelty and destruction at the hands of vindictive Admiral Cockburn. Wishing to teach the Americans a lesson for waving an American flag at him as he sailed by in his frigate, Cockburn unleashed a contingent of British marines on the town with orders to destroy and pillage. Armed with hatchets, the soldiers burned or demolished forty of the sixty houses, two taverns, a blacksmith shop, and numerous other buildings.

But even the threat of harm at British hands could not deter Samantha from pursuing her objective. Pulling her hands from Adam's grasp, she tossed her head back defiantly, nearly upsetting the straw bonnet perched atop her chestnut hair.

"You know why I've come, Adam. Senator Pickering promised that he would look into Robbie's disappearance. I have little patience to sit around and wait for some word of my brother. I want to know where he is."

11

Guiding her to the gold brocade settee, Adam urged her to sit, occupying the space next to her. "Samantha, I know how worried you are about Robert. I feel the same way. He is my best friend, after all. But you mustn't throw caution to the wind. What good would it do if you were to become harmed in the process?"

"If you're worried about those fool Englishmen who are parading up and down the Chesapeake Bay, I wouldn't. They don't scare me a bit. They're just trying to frighten us off. They would no more invade Washington than we would invade London. Why should they? There is no commerce or industry here."

Rising to his feet, Adam crossed to the window, presenting her with his back as he looked out. The sun at its zenith streamed in through the open window, making the small room uncomfortably warm. "I had hoped to spare you this news, Samantha; but you are so adamant, I feel I mustn't keep it from you."

Samantha's eyes widened in alarm. Jumping to her feet, she rushed forward, grabbing on to Adam's arm. "Please, you must tell me if you have news of my brother." She turned him toward her.

"The news isn't all that good, I'm afraid. Senator Pickering has just received word that there were twenty-one casualties aboard *The Chesapeake;* four of the men were impressed and taken to Halifax."

Samantha gasped, the natural pink blush in her cheeks paling white. "And Robbie? Was he one of those casualties?" She held her breath, fearful of the answer.

Adam shook his head, concern clouding his clear gray eyes. "We've no way of knowing."

She released the breath she was holding; an ember of

hope sparked in her breast. It was entirely possible that Robbie was still alive. She refused to believe that her impetuous, headstrong brother was dead, no matter the gloomy picture Adam painted.

"Damn war!" she cursed, not realizing she had uttered the epithet aloud.

"Really, Samantha!" Adam pursed his lips, an indication of his displeasure. "A lady of quality does not use profanities—no matter the circumstance."

The brown eyes darkened from the color of warm sherry to the volatile shade of brandy. Was it any wonder that she'd refused Adam's proposal of marriage on three separate occasions? As dear a friend as he might be, the prospect of stifling her natural inclinations for a lifetime was unthinkable.

"Forgive me; I must have lost my head." She crossed to the door, pausing before it. "I have to be going. I promised Grandfather I wouldn't be gone too long."

Adam smiled at her capitulation. "That's a good girl. You run along home and let me worry about finding Robert. There's no sense in worrying needlessly until we find out something more definite."

Afraid to respond to Adam's patronizing remarks, lest she tell him exactly what she thought of his condescending attitude, Samantha hurried out the door, shutting it firmly behind her. Alone in the hall she paused, taking deep breaths to calm herself. Botheration, but Adam was annoying! Home indeed! She had no intention of going home. She was going to pay a visit to Mr. Gales down at his newspaper office. Perhaps the editor of the *National Intelligencer* would be better informed than the senator and his opinionated secretary.

13

Walking briskly down the main thoroughfare, Samantha dabbed at the droplets of sweat pouring off her brow. June in Washington was proving unbearable. It was dreadfully hot and horribly humid. The heat had settled over the city like a heavy quilt, wet with unshed moisture. Her clothes felt damp and sticky. And although the Lombardy poplars lining Pennsylvania Avenue did offer a modicum of relief, they weren't enough protection from the scorching rays of the afternoon sun.

Wouldn't old Mrs. Dinker be surprised to learn that people actually sweated, she mused, thinking of the stodgy headmistress at the boarding school she had attended in Boston. According to Mrs. Dinker, young ladies did not sweat or perspire; it wasn't allowed nor was it considered ladylike. Instead, they glistened.

Pulling up her skirts to avoid the animal droppings on the footpath, she smirked, thinking that she certainly had been doing her fair share of *glistening* lately. How she would love to pit Mrs. Dinker against a Washington summer; it would be interesting to see who came out ahead.

The office of the *National Intelligencer* was housed in a modest brick building halfway between the Capitol and the President's House, directly across from Blodgett's Hotel. Samantha entered to find a short, unimposing, red-faced man whose kind brown eyes reflected a keen intelligence. He had dark, wavy hair generously sprinkled with gray and a friendly smile when he greeted her.

"Good day to you, miss. How may I be of assistance?"

"I'm looking for Mr. Gales. Would you happen to

14

know where I could find him?"

Wiping his ink-stained hands on the corner of his leather apron, the man nodded. "Indeed, miss, I do. I'm Joseph Gales. How may I help you?"

Samantha felt her cheeks warm. "Excuse me, Mr. Gales. I just assumed by your appearance that . . ." Her words trailed off at his understanding smile.

"My assistant, Willy, is home sick. But even when Willy's here, I assist in putting out the paper. I love the feel and smell of printer's ink. It's in my blood. I've often said that if I were to bleed, my blood would run black not red." He chuckled at his witticism. "But that's enough about me. What is it you wish to speak to me about?"

Toying with the strings of her reticule, Samantha weighed her words carefully. "I've come in the hope that you will be able to help me, Mr. Gales. I'm in need of information."

"That's the business I'm in, Miss . . ." He paused expectantly, waiting for her to complete the introduction.

"Wilder . . . Samantha Wilder."

"I collect, procreate, and disseminate information on a regular basis, Miss Wilder." He walked toward the rear of the shop, passed the huge black printing press, and motioned for her to follow.

They entered a plain but cozy room with a scarred pine table, four spindle-backed chairs, and a free-standing Franklin stove. Samantha seated herself in one of the chairs.

"Care for some tea? I was just about to have some."

She shook her head, noting the copper tea kettle that whistled softly on the stove. "Thank you, no. I'm afraid the weather is a bit too warm for me." In truth, the pungent smell of ink was rendering her lightheaded.

"You're right about that, young lady. It's hotter than Hades today. We usually don't heat up like this until August."

The editor's words, softly drawled, depicted the North Carolinian accent of his childhood, though she could still discern a trace of his English heritage. Although they had just met, Mr. Gales's background was no secret to her. He had been a frequent topic of conversation at many of the dinner parties she had attended with Adam.

Taking the seat next to her, Joseph Gales studied the young woman across from him while waiting for her to speak. Miss Wilder appeared to be of the upper classes; the cut of her clothes and manner of her speech told him that much. Her soft, well-modulated voice reflected a refinement only years of schooling could produce. She was definitely a lady of quality . . . a Northern lady, if his ear proved in tune. That same well-modulated voice jarred him from his observations.

"I've read many of your editorials, Mr. Gales. I was particularly impressed by the articles you've penned on Admiral Cockburn." His dislike for the British officer was apparent; one didn't need to read between the lines to gage the editor's sentiments toward the British, and Admiral Cockburn in particular.

Gales threw back his head and laughed. "That popinjay deserved to be taken down a peg. Don't you agree?"

"I'm afraid that I'm not very political, Mr. Gales, nor am I particularly interested in this war, which I find

16

totally ridiculous. What I am interested in is locating my brother."

The editor's bushy brows wrinkled in confusion. "Your brother? I'm afraid you have me at a loss, Miss Wilder."

"My brother, Robert Wilder, was aboard the U.S.S. *Chesapeake.* He's missing, and I was hoping you might have information that could help me locate his whereabouts."

He stirred his tea absently, digesting her news. "Have you sought help elsewhere?"

"I've just come from Senator Pickering's office. What I learned there was not very encouraging."

The editor's face reddened; he set down his cup. "You went to Timothy Pickering? That self-serving, bigoted Federalist who spews forth nothing but treason?"

Unprepared for Joseph Gales's vehemence, Samantha shifted uncomfortably in her chair, her face warming under his condemnation. "I . . . I am from Massachusetts, Mr. Gales. Senator Pickering is the senator for the Commonwealth. It was only natural that I go to him for help."

"And do you espouse the same views as Pickering?" He studied her face intently.

She shook her head. "As I told you, I am not political. But in all fairness you should know that my grandfather, with whom I reside, is a very staunch Federalist. He hates this war as much as I do, Mr. Gales, but for entirely different reasons."

Gales's expression softened. "You're in a bit of a tight spot, Miss Wilder . . . between a rock and a hard place, so to speak."

Samantha sighed inwardly. The editor's assessment was more accurate than he realized. Putting up with her grandfather's constant diatribe on the evils of the Madison administration and the foolishness of the war was at times, more difficult than she could stand.

"Will you help me, Mr. Gales? I can pay . . . if the amount you require isn't too great." Grandfather kept a tight rein on the purse strings, only doling out what was needed for food and the bare necessities. She had managed to put aside some emergency funds for situations such as this, squirreling away some of the grocery money now and then. It was what she had used to purchase the new gown she would wear to the Madisons' fete tonight.

"You insult me, Miss Wilder. I wouldn't think of taking your money." Scratching his chin, he pondered the situation for a moment. "I'll need to make some inquiries. I have reliable connections who may know something more than the official government report." He thought of Daniel Fortune and smiled confidently. Daniel just might be the man to help him. As agent to President Madison, Fortune had access to information unobtainable to the general populace.

Samantha's face brightened. "That would be wonderful. 'Tis the first hope I've had in weeks."

Taking hold of her gloved hand, Joseph patted it comfortingly. "Don't get your hopes up, my dear. There may be no news to tell."

She nodded at the truth of his words but still felt confident that he would be able to help her. It was rumored that Mr. Gales was a close friend of the President—a confidant. If anyone could help her, he could.

"I trust I can rely on your discretion, Mr. Gales. I

don't want Senator Pickering's secretary, Adam Bainbridge, to know of my efforts." If Adam found out what she was up to, he would put a stop to it. And she had no intention of stopping, not until her brother was found.

"You're acquainted with Adam Bainbridge?" Joseph asked, unable to disguise the rancor in his voice. The man was as bad as Pickering; they were two of a kind in his estimation.

"Why, yes. We've been friends since childhood. Do you know Adam?"

"As well as I care to, Miss Wilder." Ignoring her confusion, he crossed to the door, pulling it open. Her unsettling revelation put a new wrinkle into the situation. Would Daniel be willing to help a friend of Adam Bainbridge? Daniel's dislike of the man was well-known. After a moment, he added, "You can rely on my discretion. I will do what I can to help."

A look of relief crossed her face. "Thank you, Mr. Gales. How will I know when to contact you?"

"Check the advertisements in the newspaper. When I have news, I will put a special notice in for you."

Repeating her thanks, Samantha exited the office, feeling better than she had in weeks. Finally, someone was going to do something about locating her brother. Eliciting Mr. Gales's help hadn't been as difficult as she had originally feared. If only her grandfather were as easy to reason with, she thought, thinking of the forthcoming argument they were sure to have when she told him of her plan to attend the Madisons' gala tonight.

Sighing, she hurried across the street to catch the coach that would take her back to Georgetown and to her grandfather who would be waiting anxiously for news of her brother.

Samantha's own anxiety increased as the horse-drawn conveyance pulled across the wooden bridge spanning Rock Creek, which separated Georgetown from Washington.

Having been settled in 1751, the bustling little community of Georgetown was a far cry from unsophisticated Washington City. With almost twice the population, Georgetown was an active trade center, its wharves lined with warehouses, its river filled with ships to export the tobacco that flourished in Virginia and Maryland.

The cobblestone streets were lined with impressive two-story, dormered brick houses and ordinaries indicative of a prosperous and civilized community.

One such ordinary, Suter's Tavern, considered by many to be *the* gathering place for gentlemen, had been frequented by such illustrious individuals as George Washington, Thomas Jefferson, and President Madison. It was the starting and stopping place of the coach, *The Royal George,* housing an entrance at the right of the building large enough to enable the coach to drive right inside.

Disembarking, Samantha paid the fare and proceeded on foot up Wapping Causeway to West Lane, passing by the Dodge Warehouses that were operated by Francis Dodge who owned many of the city's commercial interests.

It was still uncomfortably warm. The thick, moist air, laden with the heady fragrance of the lilac and honeysuckle bushes she passed was cloying. Turning right onto Cecil Place, she continued up the steep incline until reaching the narrow winding street known

20

as Cherry Hill Lane.

The houses, all made of brick, were built in the Federal style, each possessing gables, dormers, and shutters at the window. The house of Ezra Lawrence, her maternal grandfather, sat in the middle of the tall row of houses on her right.

The house had been in the Lawrence family for years, handed down by some obscure relative of her grandfather's of whom Samantha had never heard. It had stood vacant for many years, until their visit had necessitated its refurbishing.

Approaching the green painted front door with the brass pineapple knocker, she took a deep breath, dreading the confrontation she was about to have with her grandfather.

Chapter Two

Closing the door behind her, Samantha removed her bonnet and kid gloves, setting them on the mahogany card table in the entry hall. The center hall, like many of the other rooms in the house, was decorated in the Sheraton and Chippendale styles, foregoing the stylish Phyfe for the comfort of the old master craftsmen. Tables and chairs of mahogany and walnut lined the blue and yellow floral-papered walls. A pair of brass sconces flanked the looking glass, illuminating the look of consternation on Samantha's face as she checked her appearance one last time.

"Samantha, is that you?" the gravely voice floating in through the doorway inquired.

"Yes, it's me, Grandfather. I shan't be a minute."

She knew how impatient the old man was. Since his last attack of gout, Grandfather had been confined to a wheelchair and had become as demanding as a small child.

Smoothing the stray tendrils of hair that had loosened from the Grecian knot atop her head, she hurried into the parlor, spying her grandfather's agitated glare almost immediately. Today's discussion was not going to be a pleasant one, she thought, sighing inwardly.

"Good afternoon, Grandfather. How are you feeling today?" She pressed a kiss to his wrinkled cheek, ignoring his rigid posture.

"A lot you care, running all over this miserable town and leaving an old man to fend for himself."

"Now don't exaggerate. You know perfectly well Dulcie was here to care for you."

"Hmph! That black heathen isn't fit to care for a dog. She's hardly a proper replacement for Mrs. Coombs."

Samantha heaved another sigh. "Mrs. Coombs has been dead for over a year, Grandfather. I would think that by now you would have accepted Dulcie as her replacement." She certainly had. Dulcie was like a breath of fresh spring air compared to Mrs. Coombs's stale and dour disposition. Small wonder Grandfather and the former housekeeper had gotten on so well, Samantha thought.

"Never!" Ezra Lawrence bellowed, staring mutinously back at her with eyes the color of her own.

Ignoring her grandfather's ill humor, Samantha pushed his chair over to the open window, taking a seat next to him in the red brocade wing chair that rested nearby. "You're just mad because Dulcie doesn't spoil you like Mrs. Coombs did. You're not able to intimidate her quite so readily."

"The hell you say! She needs to learn who her betters are. I'm her commanding officer. She should show me the proper respect."

"First of all, Dulcie is a free woman, and we are lucky

23

to have found someone as competent as she is. Secondly, you are not commanding a Revolutionary War unit. Your days of giving orders, Colonel Lawrence, have long since passed."

"You're a brash young woman."

Samantha grinned, displaying even white teeth and two charming dimples on either side of her face. "I'm just like you, which is why we understand each other so well." Reaching for the pitcher of lemonade that rested on the card table, she poured two glasses, handing her grandfather one. "What news is there?" Ezra demanded, choosing to ignore her impertinence.

"Nothing good, I'm afraid. There were twenty-one casualties and four men taken off *The Chesapeake.* I have no concrete information as to the identities of the men involved." Noting the anguish in her grandfather's eyes, she felt her own eyes mist.

Robbie was his pride and joy. He had never let his feelings of animosity toward Patrick Wilder color how he felt toward his grandchildren. Their feud had been a long-standing one, commencing the day her mother had drowned in the Charles River while on a fishing trip with her father.

"All of this is Madison's fault," Ezra said, his expression as acerbic as the lemonade he sipped. "Had he not let himself become a pawn of Napoleon, this war would never have taken place."

"Be reasonable, Grandfather. I hardly think Robbie's disappearance is President Madison's fault. There were many in Washington who favored going to war with England. It wasn't a decision he made lightly."

"War hawks!" Ezra shouted, slamming his glass down on the table, the contents spilling onto the red and green patterned Turkish carpet beneath. "Those young fools who did not see the black days of the revolution firsthand were inspired by boundless confidence—by their misplaced patriotic fervor. Henry Clay should be strung up as a traitor."

Recognizing the stubborn set of his chin, Samantha shook her head in disgust. Why she had thought she could reason with her grandfather was beyond her understanding. The old man was adamant in his beliefs. Nothing she could say would change them. His position was as rigid as the marble pillars gracing the halls of the Capitol—hard, cold, unyielding. And he wasn't alone. There were many like her grandfather who were opposed to the war with Great Britain. Many who called it, "Mr. Madison's War."

Setting her glass down, Samantha stood. "I'm going upstairs to take a nap. I want to rest before the Madisons' gala this evening."

Ezra Lawrence's face darkened to the scarlet shade of the brocade chair, contrasting markedly with the snow white of his hair. "I'll not allow it. How can you think to dance attendance on our enemies?"

"I don't consider the Madisons our enemies, Grandfather. Mrs. Madison was most gracious to invite me to her party, considering your staunch political beliefs." Ignoring his snort, she continued, "Besides, I'm going for a purpose. I may be able to learn something about Robbie's whereabouts. What harm can it do? Adam will be there to protect me."

She knew her last statement was a lie. Adam had told her only today that he would be unable to attend due to a pressing engagement. In truth, she was relieved. His presence would have proved detrimental to what she would attempt to achieve tonight. She intended to play whatever role she must to gain the confidence of some of the more influential men who would be at the Madison's home this evening. For Robbie's sake, she hoped she was successful.

The light of a thousand candles sparkled brightly against the mullioned windows of the President's House, echoing their brilliance within the depths of Daniel Fortune's dark blue eyes, which, at the moment, were trained on the lovely woman standing before the French doors of the saffron-colored drawing room.

She was dressed simply, but elegantly, in a gown of white gossamer silk that shimmered in the glow of the candlelight. Her peaches-and-cream complexion and rich chestnut hair beckoned his attention from across the room, where he stood in conversation with Joseph Gales.

"I see you have spotted the lovely Miss Wilder," Joseph remarked, following Daniel's gaze and smiling appreciatively.

Daniel's eyes widened. "That is the young woman you told me about? The one searching for her brother?"

Joseph nodded. "One and the same. Pity that she's acquainted with Bainbridge. As far as I could ascertain, it's the only flaw in her character."

The blue eyes narrowed imperceptibly. If the woman was a friend of Bainbridge, then she had more than one flaw to her character. Adam's taste in women was well-documented: he liked experienced, big-breasted harlots. Miss Wilder failed in one category; did she succeed in the other?

Tearing his gaze away from the beautiful woman, he turned to face Joseph. "Do you believe this woman's story about her brother? For some reason, I find it hard to accept that she can be as sweet and unassuming as you have led me to believe."

Taking a sip of his claret, Joseph shook his head. "You're letting your animosity toward Bainbridge color your opinion where Samantha Wilder is concerned. I pride myself on possessing a keen sense of judgment. I couldn't be wrong about her."

"Well, then, can you explain why she is twirling about the room in the arms of such a disreputable rogue as Edward de Crillon? I don't care if he does wear the ribbon of the Legion of Honor. If that man is the son of a duke, then so am I."

"But you are, dear boy. Did you forget?" Joseph's eyes twinkled merrily.

Daniel smiled sheepishly. He was indeed the son of a duke—the duke of Blackstone to be correct. But it was damned difficult to remember that fact. His father, Nicholas Fortune, had left behind his estates in England to fight for American independence. His stand was deemed traitorous by the Crown, and Nicholas had been stripped of title, fortune, and estates for the second time in his life.

Small wonder that he, Daniel, had little use for the nobility, the English, or the damned Federalists. But he knew with a certainty that Adam Bainbridge's opinions were quite to the contrary, and he would bet money that the lovely Miss Wilder was of a similar persuasion.

His eyes wandered over her lithe form once more, landing with undisguised pleasure on the swell of the creamy white mounds which peeked provocatively over the low cut of her gown. Samantha Wilder would bear closer scrutiny—much closer scrutiny.

Samantha had been flirting shamelessly with Count de Crillon for the better part of an hour. She knew his reputation was not above reproach. She had heard the rumors of his feud with Napoleon and how he had charmed his way into the good graces of President Madison and his Secretary of State James Monroe. But she was determined to find someone that could help locate her brother, even if it was this pompous, strutting peacock. It couldn't hurt to enlist the aid of someone with international connections, she thought. If she must cast herself in the role of femme fatale, then so be it.

Returning her attention to the fawning Frenchman, whose beady brown eyes reminded her of a snake's, she laughed at the outrageous remark he was making. "Careful, monsieur, you will turn my head with your pretty compliments."

"That is easy to do. You are so very beautiful."

"*Merci.* Tell me, Comte de Crillon, have you news of the war?"

"Bah, no!" he replied with a wave of his hand, the lace ruffle on his red satin sleeve billowing out like a ship's sail. "I have lost all interest in such a debacle. But come, surely we can think of more pleasant conversation, no?" He lifted her hand to his mouth, placing a wet kiss to her palm.

Samantha fought the urge to vomit. In his overstated finery, the count reminded her of a gaudy window dressing. She masked her annoyance with a sweet smile. "Of course."

"Mademoiselle Wilder, I find you to be the most enchanting of creatures. How is it that you find yourself unescorted this evening?"

Seeing no point in continuing her performance with a man who obviously was not going to divulge any useful information, she replied, "My escort, Mr. Bainbridge, was unavoidably detained. He will be joining me later." She saw the look of dismay on his pudgy face and smiled inwardly. Apparently, the count thought she would be an easy conquest; little did he know. "Perhaps another time?" Her smile held promise.

Realizing that his plans for the evening were thwarted, it didn't take long for Edward de Crillon to mumble his apologies and cross to the other side of the room, seeking his next prey in the form of a voluptuous redhead who had just entered.

Samantha breathed a sigh of relief. She was going to have to be more careful. At twenty-two, her lack of experience with members of the opposite sex was painfully obvious. She didn't want to make any mistakes she would regret later.

When the marine band interrupted their musical repertoire to take a break, Samantha inched her way toward the French doors, pausing briefly before making her way outside to the terrace. The night air, though still warm, was a welcome relief after the stifling closeness of the drawing room. She inhaled deeply, filling her lungs with the sweet scent of jasmine that perfumed the air. The eager mating call of the crickets' shrill chirp and the deep croaking sounds of the tree frogs serenaded her with as much enthusiasm as the band had a few minutes before.

Mulling over her less-than-satisfactory progress, she

took a seat on the stone bench that rested beneath a hanging lantern, watching as a persistent moth neared the flame, then retreated, beating its wings against the glass, trying to gain entry.

She felt as helpless as the moth at the moment. Thus far, her attempts to discover anything useful about her brother had proven futile. All of the gentlemen she had danced with tonight, including the Frenchman, had little to add to the information she had already obtained. It was proving awkward to talk about anything of a political nature with men who were more intent on discussing the latest fashions from Europe than the war that was going on around them.

Why was it that men still viewed women as empty-headed chits? she wondered. Not that she was particularly well versed in the art of politics, but she was a sight better informed than some of the dandies she had met here tonight.

If only President and Mrs. Madison would arrive, she thought, fidgeting anxiously with the satin ribbons of her gown. Perhaps then, she would be able to discover some bit of information about her brother's disappearance.

The President's majordomo, John Sioussant, had announced earlier that the couple had been unavoidably detained but had given no further explanation. Rumor had it that the delay was caused by Dolley's son from her first marriage, Payne Todd, a handsome, high-spirited lad who was given to excesses of gambling and womanizing, and who had been dubbed "The American Prince" by the newspapers. He had caused his mother considerable distress and embarrassment since his arrival a few weeks ago.

The sound of cheers and clapping alerted Samantha to the Madisons' arrival. Rising from the bench, she reentered the house to find the presidential couple stepping into the room.

Smiling with genuine pleasure, she observed Dolley being trailed by her diminutive husband, James, or Jemmy as he was usually called. Though the President stood at least three inches shorter than his wife and was nearly seventeen years older, their differences seemed to matter little; the love shining on their faces told her that much.

Mrs. Madison was resplendent in a pink satin gown trimmed in ermine. She sported a white satin turban with several white ostrich plumes cascading from it; dark bangs peeked out from beneath it. She was large framed and full busted, with a soft oval face, an impish mouth turned up into a smile, and widely set blue eyes. She was a handsome woman, not beautiful in the classical sense, but pretty just the same.

James, in contrast, was dressed very soberly and out of fashion in short black breeches with buckles at the knee, black silk stockings, and shoes with strings. He wore his hair powdered, dressed full over the ears, and tied behind his neck. His dress and manner bespoke a sedentary, studious man. He was as small and delicate as Dolley was big, and together they made an incongruous pair.

The room pulsated with life as soon as the Madisons entered. The weekly "Drawing Rooms" made up an important part of Washington society, attracting young people eager for a minor flirtation, social dowagers bent on obtaining the latest gossip, and politicians and deal makers hoping to strike an advantageous business arrangement. No invitations were necessary, but when one was issued, as it had been in Samantha's case, it was politic to attend.

As the presidential couple lined up to greet their guests, Samantha made her way forward through the throng of jubilant well-wishers to pay her respects. Butterflies danced in her stomach as she crossed the highly polished parquet floor. This was her first time meeting the President and his lady, and although she had heard of their friendly, warm manner, she was still uncertain what type of reception the granddaughter of Ezra Lawrence would receive.

She needn't have worried. Dolley's effusive greeting put her instantly at ease.

"My dear, we're delighted that you were able to come. Jemmy and I always enjoy being surrounded by the young people of Washington City."

The President nodded in agreement but said nothing, and Samantha surmised that he probably didn't get much of a chance to speak when the gregarious First Lady was by his side.

"Have you met my son Payne?" Dolley continued, indicating with a wave of her hand the curly-haired young man to her left. "He certainly noticed you right off." Her lilting laughter at Payne's embarrassment filled the air.

Samantha almost felt sorry for the young man until she noticed the erotic glitter in his eyes, the way they raked over her in a frankly assessing manner. Pasting on a smile, she offered her hand only to have it snatched up by the tall man standing next to him.

At a loss for words, she could only stare as the long, tanned fingers wrapped themselves around her much smaller ones. They were the hands of a gentleman, yet she could see they were not immune to a day's work. Slowly, she lifted her eyes to gaze into the most startling blue orbs she had ever encountered. They were like deep, placid pools of blue water, and she thought if she looked into them long enough, she'd be able to see all the way into his soul. His hair, as black as a raven's wing, was worn short, coming to rest on the collar of an immaculate white ruffled shirt.

"Allow me to introduce Daniel Fortune," she heard Mrs. Madison say. "The Fortunes reside in Williamsburg and have been friends of ours for years. Jemmy thinks of Daniel as a second son. He's watched him grow into a strapping young man."

Strapping wasn't quite the word Samantha would have used to describe Daniel Fortune. Muscular. Godlike. Beautiful. All those words came to mind as she stared into his handsome face. He was Adonis come to life.

Suddenly aware that she was gaping open-mouthed at the stranger, Samantha recovered herself enough to reply, "How do you do, Mr. Fortune. I'm pleased to make your acquaintance." Her voice sounded breathless, as if she had just been kicked in the stomach by a mule. The feeling was compounded when Daniel Fortune's tanned face and compelling lips broke into an engaging grin.

"The pleasure is mine, I assure you, Miss Wilder. Would you care to dance?"

Staring helplessly at Dolley, who was nodding her encouragement, Samantha let herself be led out onto the dance floor. They joined three other couples for a quadrille, and Samantha soon found that Daniel For-

33

tune was not only handsome but an accomplished dancer as well. By the time the spirited dance ended, she was lightheaded and breathless, a condition she was certain was not caused by the lively steps.

"Would you care for a bit of refreshment?" Daniel asked. Not waiting for her reply, he propelled her toward the far end of the room and seated her on the Empire sofa, promising to return momentarily.

As if caught in a whirlwind, Samantha rested against the bright yellow damask upholstery, taking a moment to catch her breath. She had never met a man so . . . so commanding before, she thought. And though it went against her independent nature to be treated with such high-handedness, she found it didn't bother her. Not wanting to delve too deeply into why this was so, she occupied her thoughts with an inspection of the room.

Gazing about the attractively furnished formal reception area, she noted the tall, mahogany secretary-bookcase standing against the opposite wall. To her right was the intricately carved, white marble fireplace on whose mantel rested a bronze-doré clock, which played pastoral music every hour on the hour. On either side of the clock, two French gilt porcelain vases contained large sprays of white magnolia, framing the Gilbert Stuart portrait of Dolley which hung above the fireplace.

Further inspection of the room was prevented by a pair of long, muscular legs housed in a pair of close-fitting, black broadcloth trousers. Her eyes traveled up the long length of him, widening slightly when they encountered a very overt male protrusion, continuing up a washboard-flat stomach, across a well-muscled chest, stopping at a pair of sensual lips that made her heart pound erratically in her chest. Daniel Fortune leaned over her, holding a glass of punch, and by the amused expresson on his face, she could tell he found her frank assessment of his person amusing.

"I hope you like sangaree. It was all I could find."

Feeling her cheeks burn, she took the glass he proffered, muttered her thanks, and drank down a large measure of the sweet, cooling liquid. A moment later, her eyes began to water. "Gracious me! Are there spirits in the punch?" she sputtered.

Removing the cup from her hand, Daniel placed it on the table, taking the seat next to her. "Sorry," he said, barely able to conceal his grin. "I thought you knew." He allowed her a moment to compose herself, then asked, "Are you new here, Miss Wilder? I don't recall seeing you at the Wednesday Drawing Rooms before."

"I arrived only this month. I'm originally from Boston."

"I see. You seem to be a long way from home. What brings you to Washington City?"

Afraid to reveal her true motives to a man she barely knew, she reached for a plausible explanation. "My grandfather and I are visiting friends."

"Anyone I know? I'm well-acquainted with most of the local populace."

"My grandfather has business dealings with Adam Bainbridge. He's a close friend of the family. Do you know him?"

"Mr. Bainbridge and I are acquainted. How is it that you're here tonight without Mr. Bainbridge?" And why didn't you mention your brother? he added silently, noting how she lowered her eyes to mask her nervousness. What did she have to be nervous about? he wondered.

"Adam had some business to conduct. Since I had already planned to attend, I decided to come alone."

"How fortunate for me." He reached for her hand, bringing it to his lips for a kiss.

Tingles of awareness darted up her arm as Daniel's lips came in contact with her skin. Pulling her hand quickly away, she sought to bring the conversation around to a more impersonal subject. "Do you have news of the war, Mr. Fortune?"

His eyes lit with suspicion. "Why do you ask? It's an odd subject for a lady to concern herself with." He noted the color that flooded her cheeks once again.

"I'm merely curious to know what the local citizens think of the war. As you may have heard, we New Englanders are not all in favor of it. My grandfather is particularly opposed."

Daniel fought to keep his anger under control. New England's sentiments against the war were well-known to him. The New England states' refusal to furnish men or money to help in the war with England was an audacious, calculated attempt on their part to cripple the federal government. It was no surprise to learn that her grandfather shared the same views. He was probably some rich merchant out to fatten his purse.

Masking his hostility, he asked, "And who might he be?"

Samantha smiled. "Ezra Lawrence. Perhaps you've heard of him. He served under General Washington during the War of Independence."

Daniel almost groaned. Ezra Lawrence. He might have known. He had read some of the letters the old coot had written to the editor of the opposition newspaper, the *Washington Federalist,* denouncing the war with Great Britain.

"No . . . can't say that I have," he lied. "But perhaps my father has. He, too, served with Washington."

"Well, then, it seems we have something in common."

"I daresay, Miss Wilder, that we have a lot in common."

The intensity of Daniel's gaze made Samantha squirm in her seat. Her throat felt suddenly dry; she reached for her glass once again. Ignoring his enigmatic remark, she inquired, "What is it you do for a living, Mr. Fortune? Do you have a trade?" Though his clothes and manners were that of a gentleman, his deeply tanned complexion and work-roughened hands indicated a man who spent a great deal of time out-of-doors.

"I am a man of many talents, Miss Wilder, adept at a great many things. If you have a particular service you would like me to perform, I'm sure we can come to some sort of an agreement."

His gaze wandered insultingly over the bare flesh of her bosom, leaving no doubt in Samantha's mind as to the kind of service he was offering. The color touching her cheeks had little to do with the potency of the drink she was sipping. Rising from her seat, she fought the urge to slap the arrogant smile off his face. "I really must be going. I have important matters I need to attend to."

"Like finding your brother?"

The question caught her off guard. She stumbled

and would have fallen had not the strong arms of Daniel Fortune come around her waist to steady her.

"I believe the punch has caught up with you, Miss Wilder."

"It is not the punch and you know it," she hissed, pulling out of his embrace. "What do you know of the search for my brother?"

Grabbing hold of her arm, Daniel led her to a private alcove near an open window. "I told you, I am a man of many talents. Perhaps I can be persuaded to assist you."

She stiffened. "Why you . . ." She lifted her hand only to have it grabbed and brought to Daniel's lips for another kiss—a kiss that burned as hot as her temper.

"Let's not make a scene, Miss Wilder. Remember, I might be in a position to help locate your brother."

His words stilled her rage for the moment. "What is it you want? I have little money." She could see she had been wrong: Daniel Fortune was no gentleman.

"I don't require your money; I have plenty of my own."

"What then?" She braced herself for his reply. She might be an innocent when it came to men, but she wasn't stupid.

"Meet me tomorrow at the edge of Parrott's Woods. Perhaps we shall be able to strike a bargain of sorts."

"I sincerely doubt it, Mr. Fortune. Why would I need your assistance? I have already enlisted the help of Mr. Bainbridge. I doubt his price will be as high as yours."

"I wouldn't count on it." Before she could reply, he added, "Don't disappoint me, Miss Wilder. Your brother's life may well depend on your capitulation." At her look of outrage, he grinned, displaying teeth as white as the finest set of matched pearls. "Shall we say ten o'clock?" Without waiting for her to answer, he stalked off, disappearing into the crowd.

Grateful for the open window, Samantha fanned herself with quick, nervous strokes. The audacity of the man! Why should she meet a perfect stranger in a secluded area of the city? Did he think she was hopelessly naive? But what if he knew something about Robbie? What if he could help her locate her missing brother?

The questions spun around and around in her head until she felt quite dizzy. Who was this Daniel Fortune that had turned her life into such a turmoil in only a few short moments? And what did he want with her?

Chapter Three

Listening with only half an ear to what Albert Gallatin, the Secretary of the Treasury, was saying about the wretched financial state of the government, Daniel observed Samantha Wilder's hasty departure from the drawing room. He smiled to himself. She was a beauty, all right! Joseph had been correct in his assessment of her looks. But what about his other judgments? Something about Miss Wilder didn't quite ring true.

She was a Northerner raised in a Federalist state among Federalist sympathizers, yet she claimed to have no political allegiance of her own. If that were true, why was she so intent on ferreting information from such an unscrupulous individual as Edward de Crillon? And why had she asked his own opinion of the war?

Could Samantha Wilder be working for Pickering and Bainbridge? he wondered. Could she be trying to gain the confidences of the politically powerful in Washington by worming her way into the Madisons' good graces, only to stab them in the back?

The blue eyes glittered dangerously. Well, it wouldn't work. He would see to that. Come tomorrow he would find out just what the mysterious Miss Wilder was up to. If she thought to spy on the government of Madison, she would be in for a big surprise. Others had tried and failed. It would be a shame to stretch such a lovely neck on the end of a rope, but stretch it he would. It would be a pity though, he thought, feeling a tightening in his loins. He could think of far more pleasurable things to do with Samantha Wilder than hang her.

Adjusting the skirts of her green velvet riding habit a bit more modestly, Samantha positioned herself upon the rented roan and proceeded north up Water Street toward the rural area known as Georgetown Heights.

Whatever had possessed her to commit this folly? she asked herself for the hundredth time as the horse picked its way along the cobblestone streets. Why had she decided to agree to Daniel Fortune's demands? The answer was always the same: Robbie. 'Twas the only thing that could make her don her heavy riding habit, she thought dismally.

Like dew to a petal, the material clung to her skin, making her feel like a wet rag. Pulling at the offending garment, she gazed up at the sky. White, fluffy clouds blanketed the heavens where only minutes before a palette of blue had appeared. The clouds offered little relief. The air was still heavy with moisture, and it wouldn't surprise her if there was a shower before the day ended.

"Easy girl," Samantha crooned, pulling back on the reins when the horse tried to pick up her pace. Molly, the mount she had rented from the livery at Suter's Tavern, seemed docile and well-behaved, but she would take no chances. There would be no wild galloping for her. She had never taken a shine to horses nor they to her, not since her brother's horse, Snuffy, had dumped her on her rear at the age of ten.

Shortening the reins and taking a firm hold, she continued at a sedate pace, enjoying the lush green countryside that surrounded her. She rode beneath a canopy of oaks and cottonwoods; vines of wild grape clung to the branches overhead, emitting a sweet fragrance.

The smell of water and the immediate drop in temperature told her that she was nearing Rock Creek. Passing the cemetery, her anxiety increased as the sound of rushing water grew more distinct, and she realized she was close to her destination.

As the horse plodded its way across the dried leaves and twigs of the bridal path, Samantha's mind wandered back to the previous night's conversation with Daniel Fortune. What motive, if not money, did Mr. Fortune have in offering to help locate her brother? What was in it for him? she wondered. Human nature, being what it was, would not allow her to believe that he didn't have an ulterior motive in mind. And it sent her pulses racing to think what that motive might be.

He was no gentleman. She had seen the lascivious glances he had directed her way. There was an animal intensity about him—an unleashed wildness hovering just beneath the surface of his polite exterior. And against her will, it had captivated her.

Spying the object of her consideration seated atop a large granite boulder, Samantha's heart pounded fiercely in her chest. Palms, that moments ago were dry, were wet with anticipation.

"Keep your wits about you girl." She could hear her grandfather's voice as clearly as if he were standing next to her, though she knew he still slept soundly in his bed. Fortunately, it was Ezra Lawrence's habit of sleeping late that had allowed her the freedom to commit her indiscretion this morning.

Swallowing hard, she pulled Molly to a halt a few feet from where Daniel Fortune sat. He looked relaxed—totally at ease, as if he didn't have a care in the world. She found his self-assured manner unnerving.

Daniel couldn't repress his grin at the sight of Samantha Wilder's awkward dismount off the most pathetic piece of horseflesh he had ever seen. He would bet money that she hadn't seated a horse more than ten times in her entire life. The jaunty plumed riding hat she wore, set at a rakish angle, looked hopelessly lopsided. Her habit, much too heavy for the warm Virginia weather, was wrinkled and damp, clinging to her lush curves in a most provocative manner. She looked miserable and utterly desirable.

Pushing himself off the boulder, he strode forward, noting the wary look on her face as she watched him approach. He smiled inwardly, relishing the fact that he made her nervous.

Samantha clung to the reins like a lifeline, as if the thin strips of leather could offer some security against Daniel Fortune's confident manner. He was dressed quite differently than he had been last night. Last night, his formal attire had provided the illusion of gentility.

43

But today, in the tan buckskin breeches and loose-fitting shirt, he was every inch the predator stalking his prey. And there was no doubt in her mind that she was the prey.

Unconsciously, her fist tightened on the reins, causing the horse to throw back her head in protest. Frightened of the snorting beast, Samantha dropped the reins, watching in dismay as Molly darted off for parts unknown.

"Damnation!" she blurted, not realizing she had spoken aloud until Daniel's deep, booming laughter filled the air, alerting her to his presence once again.

"It seems your steed has decided to return home, Miss Wilder," Daniel remarked. "And from the frightened look on your face, I can see you are entertaining similar thoughts."

Throwing her shoulders back, she tilted up her chin, staring defiantly into the twinkling blue eyes that mocked her. "Don't flatter yourself, Mr. Fortune. I'm not scared of you, but merely upset about Molly. She belongs to Suter's Tavern."

"Molly?" He threw back his head and roared, causing Samantha to grit her teeth in exasperation.

"I'm glad you find my predicament so amusing, Mr. Fortune. I, for one, do not relish the idea of a two-mile walk home."

"Come, sit down, Miss Wilder," he said, indicating the gray boulder, amusement still evident in his voice. "It will help prepare you for the arduous journey ahead." Taking her hand, he pulled her toward the rock. "I must admit, I'm surprised you showed up today. Apparently, I underestimated your determination."

44

"There is nothing I won't do to find my brother."

His right eyebrow shot up. "Nothing, Miss Wilder? Well, that will make what I have to propose that much easier."

Jumping to her feet, her eyes flashing fire, Samantha incinerated him with a look meant to kill. "Really, Mr. Fortune, you insult me! What kind of woman do you take me for? I will not stand here and allow you to malign me further." She turned to leave.

Daniel smiled. Samantha was really most extraordinary when she was angry. With her pert breasts heaving in indignation and her cheeks flushed rosy, he caught a glimpse of the real woman behind the icy facade, and he liked what he saw.

"You wound me, Miss Wilder. I wasn't aware that I had made any improper suggestions. What was it I said that upset you so?"

His look of innocence didn't fool her a bit. He could mask his sly innuendos behind unfailing politeness, but she had seen the unguarded lust in his eyes more than once. "You intimated that you would be willing to help me locate my brother for a price. I'm not naive, Mr. Fortune."

"It's not that I don't desire your lovely body, Miss Wilder, for I do, let me assure you. But I had other services in mind when I suggested that we could strike a bargain."

Samantha gasped, her face turning red in the process. She brought her hands up to cover her flaming cheeks.

"No need for embarrassment, Miss Wilder. I'm well aware that you and Mr. Bainbridge have an, shall we say, an arrangement. I wouldn't think to stake claim to

45

another man's territory."

Samantha stared wide-eyed and open-mouthed at the innuendos Daniel was making. She started to deny them, but then thought better of it. Why not let him think she was under another man's protection? It would keep their own relationship strictly business, and that's the way she wanted it. She quickly regained her composure.

"You haven't told me what it is you desire of me, Mr. Fortune."

"First off, you can start by calling me Daniel, and I will call you Samantha. I'm not one to stand on formalities." At her nod of acquiescence, he continued, "I understand that you are searching for your brother . . . that he was impressed off the *Chesapeake* earlier this month."

"That's correct. I've enlisted the aid of Mr. Gales, the editor of the newspaper. Is that how you found out?"

"I never reveal my sources, Samantha. It's unimportant where I get my information. If you're interested in helping me, I might be able to locate your brother for you."

"I don't know what it is you want from me, Mr. . . . Daniel. I've only just arrived in Washington City. I'm not well acquainted with the workings of the government nor the people who run it."

Her innocent posture fascinated him. He watched her reel off lie after lie and never bat an eyelash. He would bet money that she was working for Bainbridge. Her alliance with him, coupled with her family's documented support for the Federalist movement, left no doubt in his mind that she was a spy. He had seen other

46

women agents before but never one as smooth as Samantha Wilder.

"You underestimate your abilities, Samantha. Your association with Adam Bainbridge and Senator Pickering could prove very useful to me."

"I don't understand. What does my relationship with Adam have to do with anything?"

"Come now, Samantha, let's not play dumb. I'm sure you are aware that Bainbridge and Pickering are involved with the Federalist movement."

"Of course," she replied, her brow wrinkling in puzzlement, "but what does that have to do with finding my brother?"

"There's always a price to pay. Nothing ever comes free, love."

She stiffened at the endearment but couldn't prevent the acceleration of her pulse.

"If you desire information about your brother," he continued, "you're going to have to trade it for information that I require about Bainbridge."

She gasped. "But I don't have any information about Adam. He doesn't tell me anything."

Daniel snickered in disbelief. "I find it hard to believe that when a man and a woman share an intimate relationship, they do not also share intimate secrets."

Samantha blushed to the tips of her toes. What had she gotten herself into? How could she deny what Daniel accused her of, when she had already led him to believe it was true? Oh, Lord, what should she do now? *Think Samantha. Think.*

Staring into Daniel's rigid features, she knew he was impatient for some type of answer. Suddenly, she knew what course of action she would take. Two could play this game, she decided.

"I had no idea you were suggesting that I spy on Adam when you first suggested we enter into a bargain, Daniel," she brazened out. "I'm not sure that I could do that in good conscience."

"I'm not asking you to reveal intimate details of your relationship with Bainbridge. All I want to know is where he goes, who he meets with—that sort of thing. I want him kept under surveillance."

"Why?"

"Adam works for a very influential man. The President feels Pickering does not have the best interests of the country at heart. He merely wants us to observe him . . . keep an eye on him. If you monitor Adam's movements, we can get a better feel for what Pickering is up to."

"So, it's not Adam that's under suspicion?"

Daniel smiled smoothly. "Of course not. We understand that Adam is merely working for the senator. It's Senator Pickering that we're concerned about," he lied.

A feeling of relief surged through her. For a fleeting moment she thought Daniel had suspected Adam of some treasonous activity. She'd known Adam long enough to know that he would never do anything to harm his country. He was a very patriotic individual— almost fanatically so.

"And if I agree to your terms?"

"I will get your brother back."

Hope poured through every inch of her being. "How do I know you can? What guarantee do I have?"

"I have new information for you, Samantha. It's only the beginning. You help me watch Pickering; I'll

48

help you find your brother."

Excitement sparked in the depths of her eyes. "What news do you have?"

He shook his head. "Oh, no. Not so fast. First we have to strike a bargain."

Samantha had no intention of spying on Adam, Senator Pickering, or anyone else for that matter. But Daniel didn't need to know that. If she could convince him that she would be his willing accomplice, she could gather enough details about her brother's whereabouts to locate him herself. In the meantime, all she had to do was feed Daniel a few bits of information that she picked up here and there. It was risky, but it just might work. It had to; Robbie's life depended on it.

"What is it you wish me to do?"

"Just keep your ears open, love. If you hear anything that you think might be detrimental to President Madison's administration, I want to know immediately. If either Bainbridge or Pickering meet with anyone you suspect might be involved with the British, report it. It's as simple as that."

As simple as that, Samantha repeated silently. Considering the fact that Adam never confided in her, and that she was perpetrating the biggest lie of her life, things weren't so simple. "And if I agree, you will tell me what you know of Robbie?"

"That's it in a nutshell, love. We cooperate with each other and each of us gets what we want."

Running her hand over the rough surface of the nearby oak, Samantha pretended to consider the proposal. After a few minutes, she held out her hand and smiled. "I agree to the terms, Daniel. I'll help you in exchange for information about my brother."

Caressing the back of her hand with his fingers, Daniel smiled into her eyes. "Don't think to dupe me once we strike our bargain, Samantha. I'm not a man who tolerates deception."

Even through the glove she wore, Samantha felt the heat from Daniel's fingers sear her skin. The words he spoke, coupled with the strange sensations she felt in the pit of her stomach, rendered her speechless. She inclined her head, hoping he did not see the confusion in her eyes.

Walking over to the black stallion who was tethered to a spindly cottonwood, Daniel reached into his saddlebags, withdrawing a sheet of parchment; he handed it to her. "This is a list of the prisoners that were taken to Halifax. As you can see, your brother's name is not among them."

"Is he dead, then?" She stared wordlessly at the paper.

"No. If you read farther, you will see the list of dead and injured. He's not among those either."

Relief washed over her, bringing tears to her eyes. "But what does it mean?"

Taking the paper out of her hands, he refolded it. "What it means, love, is that you need to bring me some information that I deem useful. Once you do, I will relay the rest of what I know about your brother's whereabouts."

Samantha's head snapped up, her eyes suddenly dry and sparking in anger. "You're hateful! I told you that I would exchange information with you. Why won't you tell me what you know of my brother?"

"I've been told many things by many women, Samantha. I've learned that women aren't always as truthful as they profess to be." Joanna Stapleton's deceitful smile flashed before his eyes. With concentrated effort, he brushed the painful memory of his former intended away. "I prefer to deal with concrete evidence not promises. When you deliver, then so shall I."

"Very well. Where do you propose to meet?"

"I have secured rooms at Suter's Tavern, which I understand is only a short distance from your home. I will arrange to contact you when the time is right."

"You mean I have to wait around until you're good and ready to meet with me? How do I know you won't disappear?"

"Really, love, if I didn't know better, I would think you didn't trust me."

"I don't trust you. I've only agreed to your ridiculous proposal to find my brother. If his life wasn't at stake, I wouldn't have anything further to do with you."

Stepping closer, he grabbed hold of her shoulders, pulling her into his chest. The smell of lilac rose up to tease his already overheated emotions. "You lie. I can see it in your eyes. You want me as much as I want you, and you know it."

"No!" she denied, shaking her head vehemently. "Let me go!" She tried to pull out of his embrace, but she was no match for his strength.

"I will, but not before I do something I've been wanting to do from the first moment I laid eyes on you." Without another word, he lowered his head, covering her lips with his own.

Her calm was shattered. The touch of his lips sent a shock wave throughout her entire body: her mouth burned with fire; the blood rushed through her veins

51

like a raging river, pounding in her brain and heart, rendering her knees incapable of support. She leaned into him. The spicy scent of his shaving soap, mixed with the masculine odors of leather and horseflesh, filled her senses. His hands began a gentle massage over her back, leaving a trail of fire wherever they touched. When she felt them move lower to cup her buttocks, she pulled back, quickly regaining her senses.

"How dare you!" she screeched, taking deep breaths to calm the wild beating of her heart. Drawing back her hand, she tried to slap his face, but he was quicker, catching it in midair.

"That is the second time you have tried to strike me, Samantha. It had better be your last."

Clutching her sides, which were heaving in anger, she replied, "You, sir, are no gentleman!"

"And you, love, are no gentlewoman. You have fires banked within you ready to burst into flame. Do Bainbridge's kisses leave you weak-kneed and panting?"

"You disgust me! You aren't fit to wipe Adam's boots. He's a gentleman. He would never think to handle me in such a fashion."

"Aha . . . that explains it, then."

"Explains what?"

His grin was infuriating. "Why, your response, of course!"

"Oooh!" Gritting her teeth and clenching her fists, she turned on her heel and proceeded to walk back the way she had come.

"Don't you want a ride back to town?" Daniel called after her.

Without turning, she replied, "I would rather walk a

thousand miles than be in close proximity to you again."

"Very well, have it your own way." Mounting up on the stallion, he rode abreast of her. "Are you sure you don't want to ride? It's an awfully long walk back."

Staring up into his smiling face, she shot daggers at him. "I've never been more sure of anything in my life, Mr. Fortune. Good-bye and good riddance."

Her last words were punctuated with a loud boom of thunder. Soon the heavens opened up to muffle anything further she was going to say on the subject. Tears of frustration mingled with raindrops as she stared up at Daniel's grinning face and outstretched hand. Swallowing her pride, she reached out, allowing him to pull her up in front of him, praying fervently that a bolt of lightning would strike him dead and put her out of her misery.

"That's better," she heard him say as his arms came around her to grab the reins. "Just settle back. I'll have you home in no time."

The feel of his chest pressed against her back was torture. She could feel the steady beat of his heart through her rain-soaked jacket; it seemed to beat in unison with her own.

They made the journey back to town in total silence. But then, they didn't need to speak. Their bodies communicated what their mouths failed to say.

Chapter Four

The arrogant jackanapes! Samantha fumed silently, slamming her hairbrush against the mahogany dressing table. Two weeks had passed, and still there was no word from Daniel Fortune. She should have known better than to trust him. What made her think that she could? She already knew he was no gentleman. Far from it. He was a scoundrel—a rake.

She touched her forefinger to her lips, remembering the kiss he boldly stole—the one she hadn't been all that reluctant to give.

"Damn the man!" she cursed in an uncharacteristic fit of ill temper. She was usually calm and controlled about most things. But when it came to Daniel Fortune, she was unable to stifle her hostility. He made her feel uncomfortable, on edge, like a horse with a burr beneath his blanket.

"Is you all right, Miss Sam?"

Catching sight of Dulcie's concerned expression in the mirror, Samantha smiled apologetically at the black maid and pushed herself up from the embroidered stool. "I'm fine, Dulcie. Just a bit on edge."

Continuing to smooth the white cotton sheets onto the fluffy feather mattress of the tester bed, Dulcie shook her head of black, kinky hair. "What's got into you, Miss Sam? You been pricklier than a porcupine since that handsome gentleman brought you home looking like a drowned kitten."

Tightening the sash of her blue silk dressing gown as if she were pulling the edges of a hangman's noose together, Samantha's eyes glittered dangerously. "That so-called 'handsome gentleman' was supposed to give me information about Robbie's whereabouts. I've been patient for two weeks; I'll not wait one more day."

Dulcie clucked softly under her breath. Miss Sam had that determined look on her face again. The one she'd seen all too frequently in the last few weeks. As sweet a child as the mistress was, patience was definitely not one of her virtues.

"What you aim to do, honey? You knows it ain't safe to go parading about by yourself. Not with them pigs sailin' about."

Samantha smiled at Dulcie's eloquent description of the British Navy. Dulcie was never one to mince words; it was the one quality that endeared the tiny, black woman to her.

"Don't worry, Dulcie. I merely intend to pay Mr. Gales another visit. Perhaps he's heard something from Mr. Fortune or has gathered some news on his own." Though she thought it unlikely, since she had checked the newspaper each day without fail and found no notice pertaining to her.

Pulling up the rose satin counterpane and fluffing the goose down pillows, Dulcie cast a critical eye at the bed and then at her mistress. "I'd best come with you."

"And raise Grandfather's suspicions? I think not. I'll be back within the hour. If not, you have my permission to form a search party." She smiled at the maid's indignant expression. "And Dulcie, do try to keep Grandfather in an even temper. I have enough to face without his ill humor."

"Hmph!" Dulcie declared, crossing her bony arms over an equally sparse chest. "That man hasn't had a moment of good humor since the day he was born."

Another perceptive assessment, Samantha agreed silently, though aloud, she replied, "Nevertheless, I'm counting on your help. I'll be back as quickly as I can."

The tinkling of the tiny brass bell over the doorway announced Samantha's arrival as she stepped into the office of the *National Intelligencer* once again. Straightening her purple velvet comet hat, she waited anxiously for Mr. Gales to appear.

A moment later, a young woman, about her own age, entered the room. Samantha's eyes widened at the woman's unkempt appearance. Her face and hands were smudged with ink; her hair, the color of carrots, peeped out from beneath a mobcap which was once white linen.

"May I help you?" the young woman asked, wiping her hands on her apron, brushing at the stray wisps of hair in a self-conscious gesture.

Samantha returned the woman's smile with one of her own. "I was hoping to speak with Mr. Gales. Might he be available?"

The red curls bobbed from side to side. "Sorry, miss.

Mr. Gales has gone to Baltimore. I'm afraid he won't be back until tomorrow."

"I see," Samantha replied, unable to hide her crestfallen expression.

"Perhaps I can help. I'm Mr. Gales's assistant, Willy."

Samantha's eyes rounded, her mouth dropping open before she remembered her manners and snapped it shut. "You're Willy?!" She remembered Gales had mentioned his assistant Willy, but she had assumed he was referring to a man.

"Yes, miss. Willy is short for Wilhelmina. Wilhelmina Matthews. I'm Joseph Gales's niece." She extended an ink-stained hand in greeting.

Staring at the hand and then at the elfin smile which accompanied it, Samantha grabbed it eagerly. "How do you do? I'm Samantha Wilder. Forgive me, I didn't realize Mr. Gales had any family."

Coming out from behind the counter, Willy motioned for Samantha to follow. When they reached the rear of the shop, she pulled out a chair, indicating that Samantha should sit.

"No need to apologize. I haven't lived with Uncle Joseph long. Just since," she paused, setting the pot of tea she was holding down on the table, "my parents died. They were killed a few months back in a hay wagon accident. Uncle Joseph sort of adopted me. We've always gotten along famously."

"I'm terribly sorry; I didn't know."

"Not many people do. I've tried to keep myself as inconspicuous as possible, seeing as how I'm a woman doing what's rightfully a man's job."

Samantha nodded, unsure of what to say. There was

57

certainly no reticence about Miss Matthews, she thought. But perhaps that was for the best, if she was going to try to compete in a man's world.

"I hope that doesn't make you feel uneasy," Willy went on to say. "I know most ladies of quality would frown knowing that I work in such an unladylike profession, but I truly love it. And I've always been a bit of a tomboy."

Remembering all the escapades she and Robbie had gotten into as children, Samantha smiled wistfully. She, too, had been something of a tomboy. Unfortunately, militant Mrs. Coombs and a stint at Mrs. Dinker's boarding school had taken care of that inclination.

"It doesn't make me feel uneasy at all. I quite envy the fact that you are able to do exactly as you please. Being a lady isn't all that it's professed to be." She thought of the confining corsets, the heavy petticoats, the uncomfortable layers of clothing she was required to wear in all types of weather, and frowned.

Her skill with a needle was suspect at best; her cooking left much to be desired. But then, Mrs. Dinker hadn't deemed those things important—not as important as learning to sit with her hands folded demurely in her lap, playing a soothing piece on the pianoforte, holding her fan in just the right position. That's what being a lady was all about, according to dear Mrs. Dinker.

"I feared as much," Willy admitted, passing a plate of oatmeal cakes over to Samantha. "But I'm afraid Uncle Joseph is going to attempt to turn me into one. He's just humoring me, or so he says, until my mourning period is done."

Studying Willy's gamine features—the large green eyes, the sprinkling of freckles across the bridge of her nose, the creamy white skin, Samantha decided that beneath the grime, Willy was quite an attractive woman. It wouldn't take much to transform her into a proper lady—one at whom society wouldn't sneer.

"Where did you live before your parents died?" Samantha asked, nibbling her cookie, suddenly realizing that she hadn't had a bite to eat since breakfast.

"We had a small farm in Virginia, near Fredericksburg."

Samantha's head popped up. *Fredericksburg.* Wasn't that the town Mrs. Madison had said Daniel was from? Perhaps Willy was acquainted with him.

"Do you know a man by the name of Daniel Fortune? I understand he lives in Fredericksburg."

"I do. But Daniel doesn't live in Fredericksburg. His family resides in Williamsburg, farther south." Smiling impishly, she added, "I see you're already acquainted with one of the most eligible men in the area."

Feeling the color creep up her cheeks, Samantha pleated and repleated the folds of her lavender dimity gown. "Mr. Fortune and I are business associates."

"Well, wouldn't I like to do business with that great hunk of a man," Willy admitted. "He fairly takes my breath away each time he comes in to talk with Uncle Joseph."

"You like him, then?" Samantha almost smiled at the rapturous expression on Willy's face. Daniel did have a way of captivating a woman. *Didn't she know?* Flustered by the direction her thoughts were taking, Samantha redirected her attention to what Willy was saying.

"I like Daniel fine, but we're just friends. He's too staid and serious for the likes of me. I'm looking for someone more . . ."

"Kind?" Samantha supplied.

Willy shook her head and laughed. "No, miss. Daniel is very kind and generous. The word I was searching for was lighthearted. Daniel's too brooding, too mysterious. It's almost as if he's harboring some deep dark secret."

Samantha mulled over Willy's revelation, waiting for her to continue.

"I hear tell his father had some trouble with the British, but Daniel never talks of it. Uncle Joseph says it's best to let dead dogs lie."

The chiming of the tall-case clock on the far wall captured Samantha's immediate attention; she gasped, fearing that Dulcie had already sent out the militia in search of her. "I had no idea it was so late. I really must be going. My family will be worried."

"In case you were wondering about Daniel's whereabouts . . . for business purposes, I mean," Willy said, following Samantha to the door. "He's gone down to Williamsburg to visit his family."

"I really wasn't wondering. I . . . I . . ."

Noting the flush covering Samantha Wilder's flawless complexion, Willy smiled inwardly, thinking that the pretty woman wasn't a very good liar. "At any rate, I've enjoyed our chat, Miss Wilder. I don't have much opportunity to talk with women my own age."

Grateful for the change in conversation, Samantha took a deep breath and smiled. "Please, you must call me Samantha or Sam, if you like. I, too, have enjoyed our visit. Perhaps we can do this again very soon."

She had learned more about Daniel Fortune in one short hour from Willy than she had learned from either Mr. Gales or Daniel himself. The young woman was a virtual font of information. And she liked her. It would be nice to have a woman friend. She hadn't made the acquaintance of many women in Washington . . . none that she cared to associate with, at any rate.

"I look forward to it, Sam. The fact that we both share boys' nicknames sort of makes us kindred spirits. Don't you agree?"

Giving Willy a hug, Samantha smiled widely. "Indeed, I do. I agree wholeheartedly. I will see you soon."

Stepping outside, she looked back and waved, feeling happier than she had in weeks. She wondered if Willy had that effect on all people. Pulling the door closed, she turned toward the street, failing to notice the impeccably dressed blond man who was standing directly in her path.

"Samantha! For heaven's sake! What on earth are you doing here? I thought I told you not to wander the streets without an escort."

Samantha recognized the voice immediately. Looking up, she found Adam's angry gaze upon her and sighed inwardly. What rotten luck! she thought dismally. Now he would want explanations, and explanations were something she was fresh out of at the moment.

He was standing smack-dab in the middle of the walkway, arms crossed over his chest, looking very much like an indignant schoolmaster. She would have laughed at his ridiculous posture, but something in his eyes, perhaps the fact that they were bulging in outrage, made her think twice about it.

"Hello, Adam," she replied, trying to keep her voice even. "What brings you outside on such a warm day?"

"Don't try to exchange pleasantries with me, Samantha. It won't work. I want to know what you were doing inside the offices of this trashy newspaper, and why you have chosen to disobey my instructions?"

"I was visiting a friend, if you must know. Though it is really none of your business."

"A friend." His tone took on a note of incredulity. "I hope you are not referring to that ragamuffin niece of Joseph Gales. The man is bad enough, but that half-girl, half-boy he employs is disgusting."

Samantha's eyes flashed like summer lightning. Grabbing on to Adam's arm, she pulled him away from the door of the newspaper office, fearful that Willy would hear his rude comments. "How dare you speak of my friend that way? You don't even know Willy Matthews. She's a very nice person. And as for Mr. Gales, he is very nice, too."

Adam stared at her suspiciously. "How is it that you are acquainted with Joseph Gales? The man is a troublemaker, no better than those War Hawks with which he associates." He thought of Henry Clay and John Calhoun, and how they'd grown more vocal with every passing day. His eyes narrowed. The fools would have to be stopped.

Pausing beneath the sign that read, "Coach Stop," Samantha plopped down on the wooden bench, trying to get her anger under control.

"Not that it's any of your business, but I met Mr. Gales at the Madisons' gala the other evening. He seemed a very nice gentleman." Adam turned so red at her disclosure, Samantha thought he was going to burst a blood vessel.

Taking the seat next to her, he impaled her with icy eyes. "Who may I ask was your escort? I wasn't aware that you were acquainted with any gentlemen other than myself."

She smiled, delighting in his annoyance. "I went by myself . . . unescorted."

"Does your grandfather know?"

"Of course not. He thinks I went with you. And if you think to tell him otherwise, remember, you're the one he's going to blame. After all, he did put you in charge of my safekeeping."

Adam's face hardened. Samantha had him over a barrel, and she knew it. If he were to confide Samantha's behavior to Ezra, the old man would have his hide. He couldn't afford to rile the old codger; he needed his political support. Ezra was well-respected among the Federalist faction. He would need his endorsement when the time came to make his move.

"You go too far, Samantha. Your childish antics may have proven amusing when we were children, but the games you play now are dangerous. Haven't I told you that is is unsafe to go about unescorted?"

Shielding her eyes from the sun, Samantha looked down the road to her right, then turned her head to look in the opposite direction. "Really, Adam, the way you are talking would make a person think that we are going to be invaded by the British at any moment. I fail to see any red-coated devils milling about the streets. Do you know something I don't?"

She noted the flush covering his cheeks, the way he dabbed nervously at his forehead with his handkerchief, and thought that his discomfort was caused by more than the warmth of the day.

"I only know what I read in the newspapers. And if I were you, I wouldn't put much credence in what I read in the *National Intelligencer*. They do not support the Federalist cause, Samantha."

Thinking of her conversation with Daniel, and Adam's odd behavior of moments before, Samantha decided to see what, if anything, she could find out about Senator Pickering. After all, when Daniel came back, he was certain to want some bit of information in exchange for news of Robbie. She asked, "What does Senator Pickering intend to do about this war? Surely, he has voiced his opinions in the Congress."

"I am not at liberty to discuss the senator's views or his plans." His brow wrinkled in confusion as he studied her. "Since when are you so interested in this war? I thought you had no political preferences."

"'Tis true, I don't give a fig about politics, but I do care about my brother. If ending this war will bring Robbie home safely, then I want to learn what I can."

"Ending this war is what some of us intend to do, my dear. Never fear, we will find a solution. Robert will be returned to the bosom of his family before you know it."

There was a self-assured air about Adam that Samantha found disconcerting. It was almost as if he knew something of great importance. But how could he? Madison distrusted Pickering. Daniel had said as much. The President would never have confided his plans to the senator, if that was the case.

Swallowing her suspicions, she patted Adam's hand and smiled, relieved to see the coach approaching.

64

"Thank you for waiting with me. I'll try to be more circumspect in the future." She stood; he followed, grabbing onto her hand.

"If things go the way I hope, Samantha, you may well be married to a very important individual."

Samantha's smile turned into a grimace. Would Adam never give up the idea of marriage? How many times must she refuse in order for him to understand that she was not interested in marriage, with him or anyone else?

Not wishing to pursue a topic that was sure to cause more unpleasantness between them, she said her fare-wells and boarded the coach, anxious to return home and put everything she had learned today into proper perspective.

The coach's steady rocking motion did little to soothe her anxiety. The sudden realization that she had been placed in the middle of something about which she knew little filled her with trepidation.

She should never have listened to Daniel Fortune, never have agreed to help him, even if she was only using him to gain information about Robbie. Using a man like Daniel was dangerous. She wouldn't be able to twist him around her finger like she did Adam.

And Adam. His cryptic comments made her uneasy. What if Daniel were right? What if Adam knew something that could harm the President?

Oh, Lord, she thought, rubbing her temples, why didn't I just stay home today and mind my own business? Adam's words came back to haunt her, *". . . the games you play now are dangerous."* If he only knew . . .

Chapter Five

Daniel leaned back in the white wicker rocker, wondering why he had bothered to make the journey down to Williamsburg in the first place. He had stopped at his sister's plantation, Meadowlark, which was situated about ten miles from the town of Williamsburg, in the hope of speaking to her husband Harold. But as luck would have it, Harold had gone to Savannah on business, leaving him to contend with his sister's inane prattle, which was driving him slowly insane.

"You are being insufferably rude, Daniel," Sarah Chastain remarked, pulling her bow-shaped lips into a pout. "Why, I don't believe you've heard a word I've said." She smoothed the skirt of her white muslin dress, her eyes rounding in indignation. It was a look he had seen many times in his thirty-six years.

Daniel sighed, trying to refocus his attention on the mundane conversation. They were seated beneath the grape arbor at the rear of Sarah's house, sharing a pitcher of iced tea together. And while the bees that hovered over his head droned on, so did his sister.

"I've heard every word you've said," Daniel reassured her, taking a sip of the refreshing liquid. "But I've not come to discuss the weather, Liza's missing teeth, nor old Mrs. Murdock's rheumatism. You know why I'm here."

"Oh, Daniel, don't be such a dunce. You know perfectly well Harold will never sell Caesar. He's one of the most productive breeders we've got. Why, Harold says—"

Slamming his glass down, Daniel jumped to his feet, his blue eyes impaling her. "I can't believe I'm hearing this rubbish from my own sister! You know our family has never countenanced slavery. It was bad enough when you up and married a slaveholder. But for you to espouse his views . . ." He shook with suppressed anger.

It was the same argument they'd had every time he visited the Chastain plantation. Harold Chastain had repeatedly refused to sell the slave Caesar, who was Daniel's childhood friend. And Daniel would not be satisfied until Caesar walked the earth a free man.

Standing, Sarah placed a placating hand on Daniel's arm. "Harold is my husband. I have no say in what he does or does not do. I am his wife and must obey in all things."

Daniel's voice filled with disdain. "Mother would slap you silly if she heard the way you were talking. She raised us to be free and independent thinkers. You're no better than the slaves your husband owns."

Sarah's face pinkened to the color of the rhododendron bushes lining the oyster shell path; her eyes filled with pain. "How *dare* you speak to me in such a fashion?! If you weren't my brother, I would have you thrown off Meadowlark."

"Don't bother," Daniel said, reaching for his hat. "I'm leaving anyway."

Her expression grew immediately contrite. "Oh, Daniel, please don't leave this way. You know I'll talk to Harold about Caesar. Haven't I done so before? I can't bear it when you're angry with me."

Daniel stared down at the raven head bowed before him and sighed. With her ebony hair and bright blue eyes, Sarah was the image of Alexandra Fortune. But there the similarity ended. Where his mother was outspoken, headstrong, loyal to the extreme, Sarah was quiet and reserved. She vacillated like a willow tree in a heavy wind. It was hard to believe she was actually part of the same family.

His father, Nicholas, had doted on his only daughter, spoiling her outrageously. Sarah was the only bone of contention between his parents, the only disharmony in an otherwise perfect marriage.

"I'm not angry, Sarah, just disappointed. I can't believe the change marriage has wrought in you in only five years."

"You've yet to fall in love, Daniel. Love changes a person and not always for the better." She stared at the toes of her Moroccan leather slippers.

"Have you forgotten Joanna?"

Her head snapped up. "I have not. And I can see by your rigid expression that neither have you. But the love you felt for Joanna is not the kind of love that I am talking about. You were young—impetuous. More in love with love than you were with Joanna. I am talking of an all-consuming love, a passion that burns hot and cannot be extinguished by differences or disagreements. The kind of love shared by our parents—the kind of love I feel for Harold—the kind of love you will one day feel."

Daniel snorted contemptuously. If love could turn a person into a mindless, blathering creature with no backbone and no mind of his own, then he wanted nothing to do with it. He'd learned his lesson early on; he had no desire to repeat the experience.

Placing his arm about Sarah's shoulder, Daniel guided her down the path that led to the rear yard where his horse was stabled. "I pray you will have success in convincing Harold to part with Caesar. I will pay whatever he asks, if only he will set him free."

Sarah heaved a sigh. "Are any of us ever free, Daniel? Don't we just exchange one form of bondage for another?"

Pausing, he stared at his sister quizzically. Her face reflected a maturity he hadn't noticed before, her eyes a hint of sadness. "Are you speaking of yourself, Sarah? I thought you just said you were happy with Harold."

Pulling his head down, she placed a kiss upon his cheek. "I am happy. But love can place a burden upon the heart as heavy as any chain of bondage. Go with God and be careful. Give my love to our mother and father. Tell them that I shall visit soon."

Watching his sister walk back up the path toward the large brick mansion, Daniel pondered her words. Women always made things more complicated than they needed to be. Friendship and loyalty were clear-cut in his estimation. He would see his friend freed or die trying. It was a vow he had made years ago; one from which he would not deviate.

Retrieving the reins from the young stable boy, he

mounted his horse, flipping the child a coin. If a man was to work, he should be paid for his efforts, he reasoned, pleased by the excited expression on the small boy's face.

Shading his eyes from the sun, he stared back down the drive, catching sight of Sarah as she approached the columned porch. With a wave of his hand, he departed, nudging the stallion into a trot down the elm-lined road that would take him the ten-mile journey to Williamsburg.

The setting sun colored the sky a purplish-pinkish hue. Guiding his horse down the broad, tree-lined main street known as Duke of Gloucester, Daniel breathed a sigh of relief. It was good to be home.

Nothing had changed since his last visit. The familiar signs of the Raleigh and Wetherburn Taverns still greeted the weary traveler. The heavenly scent of gingerbread still wafted through the air from the bakery behind the Raleigh, and the disgruntled sounds of pigs and sheep could still be heard as they rooted through neatly fenced yards.

Turning his horse down Nicholson Street, he spotted the house of his birth. It was still painted white, trimmed with blue shutters, and surrounded by a white picket fence. The flowers that hugged the pickets— white and red hollyhocks, azure blue larkspur, looked the same as they had when he was a lad of ten, playing within the confines of the yard.

Stabling his horse, he headed for the house and was greeted by his very surprised mother who rushed forward when he entered.

"Daniel," Alexandra Fortune shrieked, "why didn't you tell us you were coming?" Her smile was ebullient and welcoming.

Enfolding his mother in his embrace, Daniel hugged her tightly. "I didn't know myself. It was sort of an impulsive gesture." And noting the happiness on his mother's face, one he was glad he'd made.

Spying his father, who had just entered the hall to investigate all the commotion, Daniel smiled and winked. "Good to see you, Father. How are you feeling?"

"Never better, son," Nicholas replied, slapping Daniel on the back. Turning his attention on his wife, he smiled indulgently. "Let him go, Alex. You'll strangle the boy."

"A child needs a little smothering every once in a while. Isn't that right, Daniel?" She beamed like a young girl.

Nicholas shook his head. "Come into the parlor, son. I was just about to have a brandy. You must tell us all the political news. We've been starved for word about the war and what's been going on inside the capital city."

"Really, Nicholas, can't we talk of more pleasant things? Daniel has only just arrived," Alexandra protested, handing her son a snifter of brandy before taking a seat next to Nicholas on the blue brocade settee.

Sipping thoughtfully on his drink, Daniel took a moment to observe his parents. They were aging, he thought sadly. He'd only been gone three months, but he noticed the new lines about his mother's eyes and mouth, the way his father's hair no longer

71

showed a trace of black.

But then, who was he to talk? He had noticed a considerable amount of gray in his own temples. With all the problems he had faced in the past few months, it was a wonder his own hair wasn't as snowy white as his father's.

Did he dare subject his parents to the worrisome news about the situation with the British? At the impatient look on his father's face, he knew the answer. They'd been through much worse and survived; they would do so again.

"The war is not going well," Daniel finally confessed. "We are outmanned by a wide margin. Our regular army contains only seven thousand poorly trained, ill-equipped men; our navy, only sixteen vessels, most of which are useless due to the British blockade of the Eastern Seaboard." He paused to take another sip of the amber liquid, then continued, "Washington City is without fortification. President Madison has ordered troops to repair Fort Washington, but I fear it's too little, too late." He shook his head. "To make matters worse, Albert Gallatin tells me that the Treasury is almost bankrupt."

"I had no idea things were so bad," Alexandra stated, her eyes rounding as she exchanged a worried look with her husband.

"Not many people know the truth of it, Mother. The President and Secretary Monroe have tried to maintain a brave front, but even that is starting to crumble."

Standing, Nicholas paced the room, making tracks in the blue and rose Aubusson carpet beneath his feet. "I won't let those bloody Englishmen take more than they already have. I've sacrificed so that this country

72

could be free of English domination. I'll be damned if I'll stand by and let them put the yoke of oppression around our necks again."

He thought of all he had given up back in England to fight for American independence—his ancestral home, Blackstone, his fortune, his title of duke. But if he had to do it all over again, he would, for the price of freedom never came cheap, and what was gained was worth far more than any material possession.

Noting the throbbing vein in the side of Nicholas's neck, the way the brown of his eyes had darkened to black, Alexandra grew alarmed. "Please, Nicholas," she pleaded, taking hold of her husband's arm, "you'll make yourself too ill to eat supper. Now sit down and relax. There's no sense in working yourself up into a dither when there's nothing to be done at the moment. Isn't that right, Daniel?" She looked at her son for confirmation.

"I'm afraid Mother's right. There's nothing to be gained by upsetting yourself. I shouldn't have said anything."

"Nonsense," Nicholas said, swallowing the rest of his brandy. "Your mother has gotten too protective in my old age. She thinks that I'm going to drop dead at the least little excitement."

About to take exception to his last comment, Alexandra opened her mouth to speak but was interrupted by the maid's call to dinner. "You're saved by the dinner bell this time, Nicholas. But I'll get you for that comment later," she promised.

Nicholas grinned. "I'll look forward to that, my sweet," he replied, squeezing her waist as he guided her into the dining room.

*   *   *

After dinner was completed, Nicholas retired to his bedroom, while Alexandra and Daniel adjourned to the study to continue their conversation. The walnut-paneled room was illuminated by several wax tapers; the fragrance of bayberry permeated the air with its distinctive odor.

Daniel stood before the fireplace, his arm braced against the mantel, staring down at his mother who was seated on the sofa in front of him. She was still a lovely woman, he thought. Dressed in the bright red lawn gown, her blue eyes shining with love, it wasn't difficult to understand why his father had given up all he possessed to spend a lifetime with her. Thinking of his father brought a worried frown to his forehead.

"Is Father going to be all right? He looks a little peaked to me."

Alexandra's face clouded with unease. "Nicholas is not really ill, Daniel. He just needs to slow down a bit. After all, he's not a young man anymore." Though for a man of seventy, he could still give many a younger man a run for his money. He certainly hadn't slowed down at all in the bedroom, she thought wickedly, smiling at the memory of that morning's encounter.

Her expression sobered when she noted the distracted look upon Daniel's face. "What is it, son? You look dreadfully unhappy."

Rubbing the back of his neck to ease the tension, Daniel heaved a sigh. "I stopped by to see Harold today about Caesar. He wasn't in."

Alexandra's eyes filled with understanding. "So that's it. I should have known you'd stop by Mea-

74

dowlark to try and convince Harold to sell Caesar one more time. I'm sorry you had no luck. Did you see Sarah?"

He grimaced. "Yes, and I'm afraid we had words."

"My dear, you and Sarah have had words since you were knee-high to a grasshopper. That is nothing new."

"I'm afraid I was a bit hard on her this time, Mother. She's changed so since her marriage to that . . . that peddler of human flesh."

Patting the space next to her on the brown leather sofa, Alexandra indicated that Daniel should sit. "You know how I feel about Harold. I've never condoned his actions." That was an understatement, she thought. She had practically dropped dead the day Sarah announced her intention to marry Harold Chastain. But seeing the look of love on her daughter's face, and knowing the bliss and pain of being in love, she had given her blessing, realizing to do otherwise would have been futile.

"Harold is Sarah's husband," Alexandra continued. "She deserves our support, Daniel."

"But Caesar is my friend. If you could have seen him, Mother. He's so despondent of late. I tell you, if I don't do something soon, I don't know what's going to happen."

Alexandra's eyes widened in alarm. "You don't think that he'd resort to violence, do you?"

"Caesar?" He looked at her in disbelief. "Never! He's as gentle as a lamb, though his size is more that of a giant black bear."

"I'm relieved to hear it. Sarah may have her faults, but I don't want any harm to come to her."

"You should have heard her, Mother. Defending her

husband, making excuses for him, all in the name of love."

Alexandra smiled knowingly. "Love causes people to behave in strange ways, Daniel." She and Nicholas had certainly been proof of that. She thought back to their own unconventional courtship, which had been prompted by an arranged marriage—a marriage between a member of English nobility and a reluctant American patriot. Those were trying times, but she wouldn't trade them for anything.

"Now you sound like Sarah. Are all women blinded by their heart's desire?" He thought of Samantha's attachment to Adam Bainbridge and smirked. "I will never understand them."

"Why do I get the impression that we are no longer talking about Sarah?" Alexandra eyed her son suspiciously, observing the color that stained his cheeks. She would like to meet the woman who could cause a man like Daniel to heat up like a flatiron, she decided.

Observing the hopeful glint in his mother's eye, Daniel shook his head, pushing himself to his feet. "Don't get any ideas, Mother. The woman that comes to my mind is a troublemaker—a Federalist, no less. Her name is Samantha Wilder. I'm trying to help locate her brother in exchange for . . ." He paused purposely, smiling wickedly.

"Daniel! Shame on you!" Alexandra exclaimed, a horrified expression on her face.

Daniel laughed aloud, then winked, adding, ". . . information. I think Samantha is connected with Bainbridge, Pickering, and their ilk."

"Is this Samantha pretty?"

A faraway look entered his eyes. "Not pretty . . .

76

beautiful. With hair the color of rich mahogany. Skin like sun-kissed peaches. And two dimples on—" He snapped his mouth shut, noting the amused expression his mother wore. "Beauty's only skin deep; I've yet to delve beneath the surface."

"But you'd like to?"

Aye, he'd like to delve into Samantha's sweet, honeyed charms, he thought silently, but aloud he replied, "There's more to Miss Wilder than meets the eye, Mother. It's my duty to find out what it is." And what a pleasant duty it will be, he thought, smiling to himself. Very pleasant indeed!

The object of Daniel's consideration was at this very moment squeezing the life out of a plump red tomato, pretending it was Daniel's head she held firmly in her hands. She had accompanied Dulcie to the Center Market, located on the south side of Pennsylvania Avenue on Eighth Street, to take her mind off her growing unease caused by Daniel's continuing absence and to buy some much-needed groceries.

Saturday morning was the traditional day set aside for grocery shopping in the Wilder household, and war or no war, today was no exception.

The sun was cast behind a layer of clouds, making the early morning task not quite as laborious as it would have been had it been the middle of the day. She would never get used to these horrid, humid summers, Samantha thought disgustedly, feeling beads of perspiration trickle down between her breasts.

"What you think of fried chicken with some of these fresh peas for dinner, Miss Sam?" Dulcie asked, holding up a handful of the green pods. "You know how Mr. Adam likes my chicken." She puffed her chest out proudly.

"Yes . . . yes, Dulcie, anything is fine," Samantha responded absently, wishing fervently that they could cancel their dinner party this evening. Fat chance, she thought, unable to hide her displeasure. Grandfather had taken matters into his own hands by inviting Adam and Timothy Pickering to dinner tonight. Thank God the senator had sent his regrets. Putting up with Adam and her grandfather in the mood she was in would be difficult enough.

Absorbed in her dilemma, she failed to notice the young woman who had sidled up next to her.

"You're going to squash that tomato to juice if you continue to squeeze it so tightly."

Glancing over her right shoulder, Samantha's eyes widened. "Willy!" she exclaimed, dropping the tomato back into the bin, "I didn't expect to see you so soon. It's only been a week since last we spoke." Taking in Willy's new blue gingham dress and straw bonnet, she added, "And how pretty you look."

Willy muttered her thanks. "It's Uncle Joseph's idea. After I mentioned that I had made your acquaintance, he insisted that I purchase some new clothes." She held the skirt open for Samantha's inspection. "It is rather nice, isn't it? I haven't had anything this pretty in years. My parents were what you might call rich of heart but poor of pocket."

Clasping Willy's hand, Samantha said, "I'm delighted to see you again. I'll tell Dulcie to finish up here, then we can take a walk in the park."

Willy smiled regretfully. "I'm afraid I can't, Sam. I'm

to meet my uncle at his solicitor's. Something about my parent's farm."

At Samantha's look of disappointment, Willy added, "I stopped at your home and your grandfather said you were here. You won't look so unhappy when I tell you why I've come." She reached into the pocket of her skirt, retrieving a wax-sealed piece of parchment. "I have a note for you," she smiled widely, "from Daniel. He came by the newspaper office late last night."

"Daniel?" Samantha mouthed stupidly, before her brain comprehended the meaning of Willy's words. Her hands started to sweat as she held the note tightly in her hand, debating whether or not she should open it.

"Well, aren't you going to open it? I'm dying to know what it says," Willy urged. "Perhaps Daniel's declaring his undying love."

Samantha laughed at the eager expression on Willy's face, and the absurd notion that Daniel harbored a fondness for her. "Why, Willy! I had no idea you were such a romantic."

The freckles on the young woman's face were made invisible by a deep blush. "Someday my knight in shining armor is going to spirit me away on his white charger," Willy declared in earnest.

"That only happens in fairy tales, Willy."

"Maybe, but I can't help but feel that someday it's going to happen to me."

How wonderful to be that naive, Samantha thought, wondering when her dream of a conquering hero had vanished to be replaced by the reality of men who never gave without wanting something in return. *"Nothing's ever free, love."* Daniel's words pricked at her subconscious like a sharp quill.

Shaking off the unpleasant thought, she opened the missive, only to be confronted by more of Daniel's arrogance. Her lips thinned in displeasure as she read the bold strokes that filled the page: *"Meet me tonight at the Tayloes' ball. I've checked the list: Adam's name is on it. It shouldn't be too difficult to finagle an invitation from him. Don't disappoint!"* It was signed, *"D."*

"Of all the. . . ." She crumpled the sheet of paper, stuffing it into her reticule, her face reddening in anger.

"Bad news?"

Samantha's eyes hardened. "Bad news doesn't describe it, Willy. Rather I would say dirty, rotten, miserable, high-handed, despicable. . . ."

Hours later, still spewing forth epithets as she paced across the green and rose Oriental carpet of her room, Samantha was still trying to figure out a way to get Adam to take her to the ball that evening.

"It shouldn't be too difficult," she mimicked sarcastically, plopping down on the counterpane. "Ha!" she scoffed, punching the pillow, wishing it were Daniel's stomach.

Laying her head down, she stared up at the lace canopy overhead. Why hadn't Adam mentioned that he was going to the ball tonight? And why hadn't he invited her? she wondered. That in itself was reason enough for her to be there, she decided. But how?

Suddenly a devious smile split her face, replacing the frown of moments before. She jumped up. *Of course! Why hadn't she thought of it before?*

All she need do was pretend that Adam *had* invited her. When he arrived, she would be dressed and waiting for him. Adam was much too polite—too correct to gainsay her assumption, especially in front of her grandfather.

Twirling about, she hugged herself. "Samantha, you're a genius . . . a true genius."

Chapter Six

Some genius! Samantha thought disgustedly, eyeing Adam across the crowded ballroom deep in conversation with Senator Pickering, Henry Thurgood, and another gentleman she had never seen before.

The orchestra the Tayloes' had hired was wonderful, not that it did her much good. She'd been planted, much like the potted palm she stood before, shortly after their arrival with explicit instructions not to budge. In the foul mood Adam had been in since she'd pulled her little deception, she didn't think now would be a good time to cross him and exert her independence.

To say that Adam had not been pleased to find her waiting to accompany him to the ball would have been an understatement. In fact, much to her surprise, his reaction had almost bordered on rudeness. Even her grandfather had raised a questioning eyebrow at his behavior.

What was so important about this affair that Adam didn't desire her company? What was he hiding? she couldn't help wondering.

Shaking her head to clear her disquieting thoughts, she gazed about the opulently furnished room. The ballroom of the Tayloes' mansion was decorated in the style of Louis XIV. Rich red damask drapery hung at the windows and was repeated on the settees and occasional chairs.

Two enormous gilt-edged, floor-to-ceiling mirrors, which hung on the far wall, reflected the lavishly dressed dancing couples in their silks and satins as they pirouetted across the black-and-white tiled floor.

Samantha tapped her foot in time to the music. Absorbed in her observations, she failed to notice that she was no longer alone.

"Good evening, love. You look lovely this evening."

Her heart raced. She turned, her mouth dropping open at the sight of Daniel standing next to her. He was grinning and looked devilishly handsome in his black formal evening attire.

Daniel was thinking similar thoughts about Samantha as he eyed her costume appreciatively. She was dressed in a peach moire ball gown, draped off the shoulder, revealing a tempting expanse of creamy white flesh. His eyes riveted on her breasts, which were lush and full like two ripe peaches. His mouth watered. He had a fondness for peaches.

"You look good enough to eat, love."

First dumbstruck, then angered by the lascivious glint in Daniel's eyes, Samantha fought to keep her temper under control. "How dare you show up here all sweetness and innocence after leaving with no explanation?!" she said through gritted teeth. "And to send that imperious note! You are despicable, Mr. Fortune."

Daniel's grin widened. "I've missed you, too, love.

83

Shall we walk in the garden before you bring undue notice onto ourselves?" Before she could reply, he grabbed her arm and gently but firmly led her out the side door, across the brick patio, toward the rear yard. When they were a safe distance from the house, he stopped.

"What do you think you are doing?" Samantha accused, pulling out of Daniel's hold.

"You must learn to curb your impulsive outbursts, love. We're not supposed to know each other very well, but you were behaving like a jealous mistress. What are people to think?"

Samantha gasped, her cheeks flooding with color. "How *dare* you!"

Noting the way Samantha's brown eyes sparked fire, the way her luscious breasts heaved in indignation, Daniel chuckled. "You really make a terrible accomplice, Samantha. I'm not sure that this arrangement we've made is going to work."

His words tempered her outrage. "Not work! But it has to work. Surely you have news for me?"

Lighting a cheroot, he inhaled deeply, blowing the concentric swirls of smoke into the air. "That depends. Tell me what you know."

Probing her mind for some bit of information with which she could entice Daniel, Samantha proceeded to tell him about her last conversation with Adam and his curious remarks about ending the war. She also revealed how odd she found Adam's behavior about escorting her to the ball. She hoped she hadn't revealed anything that would be damaging to Adam. His conduct had been odd of late, and perhaps Daniel could clarify things for her, but she didn't want to cause

Adam any trouble.

She searched Daniel's face, trying to determine if what she had told him had made any difference, but found his expression noncommittal.

"Interesting, but hardly anything new," Daniel remarked, grinding the cheroot beneath the heel of his shoe. "Is that it?"

She nodded. "I'm afraid so."

"Do you know the man that accompanied Pickering here tonight? The one with the scar on his left cheek?" He watched her reaction closely. John Henry, former American Army officer turned British spy, was attempting to alienate New England and New York from the rest of the country by promoting their allegiance to the Crown. He had been under surveillance for some time.

She shook her head. "I was not introduced."

Her eyes were guileless, her manner forthright. He could tell she was speaking the truth. A feeling of relief swept over him. Had she known the man Pickering brought was a British agent, he would not have had anything further to do with her. He was taking a chance as it was.

At the sound of voices, Daniel grabbed Samantha's hand, leading her deep into the boxwood maze at the rear of the garden. It was very dark.

"How will we find our way back?" she asked finally. "I can't see a thing." They were surrounded on all sides by tall, compact, boxwood hedges, which, much to Samantha's dismay, provided an inordinate amount of privacy.

Daniel's teeth flashed white against the darkness. Leading her to a stone bench, he pulled her down beside him. "As a child I often played in the maze at the Governor's Palace in Williamsburg. This maze is simple compared to that one."

Aware that she was alone in the dark with a man of questionable motives and that they were a considerable distance from the house, she shivered.

"Are you cold?" Daniel asked, placing his arm around her shoulders.

The feel of his warm hand on the bare flesh of her arm sent tingles of awareness up and down her spine. His fingers caressed the satin of her skin, creating a warm sensation in the pit of her stomach. Her mouth suddenly went dry; she couldn't formulate the reproach she knew she should utter. Turning to face him, she saw the glow of desire burning brightly in the depths of his blue eyes; her heart pounded a cadence, loud in her ears.

"You're beautiful, Samantha. Beautiful, warm, and wonderful. You know that I'm going to kiss you, don't you?"

She nodded mutely, mesmerized by the velvet sound of his voice and the tender feel of his fingers on her flesh. His lips were like magnets, drawing her closer, ever closer, until they covered hers, branding her with fire. A rush of pleasure surged through every inch of her being, and suddenly she realized that she wanted to be kissed, had wanted to since the first time Daniel had kissed her beneath the trees in Parrott's Woods. Forgetting who she was and where they were and what had brought them together, she responded with an urgency that surprised and frightened her.

Wrapping her arms about the firm muscles of his back, she leaned into him. Her nipples, pressing into the hard planes of his chest, pulsated painfully, growing pebble hard. She didn't protest when, a moment later, she felt his hands insinuate themselves into the bodice of her gown, freeing the aching globes from their corseted confinement.

"You're exquisite," she heard him say through the veil of desire settling over her. "Mmmm. "Ripe, red cherries, ready to be picked."

His mouth replaced his hands to suckle the hardened nubs, his wet tongue laving the stiffened peaks until she thought she would explode with want of him. She ran gentle fingers through his thick hair, urging him, needing him, to inflict this torture she craved.

Like manna from the heavens, Daniel savored the plump, puckered morsels, unable to get his fill. When Samantha dropped her head back, moaning in ecstasy, allowing him access to her yearning flesh, he felt himself grow rigid with a hunger that could no longer be denied. He cradled the heavy mounds, marveling at their perfect beauty before setting his mouth to suckle the swollen buds with tantalizing possessiveness once again. Desire drove all conscious thought from his mind; his need to drive his hardened shaft deep into the soft recesses he knew would be wet and waiting dominated his actions.

Painful pleasure settled in the apex of Samantha's thighs, creating a burning hunger unknown to her before. She felt herself grow moist, grow unbearably taut, and she craved the release she knew Daniel could provide. Rendered senseless by her body's traitorous response, she lost all inhibitions and all track of time until the distinct sound of voices pierced through her shroud of passion.

Slowly her mind began to clear, and she became aware of what she and Daniel were doing. Taking deep breaths, she tried to still the persistent throbbing in her loins, pushing at Daniel's broad chest, she struggled to sit up.

"Samantha, are you out here?"

Recognizing the voice, panic rioted within her. "My God! It's Adam," she whispered.

Feeling the rush of cool air on her naked breasts, she covered herself with her hands, blushing furiously at the seductive smile on Daniel's lips. When he lowered his head to place a kiss on each of her hands, her heart caught in her throat, her body frozen in limbo.

"Pity we were so rudely interrupted, love. I was just beginning to enjoy myself." His pained expression belied his flip remark, but Samantha was too incensed to notice.

Her eyes blazed with sudden anger. "Why, you . . . !"

He placed his finger gently across her lips. "This is where I take my leave. I will see you soon. Perhaps then we can continue what we started." Like a phantom—a figment of her imagination—he was gone, disappearing into the night.

Choking on her outrage, Samantha readjusted her corset, pulling up her dress to cover her nakedness.

"Samantha?" Adam's voice rang out in the stillness.

"Yes, I'm here," she replied, her voice breathless. "I got lost in the maze." Her explanation sounded feeble to her own ears, but it was the best one she could come up with on the spur of the moment. She tried to smooth her hair, which had come loose from its knot, into some semblance of order.

"What on earth are you doing out here all alone?"

Adam asked when he finally arrived, holding up a lantern to check the surrounding area. "You are alone, aren't you?" He took in her disheveled appearance, eyeing her suspiciously.

Rising to her feet, Samantha smoothed her dress, which was horribly wrinkled. "Of course, I'm alone . . . as I have been for most of the evening," she accused, purposely putting him on the defensive. "If I hadn't been left to my own devices, I wouldn't have wandered out here alone." If she hadn't been so upset, she would have smiled at the look of chagrin that crossed Adam's face.

"I'm terribly sorry, my dear, but I had business to discuss with the senator."

"Well, I don't know why you bothered to invite me in the first place, Adam, if you had no intention of spending any time with me."

He looked puzzled. "Well, I . . ." Noting Samantha's pique, he changed his mind about his reply and said instead, "Shall we go back to the party, my dear? I promise to make it up to you."

Later, as they rode back to Georgetown in silence, Samantha had time to think about her shameful behavior with Daniel. She felt her cheeks burn each time she thought of the disgraceful way she had responded to his touch and was grateful for the darkness that hid her humiliation.

How could she have forgotten herself that way? How could she have succumbed to his practiced charms?

She came to the painful realization that she was out of her element when it came to a man like Daniel Fortune. She wasn't experienced enough to handle a womanizing rake such as he.

She also realized something else: he had not told her one thing about her brother Robbie.

Pulling his cravat around twice, then knotting it, Daniel smiled in satisfaction at his reflection in the mirror. Last night had been a revelation for him, and he was sure for Samantha as well. He'd been both surprised and delighted by her ardent response to his love-making.

She had excited him almost to the brink of no return. It was only an inordinate amount of self-restraint on his part that prevented him from taking her then and there. And from her response, he didn't think she would have minded. There was a wealth of passion hidden beneath the folds of her stiffly starched skirts.

He chuckled, remembering her look of outrage when he had departed so abruptly. If she only knew the amount of pain he had suffered when Adam had made his unwelcome presence known. He'd spent a restless night on account of her and that miserable bastard.

At the thought of Adam, his lips thinned. Imagining Samantha doing those same things with Adam that she had done with him twisted his gut into a knot. Did she moan when Adam kissed her? When he fondled her breasts?

"Bloody hell!" he cursed, using the epithet he had learned so well from his father. He shook his fist. He had no right to care. He was using her, just as she was using him. But still the thought of her with that traitor made his blood boil.

Taking a deep breath to calm himself, he continued his toilette. Today he would visit the sweet little seductress, and he could just imagine what her reaction was going to be. He bet she was fit to be tied last night when she realized he hadn't told her anything about her brother. Shrugging into his jacket, he smiled, anticipating this morning's encounter.

Standing on the front steps of the Wilder townhouse a short time later, Daniel whistled cheerfully, keeping accompaniment with the sparrow nesting in the large gum tree, while he waited patiently for his knock to be answered.

He smiled in greeting when the door was flung open, but to his disappointment it wasn't Samantha who answered but her black maid.

"May I help you, sir?" the woman asked.

Removing his felt hat, he twirled the brim between his fingers. "Please tell Miss Wilder that Daniel Fortune is here to see her."

Dulcie didn't need to be told who the gentleman was that graced her front porch. She remembered quite vividly the afternoon he had brought Miss Sam home soaking wet and the vile curses the mistress had flung at his head.

Ushering him into the hall, she took his hat, hanging it on the hall tree. "I'm sorry, Mr. Fortune, but Miss Sam's not at home. She went to the post office."

Before Daniel could reply, a thunderous query boomed forth into the hallway from the parlor. "Dulcie! Who is it?"

Smiling apologetically at Daniel, Dulcie excused herself, returning a moment later to say that Mr. Lawrence would like a word with him.

91

Surprised by the request, but too polite to refuse the gentleman he knew to be Samantha's grandfather, Daniel did as requested and followed the maid into the parlor. He found Ezra Lawrence seated in a wheelchair by the front window, his right foot propped up on the stool in front of him. He had a permanent hunch to his shoulders, as if he carried the weight of the world upon them. His skin was as white as his hair, and he looked every bit as irascible as his letters to the newspapers made him out to be.

"Good morning, sir. Your maid said you wished to see me."

Ezra squinted, staring intently at the stranger before him. "You related to a Colonel Fortune—a Col. Nicholas Fortune?"

Nodding, Daniel came forward to take the seat Ezra Lawrence indicated. "Yes, sir. Nicholas Fortune is my father."

"I knew it!" Ezra cried, slapping his knee. "Your name is not that common. I thought perhaps you might be related."

Daniel smiled inwardly at the old man's delight. "Your granddaughter tells me that you served under General Washington during the War of Independence. Is that where you met my father?"

"Aye. Nicholas Fortune saved my life. 'Twas when we were encamped at Valley Forge. I nearly froze to death." He readjusted the blanket covering his legs, seemingly lost in another time. "I had fallen through thin ice on a pond that wasn't quite frozen. Your father jumped in and saved me."

Daniel's eyebrows arched in surprise. His father was a hero, and he'd never even mentioned it.

"I see by your expression that you were unaware of your father's heroic exploits." At Daniel's nod, he continued, "Let me tell you, Nicholas Fortune was a brave soldier. Washington thought very highly of him; we all did."

"Thank you for telling me, sir. My father has never been one to blow his own horn."

Ezra chuckled, wheeling himself over to the piecrust table to pour himself a cup of coffee. "Care for some? I don't drink tea. Can't abide the stuff. The war, you know."

Daniel smiled knowingly, thinking how his mother's sentiments toward the British and their tea closely matched Samantha's grandfather's. To this day Alexandra Fortune would not serve tea in her home.

"No thanks. I really can't stay. I only stopped by to give Miss Wilder a message."

The old man's eyes grew assessing. "How is it that you're acquainted with my granddaughter? She's never mentioned you before."

That wasn't surprising, Daniel thought, considering her low opinion of him. "We met at the Madisons' Drawing Room some weeks ago. Mrs. Madison introduced us."

Ezra scowled. "Bah!" he replied with a wave of his hand, as if to dismiss the whole affair. "Parties and pleasures are all that these Southerners are good for. Useless pastimes, if you ask me."

Daniel didn't see any point in taking offense at Ezra Lawrence's unflattering opinion of Southerners, nor did he see any point in mentioning the fact that Dolley Madison, schooled as a Quaker, had been raised in Pennsylvania.

Rising from the Chippendale side chair, Daniel held out his hand, grasping Ezra's gnarled one. "Thank you for your hospitality, Mr. Lawrence. I shall give your regards to my father when next I see him."

Ezra inclined his head, then as an afterthought, said, "Why not come to dinner tonight, boy. My granddaughter is entertaining a few friends. Are you acquainted with Adam Bainbridge?"

Daniel fought to keep his face perfectly impassive. "Indeed. Mr. Bainbridge is quite well-known to me." Well-known and well disliked.

"Splendid! Then you must come and sup with us. It will be a delightful surprise for Samantha." He went on to explain, "My granddaughter had been under a great deal of strain lately, due to my grandson Robbie's disappearance. It will be good for her to pass the time with friends her own age. I'm afraid I'm not much company for her. Too set in my ways and all. What do you say?" Ezra prodded. "Shall we put one over on her?"

Daniel had to smile at the old codger's deviousness. "What about your maid?"

Crossing his arms firmly over his chest as if the matter were already settled, Ezra replied, "Leave her to me."

"Very well, I accept. I'll look forward to this evening." And to seeing the look on Samantha's face when she found out who had been invited to dinner.

Stepping back to admire her handiwork, Samantha smiled, pleased with the way the dining room table looked. She had used their best Canton china and Waterford crystal. The yellow and blue floral pattern

94

looked lovely on the white linen tablecloth. She wanted everything to be perfect for Willy's first dinner party.

The wax tapers in the center of the long mahogany table glimmered brightly, reminding Samantha of the excited sparkle in the young woman's eyes when she had extended the invitation. Though excited, Willy had also been full of dismay.

"I couldn't possibly accept, Sam," Willy had protested. "I haven't a thing to wear."

Samantha looked skeptical. "What about all those new clothes your uncle just purchased?"

At the question, Willy turned as red as her hair. "You've caught me in a lie, so I might as well confess: I don't have the social graces to attend a dinner party. I was raised on a farm not a plantation. We didn't do much socializing."

"Didn't you tell me that once your parent's farm was sold, you would be inheriting a tidy sum of money?"

"Yes, but—"

"No buts about it," Samantha interrupted. "If you're going to have the means to go into society, then you'll have to learn the ways."

And so, on the pretext of going to the post office, Samantha had gone instead to the little brick house behind the newspaper office to give Willy a quick lesson in table etiquette. She was determined that Adam would not look down his nose at Wilhelmina Matthews again.

Satisfied that everying was going to go her way tonight, Samantha hurried to the door to greet her guests.

Though the evening had started off somewhat strained, Samantha was finally beginning to relax.

Adam had been reserved but polite, making small talk with Willy when necessary. Grandfather, having taken a shine to Willy's effervescent nature, had spent the last twenty minutes regaling her with his war stories. Everything was going remarkably well until Dulcie came into the room.

"Miss Sam?"

Samantha turned, noting Dulcie's agitated expression. "What is it, Dulcie? What's wrong?" She stared quizzically at the maid.

"I'm afraid that I am what's wrong."

The deep voice made the hairs on the back of Samantha's neck stand on end. Turning, her eyes widened at the sight of Daniel, hands in his pockets, strutting casually into the room as if he didn't have a care in the world.

She drew a sharp breath before recovering herself. Glancing quickly at Adam, who hadn't seemed to notice her reaction, she rose to her feet. "Good evening, Mr. Fortune. Was there something with which we could help you?" He was poised, not the least bit disconcerted, which was in opposition to how she felt at the moment.

He looked terribly handsome in a jacket of blue superfine that defined the broadness of his shoulders and matched his eyes exactly. She fought to keep her emotions under control. Seeing Daniel so soon after their passionate (she felt her cheeks warm at the word) encounter brought forth memories—unwanted stirrings—deep within her breast. She wasn't ready to face him yet. Her grandfather's loud guffaw jolted her out of her disquieting reverie.

"Come in, Daniel," Ezra commanded. "You're just in time to hear the story of Washington's march to Yorktown."

Samantha almost groaned. Not wishing to embarrass herself or her grandfather in front of the other guests, she made the introductions as quickly as possible.

Why was Daniel here? She noted the easy camaraderie between him and her grandfather. How did they meet? she wondered. Now wasn't the time to get to the bottom of things, she decided. But she would, by God, she would.

Supper had become a nightmarish event. Daniel was enjoying his role as the "devil's advocate" by purposely instigating topics he knew would be inflammatory. Listening to the heated conversation going on between Daniel and Adam, who had glowered at her throughout most of the meal, Samantha almost gagged on the piece of crab cake she was chewing when Daniel brought up the recent invasion of Hampton, Virginia, by the British.

"I don't understand how you can sit there, Bainbridge, in front of these ladies and tell me that the pillaging of Hampton was the fault of the United States. By God, that bloody regiment of Royal Greens raped innocent women such as those sitting here at this table."

At the sight of the vein throbbing in Adam's temple, Samantha took a large sip of her bordeaux and smiled apologetically at Willy who was staring wide-eyed at the entire exchange. The evening was definitely going from bad to worse.

"How dare you speak of such vulgarities at the table?" Adam accused. "Are you Virginians so uncouth?"

Ezra leaned back in his chair, his puckered lips twitching in amusement. He looked from one side of the table to the other, waiting eagerly for the next argument. If there was one thing he enjoyed, it was a heated discussion. And by God, this one was as hot as Dante's *Inferno!* He leaned forward to hear what Daniel was saying.

"I dare to speak my mind like any patriotic American," Daniel retorted. "I'll not bow down to British threats or Federalist insurrectionists. This is a free country, and I'll speak as I see fit. My father and Mr. Lawrence, here, fought for that very freedom."

"Bravo!" Ezra remarked, clapping his hands together. "You sound just like your father. By God! The two of you are cut from the same cloth."

Samantha stared at her grandfather in disbelief. She hadn't seen him this animated in years. And how did he know Daniel's father? she wondered.

"How can you defend him, Ezra? You're a Federalist, for heaven's sake." Adam stared at him accusingly.

"So I am. But first and foremost I'm an American. I've forgotten that of late; it's good to be reminded. Sometimes we lose sight of what's important."

Pushing his chair away from the table, Adam stood, unable to hide his animosity. "If you'll excuse me, I have to be at the Capitol early in the morning." Turning toward Samantha, he said, "Thank you for dinner, Samantha. I'm sure that we'll see each other soon."

He left, leaving Willy and Samantha staring open-mouthed after him.

"My goodness!" Willy exclaimed after Adam had departed. "And here I thought I was the one who didn't have good table manners."

Daniel and Samantha exchanged amused glances, then burst out laughing, lessening the tension in the room.

"My dear," Ezra said, reaching for Willy's hand, "your manners and your demeanor are both delightful. Please don't change a whit. Now, if you young people will excuse me, I think that I shall retire. I fear all this excitement is too much for an old man."

Ha! Samantha thought, noting the gleam in the old reprobate's eyes. He enjoyed every minute of it.

Daniel stood, maneuvering Ezra's chair away from the table. "Thank you for inviting me, Mr. Lawrence. It was delightful."

Slapping Daniel on the arm, Ezra chuckled as he wheeled by. "It was that, boy. I'm sure we'll see you again. Isn't that right, Samantha?" He turned toward his granddaughter, noting how flushed her face had become.

"Of . . . of course. Mr. Fortune has proven to be a very stimulating dinner conversationalist." She meant it as an insult, but by the amused grin on Daniel's face, she could see that he wasn't affected by it.

After her grandfather was out of earshot, and Willy had crossed to the other side of the room, Daniel leaned over and whispered, "I find you extremely stimulating, as well, love."

Gooseflesh erupted over her arms and neck as his

warm breath tickled her sensitive skin, and she recalled just how *stimulated* she had been the other night. Taking a deep breath, she rose from her chair, putting distance between them. She wouldn't be foolish enough to make the same mistake twice.

"Why don't we adjourn to the parlor?" she finally suggested, a little too eagerly. "Perhaps we could play a game of loo. You do play, don't you, Mr. Fortune?"

The light from the candles overhead reflected the passion in the depths of Daniel's eyes. Samantha's blood rushed through her veins, warming her face and causing her heart to skip madly in her chest when his tongue reached out to lick his lips, his mouth tipping into a wildly erotic smile.

"I would love to play with you, Miss Wilder." His eyes raked boldly over her body, leaving no doubt to his meaning. "But I caution you to take care in what you bet; I'm not a very gracious loser, and I keep all that I win."

Part Two

Flames of Freedom

These things shall be—a loftier race
Than e'er the world hath known
Shall rise with flame of freedom in their souls,
And light of knowledge in their eyes.

John Addington Symonds
"The Days That Are To Be"

Chapter Seven

Walking the short distance back to Suter's Tavern, Daniel reflected on the entire evening. If not for Adam's tiresome company, it wouldn't have been half bad, he decided. Willy was a delight. And Ezra. The old gentleman had really taken him by surprise with his patriotic remarks. Perhaps Ezra wasn't quite as bad as he had originally thought, though he could definitely see from where Samantha inherited her stubborn nature.

She hadn't given an inch all evening. For every innuendo and teasing remark he had directed at her, she had retaliated with seeming indifference. And it grated! Oh, how it grated. He knew she wasn't immune to his charms. Why then, did she pretend otherwise? She acted like some silly virginal schoolgirl, and unfortunately, he knew differently.

Tossing his cheroot into the road, he turned, heading for the courtyard at the rear of the tavern. Pushing open the gate, he paused, unsure of what he had heard. Years of hunting both man and beast had fine-tuned his senses. The night whirred about him in a cacophony of sound, but there was something else. A scraping noise. He reached for his pistol, only to be reminded that he had not taken it with him this evening.

Damn! How could he have been so stupid? He listened more intently this time. There was nothing, save the mournful cry of a whippoorwill and the flapping wings of the cicada. Deciding that the noise he'd heard was only a product of too many brandies and an overactive imagination, he entered the courtyard. He'd no sooner shut the gate when a hand reached out, grabbing his shoulder. Doubling his fists, he spun about, his eyes widening in disbelief.

"Caesar!" he yelled, recognizing the familiar face at once; he quickly lowered his voice. "What the devil are you doing here? Is something wrong? Has Sarah sent you for me?"

The large, black man hung his head. "No, Mr. Dan, nothing like that. I've run away; I came here to be free."

Looking about to make sure they were alone, Daniel led Caesar into the coach house. The interior was dark; the odor of soiled hay mixed with leather and horseflesh rose up to assault their senses as they made their way back toward the stalls where the inhabitants whinnied in greeting.

"I was afraid something like this was going to happen," Daniel said, more to himself than to Caesar. He rubbed the back of his neck, wondering what the hell he was going to do now.

Spying a lantern hanging on a peg near one of the stalls, he lit it, giving the interior a golden glow, illuminating the uncertainty on Caesar's face. Pity and fear for the black man assailed him—pity at the futility of

104

Caesar's brash behavior, fear that he would die because of it.

"You know you can't stay with me; it's too dangerous," Daniel tried to explain. "You'll be caught. And until I can figure out just what it is that we're going to do, I don't want you getting into any more trouble than you're already in. You took a big chance coming here. Blacks found on the streets after ten are fined, flogged, or worse. And you have no papers."

"I done told you last time we spoke, Mr. Dan, I can't stay no more in bondage. I gotta be free. I ain't no stallion. I'm tired of being forced to mate with women I don't even like. It's degrading. You said so yourself."

Nodding at the truth of Caesar's words, Daniel sighed. "So I did. But that doesn't help us in figuring out what we're going to do. Harold isn't going to just sit back and let you go. As soon as he discovers your absence, he's going to hunt you down. And the first place he's going to search is here. He knows you'd come to me."

"I'm powerful sorry, Mr. Dan. I don't want to cause you any trouble. I'll just make my way as best I can." His shoulders slumped in defeat, he turned to leave.

Grabbing on to Caesar's arm, Daniel's voice hardened. "Don't be ridiculous. You'll be caught before you can make it out of Maryland." At Caesar's look of dismay, he hugged him, adding in a gentler tone, "I have another idea."

Samantha had just laid her head on the pillow when she heard a loud banging at the door. Climbing out of bed, she fumbled in the dark for her wrapper, wondering if perhaps Willy had forgotten something. She had tried to tell the young woman to stay, but Willy was adamant about returning home to help her uncle with the morning paper and had hired a hackney cab to take her home.

The banging grew louder. Fearful that it was going to wake her grandfather, she tied the ends of her sash together, feeling her way toward the door.

"I'm coming," she shouted as she reached the first floor, pausing in the hallway to determine in which direction the sound was coming from. Deciding it was the rear and not the front, she turned toward the kitchen, pushing open the door to find Dulcie already there.

"Who's at the door, Dulcie? Do you know?"

The black woman shook her head. "I expect we're not going to find out, Miss Sam, unless we open it." She headed for the door, but not before grabbing a rolling pin off the work table.

"Be careful! It's late. There could be all kinds of riffraff running about at this hour of the night."

"Who's there?" Dulcie cried out. "You'd best announce yourself; I have a weapon." She brandished the rolling pin at the door.

"It's Daniel Fortune. Open up. I need help."

Samantha and Dulcie exchanged startled glances before Samantha indicated with a nod of her head that Dulcie should open the door.

Daniel stood in the doorway, mouth agape, at the vision of Samantha in her nightclothes. Momentarily forgetting the urgent nature of his visit, he drank in the sight of her. Her hair hung down about her waist in soft brown waves. Her face, flushed with excitement, looked as pink as the small toes peeping out from beneath the hem of her wrapper.

"Are you going to stand there and gawk, or are you going to come in?" Samantha asked, her eyes rounding at the sight of the huge Negro following in Daniel's footsteps. The man was as black as night with massive arms the size of stovepipes. He was incredibly tall, probably three inches taller than Daniel, and had to stoop as he made his way through the doorway.

"Now who's gawking?" Daniel retorted, smiling at her reaction to Caesar's immense size. At five inches over six feet and close to three hundred pounds, Caesar's appearance had caused many a shocked expression over the years.

Blushing to the tips of her toes, which she now realized were uncovered due to her hasty departure, Samantha curled them under self-consciously, saying, "Please come in and sit down." Turning to the indignant black maid who was eyeing the stranger with unconcealed aversion, she ordered, "Dulcie, fix some coffee and sandwiches. Mr. Fortune's friend looks like he hasn't eaten in awhile."

"Fixin' food in the middle of the night for no-good trash," Dulcie mumbled, shaking her head in disgust as she hastened to do Samantha's bidding.

Ignoring the woman's rudeness, Caesar smiled in appreciation. "I'se grateful, ma'am. It's been a spell since I last supped."

Seating herself at the old maple table, Samantha tightened her sash more securely about her, feeling suddenly naked under Daniel's scrutiny. Staring into the fathomless blue pools, she felt her heart quicken. What power did he possess to make her feel this way?

107

she wondered. Annoyed by her thoughts, her voice was sharper than she intended when she remarked, "You said you needed help. I can only surmise that this has something to do with this gentleman." She inclined her head toward the giant.

"This is Caesar. He's a runaway from my sister Sarah's plantation."

"Your sister! She owns slaves?" Samantha could not repress the revulsion she felt at the thought of one human being owning another.

"Actually, it's her husband Harold. My sister is merely another in his long list of possessions."

The way he spat the words out, it wasn't difficult for Samantha to see that Daniel's view of slavery mirrored her own. A feeling of relief swept over her. "Harboring a fugitive slave is a serious offense. You could be fined or publicly whipped."

"I know. That is why you must weigh carefully what I am going to ask you." He studied her face, noting the apprehension that skittered across it. "I'll understand if you refuse to help."

Setting the cups down on the table, Dulcie filled each one with steaming black coffee. "I don't like the sound of this, Miss Sam. You'd best be careful. I wouldn't put yourself out for this here worthless nigger."

"Dulcie! What an awful thing to say." Samantha smiled apologetically at Caesar. "I'm sorry."

"That's all right, ma'am." Caesar cast an assessing gaze at the black woman, bringing a blush to her cheeks. "She's right. I'm worthless. A man ain't nothin' if he ain't free."

Samantha studied the worn surface of the table, tracing the nicks and dents with her index finger. What

Daniel intimated was dangerous. Why should she put herself in danger for a man she didn't know? Perhaps Dulcie was right. She ran her finger around the edge of the coffee cup. She'd always taken the middle road before; it was safer than taking a stand. Still, slavery was wrong. There was no gray area where it was concerned. It wasn't like this stupid war. At least there was some sense in trying to right a wrong.

Taking a deep breath, she returned Daniel's stare, surprised by the admiration she saw reflected there. "How can *we* help?" She emphasized Dulcie's role as well as her own and was rewarded with a smile from Daniel that left her breathless and a scathing look from her maid.

"I had a feeling you'd help," Daniel said. "That's why I came to you."

Warmed by his praise, she was too embarrassed to respond.

"I have to travel north tomorrow; it's urgent. I may be gone for several weeks. I need a place for Caesar to stay."

"Of course. But what of my grandfather? He may grow suspicious." It had been difficult enough to gain her grandfather's acceptance of the tiny black woman. What on earth would he say about this behemoth of a man? she wondered.

"I've thought of that. I'm having papers drawn up for Caesar, forged, if you will, naming me as his owner. They will be delivered in the morning. If you explain to your grandfather that you're keeping Caesar as a favor to me, he won't object."

Her eyes narrowed suspiciously. "What makes you so sure?"

109

Daniel smiled confidently. "Let's just say that we have more in common than meets the eye."

Before Samantha could respond, Dulcie blurted, "Where's he going to stay, Miss Sam? I can tell you right now, he ain't stayin' in my room!"

Daniel and Samantha exchanged amused glances. "There's room in the basement, Dulcie. We'll fix up the cot that's down there. It'll be cramped, but Caesar won't attract much attention if he's living in the house."

"The basement! Is you crazy? Why, the basement door's right next to my bedroom. How do I know he won't sneak up some night and attack me?" She cast a baleful glance at the black man who snickered in return.

"I been forced for years to bed women I dislike; it ain't likely I'm goin' to pick one out by choice," Caesar retorted.

Shaking her fist, Dulcie cried, "You hush your vile mouth, nigger. You ain't good enough to bed down with the likes of me. I'm a free woman of color. I choose who I lay with, and believe me, it ain't going to be you!" With that, the angry woman stormed out of the room, slamming the door to her bedroom behind her.

Daniel smiled into his coffee. "'The lady doth protest too much.'"

Samantha knew he was speaking of Dulcie, but for some reason she couldn't help feel that part of his comment was directed at her. She straightened her shoulders, tilting up her chin. "'Hell hath no fury like a woman scorned.' Perhaps Dulcie has had some bad experiences with men."

He raised a questioning brow. "Have you?"

110

The brown eyes darkened. "Only one, Mr. Fortune."

Noting the heated look on Daniel's face, Caesar pushed his chair back. "I think I'll go down to the basement and checks on my quarters, Miss Samantha, if that's all right with you."

"Of course, go right ahead. It's the door on the left. Please don't get it confused with Dulcie's, or we'll never hear the end of it."

Caesar chuckled. "Yes'm, you're right 'bout that. I be careful."

Reaching across the table, Daniel grabbed hold of Samantha's hand. "You don't know how much I appreciate what you're doing. Caesar means a lot to me. We grew up together. He belonged to a widow woman by the name of Phelps who lived next door to my parents. She treated Caesar like a son. Taught him to read—to write. Everyone was shocked when Mrs. Phelps died without leaving Caesar his manumission papers. My mother said it was propably an oversight, that Mrs. Phelps was old and getting senile. At any rate, he was sold at auction to my brother-in-law. It was a travesty. Caesar's like a brother to me."

Samantha fought to keep her emotions in perspective. As touching as Daniel's story might have been, he needed to understand what motivated her in her quest to find Robbie. "Perhaps, now, you can understand why I've been so anxious about my brother." She leveled her gaze on him, content to find her barb had hit.

"I've been meaning to talk to you about that. We got sidetracked the other night." He stared at her meaningfully, running his finger up and down her arm, delighting in the way her cheeks filled with roses. "I'm sorry I had to leave so abruptly." His voice took on a husky note.

Feeling as if she'd been scorched, she pulled her hand out of his grasp, jumping to her feet. She tried to keep her voice steady. "Really, Daniel, it's most ungentlemanly of you to bring up the other night. It was a mistake; it shouldn't have happened. I take full responsibility for my unseemly behavior."

Rising from his chair, he came to stand behind her, caressing the nape of her neck with his fingers. "You mean your womanly behavior, don't you?" He ran his lips over the tender skin just below her right ear, causing goose bumps to break out over her neck and arms. "I want you, Samantha. I have from the first moment I laid eyes on you."

Trying to ignore the sudden fluttering in her stomach, she turned, confused. "I . . ."

Pulling her into his chest, his lips whispered gently over her forehead and eyes. "I'm a considerate lover, Samantha. I would treat you better than Adam."

As if a bucket of ice water had been dumped on her head, Samantha's burgeoning ardor was doused. She pulled back, sucking in her breath before spitting out her words. "You take much upon yourself, Mr. Fortune. Adam and I have a great deal of history between us. Would you have me throw it all away for a tumble in the hay with you?" She felt a small measure of satisfaction at the look of outrage on his face. How she'd had the nerve to say such a thing, she would never know.

"I was not speaking of a tumble. I was referring to a more permanent alliance."

112

Her eyes widened. "You were?"

Picking up the curl that lay against her breast, he felt the pounding of her heart beneath his hand. "I would be willing to set you up as my mistress. You would have a house. A small sum of—"

She shook with suppressed fury. "Please leave, Mr. Fortune! I do not wish to hear another word."

He grabbed her shoulders, his voice suddenly hard. "Why not? You're perfectly willing to accept Bainbridge's protection. Why not mine?"

She swallowed the lump that formed in her throat. "I do not love you."

He rocked back on his heels as if slapped, then recovered himself and asked, "Love? What's love got to do with anything?" Was she trying to tell him that she was in love with Bainbridge?

"Everything, Mr. Fortune. Now, if you will be so kind as to leave." She indicated the door.

"Don't you want to know why I'm going north tomorrow? You've never asked me about your brother."

She stopped struggling and looked up at him, hope shining bright in her eyes. "You know something about Robbie? Oh, Daniel, please tell me."

The blue eyes glowed with an inner fire. "What's it worth to you?"

"I . . . I don't understand." But she did. Oh, God, she did.

Sliding his hands down, he cupped her breasts, gently fondling the soft globes through her thin nightclothes. Feeling her nipples harden, he smiled in satisfaction, increasing the pressure when she tried to pull away. "I want you, Samantha. I won't deny it. If you

113

won't come willingly, then I'm not above using other means."

Lowering his head, he kissed her with an intensity that left her breathless. His tongue traced the soft fullness of her lips before plunging inside to taste the sweetness within. It glided over her teeth, over the soft texture of her mouth, darting in and out repeatedly, until he heard her soft moan of pleasure. When her arms moved up to encircle his neck, he knew he had won.

Untying the satin robe, he ran his hands over the thin material of her night rail, plying the puckered peaks of her breasts with his fingers. Moving lower, he insinuated his hands between their bodies to cup the pulsing mound that pushed eagerly against his hardness. He could feel her wetness, her desire, and at that moment, he wanted her more than he had ever wanted any woman.

And he would have her, one way or the other.

But not yet.

Drawing a ragged breath, he pulled back, noting the confusion on her face. Their eyes locked for what seemed an eternity. After a few moments, he broke the spell. "I will be gone for many weeks to search for news of your brother. There is a man—a contact that may have information concerning Robert. I'm going to meet with him."

Samantha's heart pounded. Daniel's words buzzed in her ears as she grappled for composure. Her mouth felt as dry as cotton as she tried to formulate the words now stuck in her throat. God, what had he done to her? She couldn't think, only feel. "Is . . . is there a possibility that this man knows something?" she choked out.

114

Running his hands down her back, he cupped her buttocks, pulling her woman's mound to press against his hardened member. "Feel what you do to me. You're driving me wild. Why should I end your torment, when you won't end mine?"

Samantha felt Daniel's desire as keenly as she felt her own. Her body burned with need. But now that she had come to her senses, she realized she could never give herself to a man who was only interested in a temporary alliance. She had brought this on herself; it was her punishment for deceiving him. With a great deal of effort, she pulled out of his embrace, wrapping her arms about herself to quell the rising torment.

"I am not what you think."

He took a deep breath, running agitated fingers through his hair. "What the hell is that supposed to mean?"

"It means that things aren't always what they seem."

"Meaning you don't really desire me?" His laugh was contemptuous. "We both know that's a lie."

The truth of his words slapped at her. Desire had brought her down this path. Desire, deception, desperation. If only she could explain. But she knew that wasn't possible, nor was it likely he'd believe her.

"Why must you torture me so?" She covered her face to hide her humiliation.

"I always get what I want, Samantha. And I want you. You in exchange for your brother. I'll be gone for some time. When I return, you must decide if you will accept my proposition."

Her head snapped up. "But what of our original agreement? This was never part of it."

"Things change, love. I have greater need of you than

115

does our country. You must decide." He kissed her long and hard, and then he left, never looking back.

Samantha stared at the wooden door long after Daniel departed. Tears of frustration and humiliation trickled slowly down her cheeks.

How could she have let this happen? How could she have let Daniel think she was another man's mistress? How could she give herself to a man that didn't love her?

The questions pounded in her brain, whirling about in a maze of confusion, until at last, despondent and defeated, she sank down into the old wooden chair, weeping piteously into her hands for the answers that weren't to be.

Chapter Eight

The main room of the Golden Anchor Tavern was filled to overflowing with sailors intent on a good drunk and whores intent on a tidy profit. Their laughter rang out in ribald merriment, accompanying the clanking pewter tankards noisily raised in toast. The scourge of humanity frequented these waterfront saloons; and unless a man wanted to end up on a ship bound for China or be found dead in some alley with his throat cut, it was wise to stay alert.

Sitting before the massive stone fireplace, Daniel sipped thoughtfully on his ale, a watchful eye on the door, waiting for his contact to make an appearance. He'd arrived in the Boston port three days ago. Both Philadelphia and New York had proven futile. His last informant, a man named Briggs, had told him to come here and wait.

Intent on ferreting out information on the whereabouts of Robbie Wilder, he'd been frequenting the various taverns and inns, but obtaining details hadn't been easy. He'd been looked upon with suspicion by these Northerners as soon as his voice revealed a distinctive Southern drawl.

These New Englanders were a tight-lipped bunch, offering little in the way of information when asked about the British capture of the frigate, *Chesapeake*. Their reticence to talk came as no surprise, considering the fact that the Massachusetts legislature deemed the entire impressment issue trifling. How six thousand impressed American sailors could be considered trifling was something Daniel had not understood nor accepted.

Governor Caleb Strong had made it clear that he would continue to trade with England, rationalizing that he would not allow his constituency to lose their hard-earned money nor their livelihood. Considering the fact that the British blockade had done little to affect the New England merchants, the governor's stand held little validity as far as Daniel was concerned.

It was a bitter pill to swallow knowing that these New Englanders had turned their backs on their own country to embrace the enemy with open arms. They had gone so far as to establish a subterranean communication network with England. Vermont had sold beef to Great Britain via Canada, and Connecticut had pulled men from the Army and Navy.

"Treasonous bastards!" Daniel muttered under his breath, shaking his head. No different than Pickering and Bainbridge. Slamming his tankard down on the table, he drew the attention of the burly sailor who sat hidden in the dark corner of the room.

Blubber Billy Michaels looked quickly about the room before pushing his enormous girth out of the banister-back chair to make his way over to the

118

Virginian. Daniel Fortune stuck out like a tit on the chest of a big-breasted harlot. Maybe not to some, dressed as he was in rough seaman's britches and a dark navy coat, but to the trained eye of an old sea dog such as himself, it was obvious the man was no sailor.

Lost in his disquieting thoughts, Daniel didn't notice the arrival of the sailor until Billy plopped down heavily on the bench next to him, nearly flipping it over.

"Hey, mate! How about buying a sailor a pint of ale?"

Daniel recognized the pass phrase at once. "The ale's all right, but a bit of Irish whiskey would be a whole lot better," he responded, staring at the mounds of flesh hugging the huge man's middle, dripping off his gold-bearded cheeks in flaccid folds.

"Aye, you've got the right of that, mate." The large man's meaty fist pounded the table. "Whiskey, bar-keep!" he yelled. "Bring a bottle and make it Irish, none of that watered-down Southern swill." He looked at Daniel and grinned, revealing tobacco-stained teeth.

Daniel quirked an eyebrow. "Billy Michaels, I presume."

The big man nodded. "At your service, mate. But call me Blubber." He patted the gelatinous mound. "'Tis me nickname. I'm a whaler by profession, in case you didn't know."

Biting back a laugh, Daniel thought the nickname as appropriate as any he'd heard. Assuming a sober expression, he lowered his voice. "Briggs told me to contact you. Said you might have some information for me."

Billy pulled at his beard, weighing his answer. "Well

now, that depends on what you're going to do with it, and how much you're willing to pay."

"If what you have to tell me is reliable, you'll be amply rewarded. On that you have my word. The information is for a friend—a woman."

A knowing light entered the bulging eyes. "Good enough. You Southern gentlemen are too honorable to back down on a deal." He downed his whiskey in one gulp, wiping his mouth with the back of his hand.

"I met a man by the name of Robert Wilder on a ship bound for the Azores. I was impressed by those British bastards, same as him, but I managed to escape. All I can tell you is that he wasn't treated the same as the others on board. A great deal of effort was made to keep him by hisself; he was locked up most of the time, like they was afraid someone was looking for him. He was a nice-looking lad, brown hair, brown eyes, and he seemed an intelligent sort, not the type that would end up kidnapped by a bunch of Brits." Billy poured himself another whiskey.

Daniel listened to Billy's description of Robbie Wilder, but it was another's face that floated before his eyes. Frowning, he drowned Samantha's image with a large drink of whiskey while waiting for Billy to continue.

"When word got out that someone was seeking information about Wilder, I figured I'd best come forward. My pockets are always empty. A seaman only earns twenty-five a month, and information usually brings a good price."

Reaching into the pocket of his coat, Daniel pulled out a soft leather pouch, pushing it across the table. "There's a hundred dollars in gold in this pouch. If you

120

hear anything else, I'll be in town for one more day. I've got a little investigating of my own to do before I head back to Washington."

Blubber Billy's eyes lit. He drew open the pouch and whistled loudly. The dark eyes glowed as bright as the gold he fingered greedily. "It's been a pleasure doing business with you, Daniel, me lad. If you need anything else, Blubber's your man. I'll not be going to sea again. Not 'til things have quieted down."

Shaking hands with the rotund seaman, Daniel bid Billy good night. Stepping out into the fog-encrusted darkness, he turned his collar up against the chill and headed back to his lodgings. Tomorrow he would begin his own investigation of Samantha Wilder.

With the address tucked securely in his pocket, Daniel walked the short distance from the White Horse Inn situated on Commonwealth Avenue toward Charles Street where, if his information proved correct, he would find the residence of Patrick Wilder.

Gunmetal-colored clouds dotted the gray sky as he strolled leisurely along the broad thoroughfare lined with stately homes and businesses. Huge maple trees, just starting to show their color, provided an awning of green and gold.

The sun was absent, as it had been since his arrival in this miserable city. Why anyone would want to live in an area where the sun didn't shine for days at a time, and in September, no less, was a mystery to him. He would take the warm, sultry days of Virginia anytime, he decided.

As he approached the common, he turned left onto

121

Charles Street, pulling out the scrap of paper with Samantha's address on it. The clerk at the hotel had been easily persuaded to part with the information he'd needed. Money was always a strong incentive to loosen a man's tongue.

He had learned that the Wilders were not in residence at this time, a fact he obviously knew; and that the Bainbridges, who lived next door, were all deceased except for Adam, who had left some months back to work in Washington. The clerk had suggested contacting a Mrs. Wimple who lived across the street from the Wilders. Apparently the elderly widow was eager for company and should be able to provide him with the information he was seeking.

The tree-lined street was dotted with quaint dormered houses, mostly clapboard, but some of brick. They were set at close proximity to each other and almost all were fenced. To keep people at a distance, he surmised. New Englanders were not known for their gregarious nature.

Pausing before the house he knew to be Samantha's, a queer feeling overtook him. He could picture her seated on the porch of the white clapboard structure or tending the small flower garden which was sadly wilted from lack of care. Everywhere he looked, Samantha's presence was keenly felt, like a ray of sunshine warming him despite the gloom of the dreary day. Shaking his head to dispel the disturbing notion, he turned to cross the street.

The Widow Wimple's house was surrounded by a white picket fence. Her yard fared much better than Samantha's. Pink roses climbed the trellis to the right of the door, and a lovely bed of yellow marigolds and red begonias blossomed to the left. He had a great appreciation for flowers; his mother's passion for gardening had been passed on to him at an early age.

He waited a few moments for his knock to be answered. When the door opened, a bespectacled, white-haired lady, whose parchmentlike skin reflected a wealth of years, offered a welcoming smile.

"May I help you?"

"I hope so. I'm a friend of Robert Wilder. I've come for a visit, but I find that the house appears to be deserted."

Taking pity at the look of dismay on the young man's face, Mary Wimple invited Daniel in, offering him a seat on the lumpy horsehair sofa. For two hours, over cookies and lemonade, they sat discussing the Wilders.

Through the talkative woman's penchant for gossip, Daniel learned of Betsy Wilder's death and the adverse effect it had on Samantha as a child. He caught a rare glimpse of the child that the woman had become, learning of her devotion to her father and brother, and how she had balked at being sent away to boarding school.

She'd been a tomboy, a ruffian, Mrs. Wimple explained, in need of having her rough edges smoothed. "Why, you should have seen the child." The matronly woman shook her head in disbelief. "She cavorted about the neighborhood like a wild Indian from morning 'til night."

Daniel smothered his smile. Somehow he just couldn't picture Samantha *cavorting*. It was certainly a side of her nature he hadn't seen, though he did detect a wildness beneath all that prim exterior; the thought produced a tightening in his loins, necessitating a shift in position.

Mrs. Wimple went on to reveal the circumstances of Patrick Wilder's death. Daniel was surprised to discover that Wilder had died at the hands of the British. He knew the merchant had died at sea, but was never told how it had happened. It was easy to understand why Samantha was so intent on finding her brother. It also made it more improbable that she was a spy. Unless, he amended, she'd been overwhelmed by Bainbridge's charms and convinced that she was helping her country.

Thanking the widow for her help, Daniel took his leave, but not before unobtrusively leaving a small amount of money beneath the lace doily on the tea table when the elderly lady's back was turned.

Mrs. Wimple's accurate recitation had been worth far more to him than the small sum he had left her. If half the agents working for Madison were as astute, there would be little difficulty gathering the vital information needed to aid the government.

Picking up his pace, Daniel hurried back to the inn, realizing how eager he was to see Samantha again. The chit had gotten under his skin; there was no denying it. He hadn't been able to keep his mind off her luscious body or compelling lips.

What would her reaction be to his proposal? he wondered. Why had he tendered it in the first place?

He wanted her. It was as simple as that. And yet, how simple was it to desire a woman who might very well be a traitor? Who might very well be in love with another man?

"Love," he scoffed, kicking at the stones in the dirt path. Did it really exist? He had thought so once, before Joanna convinced him otherwise. Joanna

Stapleton. The opportunist who had married for money and position and not for love—the woman who had taken his foolish heart and desecrated it.

He'd gotten over Joanna. He could even understand her motives, for weren't all women opportunists at heart? Wasn't each out to gain what she could, not caring who was hurt in the process?

Samantha's warm smile suddenly plagued him.

How could he hurt such a sweet, seductive woman? He heaved a sigh. How could he not?

Throwing her copy of Parson Weem's *The Private Life of George Washington* that she had just purchased for the outrageous sum of eighty-five cents across the room, Samantha smiled in satisfaction as she watched it bounce off the wall. It was drivel. And as far as she was concerned, she needn't have wasted her time nor her money on it.

Rising to her feet, she paced across the dark pine planks of the study; she was too preoccupied to read anyway. It normally gave her great satisfaction to escape into the paneled sanctuary, surrounded by her grandfather's vast collection of leather-bound books. Reading had always been one of the greatest pleasures in her life.

It probably was for most spinsters, she thought, smiling ruefully. But her state of spinsterhood had occurred by choice, not by chance. She could have accepted any number of proposals over the years, but had chosen not to. Duty to her family came first, as it should, and she hadn't regretted her decision. Besides, she could still have Adam. She had only to say the word, and he would gladly marry her. But that notion held little appeal.

And then there was Daniel's proposal.

Daniel. He'd been gone for weeks and despite everything—his cavalier treatment of her, his indecent offer—she missed him. She didn't want to, had tried desperately not to, but still his tender smile invaded her waking moments, while the memory of his passionate kisses and caresses tormented her nights. She had actually woken up on several occasions doused in sweat, shaking with want.

Want. An apt word, she decided. What did she want? To be some man's mistress, his plaything, until he grew tired and moved on to greener pastures?

She paused before the open window that looked out over the rear yard. A refreshing breeze caressed her skin, ruffling the bodice of her blouse. Observing Caesar and Dulcie arguing over the garden hoe as they attempted to tend the vegetable garden that Caesar had recently planted, her mood brightened. Like two dogs with a bone between them, they tugged on the hoe until Dulcie caused Caesar to lose his balance, and he stumbled backward, stepping into a newly planted row of squash.

"Damn stubborn woman!" he shouted, raising his fist in protest.

Dulcie smiled, her white teeth flashing victorious against her ebony skin. "That'll show you to mess with me, you big ox."

Samantha covered her mouth to stifle the giggles threatening to erupt. Those two had been at each other's throat since the night Daniel dropped Caesar off on her doorstep, and they showed no signs of calling

126

a truce. Suddenly her laughter bubbled up; there was no containing it. And it felt good, so very good.

In truth, there hadn't been much to laugh about lately. Shortly after Daniel's departure, British ships had moved up the Potomac, coming within sixty miles of Washington City. It had been previously believed that their navy would be unable to reach the Capital due to the shallowness of the water and the difficulty in navigation. Thus, when they reached such close proximity, panic resulted.

Earthworks began at Greenleaf Point and the Navy yard; frigates and gunboats of the U. S. Navy sailed at once. Thousands of troops assembled; many were senior volunteers over the age of forty-five. Samantha smiled, thinking of how her grandfather had called for his saber to be brought down from the attic. She shook her head at the recollection. Had her grandfather's request not been so serious, it would have been downright comical.

Area residents worried that slave uprisings would occur due to the British promise of freedom to all slaves that joined their cause. This prompted Mayor James Blake to appoint a night watch to patrol the streets.

Fortunately, nothing came of the advance by the British. They soon turned their ships around and sailed back the way they had come, and the militia returned home.

When would all the madness stop? she wondered, pressing her forehead against the mullioned panes of glass. When would Robbie be brought safely back to her? When would Daniel?

Chapter Nine

"I don't know what we is supposed to do with all these pickled beets, Miss Sam. I done told that fool Caesar he was planting too many of them," Dulcie said, wiping her forehead with the edge of her apron before placing the earthenware containers on the shelf.

Glancing at the row of crocks lining the shelves of the kitchen dresser, Samantha tried to hide her look of dismay. "I guess we should be grateful that we have so much to eat. With times as uncertain as they are . . ." Her words trailed off.

With each passing week the British blockade was proving costly to those living in the South. Flour had increased to four dollars a barrel, sugar, when available, to nine dollars a hundredweight, and salt was rapidly becoming a scarce commodity.

"I know you're right, Miss Sam, but I still don't see why that worthless nigger gets to set inside the parlor, cool and comfortable, playing chess with your grandpa when we is doing all the work. No, sir, don't seem right to me."

Samantha smiled, wiping her hands on her beet-splattered apron. Quite in contrast to her original fears, Grandfather had taken to Caesar like a tick to a hound. He had accepted the black man's story and friendship without hesitation. The two spent almost every evening playing chess; Grandfather had found a willing pupil in the black slave and an eager listener to his war stories, as Samantha liked to call them.

Leaving a disgruntled Dulcie to clean up, Samantha tiptoed her way down the hall, pausing in the doorway of the parlor to observe the heads bent over the chess board in concentration. A study in contrast if ever there was one, she concluded.

The soft knock on the front door caused a queer fluttering in her stomach. Daniel, she thought, her heart pounding as she hurried to answer the summons, flinging off her apron in the process. Daniel had been gone six weeks, and for the last two, she had lived in anticipation and dread that, at any moment, he would come walking back into her life.

Pulling open the six-paneled door, she tried to hide her disappointment at the sight of Adam standing there. She knew she should be happy, he was an infrequent visitor at best these days, but still she found it difficult to summon a smile.

"Hello, Adam, it's been awhile."

Taking hold of Samantha's hands, Adam placed a courtly kiss upon them. "My dear, you're a sight for these work-weary eyes. Might Ezra be at home? I have need to talk to him."

"Why . . ." She started to answer, then paused. What of Caesar? If Adam were to find him in the parlor with Grandfather . . . "I'll go see if he's resting," she answered finally.

Hanging his hat on the hall tree, he smiled. "Don't

bother; I'll just go in and wake him myself."

"But—"

"Don't worry. Ezra's never minded a visit from me." He headed directly for the parlor, Samantha close on his heels. At the sight of the huge black man, Adam stopped so abruptly, Samantha almost plowed into the back of him. "Who the devil is that?" he demanded, pointing an accusing finger at Caesar. He was rewarded with total disregard by both competitors as they concentrated on winning their game. Samantha, unsure of how to explain Caesar's presence, said nothing.

After the moves had been completed and he was satisfied that Caesar would not be able to capture his rook, Ezra lifted his head, impaling Adam with watery eyes. "Don't like being shouted at when I'm absorbed in a game of chess." Wheeling himself about, he caught the grin that tugged at the corner of his granddaughter's mouth. "What's so darn important that you had to interrupt our game?"

Rocking back on his heels before regaining his composure, Adam stepped forward. "Excuse me." There was a disdainful note to his voice as he cast another curious glance at Caesar.

"Haven't you seen a black before, Adam?" Ezra questioned. "You'd think the man had two heads the way you're staring at him."

The twinkle in Caesar's eye was unmistakable, and Samantha found it difficult to hide her own amusement.

"Who is this man? Why is he here?" Adam demanded.

"Not that it's any of your business, but this man, as

130

you call him, is a friend of mine . . . a good friend," Ezra amended. "And a damn sight better chess player than you'll ever be."

Noting the purple outrage on Adam's face, the way his hands shook in anger, Samantha intervened. "Caesar, would you please give Dulcie a hand with those beets she's putting up?" She smiled gratefully when the big man nodded in understanding and excused himself. Turning back to face Adam whose purple had receded to a reddish hue, she asked, "Would you care for a brandy, Adam? Or perhaps some ratafia?"

"Nothing, thanks. Is anyone going to tell me who that man is?"

Samantha and her grandfather exchanged worried looks. Her grandfather's protective attitude toward Caesar surprised her. She was positive he knew more than he let on, though he hadn't commented on it until now.

"He's a servant—a friend of Daniel Fortune."

"Fortune!" Adam snickered. "I might have known that piece of planter aristocracy would foist his nigger off on you."

"Really, Adam, must you be so—"

"Bigoted!" Ezra finished. "I believe the word that you're searching for, my dear, is *bigoted.*"

Adam reddened again, his mouth thinning in displeasure. "I didn't come here to be insulted; I came to share the latest news of the war."

Samantha rushed forward, taking a seat beside Adam on the green brocade settee. "What's happened? Not bad news I hope."

"The worst. Perry has defeated Barclay. The United

131

States has taken control of Lake Erie. General Proctor has been forced to withdraw all British troops from Detroit."

Samantha's forehead crinkled in confusion. "But why is that bad news? Surely you don't want the British to win this war."

"Don't you see, Samantha? With the Americans' victory, the war will be prolonged. A British victory at Lake Erie and Detroit would have ended things that much sooner."

"But at what cost?" Ezra demanded. "We're talking about American lives. This isn't just an issue between two opposing political factions anymore. For God's sake, Adam, American blood is being spilled just as it was thirty-six years ago. This puts a new light on the situation; things have changed."

"So have you, Ezra. You were one of the staunch supporters of the Federalist government. Surely you don't mean to embrace the other side."

"Daniel Fortune was right; political policies matter little when the honor of our country is at stake."

"Fortune again!" Adam's lips twisted into a sneer. "How can both of you be so taken in by him? He's not what you think."

"Perhaps none of us are," Ezra responded, staring coldly at the vehement idealist, bringing two splotches of color to the young man's cheeks.

"I must take my leave," Adam announced, rising. "I can see myself out."

Samantha stared first at Adam's retreating back, then at her grandfather, whose expression could only be described as gloating. Rendered speechless by the exchange, she found her voice a moment later. "Would you mind telling me what that was all about? I fear you've made Adam quite angry."

Ezra smiled softly. "My dear, age gives a man wisdom; it also allows a blind man to see clearly. I believe your Daniel Fortune has given me back my sight." With that, he wheeled himself out of the room, leaving Samantha to stare open-mouthed after him.

"Politics," she said, shaking her head in disgust. "Lord save me from lawyers and politicians." And blue-eyed Virginians, she added silently.

Adam never broke his stride as he hurried up the granite steps of the Capitol, eager to share his concerns with Senator Pickering. Anger fueled his movements as he took the steps two at a time. Reaching the top, he paused but a second to catch his breath before continuing inside.

The senator was in his office, seated behind a massive mahogany desk when Adam entered, smoking a foul-smelling cigar while he poured over a stack of official-looking documents.

"Senator Pickering," Adam called, closing the door behind him. "I fear I bring bad news."

"Huh? What's that you say?" Pickering pushed his glasses onto his nose. "Oh, it's you, Adam." His bushy brows drew together; the glow from the candles in the chandelier overhead created a shimmering effect on the gray of his hair. "What's wrong? You look as if you've just run a foot race and came out the loser." Puffing on his cigar, he leaned back in his chair, patting his paunch.

Coming forward to take a seat in the black leather

chair before the desk, Adam wrinkled his nose, waving absently at the smoke burning his eyes. "I've just come from Ezra Lawrence's home. I fear we can no longer count on his support."

"Be serious, Adam," the senator replied, his face masked in disbelief. "Ezra's been with us from the first. 'Twas only my father's connections that got me this seat in the Senate; by all rights, it should have been his."

Removing his handkerchief, Adam wiped the beads of sweat from his upper lip. "I tell you the old man's changed. He's turned into a damned patriot, spouting off about national honor."

Pickering steepled his pudgy fingers under his chin; a gesture Adam had seen him do a thousand times since joining the senator's employ two years previously. He'd been handpicked by the senator to fill the vacancy left by Pickering's former secretary Henry Lassister.

Adam had worked hard to gain the senator's favor, working late into the night, running errands no sane man would have ever considered; he would not risk losing all because of one near-sighted old man.

"What brings about this change of heart? Do you think Lawrence has joined forces with Madison?" Pickering questioned, adding, "I find that extremely difficult to believe, considering the fact that Ezra despises the man."

"'Tis not Madison that he's aligned himself with but a man by the name of Fortune—Daniel Fortune."

"I've heard the name. He's from Williamsburg. His father was an English duke—a regular lord of the realm—but he gave it all up to fight for democracy."

"A duke?! Fortune's an Englishman?" Adam's sur-

134

prised expression turned calculating. "How interesting."

"What's Fortune got to do with all this?"

"I'm not sure. All I know is that Ezra has taken a liking to him. Fortune's had an adverse influence on him. Why, he's even gone so far as to put up the man's nigger slave."

Scratching his head, a bewildered expression crossed the senator's face. "You must be mistaken. The Fortunes have long been opposed to slavery. I've read several of the articles Nicholas Fortune has penned for the newspaper. It seems unlikely his son would advocate slavery, let alone own one."

Now it was Adam's turn to look confused. "But if the black isn't Fortune's . . ."

"Probably a damn runaway. These reformers are always interfering in the natural order of things."

"But I thought you opposed slavery. In your last campaign . . ."

Pickering waved off his comments, the ash from his cigar falling unnoticed onto the desk. "Don't be naive, Bainbridge. You must learn that in politics, one says what is expedient at the time. Personally, I despise the black bastards. Wish we could ship them all back to Africa. But since they're here, bondage is as good a solution as any. We wouldn't want them roaming the streets, now would we?"

Pouring two brandies, Pickering handed one to his secretary. "Let us drink to what's really important in life: Federalist supremacy, success of our friends, the British, and death to the opposition, whomever they might be."

A fanatical light entered Adam's eyes. "Yes. Death

to the opposition, whomever they might be," he repeated, raising his glass in toast. Daniel Fortune's face loomed before him. He smiled malevolently, drinking down the devil's own brew.

Samantha's hands shook as she read, then reread, the note from Daniel that had just been delivered by messenger. He was back, had returned only this morning, and he wanted to meet with her. She was to go to the gazebo in the rear courtyard of Suter's Tavern at midnight tonight. Caesar was to accompany her.

Why, she wondered, had he sent her such a curious missive? And what was so important that it had to be tonight? *Robbie.* A flicker of apprehension coursed through her. Had Daniel found something out about her brother? And if so, was it good news or bad?

Biting her lower lip, she gazed out the window of the kitchen, wiping away the condensation that had formed on the small panes of glass with the heel of her hand. It was raining—pouring really, as it had been for the past two days. And from the looks of the blackened sky, it had no intention of letting up.

Glancing at the Massachusetts case clock that stood on the corner shelf, she watched the hands tick off the minutes, her heart pounding in time as they moved closer to the hour. It was nearly four o'clock. Eight more hours until she had to meet Daniel. What would she do with herself until it was time to go? she wondered, pacing back and forth nervously.

Dulcie and Caesar had gone to the market to fetch some fish for dinner. Grandfather was upstairs napping. She had been in the midst of making an apple pie when the message arrived, but that prospect had lost its appeal.

Staring at the pile of dough sitting on the worktable, she sighed. Sugar and flour were too expensive to waste; she would have to finish it. At least it would help take her mind off Daniel's strange summons.

Flouring her hands, she patted the dough into a smooth round and picked up the wooden rolling pin. After a couple of swipes, she paused, her face whitening to the color of her floured hands. What if Daniel wanted her answer tonight? What if his damned proposition was the reason he was dragging her out in the middle of the night and not to give her news about Robbie? Slapping the wooden pin against her palm, her eyes narrowed. He wouldn't dare!

But she knew he would. She thought of the fierce determination in the depths of his blue eyes the last time she had seen him, the huskiness of his voice as it poured over her, filling her with longing.

"I want you . . . I want you . . . I want you. . . ."

The rolling pin clattered to the floor, sliding unnoticed beneath the table as she clutched the sides of her head to black out the torturous litany.

What was she going to do? What was her answer going to be? For, God forgive her, she wanted him too.

An autumn chill nipped the night air as Samantha and Caesar made their way down the rain-soaked road toward Suter's Tavern. Fortunately, the rain had stopped, leaving in its wake plunging temperatures and a mire of mud. The air smelled clean, as it always did after a cleansing shower. Even the piles of garbage littering the sides of the road had had their noxious odors diffused by the steady downpour.

Samantha cast a sidelong glance at the large man beside her. His expression, illuminated by the glow of the street lamp, was unreadable, giving no indication as to what he was thinking. If Caesar thought it odd that they had been summoned out in the middle of the night, he made no mention of it. He was a man of few words, she had discovered.

In the two months Caesar had lived with her, she hadn't really learned much about him, other than what Daniel had confided. But then, she hadn't taken the time to get to know him. It was her fault. Absorbed as she was in finding her brother and in Daniel's ridiculous ultimatum, she had been remiss.

From the few conversations they'd had, she could tell he was an intelligent individual, not book smart like some, but learned in the practical ways of life.

Caesar's skill as a carpenter was amazing. He had built Dulcie a lovely oak nightstand for her bedroom, which the black woman had accepted grudgingly and most ungraciously to Samantha's mortification. They had an abundance of fresh and pickled vegetables, attesting to his skill as a gardener, and he had rigged up a device whereby the leather fire buckets that hung in the kitchen could be filled from a cistern outside with a minimum of effort or delay. This was especially important, since every household had to keep a bucket capable of storing two and a half gallons of water for each story of the house or pay a one dollar penalty.

"We're here, Miss Samantha," the deep voice intruded into her musings.

Drawing her blue wool pellise tight about her to

138

ward off the sudden chill that pervaded her body, she nodded, her throat suddenly dry.

Pushing open the gate to the rear yard of the tavern, they entered to find a copious and elegant garden. Walkways covered by fragrant grape arbors led to various directions. They followed the oyster shell path to the right which led to the white painted gazebo in the far corner of the garden.

Apprehension gnawed at Samantha's composure with every step she took. When they reached the small wooden building, Caesar seated himself on the marble bench outside.

"I wait here and keep watch, Miss Samantha."

Hiding her dismay that Caesar wouldn't be accompanying her inside, she smiled weakly and entered the building, pausing in the doorway until her eyes adjusted to the dark.

"Come in and close the door."

She searched the darkness for the sound of Daniel's deep voice; she could barely make out his intimidating form in the far corner of the room. Her feet felt planted to the floor; it took a moment for her body to comply with his demand.

Closing the door, she breathed deeply. "Why did you send for me? Is there news of my brother?" She tried to keep her voice steady, businesslike. In the small confines of the gazebo, Daniel's presence surrounded her like a warm cloak. She could smell the spicy scent of his cologne; it assaulted her senses as effectively as a caress. She wanted to go to him to tell him she had missed him, but she couldn't. They were playing by his rules, and she wouldn't give him the upper hand; the stakes were too high.

"Come to me, Samantha; I've missed you."

His words poured over her like warm maple syrup, sweet and thick. Her palms began to sweat; she wiped them on her pellise. As her resolve began to weaken, she took another deep breath of the cool night air to fortify herself. "I think it would be best if I stayed where I am. 'Tis safer that way."

"Of whom are you afraid? Me?" His laugh was derisive.

She was afraid of herself—of the effect he had on her emotions, but she wasn't about to admit that to him. "Should I be?" She tried to keep her voice light.

Lighting a cheroot, he stepped forward; the glow of the match illuminated the portentous expression on his face. "Most definitely, love. If I were you, I'd be scared to death."

She swallowed. "I fear little. Now, if you would be so kind as to tell me why you have dragged me from a warm bed . . ."

"How can your bed be warm when I am not there to set your heart on fire?" he asked, stepping forward until he was mere inches from where she stood.

His nearness was unsettling. "How arrogant you Southerners are. What makes you think that I desire you?"

"I don't think; I know." He ground out his cheroot.

Samantha was tempted to turn tail and run, but she stood her ground, unwilling to be intimidated by Daniel's arrogant manner. "Perhaps you are right," she admitted, "but that doesn't mean that I intend to sleep with you."

"Who said anything about sleeping?"

She could feel the heat upon her cheeks and was

grateful for the darkness. Noting the whiteness of his teeth as he stood there grinning, she choked back her anger. "I am not as adept at hypocrisy as you, Daniel. Which is why I've decided that I cannot accept your proposition."

"Not even if I tell you where your brother is?"

She sucked in her breath. A silence stretched between them, growing tauter with each passing second. Swallowing the lump in her throat, she blurted, "I lied to you! I've never been with Adam." He threw back his head and laughed, the sound so chilling she felt a shiver of fear run up her spine.

"Come now, Samantha. You can do better than that."

"I don't consider my deception very amusing, nor do I appreciate your laughing in my face."

His expression hardened; his voice became velvet steel as he grabbed her shoulders. "Why would you tell me such a thing if it weren't true? Do you value your reputation so little? I warned you once, I'm not a man that tolerates deceit."

"I wanted to keep our business arrangement just that: business. I thought that if you believed I was Adam's mistress, you would leave me alone. Unfortunately, my plan backfired and had just the opposite effect." Noting the look of disbelief on his face, she continued, "Perhaps now that you know that I'm not some lightskirt, we can resume our original arrangement."

"You've never slept with Bainbridge?"

She shook her head, blushing to the tips of her toes. "Nor with any man."

He stared at her, wanting to believe her, wishing that

he could, but his pride would not accept what she told him. "Your actions, both in the garden at the Tayloe's party and in your own kitchen, would indicate otherwise, love. You don't behave like an untried virgin."

Unable to deny that she had acted like some shameless hussy, Samantha felt powerless to resist when Daniel untied her pelisse, dropping it to the floor.

Lowering his hands, he cupped her breasts, feeling the nipples harden as he stroked the pebbled points. "Even now your body responds like a woman who knows what she wants. Do you deny it?"

Regaining her senses, she stepped back, putting distance between them. "I am a virgin. And I don't particularly care whether you believe me or not. The fact that my body... *my body,* Daniel, not me, responds to your practiced advances, is not an indication that I am not."

"Well then, there is only one way to find out, isn't there?"

Her mouth fell open. "You're insane!"

"That's my price, Samantha. Your so-called virginity in exchange for your brother's life. A small price to pay, is it not?" Retrieving her cloak, he handed it to her.

Anger flushed her cheeks, lighting her eyes to an amber glow. "You are shameless—vile. I will never submit to your disgusting demands. Why I ever thought I could—" She clamped her mouth shut and turned toward the door.

"Think long and hard, Samantha, before you throw your brother's life away. I am the only one who can help you; I know where he is."

She turned back to face him, sucking in her breath. "I don't want your help; I'll find him myself."

142

"Is your virtue so precious that you would condemn your brother to hell? For that is what you are doing."

"I hate you!" she screamed, sobbing into her hands.

He smiled smoothly, belying the inner turmoil her words inflicted. "So it would seem. But then, you've lied before, haven't you? Since I consider myself a fair man, I will give you some additional time to get used to the new proposal. You may have two weeks. On the day of—"

"Two weeks!" she blurted, her head jerking up, her cheeks streaked with tears.

He ignored her outburst. "As I was saying, on the day of the Jockey races I will expect your answer. If you decline my offer, I will wash my hands of both you and your brother. Is that clear?"

"Perfectly!" she spat before slamming out the door.

Daniel winced as the door banged shut. Reaching into the pocket of his waistcoat, he extracted another cheroot, lighting it. If Samantha was telling the truth, it would put a whole new light on whether or not she was really a British agent. If she was a virgin as she claimed, then her alliance with Bainbridge could be discounted. If not . . .

He drew deeply on his cheroot, the puffs of smoke swirling about his head like a silver mist. It was his job to expose traitors. He had to know if Samantha could be trusted. And there was only one way he could find out. A pleasurable one, he must admit, but all in the line of duty.

In two weeks time, he would have his answer. And willing or not, he would have Samantha and finally get at the truth of the matter.

Chapter Ten

"What are you doing to do, Sam? The race is only two days away, and you've yet to come to a decision."

Shrugging her shoulders, Samantha smiled weakly at Willy. She had come to the newspaper office every day for the past week, hoping her friend would be able to offer some answers to her predicament; but as yet, neither herself nor Willy had been able to come up with any sort of viable solution. The truth was: she wasn't entirely sure there was a solution.

Stacking the sheets of cream-colored stationery Willy had just finished printing for Mrs. Madison into neat little piles, Samantha finally replied, "I wish I knew. I have little choice in the matter. As your uncle is so fond of saying, 'I'm stuck between a rock and a hard place.'"

Willy turned. "I can think of worse things to be than Daniel Fortune's mistress."

Samantha's lips thinned. "The man is a vile black-mailer, using my brother as a weapon against me. He's despicable!"

Tying a string around the stack of paper, Willy added the bundle to the growing pile that sat in the corner. "I would never have believed Daniel would do such a thing. He always seemed such a perfect gentleman."

"Perfectly awful you mean!"

"Now, Sam, be fair. You've already admitted that you brought this whole affair upon yourself by lying to him in the first place. Daniel is merely thinking with an organ other than his brain." She smiled impishly at Samantha's shocked expression.

"Willy Matthews! What an awful thing to say," Samantha chastised. Awful, but true, she suspected. She had been so careful to heed the advice of Mrs. Dinker and Mrs. Coombs over the years: *Men are out for one thing, Samantha. Never succumb to your body's weakness; it's the ruin of many a young girl.*

Too bad the old biddies hadn't offered any advice on how not to succumb. It was growing more difficult to say no. Daniel's lips and hands had proven persuasive more times than she cared to admit. Like a magician, he had cast a spell over her, one she was unsure how to break.

"From the look on your face, I'd say you were having the same difficulty as Daniel," Willy added.

Her cheeks flaming as bright as Willy's hair, Samantha plopped down on the nearby chair, sighing in resignation. "'Tis true, I must admit. Daniel's charms have overwhelmed me on occasion." She looked up, her expression suddenly feral. "But only because he's far more experienced at this game of seduction."

"But if that's true, how will you resist his demand to

145

become his mistress? Once you give yourself to him, you've nothing with which to bargain."

A long silence stretched between them. Samantha cradled her head, her face a study in abject misery. Finally, lifting her chin, she managed a tremulous smile and said in a voice barely loud enough for Willy to hear, "I've decided to accept Daniel's offer."

The heavy lashes shadowing the green eyes flew up. "What! You can't be serious! You're a gently reared woman, not some street-side doxy. You've no idea what you're getting into. You'll be throwing away your chance for a decent marriage. No man marries another man's mistress."

Staring at the vehement young woman, Samantha chewed her lower lip. Willy's arguments were no different than the ones she'd had with herself, over and over again. But if giving herself to Daniel would save her brother's life, it was a small price to pay.

"I've thought of all you've said, Willy. But the fact remains that Robbie's life comes first. 'Tis only a piece of skin that we're discussing; I was bound to lose it someday." Her eyes darkened. "Daniel Fortune may take my virginity, but he'll never truly possess me. Once Robbie is safely home, the bargain will come to an end."

"Perhaps you need to think on it a bit more. Maybe you'll find another way."

Samantha shook her head. "I've thought long and hard and have come up with no other solution."

Willy's look was commiserating as she placed her arm about Samantha's shoulders. "I know Daniel will be kind to you; he's a good man deep down. I'm just sorry that he's going to win. I thought for sure you'd be

146

able to outwit him."

A secretive smile tugged at the corners of Samantha's mouth. "Perhaps there is still a way. I may agree to become his mistress, but I didn't say I would make it easy for him. There'll be hell to pay yet; you can be sure of that."

Willy's look was clearly skeptical, if not alarmed. "Something tells me that you're playing with fire; something tells me that you're going to get burned."

A warning voice whispered in her head that Willy was probably right, but Samantha refused to listen. She had already been burned—her emotions set aflame, seized by a fire so hot, it threatened to destroy her. She couldn't stop now. Something within her—some perverse desire—pushed her on. She'd walk right through the flames of hell with Daniel Fortune if necessary. For hadn't he already seared her soul?

The day of the horse race dawned crisp and clear, not a cloud marred the azure blue sky, nor the hint of a breeze ruffled the colorful autumn leaves that clung tenaciously to the branches overhead.

Samantha had accepted Adam's invitation to attend the race late the previous evening when he had stopped by to speak to her grandfather on some urgent political matter. Feeling guilty that she and Adam hadn't spent much time together of late, she had grudgingly agreed to his escort. Now she wondered at the wisdom of her decision.

Listening to his unrelenting discourse on the questionable character of Daniel Fortune was driving her to distraction. As if she didn't already know that Daniel was rife with flaws, she thought, nodding at the appropriate times while the open-air carriage rolled unsteadily along the rutted road toward the Jockey Club racetrack.

The Jockey Club field was situated north of town. The three day meets were held biannually, every summer and fall. She had wondered about the propriety of a woman attending such an unconventional event as a horse race, but Adam had assured her that ladies made up at least one third of the audience.

Samantha hadn't bothered to explain that she had more serious games to contend with other than watching a group of horses and jockeys run around a mile-long track. She was playing for greater stakes than the two dollar bets being placed by the hopeful spectators.

"We're here," Adam announced, guiding the horses to a clearing near the track where they could watch the race from the comfort of their carriage.

Looking about, Samantha was astonished to discover the multitude of people milling about. There were literally thousands of men, women, and children. There were no color barriers here; both blacks and whites attended as equals. Nor were there class distinctions; senators and congressmen mingled freely with their constituency.

The only concession made to the more affluent was that they were allowed to park their carriages and conveyances on the western side of the field, while the rest of the crowd had to be content with sitting atop the roofs of the various refreshment booths that lined the track.

Excitement crackled the air, and Samantha found it to be contagious. This was her first horse race, and she was as eager for things to get started as the gamblers who had placed bets on their favorite to win.

"Who's riding in today's race?" she asked, craning her neck to get a better view. "Do you know anyone who's entered?"

"Actually, someone you know is riding today."

Casting a quizzical glance at Adam, she turned back toward the riders who were lined up at the starting gate. Spotting the big black stallion who looked vaguely familiar, she sucked in her breath when she recognized its rider.

"I see by your surprised expression that you didn't expect to see Fortune here today. I don't know why. These damned Virginians are known for their idle pursuits and useless pleasures. Horse racing is but one."

Adam's air of superiority nettled her. "Why are you here if you find the races so distasteful?" She noted the sly smile that crossed his lips and felt the hairs on the nape of her neck stand on end.

"I have other, more important, reasons for being here."

The loud bang of the starting gun prevented further questioning, but Samantha made a mental note to find out later just what Adam was up to.

Six horses and riders took off at the sound of the gun. Samantha's heart raced wildly as the stampeding horses circled the track. Clumps of dirt and dust flew up everywhere as the horses' hooves pawed feverishly at the ground. She watched as Daniel moved forward, edging his way toward the finish line. When the riders cleared the halfway point, Samantha observed that Daniel was having trouble controlling his mount; his saddle appeared to be slipping out from under him.

Her eyes widened in fear as she watched Daniel drop the reins and grab onto the horse's neck, leaning down over the top of the snorting beast. Horse and rider became one blur as they galloped toward their destination.

Samantha's heart pounded as loud as the horses' hooves beating against the packed turf. Unable to contain her excitement, she stood, jumping up and down as the horses drew closer to the finish line. The carriage swayed slightly, causing Adam to remark, "Really, Samantha! You're making a spectacle of yourself." He eyed her with distaste.

Ignoring Adam, she clapped her hands, cheering loudly as Daniel crossed the finish line a nose ahead of the rider on a sleek bay. She didn't see the way Adam's eyes narrowed, nor the way he clenched his fists when the winner of the race was announced.

Turning to face him, her eyes bright with pleasure, she smiled. "Isn't this wonderful? Someone we know actually won." Her smile faded slightly at the annoyed expression on Adam's face. Whatever was the matter with him? she wondered.

A few moments later, Adam excused himself and wandered off in the direction of the stables, leaving Samantha to stare quizzically after him. She shook her head. The man was impossible. She didn't have time to ponder Adam's queer behavior, for Daniel was striding in her direction with quick, purposeful steps.

A large knot formed in the pit of her stomach. Swallowing a similar knot that had lodged in her throat, she pasted on a smile. He was sweaty and smelled of horseflesh; his buckskin breeches hugged his muscular thighs like a second skin, and she thought that she had never seen a more handsome man in her life.

"Hello, love. I see you made it. Did you come alone?"

His nearness made her senses spin; her pulse pounded like a blacksmith's anvil. "No . . . I . . . Adam is with me." She noted the way his eyes narrowed at the mention of Adam's name and wondered if perhaps he was jealous. The thought bolstered her courage. "Actually, he was with me; I'm quite alone, now."

Smiling appreciatively, Daniel's eyes traveled over the green taffeta morning gown that enhanced the reddish highlights of her hair and the blush of her cheeks. The blue eyes glowed in admiration. "We can't have that, now can we?" He held out his hand. "Shall we adjourn to a more private area where we can talk?"

Her moment of reckoning was upon her. Nodding in acquiescence, she leaned forward, noting the satisfied light that entered his eyes, the slow, secret smile curving his lips that told her he had won. His hands on her waist felt alarming as he lifted her from the carriage, sliding her down the length of him in a most provocative manner. She felt an unwelcome surge of excitement and pulled away as soon as her feet hit the ground.

Talk. Did he really think she was so naive she would actually believe that he merely wanted to talk? Well, she would talk, but she wasn't sure he was going to like what she had to say.

They walked in the opposite direction of the stables, away from the crowds, away from the racetrack, away from the security of the life she had known. She was embarking on a dangerous path. Where it would lead, she didn't know. She was pitting herself against a man more powerful, more adept at subterfuge than she

151

could ever hope to be. What made her think she could win?

Absorbed in her reflections, she failed to notice the glacial gray eyes staring after her. Had she known what Adam was thinking, she would have felt even less confident about her momentous decision.

Samantha and Daniel walked hand in hand, like two young lovers off for an afternoon stroll. But Samantha knew this was no afternoon walk in the park. There was a purpose to everything Daniel did. Why should today be any different?

A few minutes later, arriving at a lovely clearing populated by clusters of black-eyed Susans and Queen Anne's lace, Samantha was surprised to discover a phaeton and horse tied up to a gnarled oak. It sat before a bubbling stream of clear blue water. The sun shining down reflected over the surface like a thousand glittering diamonds, and she thought that she'd never seen a lovelier spot for a picnic.

"I hope you're hungry," Daniel said as he approached the carriage, reaching into the interior to extract a large wicker basket. "I've brought lunch."

For a fleeting moment she was warmed by the gesture, but then, deciding he was only giving the condemned a last meal, she tossed her head back. "I'm not really hungry."

"Pity, I'm starving. And I've brought fried chicken, potato salad, and two large slices of pecan pie." Spreading the blue and white star-burst quilt on the ground, he placed the basket upon it.

Samantha felt her stomach rumble; she looked up to discover that Daniel had noticed it too and colored fiercely at the amusement on his face. "I guess I could eat a little bit . . . since you've gone to so much trouble."

"There's something I must do before we eat," he said, pulling his shirt up and over his head. "I smell like horse and sweat; I need to take a bath."

Samantha's mouth fell open. "A bath! You mean to undress and bathe in front of me?" Was he so eager to consummate their agreement, he had lost all sense of propriety?

"I'll leave my smallclothes on, if that will soothe your ladylike sensibilities, but I won't ruin a perfectly good lunch because of what you consider my lack of decency."

She didn't have time to retort, for he jumped into the water, ending their conversation. Seating herself on the blanket, she thought for one small instant that it would be quite lovely if he drowned. But then, fearing that she would be struck dead for such unkind thoughts, she silently recanted her wish.

It was really too pretty a day to have such nefarious thoughts anyway, she decided, holding her face up to the warmth of the sun. The large oak and beech trees formed a lacy veil overhead, allowing the big orange ball to filter down through the red and gold leaves in intricate patterns. Squirrels scampered to gather the acorns they would store for the coming winter, while a flock of Canadian geese in perfect V formation headed south toward more temperate climates.

It was an idyllic picture. But unfortunately reality intruded, as it always did, to shatter the illusion. She turned her head at the sound of footsteps crunching through the dried autumn leaves that littered the ground.

Daniel emerged like Neptune rising from the depths of the ocean; water glistened like dewdrops off his naked chest and muscular arms.

Samantha had to fight to keep her mouth from gaping open at the sight of his smallclothes, which were practically transparent and plastered to the lower half of his body. There was no denying the enormous bulge that jutted forth between his legs; she had to jerk her head up to keep from staring at it. Unfortunately, when she raised her eyes to gaze into his face, he was grinning at her with a knowing look that didn't leave a doubt in her mind that he knew just where she'd been staring.

"Did you enjoy your swim?" she choked out, busying herself with the basket, trying to act nonchalant. The sight of his bronze chest, thickly matted with dark, curly hair, was doing strange things to her insides.

Wringing his hair out, which looked like wet obsidian, he hunkered down next to her. "I really hate staying in these wet underclothes. Are you sure you would mind if I removed them?"

"No! I mean yes, I would mind. Please leave them on."

He chuckled at the way her words got all tongue-tied in her sweet, kissable mouth. Good thing he had an excuse for the bulge between his legs, for he didn't think he'd have been able to hide it. Not the way she'd been looking at him for the past few minutes with those big brown eyes and rosy, flushed cheeks. God, she was beautiful!

"Care for some chicken?" she blurted, practically tossing the crispy hunk of meat at him. "It's very good."

"Mmmm," he responded, taking a bite. "I love breasts. They're so succulent and tender. But then, you

154

know that already, don't you?"

Pulling her knees up under her chin, Samantha smoothed her dress down, vowing she wouldn't let Daniel's teasing remarks nettle her composure again. "I thought you wanted to talk. Isn't that why you brought me here?"

"Among other things."

A soft breeze caressed her heated cheeks. He didn't mean to throw her down on this blanket and have his way with her . . . out here, in front of God and everybody, did he? She swallowed, her heart pounding so loud in her ears she thought for sure he could hear it.

As if he could read her thoughts, Daniel replied, "Tempting idea, love, but I prefer a more comfortable bed to lie upon."

She turned away from his wicked grin, staring out at the water which shimmered in the afternoon sun as it cascaded over the smooth rocks and crevices. "Why do you persist in tormenting me so? Does it give you so much pleasure?"

Leaning toward her, he reached out to grasp her chin, turning her back to face him. "You give me pleasure, love. You and your tempting body and your kissable mouth." Like the whisper of a gentle wind, he placed his lips upon hers. "God save me, but I want you."

Her mouth burned with fire. She sucked in her breath, edging her way over to the far end of the quilt, fighting her overwhelming need to be held in his arms. "I've come to a decision . . . about your proposal." The eager look on his face was almost touching. Almost. But she wasn't about to forget that he had brought her to this humiliation because of some selfishly motivated sexual perversity. She hardened her resolve.

He arched his brow expectantly. "Do I dare ask what it is that you've decided?"

"You've left me little choice in the matter." Her accusing words stabbed the air, but if he felt their prick, he didn't show it.

Daniel's heart pounded as foolishly as any young schoolboy in the throes of his first passion. What madness was this that made him eagerly await the decision of a woman who most likely was a traitor to her own country? And what greater madness in the fact that he just didn't give a damn anymore?

Samantha observed the myriad of emotions flitting across Daniel's face. He seemed nervous. Almost as if she held the fate of his life in her hands. A heady feeling, if only it were true. But she knew differently, or at least, she thought she did.

"Are you going to tell me what it is you've decided? Or do I have to guess?"

His question brought her back to the reality at hand. Staring at him with determination lighting her eyes and resolve strengthening her will, she answered in a voice as soft as a petal on a newly formed rosebud, "I have decided to become your mistress."

Chapter Eleven

His smile fairly took her breath away. "I have two conditions," she added, watching it fade.

"Conditions?" His expression grew wary.

"Yes. If I'm to become your mistress, there must be an agreement regarding my brother. I will not give all and receive nothing in return."

"That seems fair. I will tell you what I know."

"There's more." She saw his eyes darken and sucked in her breath. "In addition to revealing all that you know about my brother's whereabouts, I want proof. Irrefutable proof that he is still alive."

"Proof! Where am I going to get proof? The man is clear on the other side of the ocean."

"He's in England, then?" She waited for his answer with bated breath and felt dismayed when she realized he was not going to tell her.

"Not so fast. We haven't reached a compromise, as yet."

"With your connections, it shouldn't be that difficult to procure the proof that I require. Robbie always wears a pewter medal around his neck. It's very distinctive. One side depicts an arm grasping a pole on top of which rests the liberty cap and the words 'Sons of Liberty,' on the reverse, the Liberty Tree. My father gave it to him; he never takes it off."

Intense astonishment touched his face. He couldn't believe what she was telling him. Her father was a Son of Liberty? A member of the group held most responsible for bringing about the Revolutionary War? It was impossible.

Wasn't it?

Before he could question her further, she went on to say, "I want you to bring the medal to me. Once you do, I will be yours to do with as you will."

The image her words conjured up produced an instant tightening in his loins, making him forget everything else for the moment. She would be his to do with as he willed. To strip naked, revealing every inch of her perfection, to suckle the luscious mounds that drove him crazy with desire, to drive his shaft deep within her velvet confines. To possess. To cherish. To . . .

Feeling his hands start to sweat, he shook himself, recapturing his wild imagination. "You do not drive an easy bargain, love. *If* I could locate your brother's exact whereabouts, and that's a big if, I would still have to figure out a way to get near him. It might be next to impossible."

"Then we have no deal. It's my way or not at all. I'm not going to be foolish enough to part with the one thing I can never replace, only to be left holding an empty bag of promises."

"You are speaking of your so-called virginity again, I take it."

"That's correct. I'm speaking of my so-called virginity as you speak of your so-called ability to find my brother. I can produce what I possess. Can you, Daniel?"

A spark of admiration lit his eyes. Samantha was a worthy adversary. Not to mention a clever one. It would take time to procure this medal. He thought of Blubber Billy and frowned with uncertainty. The man would drive a hard bargain, but would he be able to deliver?

"I see that you have thought this out very thoroughly, Samantha. I take it that you also realize it will take me some time to gather this proof that you seek. It's what you are counting on, is it not?"

"Naturally I am anxious to learn of my brother's whereabouts and see the proof that he is still alive, but I am a patient woman, Daniel. I will give you more time than you gave me to produce what I desire."

"And when I do, you will come to me willingly? No strings attached?"

"As I said, I will be yours until such time as my brother is returned safely home. Then our arrangement will come to an end."

"Are you so certain that you will be able to end it, love? Are you so certain that after you lay in my arms, let me make love to you, you will be able to walk away as if nothing has happened?"

A heat so intense that it threatened to ignite flared within Samantha's breast. She paused to catch her breath, struggling with the uncertainty aroused by his questions. When she spoke, her voice reflected a calmness totally contradictory to her inner turmoil. "No strings attached, remember?"

A humorless smile twisted his lips. "So be it."

Like the falling autumn leaves, the days passed quickly by, dropping off the months, one by one, until October was only a memory and the Thanksgiving holiday rapidly approached.

The passing weeks had brought about changes. Changes in the course of the war, changes in relationships.

Lord Castlereagh had sent President Madison a letter earlier in the month, offering direct negotiation to end the war. Madison accepted the proposal, sending John Quincy Adams, Henry Clay, Albert Gallatin, and Jonathan Russell as peace commissioners.

The overture by the British, however, hadn't prevented their extension of the blockade along the American coast, which now included Long Island. Only ports north of New London, Connecticut, remained open, and American commerce was virtually at a standstill.

With the blockade came shortages, and Samantha, seated at the worn worktable in the kitchen, wondered how she would put together a Thanksgiving meal with no flour and sugar to bake pies and no Maine cranberries to serve for relish.

She gazed at her copy of Amelia Simmons's *American Cookery,* then surveyed the menu in front of her, sighing disgustedly. There were only two items on her list: turkey, which Caesar had mysteriously procured and penned up the previous week, and beets. She screwed up her face. The thought of eating another

160

pickled beet made her stomach roll. She was surprised that her skin, and that of her grandfather's, hadn't taken on a reddish hue.

"What are you lookin' so upset about, Miss Sam?"

At the sound of Dulcie's voice, Samantha looked up to find Dulcie and Caesar standing quietly by the table, holding hands. Dulcie barely came to Caesar's waist, but by the blissful look upon her face, Samantha didn't think she noticed. Caesar wore a smile that seemed a permanent fixture of late.

Things had certainly changed between those two. They'd gone from a pair of screech owls to a couple of cooing doves, all in the space of a few weeks. Samantha had even observed the young maid sneaking down the cellar stairs on two different occasions when she'd gone to the kitchen for a late-night snack.

Noting the expectant looks on their faces, Samantha replied, "I'm in a pickle about what to fix for Thanksgiving dinner this year. Besides the turkey," she paused, noting the way Caesar studied the toes of his shoes, "we've little else to eat."

"Doan you be worrin' about that, Miss Samantha. Caesar's going to take care of everything."

She fixed her gaze upon the black man, eyeing him suspiciously. "What do you mean, fix? You know stealing is a crime, Caesar. I don't hold with fattening our larder at others' expense."

He shook his head emphatically. "Oh, no, ma'am! I wasn't fixin' to steal nothin'."

"What then?" She observed the big man cast a nervous glance at Dulcie.

"I'm not supposed to say, ma'am."

"Caesar, I have taken you into my home, given you a

161

place to stay, and treated you like one of the family. I think you owe me an explanation."

He nodded. "Yes, ma'am, but Mr. Dan's going to have my hide if I tell."

Her lashes flew up. "Daniel? What's he got to do with this?" She hadn't seen Daniel since their agreement had been struck. She assumed his absence had something to do with wounded pride and male ego. Hearing his name on Caesar's lips made her realize just how much she had missed him.

"Mr. Dan made me promise I wouldn't tell. He said it was a secret."

Crossing her arms, she tapped her foot impatiently, prompting Dulcie to respond, "You'd best tell her, Caesar. Miss Sam's got that look on her face again."

The big man scratched his head, thought for a moment, then, deciding that he'd rather face Mr. Dan's wrath, than Miss Samantha's, who had quite a temper beneath all that sweetness, he finally replied, "Mr. Dan done said that he'd be bringing provisions back from up North. He's been gone a few weeks; I expect he should be back anytime."

She was unable to hide her surprise. "Daniel's gone north? But he didn't even say good-bye." Observing the couple's sudden interest in her statement, she quickly added, "You'd think he'd keep me informed of his whereabouts. You are my responsibility, after all, Caesar."

"Yes'm." The big black inched his way toward the door. "I best go cut some firewood."

Samantha almost smiled at the frightened expression on Caesar's face as he scurried out, slamming the door behind him. Obviously, she was more intimidating than she thought. Staring thoughtfully at the door, her smile suddenly faded. What if Caesar's deception was discovered? The possibility had plagued her of late. Thank goodness no one had come to investigate his presence. Even with the forged papers she kept locked in the drawer of her desk, she couldn't help but worry that someday someone was going to show up on her doorstep and haul the big kind-hearted giant away.

Observing Dulcie as she prepared the haunch of venison for the evening meal, Samantha wondered if she held the same fears. "Dulcie, you and Caesar appear to be getting along much better. Isn't that true?" Samantha saw a faint blush cross the woman's cheeks.

"Yes, Miss Sam, we're getting along just fine." Wiping her hands on her apron, Dulcie took a seat opposite Samantha at the table. "Truth is, I'm in love with that big black fool."

"That's wonderful!" Samantha said, her smile fading when she noticed the look of sadness on Dulcie's face. "Aren't you happy about it?"

Dulcie sighed, fidgeting nervously with the ends of the tablecloth. "Yes, I am. But Caesar's a wanted man; they could come and get him anytime. Then where would I be?"

Samantha chewed her lower lip at the truth of Dulcie's words. Apparently, Dulcie did possess the same fears about Caesar and for much more personal reasons. Patting Dulcie's hand comfortingly, she said, "My mama, rest her soul, used to say, 'The good lord works in mysterious ways.' I can't believe he'd let harm come to someone as fine as Caesar."

"Your mama must have had a good heart, Miss Sam,

but she didn't know nothing about being a slave. My own mama was a slave. She died giving birth to me."

Samantha sucked in her breath at the revelation but said nothing.

"My papa, it was said, was her master, which is why I was sent north when I was no bigger than a mewling kitten."

Samantha gasped aloud this time. "I had no idea!"

"Didn't see much point in discussing my past. I'm a free woman now. I have the papers to prove it. But Caesar's not. He claims that Mr. Chastain is a greedy man. And although he was treated better than most, he was forced to couple with women of Mr. Chastain's choosin', slaves who had no more rights than he did. Caesar was a breeder, fattening Mr. Chastain's pockets by producing innocent little babies that the man sold for profit."

Covering her mouth to hold back the bile that rose to her throat, Samantha's voice shook with anger when she spoke. "I won't let them take him back."

"You a fine woman, Miss Sam, kind to a fault. But they gots the law on their side." Dulcie shook her head sadly.

"Someday the law will be changed, Dulcie; mark my words." The reformers up North would not rest until the institution of slavery was a thing of the past.

"Yes'm. I guess that's so. But in the meantime, what we going to do?"

What was she going to do? Samantha wondered, noting the hopelessness dulling the young woman's eyes. She wouldn't let Caesar be returned to Harold Chastain; she knew that with a certainty. But how could she prevent it? There had to be a way. And between she and Daniel, they would find it.

Squeezing Dulcie's hand, she smiled with more bravado than she felt. "Trust me, Dulcie. Caesar will be a free man. This I promise."

The Center market was crowded the day before Thanksgiving. Shoppers milled about the sparsely filled stalls, scanning the bins in search of items to buy for their holiday feast.

Thanksgiving had become an institution in the New England states, especially in Massachusetts where the pilgrims had landed so many years before. Samantha was happy to see that the tradition was celebrated elsewhere, as more and more people chose to recognize the sacrifices their forefathers had made.

Pulling her cloak tightly about her, she wiped at the flakes of snow landing softly on her cheeks. The snow had started early in the morning, falling steadily throughout the afternoon until, now, over an inch of the fine white powder blanketed the ground.

She was grateful for the quilted pellise that kept her warm and for the black giant next to her that kept grabby shoppers at bay. Caesar was like Moses parting the Red Sea. One intimidating look from him and the crowd stepped back to let them pass. At first, she'd been embarrassed by this, but after being shoved and pushed, to and fro, she soon found the advantage of having him along.

The shortage of food had made tempers short, and Samantha prayed silently that the hostilities between the United States and Great Britain would soon come to an end.

Placing several potatoes into her wicker shopping basket, she moved down the stalls, observing Caesar eyeing a bin of chestnuts with unconcealed longing.

"Shall I get some of those chestnuts, Caesar? There's nothing like the smell of roasted chestnuts during the holidays." Her eyes took on a faraway look as she remembered back to other years, other Thanksgivings, when she had roasted chestnuts with her family around the big stone fireplace in the little house on Charles Street. She swallowed, turning her attention back to what Caesar was saying.

"I'd be mighty pleased, Miss Samantha. I know Dulcie has a particular fondness for them; she done told me so."

Seeing the childlike excitement on his face, she smiled. "Well, then, we wouldn't want to disappoint her, now would we?" Reaching into her reticule, she handed the jowly cheeked shopkeeper a quarter.

"No, ma'am. But don't be spendin' too much of your granddaddy's money. Mr. Dan's goin' to be bringin' provisions."

Caesar spoke with such conviction, Samantha didn't have the heart to tell him that Daniel wouldn't be home in time to provide them with food. He was already a week overdue. The snow was sure to slow him down, if he was, in fact, on his way.

Handing him her basket, she smiled. "We've got plenty of beets, potatoes to mash, and a nice, plump turkey, thanks to you. I guess we'll do just fine. Besides I . . ." She stopped in mid-sentence as she caught sight of Adam coming her way.

A wave of guilt swept over her at the awful way she had treated him the day of the Jockey races. Leaving like she did, with no word of explanation, she couldn't really blame him if he never spoke to her again. Which looked like a distinct possibility, considering the fact that, although she had written Adam an apology, he hadn't seen fit to call, and her invitation to Thanksgiving dinner had all but been ignored. She guessed she deserved it; she had treated an old friend shabbily.

Determined to right a wrong, she raised her hand but quickly lowered it when she saw that Adam had stopped to talk to a tall dark-haired man. The man looked familiar. Hadn't she seen him somewhere before? And then he turned his head and she noticed the jagged scar that ran from the corner of his left eye down to the edge of his mouth. It was the man from the Tayloe's party, the one Adam had been so determined to meet in private.

Suddenly, Daniel's words stabbed at her subconscious like a sharp knife. *"If either Bainbridge or Pickering meets with anyone you suspect might be involved with the British, report it."* The man did look disreputable, hardly someone Adam would normally associate with, unless . . . She pushed the thought away, unwilling to face its implication.

Edging forward, she tried to get closer so she could listen to what they were saying but the crowd had thickened, and even with Caesar's intimidating presence beside her, she couldn't push her way through. A moment later they were gone, disappearing around the corner.

"Botheration!" Daniel was right, she made a terrible accomplice.

"Is something wrong, Miss Samantha?"

Heaving a sigh, she shook her head. "No, Caesar,

nothing's wrong." But everything was. Adam detested her, Daniel hadn't returned yet, and worst of all, they were going to have to eat beets for Thanksgiving dinner . . . lots of beets.

Later that same evening, seated before the massive brick fireplace of the parlor, Samantha stared into the crackling flames, rubbing her arms against the chill that beset her. The snow had piled in drifts halfway up the door, but she knew it wasn't the inclement weather that had formed an icy casing around her heart. She couldn't stop thinking about the man with the sinister scar on his cheek; she couldn't stop wondering if Adam was somehow connected with him.

Twice now, she had seen them together, once at the ball and today at the market. Both times had been in public places, but their furtive, almost secretive, manner alarmed her. Perhaps she should confide her fears to her grandfather. She turned her head to stare at him.

He was seated across the room, hunched over his chessboard in concentration. Caesar sat across from him, a determined look upon his face. Should she mention her . . . what? Suspicions? Did she really suspect Adam of complicity with this questionable character? Doubt plagued her mind. Grandfather would most likely laugh off what she realized was probably only an overactive imagination. Still . . .

Dulcie's blood-curdling scream split the quiet, making Samantha forget all her misgivings. She pushed herself to her feet, her heart racing in apprehension. Caesar, who had heard Dulcie's scream at the same time Samantha did, bolted from his chair, knocking the chess pieces to the floor in the process, causing

Ezra to shake his head in disgust.

"Damn woman!" he shouted, pounding the table. "She's ruined our match."

Casting her grandfather a reproving look, Samantha hurried out of the room, skidding to a halt when she reached the doorway of the kitchen. Her eyes widened to the size of saucers. Standing in the center of the room, caked with snow, looking very much like some prehistoric Arctic creature, was Daniel.

He gazed at her with eyes unknowing; he tried to speak, then crumbled to the floor in a heap.

"Daniel!" she screamed, rushing forward to help Caesar who was lifting him up off the floor.

"He's bad off, Miss Samantha. Plumb froze inside and out."

Fear, stark and vivid, gnawed at her composure as she stared at the still form cradled in Caesar's arms. Like shooting stars hurtling through space, questions darted around her mind, but she pushed them away; now was not the time for them. Knowing that they would have to act quickly if they were to save Daniel's life, she forced herself under control.

"Take Daniel upstairs to my room and get him undressed. Then go outside and take care of his horse. I'll be right up." She had seen men die from exposure. Her own father had almost succumbed during the blizzard of 1800 that hit Boston when she was a small child. Only her mother's quick thinking had saved his life; now, she must do the same for Daniel.

"I don't think it's proper for you to be tendin' that man, Miss Sam." Disapproval etched Dulcie's face.

"Oh, for heaven's sake! Now is not the time to lecture me on propriety. Go and make some coffee, lots of it."

"That old man ain't going to like you undressing some man that ain't your husband."

Dulcie's words made her pause momentarily. *Grandfather.* In all the excitement she had forgotten about him. "After you're finished making the coffee, I want you to go into the parlor and tell Grandfather what's happened. Explain that Daniel has taken ill."

Wagging her head, Dulcie replied, "I'll explain, but he ain't going to like it. You an unmarried woman, Miss Sam."

Alarmed for Daniel's life, Samantha's words were sharper than she intended. "Well, tell him we're engaged, then," she shouted, heading out the door. "Tell him anything. I don't care."

Rushing up the stairs, she passed Caesar on his way down. "I'll go and take care of the horse, Miss Samantha. Mr. Dan mighty fond of that stallion."

"Bundle up, Caesar; it's far below freezing outside. When you're done, please help Dulcie put my grandfather to bed. I'm not sure she'll be able to handle him alone. Then bring up the coffee. Raising Daniel's temperature is our first priority. I fear that it's going to take most of the night."

After Caesar left to do her bidding, Samantha paused before the open door to her bedroom, her eyes rounding at the sight that befell her.

Daniel was sprawled atop her rose satin counterpane, naked as the day he was born. Rooted to her spot like an venerable oak tree, she stared, mouth agape. He was magnificent, like some bronze statue that adorned the hall of an ancient Greek temple. But she knew he was no statue. He was all man—every intimidating inch of him. Her face reddened at the realization of where she'd been staring.

She shook herself as the sound of his moan propelled her into action. Forgotten was her maidenly modesty of moments before. With quick efficiency and a detached air that would have made Dr. Chase proud, she lifted Daniel's legs to draw the counterpane back; his limbs were like two long icicles. Realizing that she needed to get the blood circulating within his body, she vigorously massaged his legs, arms, and chest.

Refusing to acknowledge the impropriety of what she was doing, she concentrated instead on bringing life back to his frozen limbs while carefully avoiding the disturbing, swollen member that jutted forth between his legs like a warrior's spear.

Her hands roamed over every masculine inch of him. With large, circular motions, she pushed against his chest, his arms, his legs, willing his blood to warm. Knowing she did not possess the strength to roll him over onto his stomach, she decided to forego the massage to his back, pulling the covers up and over him instead. Putting her ear to his chest, she listened. He breathed easier.

Satisfied that her ministrations were beginning to work, she stepped over to the fireplace, throwing additional logs onto the fire to increase the temperature in the room. Taking two bricks that rested on the hearth, she wrapped them inside a piece of warm flannel, placing them against Daniel's frozen feet. She heard his sigh of pleasure, but he didn't awaken.

A moment later, Caesar entered, carrying a large enamel pot of coffee and two metal cups; he set them on the table before the fireplace.

"How he doing, Miss Samantha?" He peered at

Daniel's sleeping form. "I do believe he's looking a mite better."

Samantha's heart lightened. "Do you think so, Caesar? I hope you're right. I've done everything I can to help him."

The big man nodded. "You're doing just fine. I done put your granddaddy to bed. You want me to sit with Mr. Dan a spell?"

She shook her head. "No. There's no sense in both of us losing a night's sleep. If Daniel doesn't improve by morning, you may need to find Dr. Chase. The way the snow's accumulating, that might not be an easy task. You'd best get some rest."

Crossing to the door, he stopped, turning back to face her. "You are a good woman, Miss Samantha. Mr. Dan is lucky to have you." With those words, he quietly shut the door behind him.

Samantha stared down at Daniel, brushing his cheek with her fingertips. She smiled a half smile, doubting that he would agree with his friend. Crossing to the mahogany tea table, she poured some of the steaming coffee, taking a seat on the edge of the bed. Lifting Daniel's head, she tried to coax some of the hot liquid down his throat. He resisted her attempts at first, but she finally succeeded in getting a small quantity down him.

Satisfied that he would rest for a while, she took a seat in the rocker next to the hearth. Soon the warmth of the fire and the rocker's rhythmic motion eased her into a restless sleep.

She wasn't sure what woke her a short time later. Perhaps the log that had fallen off its grate or the sputtering of the candle on the nightstand. Rising, she chafed her arms against the chill, throwing more wood onto the fire. Cursing at her own stupidity for falling asleep, she rushed to the side of the bed.

Daniel lay there, his teeth chattering like a determined woodpecker, while he shivered beneath the quilts. "Damnation!" she swore, placing her hand on his forehead and cheek, feeling the cold skin beneath it.

Staring down at Daniel, tears filled her eyes. Tears for the fear that he wouldn't recover, tears for the fear that when he did, she would have to face the truth that had suddenly hit her like a ton of bricks: she loved him. How did it happen? When? She cradled her head in her trembling hands.

Realizing that now was not the time for self-examination or recrimination, she took a deep breath. She must concentrate on getting Daniel well.

Knowing that there was only one thing left that could help to raise his body temperature, she bit her lip in indecision. Her mother had administered to her father in a similar manner when he had suffered from chilblains. Of course, they had been married. If someone were to find out what she was about to do, her reputation would be ruined permanently.

"Ha! As if it mattered," she muttered, thinking that when she became Daniel's mistress, her reputation was going to be tattered anyway.

Fearing for Daniel's life more than her reputation, she went to the door and turned the key in the lock. Stripping off her dress and petticoats, until all that remained was her shift, she climbed beneath the covers, placing her body next to Daniel's and blew out the candle. She shivered as his cold flesh came into contact with hers; he felt like a block of ice. Well, she would

173

warm him up, she vowed, and he would never be the wiser.

The feel of his naked body pressed so intimately against hers sent warming currents barreling through her. Her body temperature rose like quicksilver in a thermometer.

At first she just lay there, too afraid to move, until she realized that Daniel wasn't going to wake up. Growing bolder, she ran hesitant hands over his muscular chest, exploring the thick mat of curling hair, relishing the way the roughened hairs felt beneath her fingertips. Trailing her fingers down his abdomen, she stopped just short of where his male organ rested. Biting her lip, she tried to halt the persistent throbbing in her loins, shutting her eyes tight against the painful hardening of her nipples. Even though unconscious, Daniel still had the power to torment her, she thought ruefully.

After a few moments, Daniel's violent spasms subsided. Relief rushed through her veins like molten lava. She smiled into the darkness, placing her head against the solid planes of his chest, listening to the even beating of his heart. Her own heart eventually quieted, matching his beat for beat, and she soon fell into a dreamless sleep.

Chapter Twelve

Daniel slowly opened his eyes to face the predawn darkness. He squinted in confusion at the unfamiliar lace canopy hanging overhead and the feel of satin beneath his fingertips as he rubbed the coverlet atop him.

He could remember nothing, only the interminable hours seated in the saddle, fighting the cold, the snow, and the lack of visibility as he made his way homeward.

Could it be that he had ended up in some whore's bed after a night of drinking himself senseless? he wondered. Turning his head on the pillow, he caught sight of a woman's head peeking out from beneath the covers. It was difficult to make out her hair color in the darkness.

Rolling onto his side, he palmed his cheek with one hand and with the other brushed back the long tresses obscuring her face. The movement caused her to stir, but she did not awaken. Suddenly, as if sensing his presence, she flipped over to face him, her mouth mere inches from his own. Unable to resist such a blatant invitation, he pressed his lips gently to hers and was rewarded with a sigh before she called out his name.

At least he had made her acquaintance before taking her to bed, he thought, peering through the darkness once again, trying to distinguish her features. But no moon shone through the shuttered windows, and the fire in the hearth had disintegrated into embers, leaving the room pitch black and the woman next to him only a shadowy form.

Deciding that touch was a far preferable sense than sight, he ran questing fingers down her hip, over her buttocks, down her thigh. The shift she wore had ridden up, leaving a tempting amount of flesh to explore. Odd that a whore would wear a shift, he thought; they usually wore nothing more than an encouraging smile.

Continuing to stroke her, he delighted in the feel of her velvet skin beneath his hands. He must have paid a goodly sum for this tart, for she was certainly delectable, not coarse or flabby like some he'd bedded. And she smelled of lilacs.

The woman grew restless beneath his exploration. When she parted her thighs, as if in invitation, he felt his manhood harden. Gliding his fingers over her lean hip, he splayed them across her abdomen, feeling the taut muscles flex in response. Moving lower, he sought the nest of curls, cupping the swollen mound, kneading it with practiced motions. Slipping his finger into her crevice, he plied the bud of her being until she grew wet with desire, and he heard her soft moan of pleasure.

Samantha fought the wakefulness that plagued her, preferring to stay in the euphoric half-awake, half-slumber state. Her dream was so real, so sensual, so forbidden, she dared not open her eyes to end it. But the persistent throbbing between her legs was becoming unbearable—the tension growing taut, like a string stretched tight on a fiddle, begging to be played.

Forcing her eyes open, she came slowly awake and with her wakefulness came the horrifying realization that her dream was all too real. She felt the hand between her legs, felt the moistness flooding her thighs, and remembered with sickening clarity whose hand it was, whose huge, stiff member pressed ardently into her leg.

Oh, my God! She grabbed at the exploring hand that had caused so much pleasure, so much torment. "Stop!" she cried out in an agonized whisper. "You must stop." Her cheeks burned at the thought of how intimately he had touched her, was still touching her. She attempted to move away, to distance herself, but she found herself unable to; Daniel's hold was too tight.

"Don't be so quick to leave, sweetheart. I wager I've paid a princely sum for a full night's pleasure between your thighs. I'm not done with you just yet."

Samantha's mouth fell open when the full import of Daniel's statement made itself painfully obvious. He thought he was in some whore's bed; he thought she was some doxy who sold herself to men. Fury ignited her temper. Fury and another alien emotion she had no right to feel: jealousy.

"Stop it right now, Daniel Fortune," she ordered, pushing hard against his chest. "You're not in some whore's bed, but in mine."

"And who might you be, my mysterious beauty?" he replied, nibbling her lower lip while he plied her nipples with experienced fingers, eliciting a gasp from her throat.

"It's me, Samantha," she choked out, grabbing on to the hand that held her breast captive. "And if you don't release me this instant, I'll be forced to scream, and then you'll be sorry. I guarantee it."

His hand stilled, but he did not remove it.

"Samantha?" His voice held a note of disbelief. "What the hell?"

He leaned over her, pressing her into the mattress to prevent her escape, while he lit the taper beside the bed. The candle flickered, then ignited, illuminating the humiliation on Samantha's glowing face.

Staring down at her, Daniel's eyes widened before he grinned most seductively. "I didn't expect to find you in my bed, love. This is quite a pleasant surprise."

"Lower your voice, and let me up, you big fool. You're going to get us both in a heap of trouble." Furious that her warning hadn't wiped the smile off his face, she added, "And you're not in *your* bed, you're in *mine!*"

Wrapping his arms tightly about her, he cradled her against him. "You're not going anywhere until you tell me how I came to be here."

"I don't think it's proper for me to discuss anything with you while you're stark naked and holding me so . . . so . . . indecently." His steel shaft rested against her woman's mound, pulsing with a life all its own, as if it knew it would not be denied entry into the slick enclosure.

"I think we're a bit past propriety, don't you?" He smiled knowingly, causing her cheeks to flame again.

She pushed harder. "Please, you must let me go."

Her voice held a note of panic.

His held a grim finality. "No!"

Samantha sighed in resignation, trying to hold her body perfectly rigid, which was next to impossible when Daniel was drawing circles around her ear with his finger, and his warm breath was tickling her face like a feather against the column of her spine.

"Very well," she answered finally. "You were ill—near froze to death. Caesar carried you up here, and I tended you."

"I vaguely remember hands vigorously rubbing my flesh; it felt wonderful. Was that Caesar?"

Turning crimson, she shook her head. "No, 'twas I."

His smile widened. "You're very skilled with your hands. I remember feeling—"

"Please stop!" she pleaded, placing her fingers across his lips. "I only did what I had to to save your life. You needed body warmth; I gave it. Nothing more."

"So we didn't . . . ?" His pause was full of regret.

"No! How can you think it?"

"Love, when a man wakes up naked in bed with a beautiful woman, and she has naught on but a thin slip of cotton, what is he to think?"

"I admit our situation looks compromising, which is why I locked the door."

"You locked the door?" The dark eyebrows arched mischievously.

She inclined her head. "I couldn't chance anyone coming in to see us like this."

"How clever of you." Brushing her forehead with his lips, he fingered the lock of hair that lay against her breast before releasing his hold on her.

"I must go. Now that you are obviously well and do

179

not need my care, I will retire to the settee downstairs."

He grabbed her arm when she made to climb off the bed. "No. I'll not have you sleeping the rest of the night in an ice-cold room. I'll go."

"But you're ill."

He coughed, taking full advantage of the worry on her face. "I'll be all right." He coughed again.

"I'll not have you undo all my efforts; you'll catch the ague or worse. That would be foolish."

"Then we'll both stay."

She sucked in her breath. "Are you demented?"

"What's the difference? We've passed most of the night in each other's arms." He smiled inwardly at her blush. "What are a few more hours?" She hesitated, prompting him to add, "I won't force myself on you; I promise."

Force, she thought, it would hardly be that. "I suppose . . . if you promise to stay on your side of the bed." What was she saying? Was she mad suggesting such a thing? Before she could recant her words, he leaned over her again, blowing out the candle. Kissing her quite matter-of-factly on the lips, like they were some old married couple, he said, "Night, love. See you in the morning."

Defeated by Daniel's logic and pacified by his promise, Samantha curled herself into a tight little ball, moving as close to the edge of the mattress as possible.

But by the time the daylight hours crept through the thin slats of the shutters and an overzealous rooster announced the beginning of a new day, she was once again plastered against Daniel's broad chest, blissfully unaware that the man who lay beside her did so with a satisfied smile on his face.

The pounding on the door caused Samantha and Daniel to bolt upright. Samantha's face turned as white as the sheet covering her. She glanced quickly at Daniel, then at the clock on the mantel. How could she have overslept? She was always up by six. *You've never had such an interesting bed partner before,* her mind answered. Noting that Daniel seemed unperturbed by the entire situation, she cast him a furious look, scrambling off the bed. She padded to the walnut wardrobe to fetch her robe.

"Lay quietly and pretend you're asleep. I'll take care of this."

Daniel lay his head back down, grinning at the ceiling. If Samantha only knew how delectable—how damned desirable she looked in the morning's light, with her hair streaming down her back in wild disarray and her thin cotton shift transparent to his view. He closed his eyes, savoring the image of her long, silky legs and full, ripe breasts.

She was an exciting, provocative woman. Her pretense of innocence had almost been convincing last night. Almost. But she was too seductive—too alluring to be the maidenly flower she protested to be. Feeling his member stiffen, he flipped over, smiling into the pillow. If she were a flower, then he was the bee, for he had the stinger to extract the honey he knew was waiting for him.

"Miss Sam, is everything all right?" Dulcie's voice floated in through the door.

Turning the key in the lock, Samantha threw open the door to allow Dulcie entry. "Ssh. Daniel is sleeping.

I've been up most of the night tending him."

Noting the rumpled sheets and the indentation on the pillow that lay next to Daniel's head, Dulcie crossed her arms, suspicion lighting her big brown eyes. She stepped farther into the room, nearly tripping over the dress and petticoats that littered the floor.

"Looks like you was in a powerful hurry to get your clothes off last night."

Staring with dismay at the clothes she had haphazardly strewn about the room, Samantha swallowed nervously, feeling her cheeks warm. "It was terribly hot in here because . . . because the fire was so large. You know . . . to keep Daniel warm."

"Is that a fact?"

A low moan, which sounded suspiciously like a laugh to Samantha's ears, came from the direction of the bed.

"Sounds like Mr. Daniel's on the mend. Whatever treatment you gave him surely must have worked, for I believe he's about cured." Dulcie crossed to the bed, placing her hand on Daniel's forehead. "Nope, I was wrong," she said, shaking her head. "That man's hotter than grease on a griddle."

A shadow of alarm crossed Samantha's face. "Is he feverish?"

"No, ma'am. What ails that boy ain't fever. But I expects you knows that."

Samantha gasped in shock. "Dulcie!"

Crossing to the door, Dulcie paused, a knowing look on her face. "You'd best get presentable and get downstairs. That old man's going to wake soon, and he's going to be askin' a lot of questions."

Staring helplessly at the door being closed in her

face, Samantha turned to look back at the bed, where she found Daniel doubled up with laughter. Her eyes narrowed; she clenched her fists. "I wished I had let you die," she said, grabbing a ceramic figurine off the mantel and tossing it at him, disappointed when she discovered she had missed her mark.

Daniel's grin was infuriating. "But love, I thought you did. For after last night, I have surely gone to heaven."

"Oooh!"

Daniel ducked under the covers just in time to miss the large volume of Shakespeare's sonnets that whizzed by his head.

"We thank thee, oh Lord, for these blessings which we are about to receive, and beseech thee to end these hostilities which burden our souls and our country. We pray that this burden soon shall be lifted. We ask this . . ."

Samantha listened intently to the prayer her grandfather intoned, thinking that, despite everything that had occurred in the past few hours, there was much for which to be thankful.

Beneath lowered lashes, she glanced surreptitiously at Daniel, who sat facing her across the dining room table, his head bowed in prayer; his black hair gleamed like polished ebony in the glow of the candlelight.

He looked completely fit; one would never know how seriously ill he had been just a few short hours ago. She marveled at his capacity for recovery, silently thanking God that he had survived the night. Smiling inwardly, she thought perhaps she should thank God for surviving, as well. It had been her most difficult test of strength yet, and she had passed unscathed, but just barely.

If Daniel knew how close she had come to yielding to his charms . . . She twisted nervously in her seat, prompting a lewd grin from Daniel, who was now staring at her and who, she was certain, had the uncanny ability to read her mind.

"Amen," she responded when the prayer ended, turning her attention back to her grandfather who was wearing a rare smile.

Lifting his glass of wine in the air, Ezra proposed a toast. "I wish to thank our guest for this bounty he has supplied us with today. At great risk to his person, I've been led to understand. We truly have much for which to be thankful."

Daniel inclined his head, feeling uncomfortable with the praise.

"'Tis a fine meal, Samantha," her grandfather added, helping himself to another portion of bread stuffing. "You and the black wench have done an admirable job."

Muttering her thanks, Samantha surveyed the table laden with food, marveling at the sumptuous feast she and Dulcie had prepared on such short notice.

She had entered the kitchen early that morning to find piles of foodstuffs littering the room. Sacks filled with flour, sugar, and salt were strewn about the table, chairs, and floor. Sides of bacon, shanks of ham, and an additional turkey still rested outside in the freezing snow, where Caesar said they would preserve better.

A large plump turkey rested in the center of the table, surrounded by a dozen tart crab apples. Bowls of mashed potatoes, candied yams, peas, butternut squash, and of course, beets, accompanied it. There were hot flaky rolls and two large pumpkin pies.

The magnificent meal they had prepared would not have been possible without Daniel's generosity and thoughtfulness. It was truly fit for a king, or a prince, she decided, bestowing a sweet smile on Daniel who winked in return.

Dulcie and Caesar had opted to dine in the kitchen, refusing her grandfather's very startling offer to join them in the dining room. She didn't know what had gotten into the old codger lately. She supposed she had Daniel to thank for that, as well, for her grandfather's improved humor seemed to coincide with Daniel's first visit.

After the meal was completed and the dishes cleared away, Samantha joined Daniel and her grandfather in the parlor. A cheery fire blazed brightly in the hearth, crackling and hissing as an occasional snowflake fell upon the logs. Not wishing to disturb the men who were still engrossed in their brandy and conversation, she crept quietly to the window, drawing the curtain back to peer out.

The snow continued to fall, the silent flakes accumulating at a rapid rate. The moon shone over the deep drifts, making them appear like soft pillows of white Virginia cotton. The trees, void of their leaves, stood like strange misshapen sentinels guarding the night. There was an eerie beauty to it—cold, stark, yet majestic in its stillness.

"There you are, Samantha," Ezra called out. "Come and stand by the fire. You'll catch your death by the window."

Samantha turned, crossing the room to take a seat in the wing chair that flanked the fireplace. The fire, however, didn't warm her as effectively as the tender smile on Daniel's lips when he greeted her.

"It's been brought to my attention," Ezra said, "that congratulations are in order. Though I do not condone Daniel's lack of decorum in observing the proprieties, I must admit that I'm pleased by this recent turn of events."

Samantha and Daniel exchanged puzzled glances, until Samantha, realizing what her grandfather was about, felt the blood drain from her face. "Grandfather, wait!" she blurted.

Totally ignoring his granddaughter's outburst, as if he hadn't heard a word she'd said, Ezra went on to say, "I'm very happy that you and Daniel are engaged, Samantha." He slapped Daniel on the back. "I admit, I was taken aback when Dulcie told me. But after thinking it over, I've decided to give you both my blessing."

Rising slowly to her feet to take her place next to Daniel, Samantha smiled weakly, afraid to look at the furious expression she was certain was registered on his face. When she did finally get the courage to glance over at him, her eyes widened in surprise, for rather than the anger she expected, his face reflected satisfaction, as if their engagement had been his idea all along. She grew instantly wary, finding his acceptance unnerving. He was up to something. But what?

Sliding his arm tightly about Samantha's waist, Daniel drew her into him. "This has come as quite a surprise to us, as well, Ezra. Hasn't it, love?" He looked down at her with adoring eyes.

She could only smile a sickly smile and nod her head in response.

"I must admit," Daniel continued, "I've been overwhelmed by your granddaughter's charms, which are innumerable, I might add."

Samantha blushed from the roots of her hair to the tips of her toes, fearful that Daniel was going to bring up the previous night's events. She fingered the folds of her green satin gown, relieved when he merely went into a boring dissertation on what he considered to be her best attributes.

After a few minutes of listening to him sing her praises, she thought she would go mad. Why wasn't he going to set her grandfather straight about their engagement? Why did he continue to perpetrate the lie?

Deciding that she'd had enough, she opened her mouth to rectify matters. She had barely gotten the first word out, when she felt Daniel's hand tighten on her waist. Looking up at him, she found a pair of dark blue diamonds, glittering with purpose, staring back at her. Her mind spun with bewilderment. He didn't want her to tell? But why? It wasn't as if he cared for her, though she wished with all her heart that it was so. Her confusion intensified when, a moment later, Daniel tendered a startling invitation.

"Since the Christmas holidays are just around the corner, and my parents have not yet had the opportunity to meet my lovely betrothed, I would like you both to journey to Williamsburg with me to spend Christmas. I plan to leave in two weeks' time."

Samantha paled, apprehension coursing through her.

Ezra smiled gleefully. "It will be wonderful to see your father again, Daniel. I vow I'm excited about the prospect. What say you, Samantha?"

Two pair of eyes stared at her expectantly. One pair, brown, tired, but lit with hope; the other, blue, eager, burning with an intensity Samantha found frightening.

Observing the heightened color on her grandfather's cheeks, the way his eyes sparkled like a young boy's, she knew she couldn't disappoint him. She was trapped. And by the smug expression on Daniel's face, he knew it, too.

What perverse game was he playing now? she wanted to ask, but instead replied, "Of course we'll go, Grandfather, if that is your wish."

Ezra let go with a shriek of delight, slapping his thigh.

Leaning over, Daniel whispered in her ear, "I look forward to our wedding night, love. Pity that we'll have to forego the ceremony." Before she could protest, he moved his mouth over hers, devouring its softness, sending the pit of her stomach into a wild swirl, making her blood boil until she thought she would melt into the flames of the fire.

No one heard Ezra's satisfied chuckle or saw the calculating gleam in his eye.

Part Three

Ashes and Ecstasy

Laurel is green for a season,
and love is sweet for a day;
But love grows bitter with treason,
and laurel outlives not May.

Algernon Charles Swinburne
"Satia Te Sanguine"

Chapter Thirteen

The Union Tavern which sat on the corner of Bridge and Washington Streets was crowded, smoke filled, and noisy that cold December night. Outside the wind howled a mournful melody as it sliced through the raging snowstorm; inside, the roar of burning pine and oak snapped and spit in defiance of the ruthless elements. But the two men bent over the table in conversation in the far corner of the room paid scant attention to either.

The smaller of the two, with light blond hair and frosty gray eyes that shone as coldly as the icicles hanging outside the window, spoke harshly to the disfigured man seated across from him. "I told you, Henry, there couldn't be any mistakes." Adam Bainbridge looked with contempt at his companion. "You were supposed to fix it so Fortune would be killed in that damned horse race. Instead, the man goes on to win and appears like a hero to everyone watching." He thought of Samantha's reaction, how she had exalted in Fortune's win, and his eyes narrowed. Women were such fools, always taken in by a handsome face and a charming smile.

The scarred man brushed nervously at his dark curly hair; his voice shook slightly when he spoke. "I tried, but the chap was too good a rider. I tell you, any other man would have been trampled to death. Fortune has nine lives."

Slamming his fist on the table, nearly upsetting the two tankards of ale, Adam leaned over, grabbing the front of John Henry's shirt. "Listen to me, you bastard, I want Fortune dead. Do you understand? It matters little to me how you achieve that end, just do it. If he's left to his own devices, our whole system could come down around our ears. I fear he's already on to us; we can't take the chance that he'll expose our plans before we're ready."

Pulling back, Henry smoothed his green satin waist-coat; an affronted expression curled his lips. "I'm a spy for Christ's sake, not some damn assassin. I only agreed to do your dirty work because you promised to send me back to England. Well, I'm ready to get out of this stinkin' country and back to where men are civilized. You Americans are all a bunch of barbarians."

Adam almost laughed. Had Henry forgotten his own heritage? He looked as menacing as any thug on the Boston waterfront, but he was really just a coward at heart. Damn the man! He would kill Fortune himself and enjoy doing it, if he didn't have higher aspirations. He couldn't afford to taint his hands with the blood of a Virginian, not and become governor of the Commonwealth of Massachusetts. No. Henry had to do the job.

"My sources inform me that Fortune has twice gone north in the last few months, probably with vital information for the American troops in Canada. We can't allow him to undermine everything for which we've worked. I'll increase the stakes. Besides your passage back to England, I'll throw in a thousand pounds." He saw the man's eyes light up with greed. "All you need do is remove Fortune; I'll take care of the rest."

"What about the blackamoor? I've seen him with Fortune a time or two. And last time, he was at the market with the brown-haired girl. I'm not fool enough to take that giant on."

Adam leaned back in his chair, his expression confident. "A bullet stops a bear as well as a rabbit."

"Aye, but I've not got a gun big enough to kill that bear. I'll remove Fortune, but not if the black's involved."

Adam's lips thinned. He had seen the black at the market with Samantha shortly before Thanksgiving. How she had the nerve to parade around town with Fortune's nigger, who he now knew to be a runaway, was beyond his ken. Was she so foolish as to believe she wouldn't be caught? He didn't want to implicate Samantha in his dealings. He had to get rid of the nigger, but without involving her. There could be no stain on the reputation of the wife of the next governor of Massachusetts.

"Leave the nigger to me," Adam said. "There's more than one way to trap a black bear." He smiled sinisterly.

Henry breathed a sigh of relief. "When do you want the deed done?"

"As soon as possible, you fool. It's nearly Christmas. Once the New Year comes, the American troops might be better equipped and supplied to handle the British forces. We need to act with all due haste in the matter."

"And then you'll give me my reward?"

Swallowing his ale, Adam smiled, patting his compatriot on the shoulder. "My dear, Henry, never fear, you will get exactly what is coming to you. On that you have my word."

The mood in the Madison sitting room was somber. The men who assembled in the President's office had just taken steps that would have far-reaching repercussions in the months ahead.

A trade embargo had been called, forbidding all trade with the British. This was in direct retaliation against the New York and New England merchants who had been provisioning the British in Canada and along the Eastern Seaboard. It was to be signed into law the next week, making all who engaged in trade with the enemy in time of war guilty of treason against the United States. This was punishable by hanging.

How did one hang an entire state, an entire region? Daniel wondered, staring at the small delicate man before him with something akin to pity. He did not envy President Madison his position. The war was taking its toll on all of them, but it had been particularly brutal on the President.

Madison's blue eyes were lackluster, his brown hair tinged with gray. Only averaging three to four hours of sleep a night, he was beginning to show every one of his sixty-two years. In fact, the President looked much older than Daniel's own father who was over seventy.

Mr. Madison's manner was mild, almost bland, but when he spoke, his voice was rich, his words melodious as they flowed from his heart like a mighty river sure in its course. Daniel turned his attention back to what the president was saying.

"Gentlemen, what we do here today will either heal the ills of our nation which have been created by this war or cause a chasm so wide no bridge we erect will ever span its distance."

Rising from the red velvet wing chair, the secretary of state smoothed back his hair and stepped forward to address the room. "Mr. President, gentlemen," James Monroe began, "what the President says may be true, but we have little choice in the matter. This treason our brethren to the north have perpetrated has been tolerated long enough. It's plain to see that Pickering and his cronies have no intention of stopping their profitable dealings with the enemy. It's time we took steps to punish those guilty of subverting our efforts to win this war."

"Hear! hear! Colonel Monroe," the tall light-haired man with the high, sloping forehead shouted as he banged his fist on the conference table. "It's about time we take steps to stop those guilty of sedition; I only hope we are not too late," Henry Clay warned. "This war, though unpopular with some, was unavoidable. We can never be a free and independent nation as long as we let others dictate their will to us. If we have to crush these Northerners beneath our boot heels, then so be it. We must stand together, knit as a whole, for surely if we don't, the very fabric of our country will unravel and ultimately split apart."

Daniel leaned back in his chair, observing the hot-headed orator from Lexington, Kentucky. Mr. Clay, the house majority leader, was well-known for his outspoken views on the war. He was tall, lean, only thirty-six, but Daniel suspected his expertise was in aging others rather than himself. Together with the congressman from South Carolina, John Calhoun, Clay had led several successful debates on the floor of the house to sway the opposition over to their "War Hawk," as they were called, point of view.

Outwardly, Clay appeared almost vulgar. His whiskey drinking, tobacco chewing, and spitting had received a great deal of negative commentary in the newspapers. But Daniel found him to be quite the opposite, graceful and dignified. In fact, Clay was quite a favorite of Mrs. Madison who was known to share her gold snuffbox with him on occasion.

Daniel smiled, thinking of what Samantha's reaction would be to Henry Clay. He was sure she would find him quite uncouth, especially if she heard his unflattering opinion concerning Northerners. He had no desire to further inflame her outraged sensibilities by subjecting her to the political machinations of a government who, like the child of legend, stuck his finger in the dike of discontent to hold back the flood of hostility that could very well drown them all.

Tomorrow they would leave for Williamsburg. Samantha was sure to be upset when he presented her with his little surprise. Why add more misery to a day they would surely both remember?

"Miss Sam, you'd best hurry if you're going to finish your packing before Mr. Daniel gets here. You know he said to be ready promptly at nine. It's nearly that now," Dulcie said, handing Samantha two freshly starched petticoats.

Samantha, fighting the urge to stick out her tongue at the bossy woman, smiled patiently instead, glancing up at the ormolu clock on the mantel. Fifteen more minutes and Daniel would arrive. She bit her lip, shutting her eyes, hoping the clock would stop ticking and time would suspend indefinitely. She had no desire to travel to Williamsburg to meet his family, to perpetrate a sham that was sure to backfire in their faces. Unfortunately, when she opened her eyes again, it was fourteen minutes until nine, and she still had not finished her packing.

"I'm hurrying, Dulcie. Why don't you go down and make certain Grandfather hasn't forgotten anything. You know how excited he's been all week."

The black maid nodded. "I ain't never seen that old man so strung up before. You'd think he never traveled anywhere in his life. He surely wasn't this pleasant on the trip we took from Boston." Shaking her head, she mumbled something under her breath and quit the room.

Dulcie was right. Grandfather was excited, and all because they were going to Williamsburg to visit his friend Nicholas Fortune. How many times had he related the incident of his near drowning and Mr. Fortune's heroic jump into the river? More times than she cared to remember, Samantha thought, heaving a sigh. Hopefully, he would not recount it again on the journey there, or she might be tempted to jump out of the coach.

Taking one last look around to make certain she

197

hadn't forgotten anything, Samantha grabbed her portmanteau and hurried out of the room. She would give Daniel no reason to find fault with her this morning. She was determined to be pleasant—accommodating if necessary—until this ridiculous charade was at an end, and they could confess that their engagement was just a silly misunderstanding. She was committed to do so for her grandfather's sake, if for no other reason.

Pausing on the last step, she frowned in uncertainty. Surely, Daniel wouldn't be foolish enough to continue this deception while they were in Williamsburg. No respectable Southern family would want their son marrying a Northerner. She had heard about the prejudices existing there, and it didn't just extend to blacks. Why, even the Southern congressmen would not share their boarding houses with those from the North. She shook her head. There was a lot more than distance that separated North and South.

The carriage Daniel had procured arrived promptly at nine. It had already been decided that Dulcie and Caesar would remain behind to care for the house, and that Caesar would stay within its confines until their return, so as not to bring notice onto himself. Willy had graciously offered to keep an eye on things while they were gone.

Standing in front of the townhouse while Daniel loaded the remainder of the luggage onto the coach, Samantha blinked back her tears as she bid farewell to Dulcie and Caesar. "I'm going to miss you; I'm not sure I'm going to like sharing Christmas with a bunch of strangers."

"You's goin' to like the Fortunes," Caesar assured her, patting her hand as if she were a child. "They fine people. Why, next to you, Miss Samantha, Miss Alexandra is just about the finest person I know."

"Don't you worry about a thing, Miss Sam. Caesar and I are going to be all right." Dulcie smiled at the big man standing next to her, her eyes aglow with love.

How lucky they were to have each other, Samantha thought, staring enviously at the happy couple. Even if their future looked dim at the moment, the love they shared would sustain them through troubled times. She cast a glance at Daniel, who was frowning back at her, making a great show of checking his pocket watch again.

Hugging Dulcie one last time, she climbed into the coach, seating herself next to her grandfather, who immediately began another one of his narratives on Washington's march to Yorktown. She didn't bother to disguise her groan this time. It was going to be a long ride to Williamsburg. A very long ride.

Daniel stared thoughtfully at the beautiful woman across from him. She was asleep, and he thought he had never seen a lovelier, more innocent face in his life. But was she truly innocent? Did she know about the unsuccessful attempt that had been made on his life the previous night? His gut twisted at the unwelcome suspicion, his mind returning to the prior evening's events.

He had left the President's meeting a little after nine, stopping by Joseph Gales's office to drop off some papers for Mr. Madison. From there, he had boarded the coach back to Suter's Tavern. Nothing had seemed amiss, until he had stepped off the coach and entered the rear courtyard of the tavern, intending to pay a visit to the taproom for a nightcap.

He hadn't heard the footsteps, hadn't heard the cock of the pistol until it was too late. Fortunately, the assailant's aim had been poor in the dark, the bullet hitting the door instead of his head.

Someone had tried to kill him. But whom?

It didn't seem like the work of a British agent. They were trained not to miss their mark. Who then? It was the second time an attempt had been made on his life. The first coming the day of the Jockey race when his cinch had been cut. He had laughed off his near fatal fall in front of the others, blaming it on his own ineptitude, but he had known Midnight's harness had been deliberately tampered with.

Samantha had been at the races that day . . . with Bainbridge. It was likely that Bainbridge was on to him. The man was as dangerous as a viperous snake. Ambition made men desperate. Was Bainbridge desperate enough to kill him? And if so, did Samantha know of his plans?

Studying her angelic face in repose, he couldn't believe she would be a party to anything so sinister. She was innocent; he was sure of it. But still the niggling doubts ate at his confidence. After all, he had placed her in a compromising position. What was it she had said? *"Hell hath no fury like a woman scorned."* Was she merely biding her time until she could exact her revenge?

Heaving a sigh, he closed his eyes and his mind to the

unpleasant prospects. Only time would prove her loyalty. But which side would she choose?

Several hours later, Samantha opened her eyes, surprised to find their journey almost at an end. The carriage followed the same route that Washington and Rochambeau had traveled on their way to meet Cornwallis at Yorktown.

Though her eyes had been closed a good portion of the time, she had listened attentively to Daniel's narrative as he patiently explained to her grandfather the various sights and landmarks surrounding them.

"It's probably changed a bit since you were on this road last, huh, Ezra?"

Ezra chuckled. "I must admit, I much prefer riding in this coach than walking every mile as I did the last time. Our feet were bloodied and swollen by the time we got to Yorktown. But, by God, I think we would have marched all the way on shards of glass if Washington had asked us to. He was a great general . . . a great president."

Daniel nodded in agreement, peering out the window. The visibility was poor, the going slow, the journey impeded by heavy accumulations of snow on the road. "It shouldn't be much longer," he stated, pulling out his gold pocket watch. "I expect another thirty minutes or so."

Thirty minutes! Good Lord, Samantha thought, clutching her reticule tightly on her lap. She would be there in thirty minutes. Oh, please, let the Fortunes be kinder than their son, she prayed silently. If they were anything like Daniel, she vowed she would turn around and board the first coach back home. She might be in love with the man, but she certainly wasn't blind to his faults. And from what she had observed thus far, he had more than the average human being.

She was soon to add one more to her list, when the carriage pulled to a jarring halt in front of what she could only surmise was a house. It was pitch black out and snowing again. She couldn't see an inch in front of her face when she glanced out the window of the carriage.

"We're here," Daniel announced. "I'll help your grandfather into the house, arrange for the driver to unload the bags and wheelchair, then I'll come back for you."

"I can hardly wait," Samantha replied sarcastically, receiving a gentle nudge in her ribs from her grandfather.

"What's got into you, girl? That's no way to speak to your betrothed. Daniel's to be your husband; you must give him the proper respect."

She shot daggers at the smile Daniel flashed at her, which was filled with so much superiority she wanted to scream. Respect. Ha! If her grandfather only knew what kind of a blackmailing blackguard the man was.

A few minutes later Daniel returned, but instead of helping her out of the carriage, he took the seat next to her, brushing the snow off his coat before draping his arm casually over the back of the seat. Immediately, her senses cried out in warning.

"Isn't it time for us to go?" she questioned, anxious to escape from his disturbing presence.

Toying with the lock of her hair that had come loose from her chignon, he replied, "I thought perhaps I would have a word with you in private. I have something for you, and it's not for others to see."

She stared wordlessly at him, her heart thumping, her brow wrinkling in confusion. What could Daniel possibly have for her? Then the most startling thought entered her mind. Had he gone out and bought her an engagement ring? Her eyes lit with pleasure. Perhaps he was in love with her. Perchance it was the reason he wanted everyone to believe in their engagement. She smiled shyly, unable to contain her excitement. "You've brought me something? A gift perhaps?"

Observing the look of childhood pleasure on Samantha's face, Daniel was tempted not to go through with his plan. But a bargain was a bargain, and he had much to gain from this one. Reaching into the pocket of his greatcoat, he extracted a small box wrapped in a piece of black velvet, placing it in her gloved hand. "This is more than a gift, love. This is the answer to my dreams."

Noting the passion in Daniel's eyes, her heart slammed madly in her chest. She was right; he had bought her an engagement ring. Oh, Daniel, she thought, her eyes misting, I love you so.

Her hands shook so badly, she had trouble unwrapping the package. Lifting the lid with impatient fingers, her mouth fell open as she stared at the contents. Displayed before her on a bed of red satin, as fine as any piece of silver or gold, was her brother's pewter Son of Liberty medal.

Chapter Fourteen

They had supped shortly after arriving, exchanged pleasantries with Daniel's parents, and were now seated in the drawing room for after-supper libations. As preoccupied as she was with her own disquieting thoughts, Samantha had paid scant attention to the time and conversation, allowing both to whiz by her as she sat dazed by the recent events.

Fighting to maintain her composure, which was rapidly disappearing, she tried to take her mind off the horrible predicament she now found herself in by concentrating instead on her surroundings.

The room was handsomely furnished in the Queen Anne style, boasting a blue brocade settee, two rose velvet wing chairs, and a lovely mahogany chest-on-chest, once belonging to Daniel's grandmother. Over the mantel, hanging from the blue paneled wall, were two gilt-framed Audubon bird prints.

Staring wistfully at the pair of painted cardinals, Samantha wished she could take flight as easily as the winged creatures in the painting and whisk herself away somewhere—anywhere other than where she was now.

Seated next to Daniel on the small confining love-seat, she felt trapped, trapped by the hand that rested so proprietarily against her neck, trapped by her own foolishness in suggesting such a ridiculous proposition to Daniel in the first place.

She had thrown down the gauntlet and Daniel had accepted the challenge of finding her brother. Now she had to pay the price for her stupidity. Why had she challenged a man like him? Did she really think he wouldn't win? Did she really want him not to?

Absently fingering the pewter chain around her neck, she thought of the consequences that lay ahead, what the reality of becoming Daniel's mistress would mean. The warm medal burned as it pressed against the flesh between her breasts, reminding her of how foolish she'd been. Daniel didn't care for her, only lusted after her like a randy dog in heat. How mindless of her to think that he would actually want to marry her—that he would grow to love her as she had grown to love him.

Observing Daniel's parents who made no pretense of the love they felt for each other as they whispered quietly, holding hands like newlyweds, made her situation all that more difficult to bear. Would she ever find a love like that? she wondered, heaving a sigh.

"No man marries another man's mistress." Willy's words came back to haunt her, answering her question bluntly and succinctly. She would never know the love a man felt for his wife, never feel a babe suckling at her breast, never experience the satisfaction of being truly cherished. She would

grow bitter and lonely after Daniel was through venting his lust upon her. Tears suddenly clouded her vision.

"My dear, are you all right?"

Samantha looked up to find Alexandra's worried gaze upon her. The bright blue eyes, so like Daniel's, were filled with kindness and concern. She had liked Daniel's mother the moment she laid eyes on her, feeling a kinship with her that she hadn't felt with another woman before, save her own mother whose memory grew more indistinct with every passing year. It made her feel that much more guilty for lying to Alexandra, for allowing her to think that she and Daniel were going to marry.

How cruel of Daniel to perpetrate this deception—to foist this lie upon his parents. But then, cruelty was Daniel's forte, and lies rolled off his tongue as easily as water rolled off the fin of a shark. Hoping to alleviate the kind woman's concerns, Samantha pasted on a brave smile.

"I'm fine, Mrs. Fortune. Truly."

Alexandra's brow knitted in disbelief as she stared at the distraught woman before her. Samantha seemed almost despondent, not at all happy like an eager bride should look. Something was definitely wrong. "Perhaps a glass of sherry would help restore your spirits, dear."

" 'Tis nothing a good night's sleep won't cure. I'm merely fatigued. The ride from Georgetown was overly long."

"You slept most of the way. How can you be tired?" Daniel remarked, running his finger over the sensitive spot beneath her ear, causing gooseflesh to break out

206

over her neck and arms. "It's only nine o'clock."

Slapping his hand as if it were a bothersome pest, Samantha's voice grew testy. "I just am."

"Leave the girl be, son. I'm sure Samantha is sick and tired of your company by now. Isn't that right, my dear?" Nicholas bestowed a conspiratorial wink upon her, eliciting a grateful smile in response.

Nicholas Fortune, for all his years, was a devilishly good-looking man, Samantha thought. His brown eyes twinkled as brightly as any youth's, and his white hair, which contrasted markedly with a healthy tanned complexion, made him appear distinguished rather than old. She could certainly see from where Daniel inherited his good looks. Both Daniel's parents were handsome people. Too bad Daniel hadn't inherited their kindness as well.

"I'm afraid that's quite true, Mr. Fortune," Samantha agreed. "Daniel does have a way of growing stale in a hurry."

She almost laughed aloud at the outraged look on Daniel's face but was soon to swallow her amusement when he replied, "Is that so? Well, there have been certain times when you haven't found me quite so tedious." His meaning was obvious; his eyes challenged, daring her to deny it.

Staring down at her toes, Samantha felt the blush rise to her cheeks. How could Daniel say such a thing in front of his parents? Her grandfather? Casting a quick glance to where her grandfather rested in the wing chair by the fire, she breathed a sigh of relief; he was still sound asleep.

She rose to her feet, smiling apologetically at her hosts. "If you will excuse me, I think I shall retire now.

207

I'm more tired than I thought."

"I'll show you to your room," Daniel offered, preparing to rise.

"No!" she blurted, then amended in a calmer tone, "There's no need. I'm sure you want to visit with your family a while longer. I can find my way."

Nicholas and Alexandra exchanged puzzled glances before Alexandra stood, threading her arm through Samantha's. Noting the odd expression on the young woman's face, she frowned. It looked suspiciously like fear. "Come, my dear, I'll show you up. Your room is at the top of the stairs on the left, right next door to Daniel's." So much for romantic notions, Alexandra thought, dismayed at Samantha's wide-eyed look of horror. The child looked as frightened as a rabbit ensnared in a trap. What on earth was going on with those two? She wouldn't dwell on it now, but by all that was holy, Daniel would cough up an explanation tomorrow.

Bidding everyone good night, Samantha turned to leave, only to be stopped in her tracks by the sound of Daniel's voice.

"Aren't you forgetting something, love?"

Turning back, she stared, baffled. "I'm sorry?"

"A kiss. Where's my good-night kiss?"

"Really, Daniel!" She tried to disguise her annoyance in front of the others but was unable to hide the two blotches of color now staining her cheeks.

"I'm waiting," he replied, a self-satisfied grin on his face.

Glancing hopelessly at Alexandra, whose look was thoughtful, then at Nicholas, whose grin was as wide as his son's, she gently disengaged her arm from Alexandra's and, as casually as she could, crossed over to where Daniel sat.

Leaning down, her lips pursed in indignation, she pressed them lightly against Daniel's cheek, too angry to feel anything but animosity. "Good night," she said aloud through gritted teeth, then added under her breath, "you vile, egotistical man."

Lifting her skirts and her chin simultaneously, she quit the room, leaving Daniel to stare after her in bemusement and Nicholas in admiration.

"I see you have chosen a replica of your mother," Nicholas remarked, reaching for his brandy, savoring the contents before he spoke. "Beauty, brains, and brazenness all rolled into one delightful package. You're a lucky man to have found a woman like Samantha to share your life. Take my advice, never let her go."

Daniel's smile was thoughtful as he stared at the empty doorway. Samantha wasn't really a part of his life. She would soon waltz out as quickly as she had entered. Unless . . .

No! he thought, turning to stare into the flames of the fire, his heart hardening. No woman would get her hooks in him again. Samantha was a pleasant diversion, nothing more. He would satiate this longing, this need he had for her, then expel her from his mind and leave her to her traitorous friends when he was done with her.

Once they returned to Washington, he would write his parents that the engagement had been broken, explaining that Samantha had called off the marriage. His mother would be upset, but she would get over it.

His expression darkened with an unreadable emotion. *Would he?*

"Never let her go . . . never let her go."

His father's words echoed loudly within his head. He clenched his fists, his face a mask of determination. But there was something else in his eyes—regret.

He felt a stab of guilt in the region of his heart. Samantha's face when he had given her the gift was childlike, full of happiness. Her joy had quickly turned to shock when she discovered the medal. What had she expected? he wondered.

He shook himself. There was no need for guilt. He had played by her rules; he had won fair and square. Why, then, did he feel so damned remorseful? Why did he feel like the loser in this little game they played?

He'd been the victor. But who had really won?

At the same time Daniel was experiencing misgivings about Samantha, she was upstairs in her newly acquired guest room having similar thoughts about him.

Seated in the rocker by the hearth, Samantha took a moment to survey her quarters. Tiny pink rosebuds repeated over the papered walls. Window curtains and a coverlet were in the same printed material. The crown molding and wainscoting were painted a bay leaf green color that matched the leaves on the roses.

Simply furnished, the room contained a canopied bed, dresser, wardrobe, and washstand. Two white cane-backed rockers flanked the fireplace.

The whole effect was very feminine. Alexandra had explained that it once belonged to Daniel's sister

Sarah. Sarah, the slave owner, who, according to Daniel, lived under her husband's thumb.

Sighing, Samantha tried not to judge Sarah too harshly. Sarah was in love with her husband, and Samantha could certainly empathize with her circumstances. Wasn't she in a similar position? In love with a man who was autocratic, despotic, and at times, totally impossible.

Staring at the bed, her stomach knotted in apprehension, her heart ricocheting off the walls of her chest. She had only to close her eyes to envision two naked bodies entwined there. A head of soft black hair bent low over an eager, throbbing breast, long tanned fingers parting supple white thighs. Her thighs—Daniel's fingers. She swallowed, placing the palms of her hands against her flaming cheeks.

"God forgive me for my sinful thoughts," she prayed quietly, rocking back and forth in self-imposed agony. And for the deeds which I shall commit, but which I do not, will not regret.

"You Southern women sure do know how to cook," Ezra remarked, piling another hotcake and sausage onto his plate. "Nicholas is a lucky man."

Alexandra smiled at Samantha's grandfather. The old man had kept them thoroughly entertained throughout breakfast. "Thank you, Ezra. I will convey your compliments to our cook Tildie." Directing her attention to Samantha, who was seated across from her at the dining-room table, she asked, "Did you sleep well, my dear? You look rested this morning."

Samantha smiled, grateful for the rice powder that

hid the dark circles under her eyes. She rarely used cosmetics, but they had been necessary this morning after her miserable night's sleep.

"Yes, Mrs. Fortune, I slept soundly," she lied. "I doubt that a cannon could have awakened me last night." In truth, she had hardly closed her eyes, for when she did, Daniel's visage was there to haunt and torment. But she saw no point in revealing that to Daniel's parents, who obviously wouldn't understand.

"Have you seen Daniel this morning, Samantha?" Nicholas asked, pouring himself a cup of coffee. He held up the pot. "Care for some?"

"No . . . no thank you. And no, I haven't seen Daniel." She quickly lowered her head to study the food on her plate, attempting to hide her pinkened cheeks. Did Daniel's father think they had spent the evening together? Surely the Fortunes were not as liberal in their thinking as their son.

"Did I hear my name mentioned?" Daniel asked, strolling leisurely into the room, dressed in a pair of brown buckskin breeches, matching jacket, and blue wool shirt. Offering his salutations, he placed a perfunctory kiss on his mother's cheek, circled the table, and settled a lingering one on Samantha's. "Morning, love."

Samantha colored as deeply as the strawberry jam she spread generously onto her biscuit, not daring to look up at Daniel, who, she was certain, was smiling wickedly at her.

Her assessment was accurate. Disappointed that he was unable to rouse a reply out of his "betrothed," Daniel turned his attention on his mother. "Have you plans for today, Mother? I thought perhaps I would take Samantha on a tour of Williamsburg."

"That's a wonderful idea," Alexandra concurred. "I need to spend part of the day helping Mrs. Murdock; she suffers so with her rheumatism. It's a perfect solution."

"I couldn't possibly leave Grandfather," Samantha blurted, smiling apologetically at the older woman. She had no intention of spending an entire day alone with Daniel. He may have won the battle, but she had no intention of conceding the war.

"Nonsense, Samantha," Ezra interjected. "Nicholas and I plan to spend the day together rehashing old times. I assure you, I don't need a nanny." He chuckled, winking broadly at her.

Samantha's heart sank. Even her grandfather was conspiring against her, she thought dejectedly. Staring at the united faces around the table, her expression grew resigned. They were all casting her to her fate, but no one knew what was in store for her, save Daniel. She stared at him and was rewarded with a smile so blatantly erotic it curled her toes.

"What about the snow?" she parried, hoping to gain a reprieve. "Surely it's too deep to drive a carriage through." She breathed a sigh of relief at Alexandra's nod; there was no arguing with the weather, even Daniel must realize that.

"I've already thought of that," Daniel replied smoothly. "We'll take the sleigh."

Samantha's face fell.

"You will be careful, Daniel. The sky still looks threatening. I fear we may get more snow."

"Samantha and I will keep each other warm. Never fear."

213

Smiling with pleasure at her son's obvious happiness, Alexandra failed to notice the sudden pallor covering Samantha's cheeks or the way her hands shook when she brought up her napkin to wipe her thinning lips.

An hour later they were on their way, snuggled beneath the warm fur lap robes as the sleigh sliced through the heavy, wet snow that completely obliterated the ground. The jingle of sleigh bells tinkled merrily as the horse plodded surefootedly through the white flakes down the main street of town.

It was cold, so cold that Samantha's cheeks felt numb, but she smiled in spite of her discomfort at the sheer joy of careening at such a rapid pace down the icy street.

She was impressed with her first glimpse of Williamsburg. Quaint dormered houses, storefronts, and taverns comprised the center street. Many of the homes were gaily decorated for the Christmas season with garlands of fresh greenery about the doors and windows. Cranberry and holly-studded front door wreaths lent a festive air and a splash of color to the snow white surroundings.

Turning right onto the Palace Green, they passed a lovely, salmon-colored brick church which Daniel informed her was Bruton Parish where his parents had married. Continuing on, they came upon the ruins of what was once an impressive, three-storied, brick structure known as the Governor's Palace, official residence to seven royal governors and home to Virginia's first governor, Patrick Henry. The Palace,

Daniel explained, had burned in 1781.

"It must have been magnificent," Samantha said, staring sadly at the rubble of charred bricks. "'Tis a pity it burned."

Daniel nodded. "I have only a vague memory of it. But from what my parents tell me, it was truly a show-place."

They picked up their pace, leaving the town proper for the open fields of the countryside, passing by several prosperous plantations, which Daniel explained, grew tobacco as their mainstay crop.

"Is that what your sister's husband grows?" Samantha questioned, wondering if that was what necessitated Harold Chastain's need for slaves.

Daniel nodded, not bothering to disguise the disgust on his face nor the disdain in his voice. "That and a small amount of cotton. Both crops require a great deal of labor, which is why Harold uses slaves. At least that's the excuse he gives."

"Do the Chastains live near here?"

"Not far. A few miles, but we won't visit today. Mother has planned a visit for Christmas Eve."

Samantha was curious to know more about Daniel's slave-holding relatives and asked, "If you are so against slavery, how is it that your sister is not?"

He sneered. "She claims it has something to do with loving her husband. I personally think it has more to do with loving money."

"You do not get along with Sarah, then?"

"As well as any brother and sister do, I guess. But this slavery issue has divided us. There's no denying that."

"I couldn't imagine not getting along with Robbie.

215

We've always been so close. I miss him very much." She felt for the medal around her throat and was instantly reminded of what it signified. Glancing over at Daniel, she could see that he was having similar thoughts. They traveled in silence for several more minutes until the wind picked up and the snow started falling lightly again.

"I think perhaps we should head back," Daniel stated. "I don't like the looks of that sky."

Following his gaze, Samantha noted the dark, angry-looking pewter clouds and nodded in agreement. They had only progressed a short distance when the snow started falling in earnest.

"Bloody hell!" Daniel cursed, wishing he had heeded his mother's warning. At the rate the snow was falling, they'd be lucky to travel another mile before the accumulation made the going impossible. Staring at Samantha, whose cheeks were red and chapped, and who shivered violently beneath her cloak though she did her best to hide it, he felt a surge of protectiveness flow through him. "We'll have to find somewhere to stop. We can't make it back in this storm before dark."

"I think that would be best." She raised her voice, trying to make herself heard above the howling winds that now ripped through the branches surrounding them. Noting the concern on Daniel's face, her own anxiety increased; she tried valiantly to hide it. At the moment, Daniel didn't need a whining woman to worry about. She shut her eyes, praying fervently that they would be delivered from the frozen hell they now found themselves in.

Her prayers were answered a moment later when she heard Daniel's voice through the din. Looking up, she found him pointing at something in the distance. Tears of relief froze on her lashes.

"I think it's a tobacco shed." He wiped at the flurries of snow blurring his vision. "I can just barely make it out. We'll wait out the storm there."

Twenty minutes later, frozen and weary, Daniel and Samantha arrived at the wooden shed. Unhitching the horse from the sleigh, Daniel led him into the building, securing the double doors with a wooden cross beam.

"Bring those wet blankets you're carrying and lay them on those poles over there to dry." He pointed to the far corner of the shed. "It's where they dry the tobacco. Then spread out the fur robes for us to sit on. I'll build a very small fire. We should be thawed out in no time."

"What of the owners? Won't they wonder who is trespassing?"

"I doubt they'll venture out in this storm. Besides, the tobacco has been cured from last season. They won't be needing use of this shed for several months yet. We have it all to ourselves." Smiling at her alarm, he wiped down the horse with bits of hay that he found lying on the floor of the barn then set about to build a fire.

Wrapping her fur-lined pellise tight about her, Samantha shivered at Daniel's words. They were alone. They wouldn't be disturbed nor discovered for hours, possibly days, if the storm didn't subside. Noting the ardent look in Daniel's eyes as he dropped down next to her, she swallowed. They were safe from the storm, protected against the elements. But who would protect her from Daniel? Who would protect her from herself?

Chapter Fifteen

"Are you cold?" Daniel asked, moving closer, wrapping his arm around Samantha's shoulders, pulling her into his warmth. "The closer our bodies are, the warmer we'll be."

If she got any hotter, she would incinerate right on the spot, Samantha thought. Daniel's hard body pressed so intimately next to her own was doing strange and delightful things to her insides. His warm breath, creeping into her ear, played havoc with her nerve endings. "I'm fine," she choked out, barely able to discern that breathless voice as her own.

"We may be here for quite a while."

"I know."

Slowly and seductively, his gaze slid over her, raking every inch of her body. "And do you also know how much I want you? Have wanted you from the first moment I laid eyes on you?"

She nodded, unable to speak, fearful that if she did, she would blurt out how much she wanted him, needed him.

Placing his fingers on the fastenings of her cloak, he undid them one by one, never taking his eyes off her as he spoke. "You knew this time would come." It was a statement rather than a question that he put to her.

"Yes," she replied, barely above a whisper. "I'm ready." But was she really? she asked herself. There could only be one answer: she loved him.

When he reached the last ornamental frog on her pellise, he halted. "You're ready, but are you willing? Although I have won our wager, I will not force myself upon you. It must be your decision to make." He saw the indecision flash across her face and felt uncharacteristically afraid. What if she refused? What if she demanded more than he was willing to give?

Blue eyes met brown, and the silence stretched between them. Samantha studied Daniel's face, looking for the cruelty in his eyes, listening for the mockery in his voice. There was none. Only kindness, concern, and something else she could not fathom. Caring, perhaps? It was her undoing. Wrapping her arms about his neck, she pressed her lips tentatively to his, answering his question in the most basic way she knew how.

Daniel's mouth covered hers hungrily. While his lips and tongue sipped the honey from her mouth, his hands gently pushed the cloak from her shoulders, his fingers deftly unhooking the bodice of her gown. She had offered herself to him; his heart swelled as did his male organ which thrust painfully against his pants, begging for the release he knew would be found in the warm, wet confines of her woman's body. She was exquisite—a gift from the heavens, and she would soon be his.

Samantha returned his kiss with reckless abandon.

219

The feel of his stubbled chin as it abraded her soft skin only heightened her senses. With a boldness she didn't think she possessed, she slipped his buckskin jacket off and set to work undoing the buttons of his shirt. A burning desire, an aching need to be possessed overshadowed all her fears and reservations.

Exploring the hard planes of his chest, the bulging biceps, the roughened hairs that lay between his pectorals, she welcomed his tongue into her mouth, mating hers wildly with his, thrusting in and out, in and out, until a fire blazed deep within her soul that no amount of snow or sleet could dampen.

A moment later, she felt the cool rush of air on her naked flesh as Daniel removed the last of her garments, leaving her totally naked to his view. She knelt proudly before him like a pagan goddess, her skin rosy from the fire, her nipples taut and dusky with desire.

"You are so lovely," he said in a choked whisper, trailing his finger from her lips to her breasts, flicking the nipples before his finger traced lower over her abdomen. They were on their knees, and he was looking at her, worshipping her with his eyes.

She blushed as his gaze fixed on the brown curly hair between her thighs; his eyes glowed like two hot coals, searing her skin. His hands followed the path of his eyes, roaming over her breasts, her stomach, pressing tenderly against the throbbing mound of her womanhood.

"You tremble with your need of me. Feel what you do to my body, as well." He placed her hand upon his hardened shaft, rotating it over and over in a circular motion. "Soon it will be inside you, stimulating you, filling you with pleasure."

His words, his hands, turned her into a frenzied mass of quivering flesh. She couldn't think, only feel, only need. When he pressed her down upon the fur robe, torrid currents of yearning flowed through her. The feel of the fur against her naked skin was wildly erotic; her thighs flooded with moist desire. "Take me, Daniel," she pleaded. "Please!"

He smiled, brushing his lips over hers as he followed her down on the robe. "You are not ready yet, love. We have a long way to go."

Stripping quickly out of his clothes, Daniel pressed his naked flesh to Samantha's, guiding his steel shaft to the entrance of her womb. Rotating his hips, he teased and tormented with the tumescent tip until she spread her legs in invitation. "That's better," he whispered, replacing his finger where his shaft so recently lay. "I need to ready you. You will enjoy our coupling more that way."

He flicked the bud of her desire, feeling it grow pebble hard beneath his fingers as her nipples did beneath his lips. He tantalized the swollen peaks, sucking feverishly while his fingers played her body like a finely tuned instrument.

Samantha arched against him, pushing against his hands, begging to be released from the torture he inflicted. When he finally lowered his body over hers, she felt relief and then a brief flash of pain as his hard shaft impaled her soft woman's core.

Daniel paused, unable to believe what his body was telling him. Bloody hell! Samantha was a virgin. Gently, ever so gently, he eased himself into her, allowing her body to accommodate his maleness. He saw her

221

bite her lower lip and felt his heart constrict, brushing at the tears now flowing down her cheeks.

"I'm sorry, love; I didn't know. It won't hurt much longer."

Soon the pain was gone, replaced by a wondrous, expansive feeling that grew, increasing in intensity. Samantha matched Daniel's rhythm stroke for stroke, riding the waves of desire higher and higher.

Passion swirled about, threatening to devour them like an undertow. Just when she thought she would drown in it, a tidal wave of ecstasy washed over her, flooding her with uncontrollable joy.

Too stunned to speak, she closed her eyes, savoring the waves of contentment that still coursed through her, allowing her breathing to slowly return to normal. After a moment, she opened her eyes to find Daniel's gaze upon her; his smile was one of complete satisfaction. He looked totally relaxed, replete.

"You're full of surprises, love," he said, brushing her lips once again. "Have you more with which to impress me?"

She colored slightly. "I tried to tell you."

His smile was rueful. "So you did. Did I hurt you?" Tenderly, he brushed back the damp curls framing her face. She was incredibly beautiful; his heart ached at the sight of her radiant smile.

"Only at first, then it was wonderful."

"It won't hurt next time."

Her eyes widened. "Next time? You mean to do this more than once? I don't think my body can take it."

He could see by her expression that she was deadly serious. He kissed her, hard. "Love, I intend to do this again and again. Loving is for what you are made." He had foolishly thought that once he had sampled Samantha's charms, he would get his fill and be done with her. He could see now that that would never happen. His hunger for her would never be satiated, no matter how many times he made love to her. She was his; he had branded her, left his mark upon her body. He was her first; he would be her last.

Noting the myriad of emotions flitting across Daniel's face, a tiny spark of hope ignited in Samantha's breast. Perhaps in time he would come to care for her. But would he ever love her? She wanted to ask him, but she knew she would not.

She would savor the time they had together. She had promised herself there would be no self-recriminations. She had made her bed; now, with Daniel, she would gladly lie in it.

The morning sun shone brightly, dancing its warmth upon the naked bodies of the two lovers so rapturously entwined on their makeshift bed.

The whinny of the horse and the impatient stamping of its hooves crept into Samantha's subconscious. Slowly, she cocked one eye open to find her head resting, not on the soft feather pillow that she had expected, but on the hard, flat surface of Daniel's stomach.

His male member, limp from exhaustion after a night of lovemaking, lay mere inches from her face. She smiled, wondering how something that innocuous could provide so much pleasure. For pleasure was something she had experienced in great quantities.

"'Twould be best to wipe that sensual smile off your

face, love, or I fear we will remain in this shed for an indeterminate length of time."

Turning her head, Samantha found Daniel's wicked grin upon her. Noting that the once-flaccid member was now rock hard and several inches bigger, she lifted her head, smiling provocatively while she trailed her finger within dangerous proximity to where it lay. She heard Daniel's sharp intake of breath and felt the power only a woman who has pleased her man can feel.

"Perhaps that is my intention. Perhaps I shall use you to gain my pleasure and then, when you are too worn out, cast you aside." She had been teasing, but by the angry glint in Daniel's eyes and the sudden tautness about his mouth, she could tell he was not amused. Perhaps he did care. The thought gave her courage.

"That will never happen. You will never be rid of me."

Her heart pounded erratically; she fought to keep her face impassive, lest he see how his words affected her. "Perhaps. But then, ours is an arrangement of mutual pleasure, is it not? I can as easily tire of you as you can tire of me. Mistresses are, after all, only temporary commodities. We have no bonds to bind us permanently."

He pulled her beneath him then, grinding his lips down upon hers before he spoke. "You are mine. I have placed my brand upon you. What is mine I keep."

"'Tis I who have placed my brand upon you, Daniel," she replied, touching his lips with her tongue, delighting in the way his eyes darkened to blue sapphires. "But I will not be any man's possession. You may take my body, but my heart remains my own."

"We shall see," he retorted, not realizing the

significance of his words, nor detecting the triumphant smile of the woman beneath him as she buried her face in the soft mat of hair on his chest.

Clutching the letter from Willy tightly to her breast, Samantha chewed her lower lip while staring out the window of the guest bedroom at the frozen vista before her.

Willy had written to say that Adam had been a frequent visitor at the Lawrence townhouse, and that Dulcie was concerned that Caesar's presence would be questioned.

"Damn Adam!" Samantha cursed, stuffing the letter into the pocket of her red wool gown. He was always meddling into things that didn't concern him. She would go downstairs and show Willy's letter to Daniel immediately. It was time they returned home. It was time to get things back to normal.

Normal. She sighed. Would anything ever be normal again? she wondered, realizing that though she would never be the same, life had gone on as if nothing had happened, as if the hours of intimacy she had spent in Daniel's arms had all been a dream.

She smiled thoughtfully. It had been. A wonderful, erotic dream.

They had arrived home to a worried but relieved family, who had gone out of their way not to question their suspicious absence, taking Daniel's explanation of the storm at face value. Her skin had been so red, so chapped by the wind, that for days her own guilty blushes had been well-concealed.

Since their return a week ago, Daniel had treated her

225

with unfailing politeness, his manner so correct, so proper, she wanted to scream—to demand that he make love to her again. Knowing the pleasure that could be found within his arms only added to her misery and longing.

Pressing her face against the cool pane of glass, she heaved a discontented sigh. There were more important things to think about than her newly found sexuality. Caesar and Dulcie needed Daniel much more than she did at the moment.

"I think it's time we had a little talk, don't you, Daniel?"

Daniel faced his mother across the sunlit room of the study, wishing he could face a firing squad rather than the determined woman seated before him. He'd been avoiding this discussion for days, since the night he had brought Samantha back from their overnight escapade. There had been few questions at first, but he knew his mother would not be content to let things lie. He had only received a brief reprieve, now he could see it was time to face the inquisition. Lighting a cheroot, he pasted on a smile of innocence.

"Talk? Did you have something you wished to discuss? It's not Father, is it?"

Alexandra's chest heaved in exasperation. "Don't be purposely obtuse, Daniel. I think you know that I am speaking of Samantha. I might be your mother, but I am still a woman. And I'm not so old as to have lost my sight, though I admit to having turned a blind eye to your escapades a time or two. I won't this time. Samantha is too fine a girl. Not to mention the granddaughter of one of your father's Army friends."

Daniel felt the heat creep up his neck. His mother's words hit closer to the truth than he cared to admit. "What is it that you're implying, Mother? You act as if I've taken advantage of Samantha. I assure you that that is not the case." She was willing. He didn't take advantage of her, he rationalized, only pressed his advantage.

"I am not going to pry into your and Samantha's personal life. After all, you are engaged to be married, which gives you certain license to behave somewhat differently than other couples." She noted the chagrined look on his face, the way he purposely stared down at the toes of his shoes to avoid facing her, and she knew. His behavior only reinforced her suspicions that he and Samantha had been intimate. She took a deep breath and continued, "But I won't sit back and watch you hurt that girl, Daniel. This engagement of yours was very sudden. I still don't understand how it all came about."

The blue eyes, so like his own, impaled him, pleaded with him for the truth. The truth. What was the truth? That he had entered into a bargain with a woman for purely selfish reasons? That now the bargain they had made seemed totally erroneous to what their present relationship entailed. That he was beginning to care for Samantha? That making love to her was an overpowering experience he had never felt with anyone else before?

"I'm waiting, Daniel." Alexandra said, tapping her foot impatiently.

"It's hard to explain the workings of the heart, Mother."

"Are you saying that you love Samantha?"

Samantha stood, frozen in the doorway, not willing to intrude on what was obviously a private conversation, not able to pull herself away until she heard Daniel's answer.

Daniel pushed himself away from the fireplace and turned to find Samantha hovering in the doorway. His face reddened. It was obvious from the expectant look on her face that she had heard his mother's last question. Bloody Hell! He threw his cheroot into the flames, taking a deep breath. Holding out his hand, he motioned for her to enter.

"Come in, love, we were just talking about you."

Samantha blushed. "I'm sorry. I didn't mean to eavesdrop. I came to discuss something of importance with you, Daniel."

Alexandra smiled, rising to her feet. "Since it was you who we were discussing, I see no reason why you shouldn't listen to Daniel's answer." Crossing her arms, she fixed her gaze upon her son.

Stepping over to Samantha, Daniel draped his arm about her waist in a very possessive fashion, placing a chaste peck on her cheek. "Mother was just questioning our engagement, love. I've been trying to explain that you and I have a very unique relationship."

"Unique?" Alexandra interrupted, her voice incredulous. "What an odd word to use with the woman that you're about to marry."

Feeling Daniel stiffen, Samantha wrapped her arm about his waist. "What Daniel means, Mrs. Fortune, is that our relationship has been quite extraordinary when compared to most others. With the war and all that is going on around us, we decided that we wouldn't submit to the traditional courting customs. We were just too taken with each other."

"Love at first sight?" Alexandra supplied, not entirely convinced.

Samantha giggled. "'Twas more like hate at first sight." She looked up at Daniel who was smiling down at her with a great measure of affection. A lump caught in her throat.

Alexandra's look was assessing. Samantha was trying to cover for Daniel. The reason was obvious: she was in love with him. But Daniel? What did he feel for Samantha? Was he capable of loving another woman after Joanna's cruel treatment of him? He was so secretive about his feelings, so reticent to discuss anything of a personal nature.

Even after Joanna had broken their engagement and his heart, he had acted as if nothing had happened. But she had seen the change in him. The once-trusting, ingenuous boy had turned into a cynical, uncaring man. She hated Joanna Stapleton for that.

Heaving a sigh, Alexandra realized there would be no answers from those two. She just hoped they knew what they were doing; she certainly didn't.

"It seems you two have your life quite under control. Not wanting to play the meddlesome mother-in-law, I believe I will take my leave." She kissed both of them on the cheek and departed the room in a flurry of blue satin and lace.

Alexandra had no sooner closed the door behind her, when Daniel sighed in relief. "That woman is more astute than any agent the President has working for him."

"She's just concerned about you, Daniel. It's a mother's prerogative."

Pulling Samantha against his chest, Daniel kissed the top of her head. "She's more concerned about you."

Samantha looked up. "Should she be?"

Instead of answering, Daniel kissed her soundly on the lips until he felt her go limp in his arms. Raising his mouth from hers, he gazed into her eyes. "You said you needed to talk to me."

Both excited and aggravated, she lowered her thick, black lashes, reached into the pocket of her gown, and handed Daniel the letter. "I think we need to get back. I don't like the sound of this."

He frowned, staring thoughtfully at Willy's missive. "You may be right. My sister's annual Christmas Eve ball is only two days away. We will stay for the party and depart the day after Christmas. Is that agreeable?"

"You're actually asking for my opinion? I'm flattered."

"You've been a good friend to Caesar. For that I will be eternally grateful."

"An eternity is an awfully long time."

He kissed the tip of her nose. "Aye. And it seems that long since I've held you in my arms."

Her heart swelled. Oh, Daniel, if only you loved me as I love you, Samantha said silently, but aloud she replied, "I think it's time we go into dinner. You may be able to satisfy your hunger in the dining room."

Giving her one last breathless kiss on the lips, he replied in a voice filled with emotion, "It's doubtful, love. It's very doubtful."

Chapter Sixteen

Samantha felt overwhelmed with relief when the Fortunes' carriage rolled into the circular drive of Meadowlark, Harold and Sarah Chastain's tobacco plantation.

The ride, though not overly long, had been dreadfully uncomfortable. Finding herself sandwiched between Daniel and Nicholas Fortune's broad shoulders, she felt like a slab of meat between two slices of bread. Alexandra and her grandfather had occupied the seat across, the extra room purposely left to accommodate Ezra's gout-ridden legs and feet.

As the carriage drew near to the house, Samantha craned her neck to see out the window. The mansion was awe-inspiring to say the least. The three-story, columned brick house sat majestically atop a slight rise. A dozen windows, each decorated with a festive wreath of pine and holly, faced the drive. The long white columns sported yards and yards of cedar garlands wrapped about from top to bottom in a spiral fashion.

Disembarking, the group entered the huge slate-covered porch, waiting for their knock to be answered. Upon the front door, circling a shiny brass knocker, hung a massive boxwood wreath decorated with apples, pomegranates, and pine cones.

Daniel's sister certainly had gone to a lot of trouble to decorate her house for the Christmas Eve ball, Samantha thought, impressed despite herself until she realized that the work was probably done by slave labor.

"What's the matter?" Daniel asked, noting Samantha's frown. "Don't you like the decorations? I thought them rather pretty myself."

"They're lovely. I was just wondering who was responsible for all the hours of labor that went into their making."

Patting her hand, Daniel smiled in understanding. "Never fear. Sarah fashioned all the decorations herself. She takes great pride in her home."

"I never meant to imply . . ."

Before Samantha could finish, the door was thrown open, and they were greeted by a diminutive, dark-haired woman with eyes as blue as Daniel's who bore a striking resemblance to Alexandra.

"Mother, Father, how good it is to see you again," Sarah gushed, throwing her arms about her parents. Her voice had a distinctive Southern drawl, much more pronounced than Daniel's, which made Samantha suspect that it was purposely affected.

After the introductions were made and they were ushered into the house, Samantha could only stare open-mouthed at the opulence surrounding her. Never in her life had she seen anything so elegant, save for the President's House.

Everywhere she looked the evidence of the Chastains' wealth was apparent, from the sparkling crystal chandeliers that hung overhead, to the exquisite French mural wallpaper that lined the walls of the formal drawing room.

The furniture was in the Hepplewhite style, consisting of ornately carved cherry and walnut pieces. There were two matching gold velvet loveseats, a scattering of red and gold brocade upholstered occasional chairs, and a massive secretary-bookcase that covered a good portion of one wall. The windows were covered in the same rich velvet as the loveseats, and beneath her feet, thick, colorful Turkish carpets of red and gold covered gleaming floors of dark polished pine.

"Close your mouth, love, you're beginning to create a draft," Daniel teased, pushing gently on her chin, his eyes twinkling in amusement.

Samantha blushed, glancing quickly about to make certain no one had observed her rudeness. Fortunately, Sarah and her mother were engaged in conversation in the opposite corner of the room, while Nicholas and Ezra were occupied at the inlaid ivory chess table. It hadn't taken her grandfather long to find a willing accomplice for his chess fetish.

A moment later, a tall blond man entered the room. He was dressed very soberly in a black suit, white ruffled shirt, and black satin waistcoat. He wore an open, friendly smile when he greeted the others, then turned and made his way to where Daniel and Samantha were seated. Bowing before them, he placed a courtly kiss upon Samantha's hand.

"You must be Daniel's betrothed. Welcome to Meadowlark, Miss Wilder. I am Harold Chastain," he drawled.

Samantha's eyes widened imperceptibly. She didn't know what she was expecting a slave owner to look like, but it wasn't this polite, urbane gentleman.

"Thank you for opening your home to my grandfather and me, Mr. Chastain."

"It's Harold, my dear, and you're quite welcome." Transferring his attention to Daniel, who was seated next to her, Harold's lips thinned ever so slightly. "Daniel, good to see you again. I suppose you've heard the news about Caesar?"

Samantha's breath caught in her throat. Not daring to look over at Daniel, she studied the plaid pattern of the green and red taffeta skirt that she wore.

"I heard." Daniel's voice was filled with contempt. "If you had sold the man to me in the first place, this never would have happened."

"And I suppose you haven't a clue as to his whereabouts?"

"Not a one," Daniel replied, shaking his head.

"I thought as much. Even you wouldn't be so foolish as to harbor a runaway. The penalty is too severe."

Samantha's chest burned; she fought the urge to wipe her sweating hands on her gown.

"I can't say I'm sorry that Caesar is gone. He was my friend."

Harold's smile never quite reached his eyes. "You always did possess strange ideals."

Daniel stiffened but said nothing. A moment later, Harold excused himself and left to join his wife and mother-in-law.

Releasing the breath she was holding, Samantha felt suddenly deflated. "He certainly wasn't what I was expecting," she whispered, staring at Harold's retreating back.

"Harold has all the sophistication of a snake and the heart to match."

Noting the fierce look on Daniel's face, the way his muscle flicked angrily at his jaw, Samantha sought to change the subject. "Your sister has a lovely home. I don't believe I've ever seen anything quite so . . ."

"Ostentatious," Daniel supplied disparagingly, though there was a hint of humor in his voice.

Samantha shook her head, casting a reproving look at him. "Shame on you. It would hurt your sister's feelings to know you felt like that."

"She knows how I feel. Everything in this house, the house itself, the lands, were all acquired as the result of slave labor. It's beautiful on the surface, but beneath, it's hideous and ugly."

Later that afternoon, having retired to her quarters, Samantha was to think about Daniel's comments more than once during the time she had to herself. Ensconced in an equally impressive guest room, she had only to look about to discover the truth of his words.

The bedroom was twice the size of hers at home; the gilt-edged, inlaid walnut furnishings were richer than anything she would ever possess. Still, she did not covet any of it. Daniel was right. It was tainted with the suffering of others.

A soft knock on the door intruded on her unpleasant observations. Crossing to the door, she opened it, surprised to find Sarah Chastain waiting patiently on the other side; a soft smile curved her bow-shaped lips.

"I hope I'm not intruding, but I didn't feel we had an adequate amount of time to get to know one another earlier."

Warming to Sarah's friendly smile, Samantha ushered her into the room. "Your home is quite lovely,

Sarah. Thank you for providing such a comfortable haven."

Her laughter tinkled merrily. "I am sure Daniel has given you an earful about my ill-gotten gains. Please don't judge me too harshly. I'm not as heartless as my brother makes me out to be."

Guilt warmed Samantha's cheeks. "I admit that I'm not very comfortable with the fact that you own slaves, Sarah. Like Daniel, I prefer to see a man paid a wage for his labors."

Taking a seat on the window seat, Sarah smoothed the folds of her rose brocade gown. "I've tried to convince Harold to get rid of the slave system, to pay them a wage, but he won't hear of it. I was raised to abhor the system of slavery; I'm not comfortable with this situation myself. But in my husband's defense, I will say that Harold does treat our people humanely. I have never seen him use a whip or mistreat any of our slaves."

"Sometimes hurts go deeper than corporal punishment, Sarah. Sometimes the wounds never heal." She thought of Dulcie and Caesar and sighed inwardly.

Sarah nodded. "That is precisely the reason that I've come here to talk with you."

Samantha raised her eyebrows in surprise, her voice reflecting her bewilderment. "Is it?"

"Mother has informed me of your engagement to Daniel. I'm very happy that Daniel has finally found someone with whom to spend the rest of his life. There were times when I despaired of that ever happening."

A deep sense of shame overwhelmed Samantha. "Thank you," she replied, hating herself for allowing the deception to continue, but too cowardly to correct it.

"I wasn't sure if you were aware that Daniel had been hurt very deeply by a woman—a woman with whom he fancied himself in love."

Samantha's eyes widened. "No. I had no idea," she replied, suddenly nauseated at the thought that Daniel had loved another woman.

"I thought not. My brother has never been one to confide in anyone. He keeps his feelings close to his chest. At times, he can be extremely frustrating."

Samantha had to smile at that. Sarah knew Daniel better than she thought.

"Because you and Daniel intend to marry, I think you have a right to know about his past relationship. Perhaps it will make it easier to understand why he acts the way he does."

"I'm not sure Daniel wants me to know about his past." In fact, she was almost positive that he didn't.

"You're probably right. But if you and that stubborn brother of mine are going to make a go of this marriage, then I want you to have every advantage. Do you understand?"

Samantha nodded mutely, feeling guilty about this entire awkward situation she now found herself in. If Daniel knew what Sarah was about to reveal, it would only add more animosity to his already strained relationship with his sister.

"About ten years ago, Daniel was in love with a woman by the name of Joanna Stapleton. She was the niece of one of the most highly respected lawyers in the area. After a brief courtship, they became engaged. Daniel was head over heels in love with her."

Samantha took a deep agonizing breath but said nothing.

"You'd never know it to see the way he is now, but

Daniel was once a different man. He didn't have a cynical bone in his body. He went into the relationship with his heart on his sleeve; Joanna took it and squashed it beneath her dainty slippers." A bitter smile twisted Sarah's lips.

"Joanna broke their engagement two weeks before the wedding. She met a man from Charleston, a lawyer with political aspirations much older than she but wealthy as Croesus. She married him the day she was to marry Daniel."

Samantha's heart ached for the boy who once was, for the man who was now. "That explains a lot of things." His distrust of her for one.

"I thought it might," Sarah said, rising to her feet. Giving Samantha a warm hug, she added, "Loving Daniel may not be the easiest task you have set for yourself, but it will be well worth it in the end."

Samantha was to relive those words over and over again in the months that lay ahead.

"It sure is good to have you home again, Miss Sam," Dulcie said, hanging the last of the garments from Samantha's trunk into the wardrobe. "It's been real quiet around here. Why, I've even missed that blustering old man fussin' at me."

Samantha smiled. "I expect Grandfather missed you and Caesar, too, though he'd be loath to admit it," she replied, pulling the brush through her long brown tresses. "I know I did."

"Did you and Mr. Daniel have a nice time?" The brush clattered noisily to the floor, causing Dulcie to turn. "What's the matter, honey? You look as red as a beet. You didn't catch a fever down there, did you?"

238

Samantha smiled weakly, shaking her head. She'd caught a fever all right—a fever in her blood. But she wasn't about to admit that to the inquisitive house-keeper. Instead, pulling her wrapper tightly about her, she answered, "Nothing is the matter . . . nothing at all."

Rising to her feet, she busied herself with the cosmetics on the dressing table, cursing herself inwardly at her childish behavior. After all, she decided, staring at her reflection in the mirror, she didn't look any different. She didn't have the mark of a fallen woman painted on her forehead. 'Twas only her own guilty conscience that made her feel as if everyone knew that she and Daniel had been intimate.

"Miss Sam," Dulcie's voice suddenly grew quiet as she came to stand beside her mistress, "I've got some-thing to tell you. Something mighty important."

Turning to stare at the maid, Samantha noted the anxious expression on her face and grew alarmed. "It's Adam, isn't it? He's been snooping around here again." Damn! She would make a point to speak with him today.

"No, Miss Sam," Dulcie replied, shaking her head. "It ain't Mr. Adam this time, though he did give us a scare a time or two while you was gone."

Puzzled, Samantha frowned. "What then?"

There was a long pause, then Dulcie blurted, "I'm pregnant!"

Samantha's eyes widened, her mouth dropping open in disbelief. Of all the things she had expected Dulcie to say, that wasn't one of them. "How did it happen?"

The young woman giggled, covering her mouth. "I expect the same way it usually does."

Samantha's cheeks suffused with color. Pregnant.

239

Dulcie was pregnant. Absently, she placed her hands over her own abdomen. Oh, God! The possibility of pregnancy had never crossed her mind. What if her illicit union with Daniel resulted in the same? In a daze, she crossed to the bed, crumbling on top of it.

"Child, what's wrong?" Dulcie cried, rushing to the bed, alarmed by the pallor on Samantha's face. She chafed Samantha's hands, which were cold beneath her touch. "You ain't going to faint, is you? I wouldn't have told you if I'd have known it would upset you so."

"It's not that, Dulcie. It's . . ." She couldn't bring herself to tell the maid what she had done.

Sitting down on the bed, Dulcie wrapped comforting arms about Samantha's shoulders. "Child, there ain't much in this life that could shock me. I might not be advanced in years, but I've seen a whole lot. If there's something you be needin' to get off your chest, I'm willing to listen."

Samantha looked up, tears blurring her vision. "I've been intimate with Daniel."

Dulcie smiled, squeezing her gently. "Is that all? I thought for sure you had gone and done something terrible."

"You don't understand, Dulcie. Daniel and I aren't really engaged. We just led everyone to believe that because . . . oh, I don't know . . . because we were stupid, I guess. He's not going to marry me. If I get pregnant, I'll be disgraced—ruined—a fallen woman."

Dulcie shook her head. "Honey, why you worrying about something that might never happen? Just because you and Mr. Daniel been making love don't mean that a baby's going to come of it."

"We only did it once." She blushed, amending, "Twice."

"Do you love that man?"

"Yes," Samantha replied, barely above a whisper.

"Doing what you did is as natural as breathing. You in love, child. It's why Caesar and I came together. I never gave no thought to getting pregnant. I only knew that I loved that man. That I had to have him. No matter what. This here baby's a product of our love." She patted her abdomen tenderly.

"It's different for me."

"Why, 'cause you white?"

Samantha reddened at Dulcie's perceptiveness. "No!" she protested. "Yes," she admitted. "I was raised to believe that submitting to a man before marriage was wrong. That I'd be cast down to hell for my sins. Society doesn't approve of babies without wedlock."

"Miss Sam, you got a powerful lot of growing up to do. I don't mean to put you down none, but if you are going to act like a woman on the outside, you gots to be one on the inside, too. You can't have it both ways. You ain't a child anymore. You can't be told what's right and wrong. You gots to decide for yourself. I think you've already made that decision; now you got to live with it."

Dulcie was right, of course. She had already made the decision. 'Twas why she had submitted to Daniel in the first place. But she never expected her decision to have such far-reaching ramifications, never expected it could lead to a child.

Rising to her feet, she wiped the tears from her face. It was time to grow up. She was a woman now. She had experienced the pain and pleasure of lying with a man, of loving him. She would experience more pain and more pleasure in the future. But would she live to regret both?

Chapter Seventeen

Samantha eyed herself critically in the looking glass. Daniel would be here at any moment to escort her to the Madison's annual New Year's Day gala, and she wanted to look her prettiest.

The amber satin gown shot with threads of gold brought out the peaches in her complexion. At least, that's what Daniel had told her when he'd given it to her on Christmas morning. She had been reluctant to accept his gift, not wanting to feel like a kept woman, but he had looked so eager, like a small boy, when he handed her the package, she hadn't been able to refuse.

Her hair, swept up in a Grecian knot, was covered with a dainty dress cap of ecru lace. She wore no jewels, only the liberty medal. Frowning at her reflection, she pulled up on the bodice of her gown, trying to cover the generous amount of flesh that spilled over the top, wondering if perhaps it was indecent to expose so much of herself on such an important occasion.

The Madisons generously opened their home to the general public twice a year—New Year's Day and the

Fourth of July. Daniel had hinted in the note he had sent that Dolley would be serving ice cream that evening. Samantha licked her lips, her eyes brightening in anticipation. She had never tasted that particular delicacy before attending her first Drawing Room, and now she had an absolute craving for it.

Ice cream wasn't the only craving she had, she thought lasciviously, her tongue rolling over her lips provocatively as Daniel's image flashed before her eyes. Staring at her reflection, she was somewhat stunned by the seductive woman staring back at her. Would Daniel be stunned too? she wondered, smiling, astonished that a few passionate hours in his arms had produced such a drastic change in her; she had gone from reserved maiden to wanton hussy within the span of a few kisses.

Daniel. She hadn't seen him in days, not since their return from Williamsburg, and she missed him, aching for him with every fiber of her being. Wrapping her arms tightly about herself to quell the familiar tightening in her loins, she was grateful for the knocker that sounded at the door.

Daniel's expression when he greeted her was worth all the time and effort she had spent in preparation for this evening's fete. His eyes, blazing with desire, riveted on the white flesh of her bosom, causing her nipples to protrude painfully while her cheeks warmed to an apricot blush.

Too stunned to speak, Daniel could only stare, mesmerized by the vision before him, muted by Samantha's beauty, her blatant sexuality. Her smile, full of warmth and promise, caused queer palpitations to form in his chest.

"Good evening, Daniel. You look very handsome this evening." His black formal evening clothes were accented by a blue satin waistcoat, the perfect foil for his sapphire eyes.

Without responding, Daniel stepped into the hall, kicking the door shut behind him. Pulling Samantha into his arms, he covered her mouth in a blood-boiling kiss. When her arms came around his neck to embrace him, he thrust his tongue between her teeth, unable to stop the madness that suddenly overtook him. They kissed for several minutes, mindless of everything but their own need for each other, until the sound of laughter intruded on their bliss. Guiltily they broke apart.

Turning to find her grandfather wheeling himself toward her, Samantha felt the blood rush to her face.

"When you two are ready to come up for air, I'd like to have a word with you in the parlor," Ezra stated quite matter-of-factly, as if finding his granddaughter in the arms of a man was an everyday occurrence. As quietly as he had entered, Ezra wheeled himself out of the room.

Taking deep breaths to quiet his breathing, Daniel shook himself, finally choking out, "That old man is going to be the death of me yet."

Staring meaningfully at the bulge between Daniel's legs, Samantha patted his cheek. "I've never heard of anyone dying of your particular affliction before, Daniel," she teased, her eyes twinkling in amusement.

Tweaking her nose, he returned her smile. "You're a saucy wench. Just wait until I get you alone. You'll think *you* had died and gone to heaven."

Placing her hand on his still-bulging member, she rubbed him provocatively, smiling at the shocked expression on his face. "You're the one who should take care, my randy stallion, for I've been desirous of taking a little ride."

First surprised by Samantha's audacity, then amused by her flirtatiousness, Daniel chuckled, slapping her backside playfully, eliciting a yelp. "You'll have your time in the saddle, wench, never fear. And it will be the wildest, most stimulating ride of your life. That, I promise." He winked broadly at her.

Passion darkened the soft brown eyes; her voice was husky when she spoke. "Are all you Southern gentlemen such good horsemen?"

"Only those who are well mounted, love, for it's the shape of the saddle that makes all the difference in the ride." He eyed her derrière with unconcealed lust, causing her to blush hotly.

Seeing that she wasn't about to best Daniel at his own game, Samantha thread her arm through his. "Shall we go and see what my grandfather wants?"

"Indeed. The sooner we're through here, the sooner we can begin your next riding lesson."

"What took you so long? I was beginning to think you both had suffocated."

"Grandfather!" Samantha exclaimed, covering her flaming cheeks with her hands as she entered the room. "You're incorrigible."

Ezra chortled. "I am, aren't I?"

Daniel couldn't repress his smile. He only hoped he

had as much spirit as Ezra when he was his age. "Is there a problem, sir? You said you wished to speak to us."

"Pour us a brandy, Daniel. What I have to say won't take long. I know you're anxious to be on your way to the big doings at the President's House." He didn't try to disguise the contempt in his voice when he mentioned the President.

Daniel ignored the aspersion, handing Ezra his drink. The old man was too set in his ways and opinions to change completely. Like the leopard, he didn't think Ezra would change his spots. He took a seat next to Samantha on the settee, waiting patiently for Ezra to speak.

"I'm not getting any younger or any healthier, for that matter," Ezra stated. " 'Tis one reason that I'm happy about your impending marriage. I want to see my granddaughter settled before I die."

"Grandfather." Samantha's voice rose in protest; she was about to interrupt when Daniel grabbed onto her hand.

"I understand," Daniel interrupted, imploring Ezra to continue.

"I've heard only today that the British have been victorious. Is that true, Daniel?"

"Yes. As much as I hate to admit it, your information is correct. Two days ago fourteen hundred British soldiers burned Buffalo, New York, and the nearby Black Rock navy yard." Ignoring Samantha's gasp, he continued, "But at the same time, the British schooner, *Bramble,* has arrived in Annapolis carrying peace dispatches."

Samantha's face brightened. "But that's wonderful!

This war may soon come to an end."

Daniel and Ezra stared knowingly at each other before Ezra spoke. "We all pray for that end, my dear. But we mustn't raise false hopes. This is merely an overture—nothing definite may come of it."

"But if they're negotiating . . ."

"Your grandfather's right, Samantha. Don't raise your hopes. This war is not over yet."

"Samantha has told me of your efforts to get my grandson back," Ezra said. "I understand that he's in England."

Daniel nodded. "Last I heard, he's in prison there. Well-cared for but heavily guarded."

"I won't ask how you know; I only want to say that I'm grateful for all that you've done for my family."

Daniel felt the heat rise up his neck; the cravat about his neck suddenly tightened. "I've done no more than any man would have in similar circumstances." He heard Samantha's sharp, indrawn breath.

"I disagree, but that's neither here nor there. The reason I've called this meeting is to discuss the plans for your wedding."

Samantha paled, leaning heavily against the back of the settee. Noting her discomfort, Daniel handed her his brandy, watching in amazement as she gulped it down.

"As I said earlier, I am an old man. I want to see my granddaughter established, know she's well-cared for. I think you should marry without delay."

Samantha held her breath, while Daniel studied the toes of his shoes with interest. After a few sickening seconds of silence, he spoke. "That is not possible right now. The war leaves too many unforeseen possibilities. My duties are dangerous and must take precedent over my personal life. If I married and was killed, Samantha would be widowed. That wouldn't be fair to her."

Ignoring the protestation, Ezra added, "I plan to settle my entire estate on my grandchildren. You would profit from such an alliance."

"Grandfather!" Samantha objected, rising to her feet on unsteady legs, having consumed the entire glass of brandy in the space of five minutes. "Please don't do this. I won't be sold like some slave at auction to the highest bidder. You can't bribe Daniel to marry me. He's right. The war stands in our way. 'Tis not the time to speak of weddings. We must worry about getting Robbie back, about ending this war. Do not place a greater burden on Daniel's shoulders; he has enough in dealing with the British."

Daniel's eyes lit with admiration; Ezra's darkened in disbelief.

"In my day young people respected their elders and did what they were told."

Placing a placating hand on her grandfather's shoulder, Samantha's voice softened. "You'll still be alive to see me walk down the aisle, to bounce your great grandchildren on your knee. I promise."

"Hmph!" Ezra crossed his arms firmly over his chest, turning to stare out the window.

Daniel listened attentively to Samantha's words, conjuring up the image of her in a white satin gown holding a bouquet of cherry blossoms. He imagined her cradling a plump baby to her breast, and his heart constricted painfully. Absorbed in his ruminations, he didn't hear her call his name.

"Daniel, are you ready to go? We're going to be late."

Looking up at the sweet smile hovering on Samantha's lips, he blinked himself back to reality. "Did you say something?"

She stared strangely at him. "I said, are you ready to go? We're going to be late."

Rising to his feet, he took her hands in his, an odd, unfathomable light shone in his eyes, as if he were seeing her for the very first time. "I'm quite ready, love. I've never been more ready in my entire life."

Casting Daniel a sidelong glance as she proceeded him from the room, Samantha wondered what strange affliction had suddenly come over him.

The lengthening shadows of twilight slashed across the heavens in streaks of purple and pink as the carriage carrying Samantha and Daniel approached the brick-walled grounds of the Madisons' home. Like a beacon, the white-washed, sandstone walls of the President's House gleamed brightly against the darkening sky.

Two giant bronze eagles stood as sentinels on tall gateposts eyeing the carriage as it rolled through the entry toward the drive fronting the mansion. There were no trees to obscure the view, no manicured lawns as befitting such an elegant structure. Instead, workmen's shanties and privies cluttered the grounds, while pools of stagnate water, used to mix the mortar for the on-going construction of the house, oozed over the landscape like a festering boil. It was said that Mrs.

Madison had complained that all she could see when gazing out the window of the mansion were brickyards and rubbish.

Upon their arrival, Samantha and Daniel were ushered into the vestibule where they surrendered their wraps to black liveried servants, who then escorted them into the "elliptic saloon" or oval drawing room, as it was commonly called.

There were already large groups of people gathered. The red-uniformed Marine band played loudly in the far corner, adding to the noise and confusion in the room.

Daniel nodded and waved to those he knew, his face whitening as he pushed his way through the throng, guiding Samantha toward the pair of long French doors at the southern most part of the drawing room. When they reached their destination, he reached into his pocket, extracting a linen handkerchief and mopping his brow, which was now covered in perspiration.

Noting his anxiety, Samantha's voice filled with alarm. "Daniel, what is it? You look ill."

He breathed deeply before answering. "I can't abide these crowds. The Drawing Rooms are one thing, but this massive number of people makes me feel closed in, as if I'm not able to breathe."

"Why didn't you tell me? We needn't have come. I certainly don't know any of these people."

"I attend for only one reason: to show respect for Mr. and Mrs. Madison. Otherwise, you couldn't have dragged me here."

"Do you wish to step outside? It's chilly out, but less crowded."

He shook his head. "We'd probably catch our deaths. No, I'll just stand here by the door. I'll be all right. I've been in closer quarters than this before."

Assuring herself that he was, indeed, all right, she turned her head to scan the crowded, blue-painted room, taking note of their surroundings. The room was quite large, owing to its unusual shape. It's perimeter was pleasantly lined with a considerable number of painted and gilded cane-seat chairs, two sofas, and four window seats, all designed in the classical revival style, all covered in crimson velvet.

"What do you think of the room?" Daniel asked. "I understand Mrs. Madison had Benjamin Latrobe design the furnishings for her."

"It's different, though I think I prefer the cozy warmth of the yellow drawing room. It's more suited to Mrs. Madison's sunny personality."

"How astute you are, love, for it's her favorite room, as well."

Engrossed in their conversation, neither Samantha nor Daniel felt the malevolence directed at them from across the room where Adam Bainbridge stood, hands folded across his chest, his eyes blazing in anger, watching them.

So that's the way of it, Adam observed. Samantha and Fortune had become more than mere acquaintances. He'd known her too long not to recognize the glow of admiration that poured forth from her eyes as she gazed up into Fortune's face, as if he were the only one in the room.

He felt his face grow hot. Damn her unfaithful hide, he cursed silently, clenching his fists. She was his; he'd be damned before he'd let another man possess her.

She was to be his wife. The perfect partner for the governor of Massachusetts. There could be no other; he had set his mind to that eventuality.

If only Henry hadn't missed the night he had tried to kill Fortune. Adam sneered. That's what he got for sending an inept amateur out to do a professional's job.

Perhaps killing Fortune was not the best idea anyway, he reconsidered. That would only make him a martyr in Samantha's eyes. Perhaps, there was another way to get rid of him. His eyes gleamed feral; his lips thinned in pleasure. He would save the killing for himself, later, when Samantha was his and no longer infatuated with the handsome Virginian.

For now, he would bide his time. Things were starting to go in his favor. The British had been victorious in New York, and it was only a matter of time before they made short work of these so-called patriots. Soon, all would be as he and Pickering had planned. He had only to be patient, only to orchestrate things a little differently. He smiled confidently, crossing the room to join his soon-to-be betrothed.

Daniel's eyes narrowed as he caught sight of Adam marching across the room in his direction. What the hell did that bloody bastard want? he wondered. Noting Samantha's smile as she caught sight of Bainbridge, his jaw tightened, as did the hand that rested possessively around her waist.

"Why, Adam, how nice to see you. How have you been?" Samantha asked, suddenly aware of the thickening tension in the room when she felt Daniel stiffen beside her.

"Never better, my dear," he replied, bending over her hand to place a kiss upon it. He smiled up at Daniel and nodded. "Fortune."

"What brings you here, Bainbridge? I didn't expect to see you at the President's gala," Daniel remarked, his voice as cool as the frigid night air.

Adam smiled smoothly. "I don't see why not. It's open to the public. I am one of the public, am I not?"

"Of course you are, Adam," Samantha supplied, casting a censured look at Daniel. "We're both happy to see you."

"It has been awhile, my dear. Where have you been keeping yourself? I stopped by the townhouse several times during the Christmas holidays, only to be told you were out of town."

"She was with me," Daniel stated, observing with satisfaction how Bainbridge's eyes had hardened into chips of ice.

"It seems grandfather and Daniel's father served in the war together. Daniel invited us down to Williamsburg to spend Christmas," Samantha added hurriedly. She could see by Adam's tight-lipped expression that the news did not set well with him.

"How cozy." Adam bit the inside of his mouth, tasting blood and wishing it were Fortune's.

"It was terribly, terribly cozy. Was it not, love?" Daniel bent his head close to Samantha's ear, nuzzling her.

Samantha blushed at the reproachful glare Adam directed at her; she swallowed nervously. "We had a delightful time. Williamsburg is a lovely town."

Forcing a smile to his lips, Adam replied, "How nice. I wonder, Samantha, if I might have a word with you in private. If your escort doesn't mind, that is." He stared challengingly at Daniel, a smirk twisting his lips.

"If Samantha desires your company, Bainbridge, she does not need to seek my permission." With that, he turned and walked through the French doors into the frosty night air.

Samantha shivered as the cool breeze wafted over her; she chafed her arms, but wasn't entirely certain that it was the weather that chilled her so thoroughly. Both Daniel and Adam acted like possessive keepers. She didn't want to become a pawn in what was obviously a long-standing disagreement.

"You wished to speak to me, Adam?" she asked finally.

Hearing the irritation in Samantha's voice nettled Adam. How dare she act as if he were intruding into her life? Feeling his animosity rise, he swallowed it, assuming a look of deep concern. "I need to talk to you, Samantha. It's very important."

Her mind suddenly congested with fear. "Is it about Robbie?"

He should have known that her precious Robbie would be her first concern. "Actually, it does involve him. I have some vital information to impart. When do you think we can meet?"

"Why can't you tell me now?"

"I prefer to wait until your watchdog is not around."

She stiffened, noting the hatred that blazed briefly in Adam's eyes before he shuttered them closed. "Would tomorrow be soon enough?"

Bowing over her hand, he kissed it, feeling her tense in response. "I'll look forward to it, my dear. Meet me at the Capitol. We'll be able to talk in private there; Senator Pickering is out of town."

Samantha bid him farewell, watching him walk away, unable to repress the feeling of foreboding that whatever it was that Adam wanted to tell her was not going to be good news. Shrugging it off, she went in search of Daniel.

The steady clip-clop of the horses' hooves as they made their way back to Georgetown seemed to echo within Samantha's chest. The dark confines of the carriage closed around her; Daniel's presence excited and alarmed as he sat next to her, his arm resting on the back of the seat, not really touching but close enough to be disturbing.

They were alone, and the tension within her that had been building all day, all evening, intensified. She had wanted nothing more than to leave the crowded gala to be alone with Daniel and was more than relieved when he had suggested that they depart.

Daniel had been quiet, introspective, since entering the carriage, as if he had some portentous problem he needed to sort out. She, on the other hand, had been restless, full of anticipation, frustration, wondering when he was going to take her in his arms and kiss her, ending the torment she had experienced since their last encounter.

The heat rose slowly to her face, then spread to her chest, building, building, until finally she felt flushed, ready to explode. Removing her pellise, she cast the offending garment to the floor.

"Daniel," she whispered, placing her hand brazenly on his thigh. "I . . . I . . ." She couldn't see his expression clearly in the dark, couldn't tell if he was mocking her with his eyes, couldn't reveal that her need of him was making her ill.

The feel of his hand as it moved down the bare flesh of her arm made her start. "What is it, love?" His voice was sweet, soft, pouring over her like rich melted chocolate. Soon his finger traveled up across the tops of her breasts, lightly caressing the warm décolletage. Her nipples hardened in response.

"I want you," she confessed, unable to contain the breathless desire in her voice.

Daniel smiled into the darkness, pleased by her ardent request. "I never deny a lady." Tapping on the roof of the carriage, he waited a moment for the driver to halt, then ordered, "We wish to take a drive through Parrott's Woods."

"Very good, sir," the driver shouted down from his perch atop the carriage.

Daniel drew the curtain back over the window. "We shan't be disturbed now, love," he said before pulling her full against him.

The caress of Daniel's lips on her mouth, along her neck, against her ear, set Samantha's body aflame. She writhed in anxious longing, eagerly accepting the warm, wet tongue that plunged so hungrily into her mouth, relishing the brandy taste, inhaling the spicy, musty scent of his cologne that was so distinctively his.

"God, Samantha, you drive me crazy. It's been so long since I've held you in my arms, made love to you." His lips brushed against her as he spoke, leaving a trail of fire wherever they touched. His mouth devoured, consumed, until she was breathless, weak with a need too long denied.

"I want you, Daniel, now, inside me," she insisted against his mouth, feeling him tense in response.

He pulled back. "You want to make love here? Inside the carriage?"

"Yes," she choked out. "In fact, I demand it."

His smile was tender. "Love, I had no idea you were serious. I thought earlier when we were exchanging sexual innuendos that you were merely teasing. We cannot make love in a carriage. It's too cold; you'll become ill."

Reaching for the fastenings that held her gown together, she undid them, one by one, never taking her eyes off of him as she spoke. "I am deadly serious, Daniel. And I am already ill. You have created this burning hunger within me; now you must drive it from me—banish the pain that torments my every waking moment."

The sight of the lush mounds displayed so enticingly before him was all the encouragement Daniel needed to comply. He reached out, fondling the heavy globes, caressing them reverently, tracing his thumbs in circular motions over the pointed peaks. "You are perfection. Your breasts are like manna from the gods."

"Then take them and be sated," she offered brazenly, arching her back, thrusting them forward.

Daniel's eyes glazed with uncontrollable longing. Like a starving man at a banquet, he lowered his head, laving the swollen nipples with his tongue, pushing Samantha down on the seat, until she lay flat beneath him. Her heartbeat pulsed beneath his ear, echoing the persistent throbbing in his loins. His tongue made a path down her ribs to her stomach, his hands pushing the satin and lace of her garments down around her feet until she was bared to his gaze.

His eyes roamed over every delectable inch of her flesh, feasting on the supple thighs, the gentle curve of her calf, the patch of soft curls at her V. Tenderly, he placed his mouth against the furred mat between her legs, hearing her shocked gasp of pleasure, feeling her tense. "Let me love you," he said, gently urging her knees apart. "There's no shame in what I do. Only pleasure, infinite pleasure."

The feel of Daniel's mouth against her woman's mound set the blood boiling in her veins. She was hot, so very hot. She writhed beneath his lips, her head lolling from side to side, her hips arching, bucking against his mouth; her legs relaxed, opening to invite his tongue inside her. She knew what they did was wrong—a violation of everything she'd been taught. But it felt so wonderful, so right, she didn't care. Only the feel of Daniel's tongue on her flesh, his lips on the very essence of her being mattered at the moment.

Soon, the pressure within her started to rise, and she could feel the hot moistness flooding her thighs. Daniel felt it too, for he raised up, fumbling with the fastenings on his breeches.

"Bloody hell," he swore, trying to undo the stubborn buttons from the buttonholes. Sweat poured off his brow, landing like a shower across Samantha's quivering stomach as he positioned himself at her entrance.

Grabbing her head between his hands, he thrust his tongue into her mouth at the same time he thrust his hardened member into her core. The musky taste of herself on his tongue coupled with the rhythmic pumping of his organ inflamed her senses, driving her to heights never before experienced.

Slowly they climbed, harder and higher, harder and higher, until finally, reaching the crest of their passion, they exploded with shuddering ecstasy.

When their breathing quieted and the gentle rocking of the carriage could be felt beneath them once more,

Daniel lifted his head, staring into the passion-lit face of the woman beneath him. "I would not trade this night for any other that I have experienced, save for the first time when I took your most precious gift."

Tenderly, she reached up, caressing the side of his face with her fingertips, thrilled with the warmth she observed in his eyes. "You have taken more than my virginity, Daniel," she whispered. *You have taken my heart, as well.*

"I . . . I . . ." He could not say the words. Not yet. It had to be right. Perfect. Tomorrow, he would tell her how he felt. Tonight he would merely show her. Leaning down, he kissed her again.

Samantha smiled into his mouth. He loved her. She knew he did. And even if he never said the words, she would carry that knowledge with her always, no matter what the future held in store.

Chapter Eighteen

Samantha fairly floated on air as she trudged briskly through the icy slush toward the steps of the Capitol. Her smile was as brilliant as the blinding sun shining overhead. Her cheeks were flushed rosy from the chilly air that nipped at her skin, but, inside, a warmth swept through her that no frigid air could dampen.

Daniel loved her! Oh, he hadn't said as much, she realized, but she knew. It was only a matter of time before he declared himself. She had felt it in his kiss, in his touch, in her heart. Last night had been all the proof she needed.

As she entered the Capitol, she noted that the building was practically deserted. Congress was still adjourned for the holiday season. Making her way down the cavernous hall, she paused before the door of Senator Pickering's office and took a deep, fortifying breath.

For some strange, inexplicable reason, she knew her meeting with Adam was going to prove awkward. He was jealous of Daniel; she had seen it in his eyes last night. Worse, he was possessive. Years of friendship had given him a false sense of proprietorship where she was concerned. He thought to marry her, and she had no intention of permitting his delusion to go on any longer. With that objective, and that of finding out what he knew about her brother, she pushed open the heavy oak door and entered.

Seated at his desk, Adam glanced up when Samantha walked in; his smile, filled with pity, sent a shiver of alarm up her spine.

"Good morning, Adam. I came as quickly as I could. You indicated that it was somewhat urgent." She took a seat in the chair he indicated.

"I'm pleased you could come, though I fear what I have to tell you might be somewhat upsetting."

A tight knot of apprehension settled in the pit of her stomach. "Has something happened to my brother? Is he dead?"

He folded his hands on top of the desk, interlacing his long fingers. "As far as I know, Robert is still missing. We have no news of his whereabouts."

"But you said—"

"I said I had important information relating to him. I do. But I don't have any details as to his exact location. I'm afraid only the British or their informants would be privy to that information."

She paled, her breath quickening. "What are you trying to say?" Adam's smug smile nettled. He was playing with her, punishing her for last evening. He'd been the same when they were children, always holding back, never giving an inch until he was sure she knew he had won.

"You and Fortune seem to be getting along quite

well. You have a *tendresse* for him, have you not?"

She felt her cheeks warm. "Daniel and I are friends, but I fail to see how that is any of your concern."

He pushed himself up from the desk, his eyes narrowing. "Everything you do is my concern. We go back a long way, Samantha; our bonds are strong, our friendship lasting. I only have your best interests at heart." Suddenly like a chameleon his manner changed, and he became sympathetic. "I didn't want to be the one to tell you; I didn't want to be the one to cause you pain."

She dug her nails into the soft leather of the seat. Foreboding swept over her. "Tell me what? What could you possibly have to say that would be injurious to me? You already indicated that you had no news of my brother."

He leaned across the desk, his icy orbs impaling her, chilling her; his voice was smooth and as hard as marble when he spoke. "Daniel Fortune is a traitor."

"No!" she shouted without hesitation, shaking her head in denial. "I don't believe you."

"I didn't believe it myself, at first. But there is proof, Samantha. The man is a British agent. He's been feeding information to the Crown. We believe he may have been responsible for the capture of the *Chesapeake.*"

Her face whitened. "Robbie," she breathed softly.

"Yes, Robert. We've had Fortune under surveillance for some time. The senator has people placed in strategic locations; they supply information. When I noticed how Fortune had wormed his way into the good graces of your family, I had him investigated. He's not what you think, my dear."

On leaden feet, she rose, shaking so badly she didn't

think she could make it the short distance to the window. Gazing out, she noted that everything looked the same, but it wasn't. Everything had changed. It was bleak—dull and tarnished as her soul. Without turning, she spoke.

"I knew you disliked Daniel. I could see it in your eyes. But I never realized that your hate extended this far."

Crossing the room, Adam turned her toward him. His voice was harsh when he spoke. "It's true. I do despise Fortune for betraying his country, for having no honor, and most of all, for deceiving you, Samantha. His father, Nicholas Fortune, is an English duke—a lord of the realm. He's titled. He owns a vast estate in England, near London, called Blackstone Manor. My dear, Nicholas Fortune is the duke of Blackstone." Her shocked expression merely egged him on. "Daniel is his only male heir who will inherit the title when Fortune dies. Don't you think they want a British victory? Do you think they will give up their heritage, their country, to fight for a backwater nation such as ours? They're traitors masquerading as loyal citizens to aid the British. You've been duped, my dear. We all have."

Her ears began to ring; her face grew hot. Sweat formed on her upper lip and forehead as Adam's hateful words receded into oblivion. She crumbled and would have fallen had Adam not been there to catch her.

Carrying her to the divan, Adam laid her down gently, patting her cheeks, chafing her hands. "Samantha! Samantha!"

After a few minutes, her eyelids fluttered open.

Adam's worried face hovered over hers. *My God! It wasn't a nightmare. This was real. This was happening.* But it couldn't be. She loved Daniel.

Adam placed a glass of sherry to her lips, urging her to drink. The warm liquid revived her.

"I'm sorry, Samantha. 'Twas foolish of me to blurt it out like that. I wanted to spare you, but I could not. It has gone too far, grown too dangerous."

He had no idea how far it had gone. She righted herself. "Why do you tell me this now?"

"Fortune trusts you. He has placed his childhood friend, a runaway, into your home." He paused at her look of surprise. "I know about the black, the man you call Caesar. Fortune has placed you in jeopardy by bringing this fugitive slave into your home. The penalty would be severe if you were found out."

Icy fingers of fear for Caesar's safety tickled her spine. "Caesar is Daniel's slave," she brazened out. "I've seen his papers."

"They're forged. He's owned by a man named Chastain. Fortune's brother-in-law, I believe."

Her heart sank. "What do you intend to do about Caesar?" She held her breath, waiting for him to answer.

"Nothing for the time being. I think it's best that Fortune go on believing that no one is on to him. That way, we can gather enough evidence to hang him."

Her breath was released in a gasp. "Hang him!" She clutched her throat, her eyes rounding in horror.

"It's what they do to traitors, Samantha."

She shook her head. "I want no part of this. I won't be involved."

"I'm afraid you already are. Unwittingly or not, you

264

may have aided Daniel in his cause to aid the British war effort. Your motives and that of your family could be suspect."

She covered her face, thinking of the information Daniel had sought on Adam and Senator Pickering. He also knew where Robbie was. How did he get that information? She clutched absently at the medal around her throat; the thin metal chain choked her. *Robbie*. Was Daniel responsible for Robbie's incarceration? she wondered, blinking back the tears that suddenly surfaced, swallowing the lump in her throat.

"What will you have me do?" Her words were laced with defeat and resignation.

Adam smiled inwardly. This was going to be easier than he thought. "Fortune has a room at Suter's Tavern. We believe he possesses maps and documents pertaining to American shipping maneuvers—naval plans, if you will. Find them and bring them to me. We must put a stop to this fiend once and for all before other innocent American victims, such as your brother and father, are lost."

The laughter bubbled up; she couldn't contain it. "You want me to spy on Daniel?" This was too cruel a joke. First she spied on Adam, now she was to spy on Daniel. *This was madness.* Her laughter intensified.

"Samantha! Get hold of yourself. The sherry has rendered you senseless."

At Adam's outraged demeanor, her laughter became hysterical.

She was going mad.

Surely, she must be going mad.

*   *   *

265

Daniel hurried past the group of Negro slaves that trundled the hogsheads of tobacco down to the wharf. He gave scant notice to the tall spires of Georgetown College that could be seen in the distance or to the brick-walled gardens of the attractive homes he walked by on his way to visit Mr. Harvey, the jeweler. He had a goal in mind, his purpose clear after a long night of soul-searching: he would purchase an engagement ring for Samantha; he would ask her to marry him.

Now that the decision had been made, his mood lightened as did his steps. He was in love. How and when it had happened, he didn't know. He only knew that he intended to spend the rest of his life with the exquisite beauty from Massachusetts. And politics be damned!

Turning right onto Bridge Street, he walked another block until he arrived at the building with the pocket watch hanging from its sign and entered.

"Good afternoon, Mr. Harvey. How are you this fine day?"

The jeweler looked up, removed the eyeglass from his right eye and squinted. Suddenly his wrinkled face split into a grin. "Mr. Fortune, come in, come in. I didn't expect to see you again so soon."

Daniel colored slightly, grateful that he and Mr. Harvey were quite alone. "Yes, well, I've come about a different matter this time, Mr. Harvey. I need to purchase a ring . . . an engagement ring."

The proprietor beamed. Mr. Fortune was a good customer. He had made a goodly sum off his last request, though the item sought hadn't been that easy to duplicate. Now it seemed the young man was thinking of settling down, which undoubtedly would mean more purchases of jewelry—expensive jewelry for his lady love. Mr. Fortune was no miser. Bending over the locked case behind him, Thaddeus Harvey produced an impressive collection of gold and silver rings.

"Check these over, Mr. Fortune. I'm sure you'll find something to your liking."

Daniel pondered, picking up one ring after another. The diamonds were too hard, not at all in keeping with Samantha's soft disposition. The sapphires, though beautiful, were too impersonal—too cold. He wanted something fiery—something hot. A ring that would reflect the deep, flaming passion that he felt for Samantha. Suddenly, his eyes lit with pleasure as they fell upon an exquisite ruby, the color so rich it changed from crimson to burgundy when he held it up to the light. It was perfect.

"An excellent choice, Mr. Fortune. I don't get many stones as exquisite as that one. The lady will be pleased, I'm sure."

Daniel smiled. "I'm sure, too, Mr. Harvey. Pleased and no doubt surprised," he added more to himself than to the jeweler. "Wrap it up. I'll take it."

Waiting for the jeweler to add up his purchase, Daniel walked to the window and stared out. The die was cast, he realized. In a few short hours, he would ask Samantha to marry him. His stomach clenched; he swallowed nervously. He had a terrible track record where engagements were concerned, but it would be different this time, he vowed. Samantha was nothing like Joanna. She was guileless, not at all mercenary. And he trusted her. It had taken him a long time to admit it, but he truly trusted her.

As soon as he paid Mr. Harvey for the ring, he would go back to his room at the tavern, change into something more suitable, other than the heavy leather trousers and wool shirt he had on, and present Samantha with the surprise of her life.

Samantha brushed back the tears clouding her vision as she hurried from the newspaper office toward the coach stop. Adam was right! Joseph Gales had confirmed it.

Taking a seat on the bench while she waited for the coach, her mind drifted back to her visit with Joseph Gales.

Not believing the passel of lies that Adam had put to her, she had gone straight to the newspaper office, knowing that if anyone was in a position to know about Daniel's heritage, it would be Joseph Gales.

Upon entering, she was relieved to find that Willy had left to deliver some flyers for her uncle. As much as she cherished their friendship, Samantha didn't think she could face the young woman right now.

Mr. Gales greeted her with such warmth and kindness, it made the words she needed to utter lodge tightly in her throat. It took a few moments to compose herself.

"Good afternoon, Mr. Gales. I hope I'm not intruding on your work."

The brown eyes twinkled. "Not at all, my dear. Won't you join me in a cup of tea? It's been awhile since you've been by to visit."

She shook her head, smiling regretfully. "I'm sorry, but I must get home. I only came by to ask you a question. I'm afraid I need your help again, Mr. Gales."

His forehead creased in consternation. "I'm afraid I still have no news about your brother, Samantha. You'll have to go to Daniel for that information."

Why, because he's a British spy? she wanted to scream, but she knew that Mr. Gales trusted Daniel. He was probably as unaware of Daniel's covert activities as she had been.

"It's because of Daniel that I'm here. I need to ask you something. I believe you have the answer to the information that I'm seeking."

He folded his arms across his chest, eyeing her speculatively. "Does this have something to do with your engagement?" The corners of his mouth tipped up. "I'm very happy for both of you."

Her cheeks burned. A heaviness settled in the region of her heart; it was an effort to keep her voice steady. "Thank . . . thank you. And yes, indirectly it does have something to do with my engagement. I heard some disturbing news today about Daniel's father. I thought you could clarify it for me."

Joseph knew what was coming. He guessed he couldn't blame the young woman for wanting to know the truth about Daniel's heritage, times being what they were. "What is it you wish to know?"

"Is Daniel's father a duke? A member of the English nobility?"

The editor hesitated, weighing his answer, wanting it to come out the right way. "Yes, but he . . ." He paused at the sound of the door opening and smiled at the heavyset man who entered. "Good day to you, George."

Her worst fears confirmed by Mr. Gales's answer,

Samantha choked back a sob and spun on her heel. She needed no further explanation. Blinded by her tears, she ran out of the office, nearly knocking into the overweight gentleman who had just entered, leaving both men staring after her open-mouthed and stunned.

Now, seated at the coach stop, she felt numb, barely able to feel the cold that seeped through her warm pellise. Adam had been right. Daniel was a traitor. How could it be otherwise? Nicholas Fortune was a duke. Mr. Gales had confirmed it. No! she wanted to scream, railing at the heavens. It couldn't be. Daniel couldn't be a traitor. But he could. He was.

She knew what she must do. She had helped Daniel wreak havoc on her own country, may have played a part in endangering her own brother. Covering her face, she shook her head. She must make amends.

She would go to Daniel's room, find the papers that Adam needed. It was the only way to right the wrong that had been done. She must put aside her personal desires. The welfare of her country was at stake.

She would exorcise Daniel from her heart, from her mind, until he was nothing more than a painful reminder of her stupidity. She'd been a fool for love. But no more. She'd play Daniel Fortune's game and beat him at it. This was war. And she had no intention of losing this time.

Humming a cheerful ditty, Daniel climbed the steps to the second floor of the tavern, patting the front pocket of his jacket to reassure himself that the ring he had purchased was still safe and secure. He smiled, thinking of how surprised Samantha would be when he presented it to her this evening.

Fumbling in his other pocket, he extracted the brass key to his room, tossing it up and catching it in midair with one fell swoop, smiling, as if he held the key to his heart in his hand. Reaching the end of the long narrow hallway, he paused, unlocked the door, and pushed it open. He froze, staring in stunned silence before a wicked grin split his face.

"Hello, love. I didn't expect to find you here. This is a surprise."

Samantha spun around, thrusting the papers she had found in Daniel's trunk behind her back. "Daniel!" Her voice tremored slightly.

Daniel moved toward her, prompting her retreat; he frowned. "Why so surprised, love? You were waiting for me, weren't you?"

"I . . . I . . ." A guilty flush spread over her body.

He stepped in front of her, so close she could feel his warm breath on her cheeks. He smelled of wet wool and tobacco; the familiar scents ignited an unwelcome memory—an unwelcome longing in her breast. But as she stared into his handsome face, she was reminded that things weren't the same. Would never be the same for either of them again.

"I've missed you, love." He reached for her, but she eluded his grasp, darting past him as she ran for the door, dropping the papers she had concealed in the process.

Daniel looked at her, then at the pile of naval maps, and finally at the open trunk. In that space of an instant, he put himself between her and the door. His eyes, bright with suspicion, narrowed.

"What have you done, Samantha? Why have you

been going through my things?" But the answer was obvious—condemning. The sensitive documents detailing American naval maneuvers were scattered at her feet. She had been caught red-handed and she knew it. Her eyes were lit with a wild, almost insane, light that he had never seen before.

"What have I done?!" she parried, her voice shrill. "'Tis not I, Daniel, but *you* who have done a grievous wrong. I was merely the pawn in your nefarious game of treason."

"Treason!" His look was incredulous as he stepped forward, grabbing onto her wrist. "What nonsense do you speak? I have not committed treason." Her laugh of contempt held a touch of madness, sending a shiver down his spine.

"The game is up. You will not use me further to achieve your vicious ends." She tried to twist out of his hold, but his grip was too strong. She feared he would snap her wrist in two, as he had her heart.

"I don't know where you got this crazy idea of yours, but you are sadly, grievously mistaken."

She shook her head. "I know, Daniel. 'Tis no use to deny it. Adam told me everything."

Daniel's eyes hardened; his lips curled. "Bainbridge!" He spat out the name. "I might have known he was behind this." His features softened momentarily. "Surely you don't believe anything that traitorous bastard has told you? He's lying to protect himself."

"You're wrong! You are the liar. Adam would never deceive me, betray his own country. I've known him all my life."

"It was Adam who arranged for your brother's capture and incarceration. He could very well have

272

been responsible for your father's death. He's an extremist—a fanatic. With no one to rely on but your elderly grandfather, you became easy prey for Adam's schemes."

She laughed. "How easily the lies roll off your tongue. And I suppose you will deny that you are working for the British? That you are an agent for the Crown?"

"I do!" Noting the purplish bruise that was beginning to form on Samantha's arm, Daniel let her go, watching regretfully as she chafed her wrist to get the blood circulating again. He cursed himself inwardly for hurting her. "Love, don't do this. Don't throw away everything that we have."

"What do we have, Daniel? A mockery of an engagement? A relationship based on coercion? An accumulation of lie after lie after lie?"

Her words slapped at his pride, their veracity too accurate to discount. "That was before."

"Before what? Before I gave myself to you like a tavern slut? Before I begged you to make love to me like the lowliest whore?" She shrugged. "I guess that's what I've become—a whore. Whore to a traitor."

He grabbed her then and shook her, hard. "Don't say that. You're no whore, and I'm no traitor."

Her eyebrow arched. "No? Then tell me, Daniel, why didn't you reveal that your father was an English duke? A lord of the realm? The duke of Blackstone to be precise?"

He stared, stunned for a moment. So that was it. She believed that his parents were traitors, too. A rage so intense that it threatened to ignite fueled his fury. How could she believe such a horrendous thing about his

273

parents after meeting them, living with them? The muscle in his jaw flicked angrily.

Noting the mutinous set of her chin, her rigid posture, he sighed in disgust. "You can believe what you like."

"You're not going to deny it? So it's true. Adam was right about everything."

He pushed her away and she stumbled; her eyes lit with surprise and then fear. "Leave before I'm tempted to do something that I'll regret."

"I already have," she threw at him, heading for the door. Pausing, she looked back, a mixture of pain and anger etched deeply on her face. "You have used me sorely, Daniel, betrayed my innocence. For that, I will never forgive you."

He stared at the door shut so abruptly in his face, then pulled out the ruby ring he had bought. Its brilliance and beauty mocked him. He closed his fist around it, fighting the pain that tore through his chest.

"Samantha," he whispered softly, "I love you."

Part Four

Hearts on Fire

We cannot kindle when we will
The fire that in the heart resides,
The spirit bloweth and is still,
In mystery our soul abides.

Matthew Arnold
"Morality"

Chapter Nineteen

August, 1814.

The months of separation between Daniel and Samantha were closely mirrored by the continuing estrangement between the United States and Great Britain.

The overthrow of Napoleon in France at the beginning of April enabled the British to concentrate their efforts on bringing the ragtag American Army to heel. The British extended their naval blockade to include additional sections of the Northeast, triggering drastic shortages, speculation, and price inflation. The severe drop in custom revenue brought the United States Treasury dangerously close to bankruptcy.

All of this, coupled with the heartbreak of Daniel's perfidy, had made living almost unbearable for Samantha. There were times, in the quiet of the night when she gazed out the window of her room to stare morosely at the moon, when she wondered if she would be able to go on. If she would be able to exist without

Daniel's love. But then her stubborn Yankee pride imbued her with the will, the determination, to endure.

Seated at the kitchen table with a very pregnant Dulcie by her side, Samantha stared at the account book before her, shaking her head dejectedly and wondering if her grandfather's monetary reserves would be enough to last until the war with England came to an end. They'd been unable to obtain any additional monies from their accounts in Boston, and the banks in Georgetown were nearly insolvent themselves. The war had taken much.

"You don't have to pay me no wages until things have improved for you, Miss Sam," Dulcie offered. "Me and Caesar have few wants. We is perfectly content just like we are."

Reaching across the table, Samantha patted Dulcie's hand, smiling softly at the generous black woman. "Don't be silly. You need the money for the baby. We've still got enough to make do, providing this infernal war ends soon."

"Mr. Dan don't think it will. Caesar says—" At Samantha's ashen look, Dulcie snapped her mouth shut. "I'm sorry, honey. I forgot."

"That's all right. I understand Caesar's need to be loyal to Daniel. I would expect no less from him."

"Caesar says you're wrong about Mr. Dan. He can't understand why you want to believe those awful things Mr. Adam done told you. I may not be book smart, but I'm a good judge of people. And I tell you right now, I'd take Mr. Dan's word over Mr. Adam's any day."

Samantha sighed. Dulcie would never understand, but she really couldn't expect her to. Adam had been part of her childhood, her life, for as many years as she could remember. She had to take his word over Daniel's. And besides, the evidence against Daniel had been too damaging. There was still the undeniable fact about Nicholas Fortune's background which Daniel hadn't refuted.

The pounding on the door prevented Samantha from having to respond to Dulcie's last statement. Advising the pregnant woman to stay put, she went to answer the summons.

A fat red-faced man stood on the porch, perspiring profusely while he stared at some official-looking document he held.

"May I help you?" Samantha inquired.

He looked up, his face growing redder. "Pardon me, ma'am. I didn't hear the door open. I'm Constable Drummond. I have a warrant for a runaway slave by the name of Caesar. I was told he was living here with you."

Samantha's face whitened momentarily before she recovered herself. "There is a slave by that name living here, Constable," she admitted, "but he's not a runaway. He's owned by a man named Daniel Fortune. I have the papers in my desk, if you would like to see them."

Removing his hat to reveal a balding pate, the man nodded, stepping into the hallway. "I believe I would. It's Miss Wilder, isn't it?"

Samantha smiled. "That's right, Constable Drummond. Samantha Wilder. Please come right this way."

Hoping that her nervousness wouldn't be betrayed by the loud pounding of her heart, Samantha walked calmly to the desk, removing the key that hung from the chatelaine around her waist. Opening the locked drawer, she retrieved the forged document that Daniel had secured what seemed like a lifetime ago.

"Here you are, Constable. I'm sure you will find that everything is in order."

Studying the document, he scratched his head, then wiped his perspiring forehead with a handkerchief he retrieved from his back pocket. "I don't understand. Mr. Bainbridge said that Caesar belonged to a man named Harold Chastain. He said you would collaborate that fact."

Samantha dug her nails into her palms. Adam's hatred of Daniel went deep, but she didn't think he would be callous enough to harm an innocent human being in order to gain his revenge. "Adam Bainbridge is wrong, Constable Drummond. He must have misunderstood. I told him that Daniel Fortune purchased Caesar from Harold Chastain quite some time ago. Caesar is owned by Mr. Fortune and has lived here as a servant and companion to my grandfather, Ezra Lawrence."

"Ezra Lawrence is your grandfather?" At Samantha's nod, the confused man whistled, shaking his head in disbelief. That old man had friends in high places, and Drummond wasn't about to risk losing his position because of what some overeager secretary claimed.

"My apologies, Miss Wilder. It appears there must be some mistake. I will have to look further into the matter, but for the time being, the slave called Caesar may remain in your custody."

Walking the constable to the door, Samantha breathed a sigh of relief as she watched him depart. She had no sooner shut the door when Dulcie came waddling into the hall, her eyes wide with fright.

"You gots to do something, Miss Sam. They's going to take my man away. My baby won't have no father if that happens." She started to cry.

Startled by the usually stoic Dulcie sobbing into her hands, Samantha rushed forward to comfort her, guiding the pregnant woman back into the kitchen.

"Sit down and rest. You'll make yourself and your baby ill. I'll fix us some lemonade." She went to a cupboard and fetched a pitcher.

"You have to go to Mr. Dan for help, Miss Sam. He's the only one that will know what to do."

The glass pitcher Samantha held slipped to the floor. The quiet and her nerves were shattered by the crash. She hopped back to avoid cutting herself on the sharp pieces that lay at her feet. "You must be joking! I can't seek Daniel's help. I told you, we're no longer friends."

"You gots to put aside your differences with Mr. Dan . . . for Caesar's sake. He needs you, Miss Sam. We both do. I know Mr. Daniel will help. He loves Caesar like a brother. He won't let nothing bad happen to him." Grabbing onto Samantha's skirts, the black woman stared pleadingly at her. "Please, Miss Sam. I ain't never asked you for nothin' before. I never will again, if only you'll help us."

"We'll go to Grandfather," Samantha offered. "He has connections; he'll know what to do."

Dulcie shook her head. "You know he ain't in no shape to help. Caesar says it's like touching a scarecrow when he helps your granddaddy with his bath."

Samantha heaved a sigh. What Dulcie said was true. Grandfather had taken to his bed these past few months, but Dr. Chase could find nothing physically wrong with him, save for his gout. The doctor had said

Ezra Lawrence suffered from a malady of the spirit, most likely associated with some recent setback or grave disappointment.

She felt her cheeks warm with guilt. Grandfather had not taken the news of her broken engagement to Daniel very well. In fact, when Adam had tried to relate Daniel's treasonous activities, Ezra had ordered Caesar to throw him out the door, stating that no son of Nicholas Fortune could be a traitor, that both Samantha and Adam were narrow-minded fools who had better remove their blinders before it was too late. Ezra and his granddaughter had spoken few civil words since.

Samantha stared stupidly at the splintered glass at her feet. The cracked and twisted pieces were like a crudely formed puzzle—a depiction of how her own life had become. Shattered. Broken. Unmendable. And all because she had loved and trusted the wrong man.

Seeing the fear, the heartbreak in Dulcie's eyes, Samantha knew she could do no less than to try and help Dulcie and Caesar. She would put aside her own disappointments and go to Daniel to tell him what had transpired; she would see if there was anything they could do to assist their two black friends. For Dulcie and Caesar had become much more than servants; they were family. And family helped each other. Perhaps her actions would help mend the rift between her and grandfather.

Tomorrow she would seek Daniel out. But first, she would find Adam Bainbridge. Her eyes narrowed. He had a lot of explaining to do.

*   *   *

"You said you would leave Caesar out of this if I agreed to spy on Daniel." Samantha's voice was full of accusation as she stared at Adam across the sunlit parlor of the boardinghouse on Massachusetts Street. The afternoon sun shone in through the open window, highlighting the silver in Adam's hair.

"That was a long time ago, Samantha, before you failed in your attempt to purloin the needed documents. Your failure has caused me a great deal of trouble, and I am still no closer to obtaining the tangible evidence I need to hang Fortune."

For that she would be eternally grateful, she decided. Though Daniel may have deceived her, broken her heart, she had no wish to see him die.

After her initial attempt at playing spy, she had refused to have anything further to do with Adam's schemes. She'd been hurt enough. She had resumed her life as if Daniel Fortune had never existed. She'd seen him only a time or two and then only at a distance. She had made it perfectly clear to Willy, Caesar, and her grandfather that she would tolerate no interference when it came to her relationship with Daniel. They had complied.

"With the terrible way things have gone with this war, I would think you and Senator Pickering would have more important concerns right now, other than hanging Daniel Fortune and harassing a black slave."

Adam leaned against the mantel, studying his nails. "Things have not gone that badly."

"Are you serious? What about the two thousand American soldiers of General Brown's army who engaged the British at Lundy's Lane? Many lives were lost. The newspapers are calling it the most violent battle of the war."

"An indecisive one at best," Adam commented, adding, "And besides, peace negotiations are now under way at Ghent. I predict a quick end to this war and soon."

She did not trust the calculating gleam she saw in his eyes. In fact, lately there were a number of things about Adam she didn't trust. His misleading statement about Caesar for one.

"I'd better go. It seems we do not see eye to eye on a number of things. I hope you will reconsider your position where Caesar is concerned. He is a big help to me and my grandfather. And right now, I can use all the help I can get."

Escorting Samantha to the door, Adam paused. "You haven't seen Fortune have you? Haven't resumed your old relationship?"

"No! How can you think it? We are done. I have no room in my life for traitors—of any kind." She wondered at the flush now covering Adam's cheeks.

"That being the case, I'll leave go of the slave for the time being. But you must know that in my position I cannot afford any type of scandal and neither can my wife." He held her chin, brushing his lips lightly across hers.

Samantha stiffened, fighting the urge to recoil. Adam's lips upon her own were cold, unfeeling, like a reptile's.

"I have waited a long time for you, Samantha." He ran his index finger down the warm flesh of her neck and across the top of her breasts. "I have restrained myself while around you, though I have wanted you in the worst way." At her shocked expression, he smiled. "I see that surprises you. It shouldn't. I want my wife pure and unsullied. When I take you to my bed and thrust between your legs, I want to feel your virginal barrier; I want to hear you cry out in pain when I tear it asunder. It is my right."

Shaking with uncontrollable loathing at the image Adam's words conjured up, Samantha swallowed the bile that rose to her throat. She felt dirty, defiled by his vile confession.

"I must go." She turned to leave.

He reached for her, pulling her into his chest, laying his mouth and hands over her in an exploratory, possessive fashion. She struggled violently as his hands covered her breasts, his questing fingers pinching at the nipples through her thin batiste gown. "Stop it," she cried, pushing hard against his chest.

His smile was lewd. "Your maidenly protests delight me, my dear. I'm going to enjoy teaching you all the hidden delights shared between a man and a woman." He thrust his thick, wet tongue into her mouth.

Biting down on the unwelcome protuberance, she felt an inordinate amount of pleasure when Adam suddenly released her and stepped back to grab his mouth in pain.

"That wasn't very amusing, Samantha," he stated, his words thick, as he dabbed at the blood on the end of his tongue with his handkerchief.

Wiping her mouth with the back of her hand, Samantha took a deep, shuddering breath and straightened her spine, replying with far more bravado than she felt, "Nor was it meant to be. I won't be pawed in a public boarding house for all to see. I care about my reputation, even if you do not."

He colored at her words. "I apologize most profusely. I lost my head."

"I have not given you leave to handle me in such a vulgar fashion. 'Tis only our long-standing friendship that prevents me from going to my grandfather." At his look of horror, she knew she had made an impression. "Good-bye, Adam. I hope you will think about what has happened here today." With those words, she slammed out the door, leaving Adam staring after her, red-faced, nervous, and unfulfilled.

Entering his room a short time later, Adam locked the door behind him. The ache in his loins was a painful but pleasant reminder of what had occurred today. Samantha was ripe for the picking, and he had waited a long time to pluck the cherry from her virgin's womb.

He smiled, rubbing the hardened bulge between his legs. He needed a whore and fast. He was nigh on ready to explode. Soon his pulsing rod would rest between Samantha's milky white thighs. But for now, the big-titted whore named Bertha would have to suffice.

But only for now.

On legs that felt as quavery as a jar of quince jelly, Samantha plodded down the main thoroughfare, hoping to reach Georgetown before the descending sun melted into the horizon. She had missed the last coach. And fearing that she would also miss Daniel before she had a chance to talk to him about Caesar, she decided to make the three-mile trek on foot. Besides, she thought, a brisk walk, even in hot weather, might clear up her thoughts and dispel the sickening feeling of disgust that Adam's words and actions had produced.

How could Adam have acted so vilely? It wasn't like him at all. At least, it wasn't like the Adam she had grown up with. He had changed.

The past few months had revealed a side of Adam that she had never seen before. He had grown demanding in their relationship. Gone was the easy camaraderie they once shared, now replaced by guarded looks, secretive smiles, and overt advances. She had explained countless times that she had no desire to marry him. But her words had fallen on deaf ears. Instead, he merely thought her coy, thought she was baiting him with silly, virginal games.

When had Adam grown to view her with romantic notions? She knew he desired her for his wife for selfish, purely political reasons. Her grandfather's connections made her an important asset to an aspiring politician. But to lust after her—covet her virginity. There had never been a suggestion, in all the years she had known him, that he harbored unchaste feelings for her.

Her lips thinned with irritation. Most likely it was because of her past association with Daniel. Adam knew that her feelings for Daniel had gone beyond mere friendship. And knowing Adam, it had nettled him.

Adam always wanted whatever someone else had. Even with Robbie, Adam had coveted. First it was the sailboat that Robbie had received from their father on his sixteenth birthday, then the horse on his eighteenth. There'd been so many things over the years. Things she had once discounted as merely friendly rivalry, but not now. Now things were out of hand. Adam had conjured Daniel up as a rival for her affections. It had made the pursuit of her that much more challenging and appealing to him.

Suddenly, a wave of nausea overtook her; she paused to lean against the lamp post. If Adam were to discover that she had been intimate with Daniel, he would find a way to kill Daniel. He would wreak havoc on those innocent bystanders that Daniel loved . . . like Caesar.

Wiping the beads of perspiration that formed on her upper lip, she silently vowed it would never happen. She had no intention of becoming intimate with Adam. He would never know that her virginity was a thing of the past. A fleeting image of being held in Daniel's arms floated by to torment her. She swallowed the lump in her throat.

No man would get the best of her again. Not Daniel, and especially not Adam, she vowed. From now on, her purpose in life was clear: she would find her brother, aid Dulcie and Caesar, and the rest of the world be damned!

She had gotten along fine all these years by herself. She needed no one. *To thine own self be true.* They were good words to live by, she decided, hurrying to cross the bridge that would bring her back to George-town.

Chapter Twenty

The tavern dining room was noisy with afternoon diners when Samantha entered. She glanced about in dismay, walking quickly to the stairs, mindful of the leering looks and suggestive whistles that followed after her.

'Twas most unseemly for an unattached female, such as herself, to be entering the tavern in the middle of the day unescorted. And downright disgraceful that she would be climbing the steps to the second level, she realized. It was a trip usually reserved for whores in search of a willing customer. Her cheeks burned as she hurried to escape the knowing smiles and ribald comments of the men who watched her.

As she approached the door she knew to be Daniel's, her stomach knotted tighter than a sailor's rope. She stood, hand poised in midair, gathering up her courage to knock.

When she finally did, Daniel's familiar voice floated through the wood separating them as he bid her to enter.

Her breath caught in her throat, her heart pounding loud in her ears as she stared transfixed from the threshold of the doorway. Daniel stood, his back turned toward her, a razor held firmly in the fingers of his right hand while he plied the blade to his cheeks.

"What is it? Is my supper ready yet?"

His questions sounded impatient, tired. It was obvious he thought she was the tavern maid. Her response clogged painfully in her throat. Her mouth grew dry, like a thick wad of cotton. Her cheeks burned hotter than the single candle that flickered on the washstand as her eyes drank in the achingly familiar form before her.

Daniel was naked from the waist up; his tanned, muscular back rippled reflexively as he continued to stroke the lather from his face, reminding her of other times she had watched him thusly.

Just as she was about to speak, he turned, and the breath she was holding expelled in a rush. Surprise, then anger, entered his eyes. He wiped the remaining soap from his face as he strode forward.

"Come in and shut the door," he ordered, grabbing his shirt off the chair.

Too stunned to do anything other than comply, Samantha closed the door behind her. Fidgeting nervously with the strings of her reticule, she waited while he shrugged into his shirt.

"What brings you here, Samantha? You haven't come to search my room for more incriminating documents, have you?" The pain in his heart made his words harsh.

She shook her head, her cheeks burning crimson.

290

"No. I've come to discuss something of grave importance."

"Has your lover dumped you on your pretty behind? Do you think to come crawling back to me, begging my forgiveness?"

His words at first startled, then a slow, fermenting fury ignited within her breast. "You are disgusting! I told Dulcie this would never work." She turned toward the door.

"Samantha, wait!" Daniel ran after her, pushing the door closed with the flat of his palm. "What has Dulcie got to do with your being here?"

"Everything," she spat out. "I would never have come if she hadn't begged me to. Dulcie and Caesar need your help."

Grabbing hold of her arm, he escorted her to the wing chair by the window, taking the seat across from her on the low wooden bench. He studied her intently, his gut twisting at the sight of the purplish smudges beneath her eyes and the wanness of her complexion. Her eyes, once bright and sparkling, were lackluster; her figure once lush and full had thinned.

Did her change in appearance have something to do with the problems Dulcie and Caesar faced? Or did it have to do with the fact that she missed him? Missed him as he had missed her?

Noting the way her hands nervously pleated and repleated the folds of her gown, he smiled inwardly. Her behavior reminded him of the first time they had met. Had it only been a year? It seemed like a lifetime ago.

"It's been a long time, love," he finally said, his memories softening his words.

She swallowed hard at the endearment, trying to retain the fragile thread of composure that threatened to snap. "Yes, it has." Eight long, lonely months, she added silently.

"How have you been? You look tired."

She smiled at that. "'Tis not a very flattering assessment to make after such a long time."

"You will always be beautiful to me."

The sincerity in his eyes sent her stomach falling to her feet. *Don't listen, Samantha. He's used you before; he'll do so again.* "Thank you."

"What's wrong? Why have you come?"

"Caesar is in trouble. We have to do something to help him."

His eyebrow arched. "We?"

"Adam is causing trouble." She paused at the lethal look that entered his eyes. "He sent Constable Drummond to arrest Caesar. I was able to convince the constable that you were Caesar's rightful owner by showing him the forged papers, but he plans to investigate further. If he does, he may discover our ruse."

Daniel pushed himself to his feet, rubbing the back of his neck. "Why didn't you just tell Drummond the truth? You've believed everything else Adam has told you. Why should you choose to protect Caesar? For all you know, he could be a traitor, too."

The hurt in his eyes touched her, and for one fleeting moment she wanted to take him in her arms and tell him that she believed him, that she knew he wasn't a traitor. But she couldn't. For she didn't. But she wanted to. Oh, God, how she wanted to.

"Caesar is a victim of circumstances. I would never hold anything he has done against him."

"Only against me, right?" He snickered, shaking his head.

"Daniel, I've come to you for help. Dulcie seems to think that you're the only one that can help Caesar."

"What of Ezra? He knows people up North."

"Grandfather is ill." The concern on his face touched her. "He's taken to his bed."

"What's wrong with him?"

She rose, turning away from his probing stare to gaze out the shuttered window. "He cannot accept the fact that we are not getting married," she replied, barely above a whisper.

Walking up behind her, he gently laid his hands on her shoulders and felt her stiffen. "Neither can I."

Her heart lurched. The feel of his lips on her neck sent shivers up and down her spine as he kissed the pulsing hollow at the base of her throat. She tried to move away, but he held her firm, turning her into his chest. Suddenly, his lips were on hers, devouring, demanding, his tongue seeking entry to the honeyed recesses of her mouth.

Feelings too long denied rose up to torment her. Parting her lips, she admitted the thrusting projection, savoring the tobacco taste of him as her own tongue matched his stroke for stroke. Her nipples hardened against his chest; her hands came up of their own volition to wrap themselves around his neck. Pressing into him, she sought to lose herself within him, to become absorbed into his being, to never let him go, for this was where she longed to be.

Suddenly, the feel of his questing fingers on her stiffened nipples brought her back to painful reality. Too shocked at her own behavior to speak, she pushed away from him, gazing up at his confused expression with one of her own. "I . . . I must go." She turned and ran, fleeing out the door as if the devil himself were on her heels.

"Samantha!" Daniel called after her, rushing to the door just in time to see her scurrying down the steps. He slammed the door, crossing the room to fall dejectedly onto the mattress. Holding his head between his hands, he shook his head, muttering in a voice filled with misery and frustration, "Bloody hell!"

A few days later, as she helped pack the remainder of the housekeeper's meager belongings into the old leather portmanteau, Samantha reflected on the missive they had received from Daniel the night before, instructing Dulcie and Caesar to prepare themselves to journey north.

It had arrived via messenger, much to Samantha's relief. She had no desire to face Daniel again. Not after the way she had humiliated herself at the tavern and especially not after experiencing all those familiar yearnings she had thought dead and buried.

"I guess that's about it, Miss Sam," Dulcie said, interrupting Samantha's less than pleasant reverie.

Samantha's eyes misted; she held out her hand to draw the black woman close. "I'm going to miss both you and Caesar. I feel like I'm losing part of my family, and I know that Grandfather feels the same way." The old man had blubbered like a baby when Caesar had bid him farewell that morning. The scene had been heartrending. Ezra Lawrence was not a man given to emotion. Sam had only seen him cry once: the day her mother had been buried.

"We goin' to miss you, too. You been good to us, Miss Sam. I ain't never going to forget you."

Walking arm and arm into the kitchen, the two women were greeted by Caesar, who waited patiently by the door with his newly acquired valise, a gift from Ezra.

"When did Daniel say he'd be arriving, Caesar?" Samantha asked, barely able to get the emotion-filled words past the lump in her throat.

"He should be here soon, Miss Sam. He said he would bring the wagon to the rear of the house as soon as the sun sets."

Gazing out the window, Samantha noted the darkening sky. "Well, we might as well eat before he arrives," she replied, glancing at the table where the supper she and Dulcie had prepared earlier waited for them. There were piles of ham sandwiches, potato salad, and a refreshing pitcher of lemonade. It had been too hot to prepare anything more substantial. The heat wave they'd been experiencing for weeks had not seen fit to abate.

"There's no sense in both of you going off on an empty stomach," she added.

Caesar chuckled, patting Dulcie's swollen mound. "I doubts very much if this woman's goin' to be able to fit much more in here."

"You hush your mouth." Dulcie slapped playfully at Caesar's hand, a tender smile hovering about her lips. "I may be fat, but I got a powerful big appetite."

Dulcie's grin was so suggestive, Samantha thought she saw a blush rise to the big man's face. Sighing deeply, Samantha fought to hold back her tears as she stared at the happy pair. She was going to miss them dreadfully.

They had no sooner taken a seat at the table when the front door knocker sounded. The three heads rose simultaneously; Samantha and Dulcie exchanged worried looks before Dulcie pushed her bulk out of the chair.

"I'll go see who it is, Miss Sam. You stay put and eat your supper."

Samantha and Caesar stared at the food on their plate, not daring to voice their suspicions on what was taking Dulcie so long. A moment later, they both released a sigh of relief when the black woman came through the door followed by a grinning Willy.

Samantha's eyes widened in surprise before she jumped up to embrace the elegantly gowned woman. "Willy Matthews, look at you. Why, you look positively genteel." Willy was dressed in a green sprigged muslin empire-waist gown with short capped lace sleeves. Her hair had been piled on top of her head in a fashionable Grecian knot, very similar to Samantha's own.

Willy blushed her usual crimson color. "I came into my inheritance a few months back."

Now it was Samantha's turn to redden. She hadn't called on Willy in months. Seeing her, being with her, reminded her too much of Daniel. And that had been much too painful to endure. "I've missed you," she confessed.

"And I you, but to be perfectly honest, you're not the reason I'm here. I came to say my good-byes to Dulcie and Caesar. And to give them this." She held out a small velvet bag, placing it in Caesar's hands.

Startled, the black man untied the bag to find a number of gold coins. He shook his head. "We can't take your money, Miss Willy. It wouldn't be right."

"You're not taking my money; I'm giving it to you . . . to make a home for you, Dulcie, and the baby. Consider it a gift for my godchild."

Dulcie covered her face, sobbing loudly into her hands; Samantha swallowed the lump in her throat and squeezed Willy's waist gently. The young woman's gesture had been generous and so like her.

A moment of awkward silence ensued, no one really knowing quite what to say. But the quiet, reflective mood was soon interrupted by a loud, insistent banging on the kitchen door. A moment later, Daniel burst into the room, looking weary and extremely agitated. He removed his felt hat, wiping the sweat and grime from his brow with the back of his hand.

Samantha's heart skipped a beat at the sight of him, but it was soon to pound in earnest when he announced, "I'm afraid there's been a change in plans."

Her brow wrinkled in puzzlement. "A change? I don't understand."

Dulcie latched on to Caesar's arm; fear shadowed her face.

"I have just received word that British ships have been sighted in the bay south of here." Ignoring Willy's startled gasp, Daniel continued, "It's too dangerous for Dulcie and Caesar to leave at this time. Things will have to remain as they are."

"Where did you get such information?" Samantha demanded, unable to mask the suspicion that gleamed in her eyes and colored her words.

Daniel's voice hardened. "That's none of your business." Turning to Willy, he said, "It won't be safe for you to stay with your uncle if the British decide to invade the Capital. Joseph's made too many enemies with his editorials, I'm afraid. I'd like you to move in here with Samantha for the time being . . . if that's all right with you, Samantha." He leveled his gaze upon her.

Samantha nodded mutely.

"Good. Caesar will be on hand to offer protection, if it becomes necessary."

"But what of my uncle?" Willy asked. "I can't leave him to face the British alone."

"He won't be alone, little one. I promise you, no harm will come to him."

Advancing on Samantha, Daniel grabbed on to her arm, tightening his hold when she started to resist. "I need to speak to Samantha . . . alone," he said to the startled trio. "We'll adjourn to the parlor for a few moments. Please excuse us." Exiting the room, he hauled the protesting woman behind him.

When they reached the parlor, Daniel deposited Samantha on the settee, then moved to lock the door.

"How dare you haul me around like a sack of potatoes?" she accused, jumping back up, her eyes widening in fear when she saw the determined look upon Daniel's face as he advanced toward her. She retreated, taking a position in front of the fireplace, thinking that the poker would serve as a weapon if she needed to defend herself.

"I'm leaving here today. When I'll be back—if I come back—is anybody's guess."

Fear twisted itself around her heart. "Don't say that; it's bad luck."

"You care, then, if I return?" He moved closer until she could feel his warm breath upon her face.

"I . . . I want no harm to come to you."

"Why? Traitors are better off dead. Aren't they?"

"Yes! No! I don't know! You're purposely trying to confuse me."

He placed his hands on the bare flesh of her arms, rubbing gently. "I need you, Samantha. I've thought of little else but the feel of your body beneath mine. The way your breasts fit perfectly in the palms of my hands." He demonstrated with aching preciseness, eliciting a sigh of pleasure. "Your image has tortured me for months. I cannot leave without possessing you once again."

She shook her head, trying to back away. "Please don't touch me that way. I can't think when you touch me that way." Her nipples throbbed beneath his fingers, causing a fluttering low in her abdomen.

Leaning his head down, he ran his tongue along the side of her neck, her ear, circling the sensitive orifice, pleased by the shudder he felt ripple through her. "I don't want you to think, only feel."

Slowly his mouth covered hers in a scorching kiss meant to melt her resistance. When he finally lifted his head to stare into her passion-lit eyes, he said in a voice as silky and seductive as his lips had been, "Don't send me away without the memory of possessing you once again."

Confusion and yearning melded together, creating a maelstrom of conflicting emotions within Samantha's breast. Her lips, still warm from his kiss, tingled. Her nipples, pebble hard and pulsating, pushed into the planes of his chest. God, how she wanted him—would always want him. And she might never see him again. Her eyes filled with tears as she witnessed the desire etched painfully, hopefully, on his face and heard the entreaty in his voice.

It would be so easy to give in, to put her convictions aside. But she couldn't. She couldn't.

Extricating herself from his embrace, she turned away from the disappointment she knew marred his features. Her voice was filled with anguish when she spoke. "I pray that you will return home safely, but the memories you carry must be those we have made before . . . before . . ."

She could not bring herself to call him a traitor. Whatever he had done, his motivations, however misguided, had been pure. She would not condemn him further for holding dear to those beliefs for a country in which he believed.

"Before what?" Daniel spat. His voice was harsh, his words cold. "Before discovering that I was a traitor?" He heaved a sigh, his hand hesitating on the cold brass of the door knob. "I pity you, Samantha, you and your prejudiced views and your unwavering faith in a man who will most surely betray you . . . betray us all. Damn your stubborn Yankee hide."

She turned then, just in time to hear him say in a voice barely above a whisper, "Good-bye, love."

When the door closed behind him, she dropped to the sofa, staring mutely ahead. Clutching herself about the waist, she rocked back and forth, trying to stem the pain that caused her heart to ache and the tears to flow freely down her face.

"Please, God," she prayed, "bring him back alive."

Chapter Twenty-One

The next day, early in the morning of August 19th, Daniel set out for the coast with Secretary of State Monroe, Captain Thornton of Alexandria, and thirty local dragoons to see what the British were up to.

When they reached their destination, an observation point along the Patuxent River near Benedict, Maryland, and some thirty-five miles east of the Capital, their worst fears were confirmed: the British Navy had entered the Patuxent and were advancing northwest toward Washington.

Gazing at the disturbing scene through his spyglass, Daniel frowned. In the distance, numerous white sails flapped wildly against an azure blue sky. As he stared at the flotilla of ships heading toward them, fear knotted his gut. Not for his own safety; he was perfectly capable of taking care of himself. But for Willy, Joseph, Caesar, Dulcie . . . and most of all, Samantha. They would all be in grave danger if the British decided to attack the Capital.

The United States was unprepared to fight a war

against Great Britain. Fear of a standing army as an instrument of despotism had rendered America's defenses practically nonexistant and ineffectual at best.

Gazing once more at the advancing British Navy, Daniel heaved a sigh. There didn't seem to be any *if* involved. The British *were* going to attack.

In the five days after Daniel's departure, near chaos reigned among the citizens of Washington. Word had finally arrived of the British advance. And although the newspapers continued to assure their readers that the brave men of Washington would afford complete protection to the city, the skeptical citizens continued their exodus.

Standing in front of the *National Intelligencer* building, Samantha and Willy watched friends and neighbors hauling wagons and carts loaded with furnishings and family treasures file by in their haste to depart the city.

"Do you really think the British will attack?" Willy asked, waving good-bye to Mrs. Langley, the minister's wife. "Your grandfather thinks it a certainty."

Samantha shaded her eyes to observe with dismay that the cashier of the Bank of Washington was waving his farewells as he passed on his way out of town. "In case you hadn't noticed, Grandfather thrives on gloom. His health has improved a hundredfold with the news of the British invasion." She sighed in disgust. "He thinks to relive past glories. But this war, though they call it the second War for Independence, has not the same support as the first. See how our brave citizens flee, rather than stand and fight."

"You can hardly blame them for being frightened,

Sam. Our militia is a nonentity, and we have a buffoon for a secretary of war." She paused, distaste marring her features as she thought of John Armstrong's repeated assurances that the British were far more likely to attack Baltimore than the Capital. "The military leaders we do have are ill-equipped and poorly trained. As far as I'm concerned, General Winder is as inept at leading our troops as Armstrong is at leading him.

"Perhaps these citizens we see before us," she made a sweeping motion with her hand, "are not so dumb after all. We may be eating kidney pie and Yorkshire pudding for Christmas yet."

Snorting in disbelief, Samantha dabbed at the droplets of perspiration pouring off her brow, then readjusted the blue satin ribbons of her straw bonnet. "I'll never believe that, and neither should you."

Squeezing Samantha's hand, Willy smiled contritely. "I'm sorry; I know you're right. It's just that you're so much better at hiding your fear than I am. I wish I were more like you."

"Posh! I'm just too stupid to be afraid and too much of a Yankee to know when the odds are against me." She returned Willy's smile with one of her own. "Now let's quit all this talk of doom and get home. Grandfather is probably bursting at the seams to know what we've found out today."

"Shall we make it sound worse than it is?" Willy asked, a mischievous gleam entering her eyes.

Samantha nodded in agreement. "Most assuredly. Grandfather would have it no other way."

It hadn't taken long for word to reach Georgetown

303

that over four thousand British troops had entered Bladensburg, Maryland, and made short work of the ragtag American army of volunteers.

Finding themselves no match for the well-disciplined, well-trained army of redcoats, the American militia had retreated, scattering themselves like buckshot over the Maryland countryside.

As the afternoon wore on, the sound of cannon fire could be heard in the distance. Alarmed by the almost assured invasion of the Capital by the British, Samantha paced nervously across the Oriental carpet of the parlor, while Willy and Ezra occupied themselves over a game of chess.

"How can you both sit there, playing that infernal game, when the entire British army is beating a path to our door?" Samantha asked, her tone coldly disapproving.

Looking up, Ezra shrugged his shoulders and shook his head at his granddaughter's impatience. "Not much a gout-ridden old man, a pregnant woman, a fugitive slave, and two hotheaded females can do, now is there?"

"Well, there's something I can do," Samantha declared, grabbing her grandfather's brass spyglass off the mantel. "I'm going up to the attic to get a better view. If the British are indeed coming, at least we should be aware so that we can better prepare ourselves."

"Suit yourself," Ezra said, "but there's naught you can do either way. And you'll most likely roast to death up there."

"Shall I come with you?" Willy asked, preparing to rise.

304

Samantha motioned her back down. "I'd never hear the end of it, if you did." She smiled at her grandfather's indignant expression. "Keep Grandfather amused; I'll be back in a few minutes."

Climbing the narrow set of stairs that led to the attic, Samantha pushed against the stubborn, humidity-stuck door with her shoulder. Once inside, a strong, musty odor assaulted her senses. It was stifling in the tiny room; she felt as if she were in the pit of an inferno and might suffocate at any moment.

Making her way past wooden crates and an odd assortment of furnishings, she crossed to the small hexagonal window, throwing it open. The air outside was only slightly cooler than within, offering little relief. Holding the spyglass up to her right eye, she focused on the horizon and was alarmed by the gray puffs of smoke she observed in the distance.

So, it was true, she thought sadly, the smoke and cannon's roar giving proof to the rumored battle said to have taken place in Bladensburg.

Was Daniel there? she wondered. Had he joined forces with the victorious British Army? Would he soon be entering the city with Admiral Cockburn and his men?

Or was he dead? The possibility brought an ache to her heart. Either way, he was lost to her forever.

Wiping the tears that mingled with the sweat trickling down her face, she knew what must be done: She would find Adam and engage his help in getting Willy and her grandfather safely out of the city. She would then find a way to help Dulcie and Caesar escape.

She thought of Dulcie so near her time and

wondered if the pregnant woman would be able to travel. She would have to, Samantha decided. They all had to leave and soon. There was no telling when the "Red Devil of the British Navy," as Admiral Cockburn was called, would make his presence known. She intended to be on her way north long before then.

Unfortunately, all did not go as planned. Before Samantha had crossed the bridge into Washington, red-coated soldiers could be seen entering the city from the east, while swarms of American soldiers exited the city in the opposite direction.

Chaos reigned, women screamed, babies cried, and an occasional volley of musket fire rang out. Fear and determination gave wings to her feet as Samantha hurried through the streets choked with people to the boardinghouse on Massachusetts Avenue.

Had she committed another folly? she wondered, noting the panic on the faces of those she passed. Willy and her grandfather had no idea she had left. Had her grandfather known of her plan to enlist Adam's aid, he would have expressly forbidden her to venture out into such a perilous situation. Cognizant of that fact, and knowing that she had to get help, Samantha had left a note, stating her purpose and her intention to return as quickly as possible.

Pushing her way past a group of British soldiers who paid her no mind, she was relieved to find herself in front of Weightman's Book Shop. Adam's boardinghouse was only a few blocks away.

Pausing to catch her breath, her eyes widened in disbelief as she caught sight of the book so brazenly displayed in the storefront window. Sitting on a bed of red velvet was a copy of *The Life of Wellington*. She would have laughed at the irony of the situation, had it not been so telling. There were many who would welcome the arrival of the British with open arms.

The lengthening shadows of twilight increased Samantha's apprehension as she walked. Turning the corner, she caught sight of Conrad's Boardinghouse. Like a lighthouse offering hope to lost ships, the candles in the windows of the boardinghouse signaled a safe haven to Samantha. She had waded through an ocean of angry, enemy faces and had landed unscathed.

Admiring the handsome white horse that was tied up to the post in front of the house, she entered the clapboard building, climbing the stairs to the second floor, comforted by the knowledge that Adam would know what to do. For all his eccentricities, Adam was level-headed and logical. Once he realized the danger they were in, he would think of a way to get them out of the city; she was sure of it.

The hallway was empty, the house strangely silent. She supposed most of the inhabitants had beat a hasty retreat by now. Approaching Adam's door, she paused at the sound of voices. Odd, she thought, that Adam would have visitors this time of evening. Odder still, that his door would be ajar. Fearing something amiss, she inched her way down the hall, flattening her body and palms against the wall.

As she grew nearer, the sounds became more distinct. The clipped British accent of the speaker sent currents of alarm coursing through her.

"You've done a splendid job, Bainbridge. Without those reports on troop strength and position, I doubt we would have been able to carry off this invasion so successfully."

Samantha gasped, covering her mouth, her eyes widening in disbelief at what the man's words implied.

"Thank you, Admiral Cockburn."

The distinctive nasal quality of Adam's voice echoed painfully within her ears, within her heart. It was full of pride and satisfaction, turning Samantha's stomach queasy as she listened.

"I've done no more than any reasonable American would have who had taken the time to consider the value of British intervention into our present misguided administration. I'm certain once the Federalists gain a foothold, Great Britain will have nothing else to fear from the United States."

Moving closer to the door, Samantha peered through the crack, observing the British naval officer whose name brought fear into the hearts of most Americans. She guessed him to be about forty-three. He was dressed in a dark blue uniform decorated with brass buttons and gold epaulets at the shoulders. There was gold braid on his sleeves and on the cockaded shako he held in the crook of his arm. His look of superiority nettled, as did Adam's fawning posture. Bitter bile rose to her throat. *Traitor. Adam was a goddamn traitor!*

"We have never feared you Americans, Bainbridge," the admiral stated, taking a sip of his brandy. "This whole sorry affair is more of a nuisance than anything else. I'll be relieved when we can leave this miserable place and return to civilization."

"Of course, you're right," Adam was quick to agree.

Anger boiled through Samantha's veins. How could

she have trusted that fanatical, power-hungry monster? she wondered. Daniel had been right.

Daniel. Oh God, how could she have ever suspected him of being a traitor? She dug her nails into her palms. Adam, that's how. The bastard had been clever. He had done a thorough job of convincing her of Daniel's so-called deception to save his own hide. And she had been stupid enough to believe him.

She had to find Daniel and tell him what she had learned. He would know what to do.

Taking a step back, she turned to leave, running smack dab into the center of a bright red uniform jacket. She gasped, her eyes widening in fright.

"Going somewhere, little lady?"

Chapter Twenty-Two

"Ross! Goddammit, what's taken you so long? I expected you back here an hour ago," Cockburn demanded of his second in command, his eyebrows raised inquiringly at the sight of the young woman held firmly in Ross's arms.

"My horse was shot out from under me, Admiral, while I carried a flag of truce. One of my men was killed." The Irish lilt could not soften the anger of the man's words.

"Who have we here?"

"'Twould seem we have a spy on our hands, Admiral."

Adam turned away from the window just in time to see Samantha place a well-aimed knee in the center of General Ross's groin. His eyes rounded in horror. "Samantha!"

"You goddamn bitch!" Ross yelled, releasing hold of Samantha to grab hold of his crotch as he doubled over in agony.

Seizing the opportunity to escape, Samantha ran for

the door, only to be stopped by the two British soldiers who had just entered.

The fatter of the two, a short man with hair the color of dirt who smelled of stale cigars and whiskey, grabbed Samantha about the waist, running his hands up and under her breasts. She squirmed, kicking at him as she tried to break loose.

"Leave her go!" Adam shouted, his eyes hardening as he observed the familiar way the soldier was touching Samantha. "That woman you so casually fondle is my betrothed. If you don't want a bullet in that thick skull of yours, I suggest you unhand her at once."

"Release the woman, Stiles," Cockburn ordered. "I told you there would be no mistreatment of the citizens here. We'll have our revenge, but not against innocent bystanders."

Stiles smiled spitefully at Adam, patting Samantha's rear before shoving her aside.

The moment the soldier released her, Samantha ran to Adam's side. However big a bastard Adam was, he professed to care for her, and she intended to use that to her own advantage.

"You know this woman, Bainbridge?" Cockburn asked, his eyebrow lifting superciliously.

Adam inclined his head. "Her name is Samantha Wilder. We are to be married."

Ross snorted. "More fool you, leg-shackling yourself to a hellion like that. Have you taught her no manners?"

Samantha bristled at the general's comments, but wisely said nothing.

Wrapping his arm about Samantha's waist, Adam smiled confidently. "There's little pleasure to be had

311

between the legs of a corpse. I prefer my women with a little spirit."

Cockburn laughed. "It's said you've drilled enough whores between here and Massachusetts to rival an overzealous woodpecker."

The comment produced a chorus of ribald laughter and brought a bright blush to Samantha's cheeks. She sucked in her breath at the crudity.

"It seems we've embarrassed your ladylove, Bainbridge," Cockburn said, turning his attention on Samantha. "Forgive us, my dear, we've been too long without the sweet companionship of the gentler sex."

"Doesn't the raping of innocent women count, Admiral? Your marines' exploits in the Tidewater have been fully documented by those unfortunates who were victimized by you British scum."

Adam paled, tightening his hold on Samantha's waist.

"Really, Bainbridge, the bitch goes too far," Ross said, stepping forward. "Curb her tongue, or I'll rip it out myself." His eyes narrowing, he stared at Samantha, rubbing his crotch. "I assure you, it would give me a great deal of satisfaction."

Before Ross could make good his threat, one of his aides, a freckle-faced, red-haired lad entered the room. "Excuse me, General, but the preparations for torching the city have been laid. Do you wish for us to begin?"

"No!" Samantha cried, trying to break free of Adam's hold. "You can't mean to destroy the Capital."

Cockburn's smile was sinister. "My dear, you are the perfect example of why we do what we do. You Americans need to be taught a lesson. Did you think that your burning of York up in Canada would go unnoticed—unrevenged? Humility is sadly lacking in the general character of you Americans." At her look of hatred, he added, "Never fear, no private homes will be burned, other than those citizens who blatantly resist."

"Like the bastards who killed my horse?" Ross interjected.

"Exactly. Only the public buildings—the President's House, the Capitol, the Treasury will be destroyed. I am not totally heartless." He laughed.

My God! My God! Samantha cried inwardly, feeling more disheartened and helpless than she had since this whole miserable episode started. They were going to torch the President's House. Poor, poor Mrs. Madison. And the Capitol! All that beauty—all those years of work up in flames.

Somebody had to stop them. Somebody had to warn the President. But whom?

There was no one. Nothing short of a miracle could save the city now, and miracles were in short supply these days.

The predawn-darkened sky was as crimson as the red-coated pestilence that had swept into the city the night before. As his horse picked his way carefully through the clutter on Pennsylvania Avenue, Daniel looked sadly about, scarcely believing his own eyes.

Smoke and flames licked the heavens, the result of the buildings that had been torched and the explosions of the arsenal and the navy yard that had been blown up by retreating American soldiers trying to prevent them from falling into enemy hands. The stench of burned powder and smoke lingered in the early morning stillness, the acrid odor tormenting Daniel's senses, bringing a painful lump to his throat and causing his eyes to tear as he surveyed the surrounding area.

Having just returned from escorting President Madison safely across the river into Virginia, Daniel had come back to ascertain the damage done to the city; he hadn't been prepared for the total devastation that had been heaped upon the fledgling community. There was little left of the government buildings, other than the smoking ruins and rubble that lay before him.

Thank goodness Mrs. Madison had been spared the sight of her home reduced to a pile of blackened stones. Word had reached him that she and her maid, Sukey, had taken refuge at Rokeby, the home of the Loves, on the Virginia side of the Potomac.

Mrs. Madison had managed to save some of the historical records, silver, books, and the Gilbert Stuart portrait of Washington that had hung in the dining room before departing the Capital. Relief and admiration had poured over him at the news of the brave woman's actions.

A loud boom of thunder echoed loudly against the red sky before the first drops of rain pelted Daniel's face. It was a miracle, he thought, holding his hand out to cup the water, washing it over his face to cool himself. The rain would put the fires out, lessening the damage to the rest of the city. Perhaps there really was a God in heaven watching over all of them, he decided.

Reining Midnight to a halt in front of the brick building that housed the *National Intelligencer* office, Daniel grew instantly alarmed at the sight of the

314

broken glass and metal that littered the yard. Dismounting, he entered the darkened building, relieved to find Joseph Gales unharmed. Joseph was bent over a pile of charred books, the remnants of what was once his personal library.

Bloody bastards! Daniel thought, observing the total destruction of the newspaper office. The presses had been smashed, the type tossed out into the street. The sad sight came as no surprise, however. Admiral Cockburn had exacted his revenge for all of Joseph's less-than-flattering editorials on the "Royal Pirate," as Gales had so frequently referred to Cockburn.

"I'm sorry, Joseph," Daniel said, his words of consolation causing the editor to turn. Joseph's face was a mask of pain and fury.

"That blackguard tried to ruin me, but by all that is holy, I'll not let him do it. Give me a week; I'll have these presses running again."

Daniel draped a comforting arm about Joseph's shoulders. "I don't doubt it for a moment. I suspect there won't be many who will take this lying down."

"What news of Willy and Samantha? Are they all right?"

The question had plagued Daniel more than once. Fear for Samantha's safety had gnawed at his gut like a cancer every day he'd spent away from the city. The only thing that had kept him going was the knowledge that Caesar was there to protect her.

"I'm on my way to the Lawrences now. But first, I have a call to make."

A knowing light entered Joseph's eyes. "I take it you're referring to Bainbridge?" At Daniel's nod, Joseph added, "So, he was the one all along. I'd always suspected him and that traitorous bastard, Pickering, but I had no idea their involvement went so deep."

"Greed and power have always been strong motivations."

"True, and there are fewer men more corrupt than those two."

Daniel's eyes hardened. "Their reign is over. I have enough proof to hang them both. And trust me when I say that the thought gives me nothing but pleasure."

With his pistol primed and cocked, Daniel kicked the door in to find Adam's room empty. He swore, banging his fist in frustration against the wooden door frame. He had purposely entered through the rear of the building, climbing the servant's stairs in the hope of surprising Bainbridge. Instead, he was the one surprised. Muttering another string of vile curses, he descended the steps, entering the deserted front hallway to find an old black man asleep on the settle bench by the door.

"Wake up, old man," Daniel demanded, nudging the man's foot gently. "I need to talk to you."

Slowly, the white head lifted, the old man's eyes widening in fear when they caught sight of the pistol pointing in his direction. "Yes, suh?"

"Do you know where Bainbridge is?"

The men shook his head emphatically. "No, suh! I don't know nothin'."

Suspecting that what the old man said wasn't quite true, Daniel decided to change his tactics. "What's your name?"

"It's Henry, suh. I'se owned by Mr. Conrad. He gots

my papers; I ain't no runaway."

"Calm down, Henry," Daniel said, sitting down next to the frightened slave. "I'm not here to cause you any trouble."

"No, suh. No trouble for Henry."

"I'm looking for a man, Henry. A man with silver hair and eyes to match. He may have been in the company of British soldiers." Daniel saw the light of recognition enter the slave's eyes.

"Silver hair, you say?"

"That's right. He's shorter than I am, slight of build."

Henry scratched his head. "I reckon I did see such a man. I'm not too sure about most of the folks that lives here; I works out back in the stable. But I do recall seeing a gentleman with hair that was whiter than mine. He was here, but he left many hours ago." He looked chagrined. "I fell asleep. Mr. Conrad done told me to guard the house, said the soldiers might try to burn it, if I was to leave. He'd be mad if he was to find out I fell asleep."

Daniel patted the old slave's hand to reassure him. "The silver-haired man . . . was he alone when he left?"

"No, suh. There were soldiers with him and a lady."

Daniel jumped up, his heart pounding. "A lady? What did she look like?" But he knew. Bloody hell, he already knew.

"She was a pretty little thing. Brown hair, eyes like a doe, big and round. She didn't look too happy."

Probably upset about her travel arrangements, Daniel thought disgustedly. "Do you know where they went?"

The man pushed his palms flat against his knees. "I heard the silver-haired man saying he was anxious to go north. The soldier, the one with the gold on his shoulders, he said they had business in Baltimore first."

Reaching into his pocket, Daniel pulled out a pile of coins, placing them in the old man's gnarled hands. "Henry, you've been worth your weight in gold. Thanks for all your help."

Henry looked at the gold in his palm, then up at Daniel and smiled, revealing a gap where his two front teeth had been. "You goin' after them, suh?"

Daniel's eyes glittered dangerously. "They're traitors, the lot of them."

The wrinkled face creased into a frown. "Even the woman?"

Even the woman? Even the woman?

The old man's question echoed like a litany, over and over, until Daniel could stand it no longer and pushed his hands, flat against the sides of his head to stop it. If only it were as easy to erase the pain from his heart, he thought.

Taking a deep breath, he finally replied, "Even the woman, Henry." He turned and walked out the door.

"Thank God you're here, Daniel."

Walking into the Lawrence parlor a short time later, Daniel removed his sweat-stained hat, wiping his forehead with the back of his hand. The violent thunderstorm had recently ended, adding to the humidity of the morning.

"I came as soon as I could, Ezra. I promised Joseph Gales I would look in on Willy. Is she doing all right?"

"Willy is fine. She's looking in on the black wench. It seems Dulcie went and had her baby late last night.

Can you believe it? Having a baby in the middle of a British invasion. Damned inconvenient if you ask me!" The old man snorted contemptuously and shook his head.

Daniel smiled wearily. "How's Caesar holding up?"

"The man's been reduced to mush. I swear, I've never seen a grown man as scared as he was last night. You'd think Dulcie was the only woman to ever have a baby."

Before Daniel could reply, Willy trudged into the room, looking exhausted. Her eyes lit as she caught sight of Daniel. "Daniel, I'm so relieved to see you. Has Ezra told you what's happened?"

"I was just about to," Ezra interjected, reaching into his vest pocket. "We found this note last night, Daniel. It had fallen under the kitchen table. It's from Samantha."

"So you know," Daniel said, dropping down onto the settee, relieved that he wouldn't have to be the one to tell Ezra Lawrence that his granddaughter was a traitor.

Ezra's forehead wrinkled in puzzlement. "All I know is that my granddaughter went up to the attic to check on the British invasion and disappeared. It wasn't until we found this note late last evening that I discovered that she had gone to Adam."

"It seems she's fooled you, too, Ezra."

"What the hell are you talking about?" Ezra demanded, wheeling himself over to where Daniel sat. He shoved the note into Daniel's hands. "If you and my granddaughter weren't so damned stubborn, you would see what perfect asses you both are. She's in trouble, man. Read the note and see if you don't concur."

Unfolding the paper, Daniel scanned the contents, finally looking up. "So?"

"Are you purposely dense, boy? The note says that she went for help, that she would return. She hasn't; she's gone."

"I'm well aware of that, Ezra. It seems your granddaughter has gone north with Bainbridge and his British friends."

Ezra's face purpled with rage. "Samantha would never have left of her own free will. She's loyal to both me and her country. I don't like what you're implying, Fortune."

"Stop it, both of you!" Willy demanded, stepping forward to come between the two men. She turned toward Daniel, beseeching him with her eyes. "Samantha is in trouble; she needs our help. If it weren't for Dulcie having her baby last night, I would have gone after her myself."

Noting the genuine concern on the young woman's face and the fear in the old man's eyes, Daniel reread the note. Pushing himself to his feet, he rubbed the tension out of his neck with the back of his hand, saying in a tired voice, "Tell me everything."

When Willy had finished her explanation, Daniel stepped over to the table and poured himself a stiff shot of brandy. It was earlier than he normally imbibed, but after the events of the last night and the day, he felt he needed it. He downed the amber liquid in one gulp, welcoming the burning sensation into his numbed body.

Turning back, his voice filled with anguish, he faced Ezra. "I'm sorry that I jumped to conclusions."

"You and my granddaughter are a lot alike in that respect, boy. I'm well aware that she thought you a

320

traitor. Damned fools, the both of you."

Daniel had the grace to blush.

"Find her, Daniel, bring her back. I know you two have a lot to work out between you. But I know my granddaughter. If she's with Adam, she's there against her will. Bring her back, boy. I love her. I only wish I had thought to tell her that a time or two."

Daniel placed the weak, gnarled hand within his two stronger ones. "That makes two of us, Ezra."

Willy wiped the tears from her eyes with the edge of her sleeve. "I'm coming with you."

Daniel shook his head. "It's too dangerous. I'll take Caesar."

"You really have no say over what I do, Daniel. I'll just follow you if you don't let me come with you. Sam is my best friend. I'm not going to sit around here twiddling my thumbs, waiting for you to come back."

"And what of Dulcie? She needs your help. With Caesar gone, she'll be all alone."

"No, she won't. She'll have Ezra," she paused at the old man's snort, "and I've already arranged for Aunt Hattie, the Morton's cook, to come over and check on her. She helped with the baby's delivery."

"I see you've thought of everything."

"I tried to." Willy's smile was triumphant.

"This is no afternoon stroll we're going on," Daniel reiterated.

"We women are far more resourceful than you men give us credit."

Daniel swallowed the lump of fear that suddenly lodged in his throat. He hoped Willy was right, for Samantha would need every bit of resourcefulness, every bit of her wits, to keep herself on an even footing with her British captors.

Chapter Twenty-Three

Dressed in rough seaman's clothing, the unlikely trio of rescuers made their way swiftly and stealthily through the darkness toward Lear's Wharf, situated on the Potomac River near the mouth of Rock Creek.

Two days had passed since Daniel, Willy, and Caesar had first laid down their plans to rescue Samantha. It had taken that long for Daniel to secure permission from President Madison to leave the Capital, the President only having returned the day before, and for Daniel to flush his contacts out to help secure information about privateers plying the coastal waters.

Though legitimate shipping had virtually shut down during the war, many privateers still managed to wreak havoc upon British ships of the line and bring supplies into the provision-starved ports.

Daniel had heard of one such ship whose master, known only as Captain Liberty, had successfully and single-handedly been responsible for damaging or destroying over thirty British warships. Daniel's contact in Georgetown, Michael O'Roarke, owner of one of the taverns down near the wharf, had relayed the information that Liberty's ship, *The Fair Betsy,* had been sighted in the Potomac. When questioned as to how the ship had managed to slip through the British patrols, Michael had smiled that gold-capped-tooth smile of his to report that *The Fair Betsy* was none other than a British schooner herself.

Daniel smiled inwardly at the cleverness of the ingenious Captain Liberty. He was looking forward to making his acquaintance.

Turning his attention to the woman at his side whose labored breathing was clearly audible in the quiet of the night, he frowned, slowing his pace to accommodate her shorter stride. Willy looked like a small boy in her baggy linen shirt, brown leather vest, and fawn-colored breeches—clothing once owned by Ezra's grandson, Robbie. A brown knit cap had been pulled low on her head to conceal the bright mop of red hair.

"Are you all right?" Daniel asked finally, staring at Willy's flushed face, wishing, not for the first time, that the stubborn, headstrong woman had heeded his advice and stayed home. Willy and Samantha shared some very annoying personality traits, he decided.

"I'm fine," she insisted. "I just haven't had much exercise of late. My wind will improve with time, you'll see."

"Caesar," Daniel said, turning to stare over his left shoulder at the black man, "how did Dulcie take your leaving? I hope she wasn't too upset."

"Dulcie says the most important thing for me to think about is getting Miss Sam back. She sets a mighty store by Miss Samantha. In fact, Dulcie's planning to

323

name our baby girl, Samantha Wilhemina Fortune. What you think 'bout that?"

Daniel grinned into the darkness. "I think your little girl's going to have a lot to live up to. Let's just hope the child is blessed with more common sense than her namesakes."

Ignoring Willy's outraged gasp, Caesar chuckled. "Yes, sir, you is right about that, Mr. Dan. Between Miss Sam, Miss Willy, and Dulcie, the good Lord done unloaded his share of stubbornness."

"Now wait just a minute," Willy started to protest.

"Ssh!" Daniel warned, motioning for them to be silent. The sound of a boatman's oar slapped the water, forcing them to halt.

"Ahoy, *The Fair Betsy*," the deep-timbred voice sounded into the darkness.

"Who goes there?" came the harsh reply.

Soon the sound of voices and crates being lifted muffled the remaining conversation.

"We're here," Daniel whispered. "Keep silent and let me do all the talking. This ship is our only chance to save Samantha. If we can't convince Captain Liberty to help us . . ." His words trailed off. He couldn't voice his fears about what would happen to Samantha if they didn't get to Baltimore in time. He trusted Bainbridge about as much as he trusted the King of England.

They would get on board, he vowed. They would convince Liberty to help them. Samantha was depending on them. And by God, they wouldn't fail her.

The fat brown cockroach scurried up the wall, then down again, seeking a way out of the dirty, dingy hotel room that was his domicile at the moment. Samantha watched in fascination from her position upon the bed as he darted across the floor to make his escape up the flue of the chimney.

Clever bug, she thought, clutching her knees as she watched him depart. She and the cockroach had been closeted together for days in the seedy Baltimore hotel room. But now it seemed she was destined to spend her days alone, save for the occasional, unwelcome appearances that Adam put in.

Rage swept through her, as it did whenever she thought of Adam. God how she despised him! When she thought of all the miserable, underhanded things he had done, and how she had believed him. It was too bitter a pill to swallow. He was no better than the filthy creature that had just escaped. But Adam wouldn't be so lucky. She didn't know how just yet, but she had no intention of allowing him to go unpunished for all the misery he had caused. There had to be a way to make him pay. And, by God, she would! If it was the last thing she did with her life, she would make Adam Bainbridge pay!

Daniel and his two companions got as far as the gangplank of the ship, then were stopped by a pair of burly seamen. The taller of the two men, who had a sinister-looking scar running from the corner of his left eye down to his chin, set down the cask he was loading and stepped forward, fingering the pistol at his belt.

"State your business," he demanded.

Motioning for the others to stay put, Daniel stepped forward. "The name is Fortune . . . Daniel Fortune. I

325

have a business proposition to discuss with the captain of your ship. I was told Captain Liberty commands this vessel."

"Is that so?" The man's eyes narrowed. "What makes you think that this is Liberty's ship? We're a British schooner out of Liverpool, mate. We don't know any Captain Liberty."

The accent was decidedly British, but then Daniel had heard that most of the men that made up Liberty's crew were escapees from Newgate prison. "I'm a government agent. My contacts tell me that this ship is the privateer, *The Fair Betsy.*"

"Hear that, Cummings?" the sailor shouted to his companion, his smile feral. "They think this here's a privateer." Turning back to Daniel, he said, "Do you see that name painted on her hull? I say you're wrong."

It wasn't unusual for privateers to disguise the identity of their ship while in port. Daniel would bet his last dollar that the name had been covered over with tar.

"I've urgent business to discuss with your captain." Daniel's features hardened. "A woman's life is at stake."

His interest piqued, the man's red bushy eyebrow raised. "A woman, you say?"

Daniel nodded. "Some days ago my betrothed, a woman by the name of Samantha Wilder, was taken prisoner by the British. I've reason to believe that she's been taken to Baltimore."

The man's eyes widened momentarily before they shuttered closed. "You say you was going to marry this woman?"

At Daniel's nod, the man pointed at the anxious pair

who waited behind Daniel. "What about those two? What have they got to do with all this?"

"They're friends of Samantha's," Daniel said, unable to keep the impatience out of his voice. "Look, if we stand here talking all night, we're going to bring attention to ourselves. Why not let me come aboard and speak to your captain. I know I can convince him of my honesty."

The man turned, winked at his companion, and said, "I don't doubt it for a moment. Follow me, mates."

Heaving a sigh of relief, Daniel complied, following the two sailors up the gangplank, Willy and Caesar trailing close on his heels. The ship creaked and groaned as if protesting the added weight of the three newcomers.

Descending the steps leading to the captain's quarters, Daniel's apprehension increased. What if he couldn't convince this Captain Liberty to help him? What if Samantha wasn't in Baltimore as he was lead to believe? He didn't have time to ponder those doubts for the door was pushed open and they were ushered into a very comfortable cabin.

The interior was paneled in dark walnut. A long oak table with benches on either side dominated the center of the room. There was a single bed, flush against the right wall, and next to it, a washstand. The large window at the rear of the compartment would provide a commanding view of the ocean, but only darkness could be viewed from its glass at the moment.

"Wait here," the man who had introduced himself as Whitaker ordered. "I'll fetch the captain for you."

Daniel nodded, not bothering to hide his disappointment that there were going to be further delays. When

327

the door was pulled shut and the three of them were finally alone, he said in a voice kept purposely low, "I don't know how reasonable this Liberty is going to be. I only know that we need this ship. I may have to take the man hostage if he proves to be uncooperative." At Willy's look of alarm, he added, "I'm hoping that's not the case."

"We do whatever's necessary, Mr. Dan," Caesar said. "Don't you fret. We's going to get Miss Sam back, one way or the other."

Daniel patted the big man's back. "Stay alert, Caesar. If things don't look like they're going well, I may need you to be persuasive."

Caesar grinned. "Yes, sir, I'm sure to be that."

Turning his attention back to Willy, Daniel noticed that her fear of moments ago had now been replaced by eager anticipation. He groaned inwardly. "Willy, you're to stay out of the way. There's no sense in these sailors finding out that you're a woman before I'm ready. Three men present more of a threat than two men and a lady."

"You constantly underestimate me, Daniel," Willy said, reaching down to pull a dagger from her boot. "I'm not as helpless as I seem, and neither is Samantha. We're both going to be just fine. You mark my words."

Daniel's eyes widened momentarily before he frowned. "I'm not going to ask where you got that; I have a pretty good idea." Ezra's furtive behavior of the night before suddenly came back to haunt him. "But I still want you to stay in the background. Is that clear?"

She saluted. "Aye, aye, Captain, whatever you say."

There was no more time for talk, for a moment later the door was swung open to admit a tall, solidly built man with dark wavy brown hair and dark brown eyes. He was clean shaven, unlike most of his crew who sported beards. His authoritative swagger bespoke the fact that he was in command.

His eyes scanned the room, taking account of the three strangers, one by one. They widened imperceptibly when they landed on Willy's slight form huddled behind Caesar's much larger one, but the expression on his face gave no indication as to what he was thinking. Finally, he turned his attention on Daniel, studying him intently.

"I understand you wished to see me." There was a New England inflection to his speech.

Daniel stared, quite confused by the feeling that he had seen this man somewhere before. He knew he hadn't but still . . . Mentally shaking himself, he held out his hand. "I'm Daniel Fortune and these are my two companions, Caesar, and," he paused, ". . . Will. We've come to enlist your aid."

"Whitaker, my first mate, has told me something of your plight. I want to hear more about this woman . . . this Samantha Wilder."

They seated themselves around the polished oak table whose benches had been bolted securely to the floor. Daniel and the captain sat at either end, facing each other, while Willy and Caesar stood in readiness behind Daniel in the event it became necessary to carry out their alternative plan, a plan which would be simple to institute since the captain had entered his cabin alone.

"Samantha is my betrothed. She's been kidnapped by a man named Bainbridge . . . Adam Bainbridge."

The captain's face reflected surprise then anger. "I

thought you said the woman had been captured by the British."

"True, but Bainbridge is working for the British. He's a traitor—an informant."

Folding his hands in front of him, Captain Liberty's voice dripped coldly with condemnation when he spoke. "If the woman was to be your wife, how could you have let another man kidnap her? Why didn't you protect her?"

Daniel's face reddened. "Samantha and I were estranged. She thought me a traitor and went to Bainbridge for help." He went on to explain the situation, leaving out only the most intimate details of his relationship with Samantha, adding, "Miss Wilder is a stubborn woman, but loyal to those she loves. Bainbridge used her sorely. I will kill him when I get my hands on him."

"Why go after a woman who has caused you so much trouble? It sounds as if you'd be better off without her."

That comment drew a strangled gasp from Willy and a deep, angry growl from Daniel. "My reasons are my own. I need help to carry out this rescue mission. If you are unwilling, I will be forced to resort to other measures."

Caesar took a step forward, but the captain stood his ground. "Your reasons, Mr. Fortune, have now become mine. They did so the moment you boarded this ship. Now, you will either tell me why it is so important to get this Wilder woman back or I'll not lift a finger to help."

"You disgusting pig!" Willy shouted, launching herself at the captain, not bothering to disguise her voice. She raked her nails down his face.

Taken by surprise, Captain Liberty grunted at the unexpected impact, but then, as if Willy was no more than a nuisance, he grabbed hold of her hands with one of his and pulled her down onto his lap, oblivious to the blood that trickled down his cheek. Surprise and admiration lit his eyes when he pulled off the knit cap to reveal a glorious profusion of red hair.

"Let me go, you . . . you ogre!" Willy shouted, struggling to free herself.

"Just as I thought," the captain said, casting a warning glance at Caesar who was ready to pounce. "I wouldn't. I can have fifty armed men down here before you can pull that pistol you have concealed beneath your coat."

The black man stared helplessly at Daniel, then took a step back.

"Leave off, Caesar," Daniel said, clenching his fists. He wouldn't risk Willy's life. "Captain Liberty is right. We're outnumbered."

"Very wise, Mr. Fortune. Now, would you care to answer my earlier question and also tell me why it is you are attempting such a dangerous mission with a she-cat tagging along?" Ignoring the squirming bundle on his lap, Liberty reached into his pocket with his free hand and extracted a handkerchief, wiping the blood from his face.

Recognizing a worthy adversary when he saw one, Daniel sighed in resignation, rising to his feet. "Although I have asked myself that very question more times than I can count, the only answer I am able to come up with is that I love Samantha, impossible though she may be. And as for Willy . . . Well, as you can see, she has a mind of her own."

The captain grinned, revealing two dimples on either side of his face. Daniel's eyes widened at the resemblance the man bore to Samantha. Staring more intently at him, his eyes narrowed in suspicion when he noticed the pewter chain dangling around his neck. Ignoring Willy's and Caesar's puzzled expressions, he strode forward, pulling the chain out from beneath the man's loose-fitting linen shirt. The Liberty Medal warmed his palm.

"I should have known. The resemblance was just too coincidental."

"What is going on?" Willy demanded, staring first at Daniel, then at the grinning features of the captain. Her heart skidded suddenly. The man was positively handsome when he smiled. She wiggled off his lap but not before a warm flush spread over her cheeks. "Is someone going to tell me what on earth is going on?"

Placing his arm about Willy's shoulders, amusement and admiration tingeing his words, Daniel replied, "Meet Robert Wilder . . . Samantha's long-lost brother."

Chapter Twenty-Four

"You're Robbie Wilder!" The green eyes widened to the size of large emeralds.

"One and the same, sweeting," Robbie replied, displaying those two charming dimples again. "And you're . . . ?"

"This is Wilhelmina Matthews," Daniel supplied. "Willy for short. She's a close friend of your sister's."

Robbie's eyes roamed over Willy appreciatively, bringing two bright spots of color to her cheeks. "Samantha always did have good taste."

Her green eyes clawed him like talons. "Well, she certainly didn't have good taste when it came to choosing Adam Bainbridge for a friend, and I'm not too sure that she's had much luck in choosing her relatives either," Willy retorted, folding her arms across her chest.

At the mention of Adam's name, Robbie's smile melted. "Tell me about Bainbridge, Daniel. I'm having a difficult time believing that Adam has turned traitor on us."

Daniel resumed his seat, indicating that Willy and Caesar should do the same. "I'm afraid that what I have to tell you is going to make your acceptance of that fact a great deal easier. Adam Bainbridge was the one responsible for your incarceration in a British prison."

Robbie jumped up, flattening his palms against the table. "How did you know I was held prisoner by the British?"

"As I told your first mate, Whitaker, I am a government agent, working for President Madison. Your sister engaged my help in locating your whereabouts. Through my contacts, I discovered the details of your capture. It seems that your impressment and eventual imprisonment by the British was all part of Bainbridge's plan. With you out of the way, and Samantha left with only the protection of her grandfather, Adam planned to aid the British with their invasion of Washington, force Samantha to wed him, and with your grandfather's political influence, gain the governorship of Massachusetts. So far, he's been partially successful."

Robbie's face purpled with rage; he banged his fist on the table, causing Willy to jump out of her seat. "That bastard! I'll kill him when I get my hands on him."

"I'm afraid that I've already set aside that privilege for myself, Wilder. However, I do need your help in finding Bainbridge and Samantha."

"Whitaker said something about Baltimore."

"We believe that's where Samantha was taken. How long she remains there is anybody's guess. It's imperative that we act with all due haste."

Crossing to the door, Robbie stuck his head out,

shouting for his cabin boy to bring food. When he turned back, a fierce gleam showed in his eyes as he addressed the disparate group of rescuers. "First we eat and then we plan. There's never been a good chart coursed on an empty stomach."

Willy's stomach took that moment to rumble in approval of the suggestion. Color filled her cheeks at the knowing smile on Robert Wilder's lips.

"It seems that we're all in agreement," Robbie stated. At Daniel's nod, he added, "Good, then we weigh anchor immediately. The quicker we catch up with that piece of treacherous scum, the sooner we'll have Samantha back where she belongs."

Aye, Daniel thought, his blue eyes turning as cold as the depths of the Potomac in January, and the sooner Adam Bainbridge will find himself on the receiving end of a bullet.

Samantha paced nervously across the small confines of her hotel room. Outside in the hall, the vile soldier named Stiles guarded her door like a vulture waiting to pick the flesh off its prey. It was how she felt at that moment: dead—lost to the rest of the world.

Did anyone know she'd been taken? Did anyone care? she wondered, flopping dejectedly onto the bed. Of course, her grandfather and Willy cared, but they wouldn't be able to help her. If only Daniel had cared enough to come after her. But why should he? She had fixed it so that he despised the very ground she walked on. Even that last night, when he had begged her to make love with him, she had spurned him. Now, she would give anything to be held in his arms, to have him make love to her again.

"Oh, Daniel," she whispered, wiping the tears that trickled slowly down her face. "Please don't hate me. Please come after me."

The sound of the key turning in the lock brought her quickly out of her maudlin state. Jumping off the bed, she wiped her face with the hem of her soiled dress, unwilling to let her captors know how dispirited she felt. She certainly wasn't going to let that fat little toad Stiles catch her sitting upon the bed. There was no telling what he would do. The pig had made it quite clear, on more than one occasion, what he would *like* to do. Revulsion brought gooseflesh to her arms, and she shivered.

"How are you today, my dear? I hope you're in better spirits."

Adam was all smiles when he entered, no doubt having been amply rewarded by the British for all his treachery. He was dressed quite smartly in a suit of black superfine with a silver brocade waistcoat and white cravat. Unfortunately, his clothing couldn't disguise the vermin that rested beneath. Looking down at her own filthy gown, once a lovely shade of pink and now hopelessly soiled, she grimaced.

"Now, now, let's not be upset. I plan to buy you a whole new wardrobe once we're settled in Boston. After all, we can't have the governor's new wife looking dowdy, now can we?" He stepped forward, fingering the long strands of hair that had fallen over her left breast.

She stepped back. "Don't touch me! And don't delude yourself by thinking that I would ever marry you. You must be addled. I'd sooner marry that repul-

336

sive pig you have posted outside my door."

Adam's eyes narrowed a fraction before he smiled smoothly. "I think not, Samantha. I've seen how you look at Stiles in fear. I've also seen how he looks at you. Would you like me to call him in here? We could put your show of bravado to a test."

She masked the revulsion she felt with a look of pure hatred. "Why don't you go back to your traitorous friends, Adam? I'm sure they desire your company far more than I do."

"My dear, you wound me," he said, stepping closer to gather her into his arms. She resisted, but he tightened his hold. "You'll not gainsay my desires, Samantha. I've waited a long time to have it all. Soon I'll be the governor and you'll be my first lady." He ran his hands down her back, over her buttocks, pulling her resisting form into his hardness. "We'll have such beautiful children, Samantha. Think of it. I'll fill you with the seeds of my ambition." He plunged his thick tongue into her mouth, bringing bitter bile to her throat.

When he released her, she stepped back, wiping her mouth with the back of her hand. "I hate you! Don't touch me."

He laughed. "Poor Samantha. There's no one here who will grant your wishes, is there? You were so spoiled as a child. First your father, then Robbie, even Ezra in his doddering fool's way. I'm afraid that is all behind you now."

"My grandfather will ruin you. He knows people—powerful people. He will see your ambitions destroyed."

"I think not." He brushed an imaginary speck of lint off his sleeve as he walked to the window. The sunlight shining in cast an eerie, almost supernatural glow over him, as if he were the devil, rising from the fires of hell. "You see, my dear, if you try to thwart my plans, I will have your grandfather killed. I assure you, it would be an easy matter. I might even do it myself."

She gasped, her eyes widening in horror. "You're evil! What's happened to you? You're not the same boy . . . the same man I knew. You are an imposter." For a moment, she thought she saw a hint of sadness, of regret, enter his eyes, then it was gone.

"People change, my dear. Circumstances often dictate that they do. You see, your family always had it all, Samantha. Money, position. While mine had nothing."

"How can you say that? Your mother and father were wonderful people; they loved you."

His features hardened. "They were groveling, stupid people who never cared to better themselves. They tried to hold me back; they never wanted me to get ahead, become someone important. My father wanted me to follow him into his profitless sailmaking business. Can you imagine? Me? Making sails?" His laughter was guttural.

"'Twas a noble profession. He did very well by you and your mother."

"By whose standards? Maybe you were content to remain in that world. I was not. I wanted more; I deserved more. Now, I have more, and you will share it with me."

The maniacal gleam lighting Adam's eyes brought genuine fear to Samantha's heart. Fear and sadness for the boy she once loved like a brother. There would be no reasoning with him. She could see that now. He was insane—totally out of touch with reality. She would have to placate him . . . find a way to escape these monsters that had ruined her life and her country.

But how?

"I don't see why we've had to put into port in Annapolis," Willy asked Robbie. They were standing on deck, staring out at the quaint, brick colonial city as the ship sailed smoothly into the harbor. The sky had turned a pewter color, the clouds dark and ominous, threatening to burst open at any moment.

Robbie stared at the lovely woman by his side. He was certain that she had no idea what a captivating picture she presented dressed in his old castoff clothes that looked far better on her than they ever did on him, her wild mane of reddish hair flying about her pixy face. He certainly couldn't remember filling out that shirt in quite that way. Realizing where his thoughts were leading, he shifted his position to hide his sudden discomfort and cleared his throat.

"I've men to pick up, provisions to unload. I've still obligations to which I must attend. I'm sure Samantha would be the first to agree that the lives of those depending on me have to be considered above all else. Also, we'll need the remainder of my crew who are in port visiting family and friends. We can't mount a rescue mission undermanned."

"Samantha may well understand, but I doubt you'll be able to convince Daniel that the delay is justified. Look how he paces the deck like a caged lion."

Robert followed her gaze, noting that Daniel did, indeed, look every inch the untamed beast. There wouldn't be much of Bainbridge left when Daniel got done with him. "The man must really be in love with my sister." He shook his head. "Poor blighter; I don't envy him."

Willy cast him a guarded look. "And what's wrong with that? You act as if there is something wrong with Samantha and Daniel being in love." His grin caused a queer fluttering in her stomach. *Seasickness. It must be seasickness.*

"Nothing's wrong, sweeting, if the two are well-matched." He cupped her chin, noting how her eyes widened to twice their normal size and smiled inwardly. "But I suspect that my sister and Daniel mix as well as oil and water. I can't believe that Samantha actually agreed to marry him. She's too independent, by far."

Twisting free of his hold, which was much too disturbing, Willy turned to stare out at the water once again. She wasn't about to reveal the unusual circumstances leading to Daniel's and Samantha's engagement. They had enough problems with which to contend without engaging the ire of an outraged, overprotective brother.

"When the right man comes along, a woman doesn't mind giving up her independence," Willy stated.

"Well, now," Robbie said, grinning, "that makes me feel a whole lot better, sweeting." He grabbed her about the waist, turning her toward him, only to have his hands slapped away.

"I said the right man, you conceited jackanapes." Willy's expression was as disdainful as she could muster, considering the fact that her heart was pounding at an alarming rate. She headed quickly for the stairway that would lead her below to the safety of her cabin, but did not escape before she heard Robbie's raucous laughter followed by his reply, "I'm about as right as they come, sweeting."

Fairly skipping down the steps as she made her way to the compartment below, Willy couldn't contain the smile that spread over her face and warmed the confines of her heart.

Seated in the common room of the White Horse Tavern a short time later, Daniel and Robbie waited nervously for their contact to appear, while presenting the appearance to anyone who might be observing them that they were just a couple of sailors out for a night on the town.

The tavern, mostly frequented by seafaring men, had an unsavory reputation for violence. Observing the vicious-looking scum that surrounded them, Daniel thought that it certainly lived up to it. The room was smoke-filled, crowded, and noisy, reeking of cheap perfume and the stench of unwashed bodies.

"You see any sign of him yet?" Robbie asked, casting furtive glances about the room. Several of his men were positioned by the bar. The rest stood outside the door, just in case any British regulars happened by. Fortunately, none had.

He was relieved that Daniel had been able to talk some sense into Willy, having insisted that she and Caesar remain behind with the rest of his crew to guard the ship. 'Twas easy to see why Willy and Samantha had hit it off so well, them being cut from the same obstinate cloth.

Quaffing his pint of ale, Daniel shook his head, wiping his mouth on the edge of his sleeve and letting

341

out a loud, obnoxious belch . . . just in case curious eyes were trained on him. "No, but then, I'm not sure just who it is we're expecting."

Robbie grinned. "I liked the belch; it added a nice touch."

Daniel returned his smile, but before he could reply, a large shadow loomed over him from behind. Turning, both men's eyes widened simultaneously. Robbie's, at the appearance of the giant before him, Daniel's, at the familiar form of Blubber Billy Michaels.

"As I live and breathe!" Daniel exclaimed, hauling the big sailor down next to him. The bench tipped slightly, owing to Blubber's ponderous proportions, bringing a smile to Daniel's lips. "What are you doing here, Blubber? I didn't expect to see you again."

"Is it really you, Blubber?" Robbie asked, peering intently at the large man. "I hardly recognized you with that beard, though I should have noticed that great mound of flesh. It seems impressment by those British bastards didn't lessen your appetite."

Patting his paunch, Blubber smiled. "I've grown fatter at the expense of those lily-livered dogs. Thanks to men like Daniel here." He swatted Daniel on the back.

At Robbie's puzzled frown, Daniel explained, "Blubber was my contact in Boston when I was seeking information on your whereabouts."

"Barkeep, bring whiskey," Blubber shouted so loudly several heads turned to stare in their direction.

So much for keeping our cover concealed, Daniel thought, noting the similar concern on Robbie's face.

"Don't worry, mates, this place is clean. I checked it out 'afore I made my rendezvous here."

"You're the contact!" both men said in unison.

"In the flesh . . . and a mite good bit of it, I might add. Aha! There's the whiskey now. Thanks, lovey," Blubber said, patting the derrière of the well-endowed tavern maid who smiled and winked in return. "A fine pair on that one, me lads. A man could lose himself a good while between the likes of tits like those."

Robbie and Daniel exchanged amused glances before Daniel lowered his voice, asking, "Do you have the information we're seeking?"

"Aye, and then some. In case you chaps haven't heard, Alexandria's been plundered. The good citizens surrendered not only their town, but their flour, tobacco, and a shit load of merchandise."

"Bloody British bastards!" Daniel shouted, pounding his fist on the table. "Haven't they done enough?"

Blubber shook his head. "It appears that their next objective is Baltimore, or so my sources inform me. Several British deserters were heard shooting off their mouths at the Fatted Goose last night. We've no time to lose if we're going to get the lady out before all hell breaks loose."

Daniel's eyes lit. "You know where Samantha is?"

"Aye. They've got her stashed in a filthy hellhole of a place. Bainbridge is with her, as well as a small group of soldiers." He poured himself another drink. "Cockburn and Ross have already left."

"It shouldn't be that difficult to get Samantha out," Robbie said. "We've got the element of surprise on our side, that and *The Fair Betsy*."

343

"Your father's schooner?" Billy asked, surprised. "I thought she and all of the crew disappeared two years ago."

Robbie's eyes hardened. "She was found abandoned and in pretty bad shape off the coast of France. Friends got her back to me. My father and his crew were never found, though."

"I'm sorry about that, lad, still, it will be lovely to sail on her."

"You're coming with us?" Daniel interjected, not bothering to hide his surprise.

Draping his arm about his companion, Blubber chuckled. "Aye, Daniel boy. I wouldn't miss this one for the world, not if it means getting my hands on that traitor Bainbridge." He fingered the ominous-looking blade at his belt. "I'd like to slit his yellow belly up one side and down the other for the part he played in my impressment."

Daniel's features hardened; his voice chilled. "No one touches Bainbridge but me. I've got my own score to settle with him."

"Because of the woman?"

"Aye," Daniel replied, his eyes darkening dangerously. "Because of the woman."

Chapter Twenty-Five

Samantha stared morosely out the window of her hotel room. Beyond the brick and clapboard buildings of the city of Baltimore, she could see the blue waters of the Patapsco River flowing gently by, seemingly oblivious to the flurry of activity occurring on its banks.

A line of fortifications were taking shape along its eastern shoreline, the most likely route for the British invasion that was forecast by the local newspapers. Hundreds of concerned citizens had turned out in defense of their city; there would be no repeat of the carnage that had plagued Washington, the editorials promised.

Samantha wished she could share their optimism. After observing firsthand the superior strength of the British army and navy, she wasn't quite as confident as she had been the first time. Adam had only been too happy to allow her the freedom to read the latest reports of the supposed British invasion in the newspapers. He wanted her to feel vanquished, hopeless, and she was sad to admit that his plan was working.

It had been over a week since she had been taken hostage by the enemy. She now considered Adam every bit as much the enemy as Stiles and the other British regulars that guarded her door. She knew it wouldn't be long before Adam made his move to continue their journey north to Boston. She had heard him talking to Stiles one evening when he thought she had fallen asleep.

As soon as word reached Baltimore that the British fleet was sighted in the Patapsco, Adam planned to flee. He needed the assurance of a British victory before he could put the rest of his preposterous scheme into action.

Did he really think that Pickering and the other Federalists, those astute and cunning merchants, bankers, and lawyers who made up the movement, would yield power to a virtual nobody? They wanted to establish a New England Confederacy under English protection, but they had men far more intelligent, far more schooled than Adam in the ways of political subterfuge to lead them. George Cabot, for one.

Cabot, the brilliant political leader of the Federalist faction, was a former Revolutionary War privateer turned politician. He, along with Pickering, had founded the Essex Junto, the nucleus of the New England conspiracy. Under his guidance, treason among the New England states had flourished during the war with England.

She shook her head sadly. If only she had cared enough, been concerned enough, to see what was going on right under her nose. She, like so many of the citizens in Massachusetts, had let this small group of